MARCH IN COUNTRY

MARCH IN COUNTRY

A NOVEL OF THE VAMPIRE EARTH

E. E. KNIGHT

A ROC BOOK

ROC
Published by New American Library, a division of
Penguin Group (USA) Inc., 375 Hudson Street,
New York, New York 10014, USA
Penguin Group (Canada), 90 Eglinton Avenue East, Suite 700, Toronto,
Ontario M4P 2Y3, Canada (a division of Pearson Penguin Canada Inc.)
Penguin Books Ltd., 80 Strand, London WC2R 0RL, England
Penguin Ireland, 25 St. Stephen's Green, Dublin 2,
Ireland (a division of Penguin Books Ltd.)
Penguin Group (Australia), 250 Camberwell Road, Camberwell, Victoria 3124,
Australia (a division of Pearson Australia Group Pty. Ltd.)
Penguin Books India Pvt. Ltd., 11 Community Centre, Panchsheel Park,
New Delhi - 110 017, India
Penguin Group (NZ), 67 Apollo Drive, Rosedale, North Shore 0632,
New Zealand (a division of Pearson New Zealand Ltd.)
Penguin Books (South Africa) (Pty.) Ltd., 24 Sturdee Avenue,
Rosebank, Johannesburg 2196, South Africa

Penguin Books Ltd., Registered Offices:
80 Strand, London WC2R 0RL, England

Published by Roc, an imprint of New American Library,
a division of Penguin Group (USA) Inc.

First Printing, January 2011
10 9 8 7 6 5 4 3 2 1

Copyright © Eric Frisch, 2011
All rights reserved

 REGISTERED TRADEMARK—MARCA REGISTRADA

LIBRARY OF CONGRESS CATALOGING-IN-PUBLICATION DATA:

Knight, E. E.
March in country: a novel of the Vampire Earth/E. E. Knight.
p. cm.
ISBN 978-0-451-46334-0
1. Valentine, David (Fictitious character)—Fiction. 2. Vampires—Fiction.
3. Kentucky—Fiction. 4. Human-alien encounters—Fiction. I. Title.
PS3611.N564M37 2011
813'.6—dc22 2010036612

Set in Granjon Roman
Designed by Alissa Amell

Printed in the United States of America

To Jim Pavelec,
the acknowledged master of Monsters from the Id

"... and chose him five smooth stones out of the brook,
and put them in a shepherd's bag which he had, even in a scrip;
and his sling was in his hand: and he drew near to the Philistine."

—First Book of Samuel 17:40 (King James Version)

MARCH IN COUNTRY

CHAPTER ONE

*F*irsch County Wayside Number Two, the Kentucky-Tennessee border, February of the Fifty-sixth year of the Kurian Order: the recent violent winter, the worst in living memory for even the tough locals, has
ebbed at last. Nothing that might be called spring warms the sky; rather,
it is a quiet between-season pause, like the lassitude between the break in
a life-threatening fever and recovery.

One winter can do only so much damage. At an old intersection between two neglected county highways, with only one route showing even
some signs of maintenance—the northbound stretch has been reduced
to little more than a horse track—the Wayside squats behind a lattice of
young fir. It might be a monument to entropy.

It is an enclave that could best be described as lumpy. No two
structures match. The central building used to be a gas station and con-
venience store, still identifiable by a few chipped logos as a BP for con-
noisseurs of pre-22 corporate branding. It stands out from the others in
that all the verticals and horizontals are square. The other structures lean
as though tired: relocated sheds, prefabricated housing, a fire-gutted strip
whose gap-toothed storefronts serve as an improvised garage and junkyard. A double layer of barbed-wire fencing, no two posts standing quite

the same, surrounds all, pulled this way and that by the growing pines. The more observant may notice dog feces among the dropped needles between the layers of wire.

Farther off, crowds of trees and brush and brown kudzu envelop what had once been a little two-street town of houses and a barn or two.

Everything in the Wayside, from crumbling brick and trailer home to boarded-up window, is painted a formerly bright shade of orange, now faded and dirtied into a rotting pumpkin color.

Wayside Number Two looks as though it would be improved by a return of the short-lived snow. You wouldn't see the mud, for a start. The garbage mound out behind the prefabs could be camouflaged into and inviting, snowy hill. The dog litter couldn't be seen—or smelled—and white would hide the slime molds coating the bricks of the gutted strip.

For all its forlorn appearance, the gas pump and parking lot in front ticked with vehicular life.

One pair of vehicles stand out. A shining new red compact truck—or oversized, high-clearance car with a lighted roll bar and stumpy cargo bed, depending how precise one's definitions—and the bulldog shape of a heavier, ten-wheeled armored car are parked so as to block the roadside gap in the wire. A tall, muscular, alert-looking black man stands beside the compact truck, radio crackling inside. The uniformed men in the armored car are more casually disposed as they wait. They blow smoke out of their lowered windows as they play cards, using the dashboard as a table. The pitiful collection of rust buckets, motorcycles, a bike, and horse wagon nearer the Wayside's main entrance look like sheep penned by a pair of wolves.

A brown truck slows as it approaches, but the bearded driver, getting a glimpse of the Georgia Control circle-and-bar logo on the doors of both vehicles—huge on the armored car, discreet on the red compact truck—thinks better of stopping. His worn tires kick up a shower of grit as he changes up after making the turn south, suddenly eager for the horizon. . . .

†

If there's one thing I hate, John Macon thought to himself, *it's grocery shopping.*

The trick, of course, was not to let on to the groceries that they were being selected. He had driven ahead, alone in his not-quite-unmarked Pooter, so the flotsam at Wayside Number Two wouldn't become alarmed at the sight of the heavier armored car holding the Reapers. Once he established there were suitable pickings at the Wayside—a quick glance through the door's glass confirmed a collection of warm bodies, none of whom looked important enough for Tennessee to miss—he'd called up the Transporter.

He strode into the dining room. They'd taught him in the Youth Vanguard how to walk authoritatively: chin up, shoulders back, a little extra strike on the bootheel. He glanced across the counter and the booths. Six hanging fluorescent fixtures containing three bulbs, two of which still managed to produce light, illuminated the sparse condiments and a desiccated piece of pie on the counter and a cash register with drawer wide open revealing only a few bills, coins, and rows of loose cigarettes, as if advertising the poor pickings a holdup would bring.

The remaining lights had a lot of work to do, despite the light of afternoon outside. What had once been enormous glass windows were filled with old sheets of aluminum siding wired together into overlapping blinds. They alternately locked and rattled in the spring wind, at least the ones that didn't have old rags stuffed into the gaps to stave off chilly drafts.

The linoleum floor interested him for a moment: there were so many cigarette burns in it one might mistake the marks for a pattern.

Macon could have described the decor on the walls without even walking in the door: the owner's business license and good conduct certificates, a tin sign proclaiming the establishment's pride in serving OneSource Foods, a glass mirror with beautiful artwork: Ringgold Beer's famous hop-picking brunette smiling over her overflowing basket, and the inevitable Royal Pep Cola sign. Probably more than one. Never mind the plates, the glasses, and a generous supply of the famous long plastic siphon-droppers for "fixing up" your beverage with flavored syrups—promising everything from eight straight hours of mental alertness to an end to anxiety to a weekend's worth of hard-ons—with the establishment's name printed on the side.

He didn't know if the English still drank their tea or the French their champagne or the Jamaicans their rum, but the people of the Georgia Control guzzled Royal Pep Cola from dawn to dusk, with the "thousand and then some" flavor variations the Royal Pep Cola company claimed could be created from six flavorings and nine additives.

As wily market-goer, Macon calculated each purchase on a cost-versus-benefit analysis. He didn't enjoy this part of the job at all—though there were worse duties. His least favorite were his rare ventures into the dripping confines of the boss's home carbuncle— but if one wanted to rise in the Control one did the Unpleasant, for no other reason than to avoid the More Unpleasant that was the lot of the groceries.

He exchanged a glance with the angular young tough behind the counter. Muscles bulged under what was once a white T-shirt, tattooing on his right hand indicated he'd done a prison term as an adolescent. Macon gave him a friendly nod.

"Water, and a menu," Macon said, taking a seat at the end of the counter where he could scan the room.

Water appeared, in battered plastic, slightly green—the water, not the plastic—no ice.

"There's the menu," the counterman said, pointing to a painted and repainted stretch of wall over the kitchen window.

If you want to rise, do the difficult, his mentor in the Youth Vanguard used to say. The old pederast had his faults, but he'd built a comfortable, and damn near inviolable, niche in the Control.

Unlike the rest of the Advancing World, the Georgia Control had humans do all the selecting of groceries. Not just the usual disposal of the inconvenient and abrasive by the top dogs in the hierarchy. Not some, not much, but all. The Directors argued to the Kurians that humans possessed a keener instinct for sniffing out weakness, wrongdoing, and rebellion. The Kurians weren't particular. As long as the vital aura of culled humans flowed, and the rest of the population remained placid and breeding, they were inclined to let their human assistants put check marks and figures into spreadsheets determining who contributed to society and who ended up a net loss at the bottom line.

Macon approved of the system. It gave the humans running the Control a little bit of leverage. There were even rumors that a

Kurian or two who'd been problematic in its demands had been removed thanks to subtle hints and pressure from the Directors.

Outside the well-patrolled borders of the Georgia Control—an area a good deal larger than the old state, and growing, its Directors were proud to report—you didn't have neat little lists and the quiet nightly pickup squads. One had to use judgement, and Macon had observed only a few excursions and the requisite grocery-selecting.

Someone had to do the difficult and nasty business of finding fodder for the Kurians. Few wanted the job, and usually the ones who wanted it sought the authority for all the wrong reasons. What sort of diseased character would want to do such a thing? Macon thought of himself as a white blood cell, keeping the system healthy and functioning. When he had to attach to and gobble up pathogens, the rest of the bloodstream was the better for it. A white blood cell that acted out of emotion, self-aggrandizement, or plain cruelty would do harm to the system.

As a junior sibling where his eldest sister was helping their father run middle Georgia's greatest city as heir-apparent urban director, he'd have to make his own way and rise on his own merit, rather in the manner of following sons in the old aristocracies.

So when a new group of Kurians sent out word that they were seeking seed-staff for expansion into Kentucky, he volunteered for the position of "Ghoul Wrangler" as the less-ambitious liked to style it. His actual title in the Control's orgbase managed to include the words "Staff" and "Facilitator" along with only a single phrasing period—if he rose to the vice-director level they'd start using commas, an elegant touch for those at that exalted level. Of course, there was that dreadful word "unincorporated" and the orgbase inactive rolls were filled with listings of ambitious Youth Vanguard souls who'd gambled their lives in unincorporated regions.

Unincorporated or no, he received a Personal Utility Transport with only 24 kils on the odometer, no visible bullet holes, and a new field-brown paint job with his name stenciled under the Pooter's driver's side window/firing slot.

His blue-black Model 18 submachine gun fit that slit quite nicely. The gun, a gift from some connection of his father at the Atlanta Gunworks, rode across his chest like a clinging bat. The counterman eyed it like a thirsty Bedouin gauging an enemy's waterskin.

He reached into a pocket of his heavy, lined-leather driving coat, and extracted a pair of antacid peppermints from a big plastic bag. He popped the button-sized tablets into his mouth and crunched them down. They tasted like peppermint-dusted chalk, but it was better than feeling that he'd swallowed hot coals. Picking out groceries always gave him a sour stomach. If he was thinking about his gut, his duties would suffer. Never mind that this particular task could be downright dangerous.

The Wayside had about what you'd expect so close to Kentucky. These backwoods Tennessee roads attracted the shady and the skeevy. Well away from the Kurians on the fringes of the Advancing World, but not quite in the limestone-cut tangles filled with suspicious, well-armed legworm ranchers who'd gut you for the half pack of cigarettes in your pocket.

Macon remembered the interview when he'd been taken on by his Kurian. Chizzb or Tschezb or something even tougher on the tongue was its name, but his small human staff called him Prince Green.

They brought him into an old security warehouse at Atlanta's barely functioning airport, perhaps the most heavily patrolled square miles in Georgia outside of the Kurian City Center downtown. The lower level still served its purpose of temporarily holding people and goods entering from outside the Georgia Control by air. The upper level, accessible only by five flights of metal stairs, looked like a giant honeycomb of ochre papier-mâché.

A Reaper, two meters of solid dreadful, smiled a black-fanged smile when he offered his ID and showed the courier-delivered summons.

Prince Green looked like a cow's liver with an umbrella top and a couple of greasy mop heads stuck into it. It pulsed as it sat, though whether this was respiration or circulation he didn't know. He'd never seen one uncloaked, so to speak—usually when a Kurian interacted with men they went out and about under heavy capes, faces hidden behind helmets or veils, sometimes not even bothering to give the illusion of feet beneath the cloak. He'd been told that when they first showed up in 2022, in the wake of planetwide earthquakes and volcanic eruptions, they'd appeared as ethereal, glowing, half-angelic aliens with all the beautiful poise of a cut flower. From such a vision, the soothing words of comfort to a stricken world may have just as well been set to music.

You will excuse the informality, a decidedly nonmusical voice breathed from an unsettling point between his ears.

Sure as shootin' I will, Macon had thought back, sinking into the spongy floor. He felt something wet pull at his ankles, like living mud. He wondered if he stepped in the wrong direction if he'd sink and leave nothing but his Youth Vanguard Leader cap floating on the living floor.

This is true: I will not present myself to you in a guise more pleasing to human eyes, the inner dialogue continued. *Preparations for the move into Kentucky have left me exhausted. Perhaps it is just as well. I see no point in trusting a man who needs such useless reality dressing.*

"I'd rather see things as they are," Macon said, trying to fill his brain with white noise. You could bullshit a Youth Vanguard Leader when he caught you with vodka in your shampoo bottle, but Prince Green had the ability to poke around in his brain.

One old hand, the Atlanta-based director who'd sponsored him in the Youth Vanguard, had told him the worst thing you could do when facing a Kurian was try to remain calm. She'd said he should give in to whatever emotion was at hand—anger, fear, revulsion. Strong human emotions confused them, and a few caused them to flee your head like a cat off a hot stove.

Macon didn't want to screw up his first real opportunity, so he went with serene competence. It had served him well with the Reapers, and weren't they just extensions of the Kurians?

This is good: I will dispense with the aphorisms. We are moving into Kentucky shortly. Our foolish cousins north of the Ohio River have thoroughly, what is your colorful expression, shit in their own front yard. They turned a minor incursion by the resistance into a full-scale rebellion thanks to the use of a heavy hand where a light stinging slap was required, then released a half-developed and virtually untested virus. They've killed half the population and made resolute enemies of the other half. We have an opportunity to pick up the pieces so carelessly broken, if we move quickly but carefully. There are to be three new Control Districts. I will have the westernmost, and you will be on my staff, if you so accept.

Macon needed to think. Were they really moving against the rebels, or was this some kind of play against their rivals north of the Ohio? They were greedy when it came to engulfing new populations and their human servants were chips thrown on the table in long shot gambles. The Georgia Control was powerful, easily the most powerful south of the old Mason-Dixon Line and east of the Mississippi, but for all that they had only a small standing army. It stood as a safeguard against a rebellion from the more numerous police and paramilitary reserve forces and was overstretched.

This is interesting: You're wondering if we have enough trustworthy forces to operate in three entire new Control Districts. We do not. But we have enough to do a thorough job of taking over one, as we did in Alabama and Florida in the days of your fathers. For the others, mercenaries, police, and a certain amount of terror will allow us to maintain our position until control is consolidated.

"There are guerillas in Kentucky, I've heard," Macon said. He'd heard a lot of talk of one beleaguered Southern Command battalion. Evidently anyone could join up under a false name. They didn't ask any questions and gave you a new identity, basically. He'd heard some mutterings that if this or that didn't work out, the person in question would run off and join the rebels.

This is true: the legworm ranchers have assembled a small army aided by a band of renegades, a smaller force from the hillbilly rabble across the Mississippi. They're in our region, camped on the Ohio near Evansville. Your brethren on the Armed Operations Staff consider the Kentuckians the more dangerous force as they are armed and numerous and know the land. I am not convinced. Nor is Director Solon, who has some experience across the Mississippi. We must move as soon as weather allows. Once my avatars are in place we will be in a position to grind them down. So: Your first task will be to convey some of my avatars to the tower I am building in Kentucky. Speak not, I already know your answer is yes.

Prince Green shifted his weight on his perch. The goop around his ankles relaxed its grip.

Go, and we will speak again when I join my avatars in Kentucky.

"Thank you for the opportunity, my lord," Macon said, formalizing their new relationship.

Prince Green showed no sign of having heard him. Some of the tentacles were rippling. Perhaps he was animating one of his Reapers, communicating the orders to his chief of staff.

Macon left the oversized hornet's nest of the hangar roof, feeling rather like a fly walking out of a spider's web.

"Looks like we have us a new ghoul-wrangler," one of Prince Green's human security staff said.

They took him out for a celebratory meal. *"Eat up. You won't see civilization again for years,"* Director Solon, Prince Green's chief of staff, predicted.

They plied him with good liquor and tantalizing promises, in that members-only restaurant that smelled like sizzling beef and cigars. When Kentucky was properly incorporated into the Control, there'd be plenty of new Director positions.

Which led him, after briefings and paperwork bookended by the usual indoctrination lectures from the churchmen about what tests he'd encounter in his new duties among the unincorporated, to Wayside Number Two. Prince Green's advance guard of Reapers needed feeding. The Reapers lived off the blood of its victim, while acting as a conduit for the *vital auras* all intelligent, emotionally resonant beings possessed.

They'd offered him a driver, but he turned them down. One of the things his father taught him was that you always needed at least one person near you at all times whose "pay chit only gets deposited if you're still breathing." He hired Casp from a reliable firm in Charleston. They bred driver/bodyguards there the way the old Roman Empire used to produce gladiators. He'd added a little extra insurance by careful selection. Casp was two meters of solid muscle and had three brothers who were also DBs. If one gave the company name a black eye, the others would suffer.

Macon judged the souls in the Wayside, and found all of them wanting in some manner or other.

Three. He'd have to take three.

Macon felt sorry for them, in a way. Or rather, he felt sorry for the person they might have been, had they not made a few bad decisions. Failure to join one of the youth movements, or to drop out of the organizations and the educational system took many down a dead end. Resentment over a relative caused a lot of bad blood. People put so much emotion into biological happenstance.

Like that heavy driver in the corner, with his patty melt. A vanabon—Macon could tell from patches all over his mesh vest. Each patch represented a key business he carried for. He probably wandered northern Tennessee, doing everything from bringing eggs to market, delivering letters and parcels and subscriptions, to making spare parts runs—probably sneaking a passenger or two discreetly among the boxes.

Macon wouldn't take him, even if the man was stuffing his food to make a hasty exit before Macon asked to look over the contents of his van. Fat men rarely were rebels.

The gal at the folding table was a possibility. He might have to talk to her to decide. Aging, weathered, still with beautiful long hair, she wore a dress of nice material in flowing patterns.

Taking his cup, he walked up to her table and she offered a welcoming smile. Her portable table was covered with spices, medicines, candles, cut-glass vials, even a couple of beautifully restored plastic dolls. She evidently made her living selling sundries to the road traffic, something nice to bring home as a surprise to the wife.

"Are the candles scented?" Macon asked.

"Scented and unscented. Cinnamon is my most popular. I have beeswax as well, you can melt the stumps down and mix in a little linseed oil and use it as furniture polish. Not cheap wicks, either, they're braided."

She was a little pushy. Macon warmed at the thought that he could snap his fingers and have her lifted out of existence. *Just stick something under my nose, babe, and you'll never see another cinnamon-scented moonrise.*

The washroom door opened, and a youth with calf muscles like horse hooves exited. Still spotty, maybe seventeen or so. His distinctive black-and-white striped shirt had a name patch—Kurt, it read—and vertical lettering in one of the white stripes read *Encom-pass* in red letters.

Encompass was one of the New Universal Church's principal periodicals for the masses, a monthly with a beautiful glossy cover and smeared pages between. Families who wanted to stay in the good graces of their local clergy would be able to discuss the month's lead article and lead editorial. The rest of it, printed on thin, soft, not very absorbent paper that almost begged to be used for sanitary purposes, made a decent sedative. Sinecured editorialists droned on and on about obscure reclarifications of a previous perceived error in Church doctrine, which, if you thought about it correctly, wasn't really so much of a mistake as it was an example of poor word choice. At the back you usually had a useful how-to or two on how to get the most vitamin value out of sixteen hundred calories or the quickest method to check your kids for lice before and after school.

Volunteers like this kid, now turning bright red for some reason as he checked his fly, sold subscriptions and delivered it. Each issue also contained a bonus offer for some household item of dubious quality the kids had to attempt to upsell and then deliver, assuming the stock ever arrived.

Tough job. Lots of miles, no pay, and plenty of headaches thanks to the summer heat.

A woman exited the washroom after the kid, fixing the two remaining buttons on her blouse. She looked like a cowboy biker, all overcoat, chain belt, and tight jeans. Smeared lipstick and short red hair, possibly dyed. Haunted, hunted eyes. No wonder the kid turned red, she was so skinny he suspected she might be a tranny. Well, no Adam's apple. Whatever her gender, the whore looked like she'd been on short commons for a while. Probably gave the kid a five-buck handjob while he felt her tits.

She clutched a rolled up copy of *Encompass* in her strong-looking hands.

Good job, kid. Never miss a chance to sell a loose copy.

Well, this whore had turned her last trick. He was half tempted to add the counterman to the bag. What kind of establishment was he running? Macon wondered what his cut was.

"Don't leave just yet," Macon told the kid, hurrying for the door and his bike.

"Th-th-th-that's t-t-t-three for you t-t-t-today, Red," a greasy-haired Indian at the counter managed.

The scarred-up Indian smelled like woodsmoke and swamp water. All the weathering made his age hard to guess, but there were a few flecks of gray in the otherwise shiny black hair.

The stuttering Indian must have had it in for the whore. Maybe he couldn't scrape together even the chump change to afford a throw. He'd all but painted a sign reading SHE'S A WHORE! TAKE HER, NOT ME.

Not quite as lean as the whore, well-muscled about the shoulders, he wore a tattered mix of legworm leather—rare down in Georgia but more common up here—and polyester felt insulated vest. He'd picked up some utility worker's canvas trousers, probably at a resale store. One of those hammer picks hung from a short chain at his belt. The legworm riders used them to peg down their mounts for the night with the hammer end, and the spike end had a slight hook to it, like a mountaineer's climbing pick. They buried that end in the skin of their mounts to pull themselves up. Macon felt a momentary doubt—the stutterer might be a deserter from one of the armies lately rampaging across Kentucky. He put one of the scented candles under his nose, turned, and took a good look at the Indian's boots.

He wore moccasins. Sort of. They looked like they had soles made out of old truck tires, fixed with thick sandal straps.

No self-respecting army would let its soldiers wear boots like that. Even the guerillas had better footgear.

The Indian glanced at Macon with wary brown eyes. "M-maybe f-f-four."

Overplaying a really weak hand, Macon thought. He spoke into his radio, ordered the Transporter to pull up and Casp to cover the door.

"Nobody leaves without my say-so," Macon said, when Casp's bulk filled the front door frame.

The Indian looked scared. Macon wondered if he'd do something stupid with the hammer pick, if push came to shove.

Everyone whispered about the Reapers, the suicides, the Resistance, and the rebels, but most of those bound for harvesting temporized and rationalized until the last few seconds, when death stared them in the face and effective resistance was impossible. Nine-tenths of the Georgia Control were inching toward harvesting, they just wouldn't see it.

Better give them a rationalization.

"I'm here to do a labor draft," he said, slowly and clearly. Some of these border types spoke English as though they'd learned it from a Scrabble scoreboard with a few letters missing. "You're all recruited. Easy work for one day, fifty Control dollars plus a week's ration draw."

"Easy how, boss?" the redhead asked. She had an odd twang to her speech, but she knew how to address Control authority.

Macon smiled. "You have to stand holding a sign with an arrow on it and make sure the arrow always points the way I tell you. We have a convoy heading up into Kentucky, our maps are iffy and signage is gone. There will be military police at the major stops and intersections, but there are still a few turns around downed bridges and whatnot that I need managed."

Macon's first job he'd supervised as a Youth Vanguard had been something very similar, near the Florida border. Only there you had to worry about hungry fauna lunging out of the Okefenokee.

"Finish up your food and have a big drink of Royal Pep on the Control, you probably won't get to eat again until midnight tomorrow morning, if our vehicles are delayed. I'm going to make a pit stop. I want you all ready to go and earn up by the time I'm finished."

He walked up to the redhead and took her by the upper arm. She cocked her head.

"You, darlin'—I've been sleeping in a seat for nine hours. How about helping me work the knots out?"

"I'd rather hold something warmer than a sign, boss," she said. "The bathroom okay? It's all I got."

Macon caught the eye of the *Encompass* distributor.

"Hey, young man. You look ambitious. Why don't you be foreman and organize some sandwiches to go." They were like sheep. Once you got one moving, the rest would follow.

The whore carefully pinched out her cigarette, held up four fingers to the Indian, and sauntered for the john. He gave her an odd salute in return, as though he were animating a shadow animal on the wall.

"What an asshole," she said. She led him into the washroom, which was cleaner than he'd expected. Apart from a few missing tiles and an overfull waste basket, the place was spotless.

She prattled about how she used to "entertain" in one of the best establishments on the Memphis waterfront and that he reminded her of a better class of men who tipped well.

The jukebox in the diner came on, some song about a long drive ahead before being reunited with absent love. Crap, he really was in the weeds. Well, he'd made his choice.

He wouldn't take any chances. He reached for her, eliciting a moan, and then patted her down, eliciting a *what gives*, looking for weapons. He found a small knife, a short blade with a nice sheep's-foot handle, with a fork and spoon wrapped up in a damp washcloth that smelled like bleach. He dumped them in the overflowing wastebasket.

"Hey, I eat with those," she protested.

"Wash 'em," Macon said. "Take off that chain belt, too. Put it in the trash with the rest."

"Who you know ever got killed with a dog chain?" she said.

Macon patted the trigger guard on his gun with his index finger. "I don't take chances in the sticks."

The whore took off her shirt so slowly you might think she was paid by the hour. Then, rubbing her nipples in absentminded eroticism, she began to talk price.

"If you know what's good for you, you'll give me one just to stay in the good graces," Macon said. He should really be enjoying this more, his chances of getting a woman in the near future weren't great.

"C'mon, boss," she said. "Five bucks. For anything and everything. That's what you tip a doorman in Atlanta."

So began a tiresome argument, her arms crossed on her chest, holding up her small, undernourished breasts. Decent muscle on her shoulders but she could use a few weeks on Georgia ham. Amazing how so many of these people who tried to scratch an existence away from the Kurians wound up thin, sick, and haggard, like wild mutts compared to the sleek German Shepherds of the Control.

Whatever she did, even if she blew him like an eight-hundred dollar private dancer at the Velvet Cloud in Limotown, he'd bag and deliver her. Macon rather liked the idea that the very last skeet dispersing in her body would be his.

After what seemed like endless negotiations, he gave her a dollar. The price of a breath mint. Plus his personal guarantee that she wouldn't have to be out all night holding up a sign.

She unzipped his fly and released his growing erection.

"This'll be the best damn dollar you ever spent," she promised, dropping her knees to the clean white tiles.

†

Relaxed, sweaty, and tired, he exited the washroom a half hour later, counted heads. The jukebox was still wailing. He shut the door to the sound of the whore fishing in the trash can for her utensils.

A fly buzzed his ear. "Wait a cyc, where did the Indian guy go?"

As if in response, the jukebox went silent.

"I think he left," the kid said.

Macon glared at Casp. He shook his head. "No one's been through this door, boss."

"Left?" Macon looked at the counterman. "Did he go out the kitchen?"

"No, boss."

"Then—"

Macon heard plastic flapping. He followed the sound to the music player. Behind a shelving unit filled with stacked boxes of dry supplies a hole in the wall, plastic-covered, flapped. He suspected there'd once been a wall-unit air conditioner, probably long since sold off, the hole then filled with a couple of layers of roofing sheet.

Well, you'd have to expect a few rats to dodge a trap. Maybe Stutters-with-Gimp wasn't as stupid as he looked.

The whore came out of the washroom.

"Anyone who doesn't want to be dead, follow me," Macon said, looking pointedly at her. "You too, Red. Casp, bring up the rear, I don't want any more stragglers."

He strode out the door. The Transporter waited in the lot near the exit. They probably wouldn't be able to see into the windowless back compartment until they were inside. He just needed them to follow him to the back doors. Half of your Authority was in how you presented yourself, walked, talked, confidence bred—

Hands swung down out of the daylight like a mousetrap snapping shut. Before Macon processed that a man—a very strong one—must be up on the Wayside roof, somehow he was in the air, swung aloft by the straps on his Model 18 and his own field harness. He sagged as his gun hitched around some invisible projection, he could just see the shoulder brace of the folding stock . . .

"Casp!"

A shadow dropped, the steel hammer pick in its hand. The Indian—

He heard Casp grunt.

Three wet strikes. Two quick, one loud and slow—a secret

knock struck by a hatchet on a melon—and Casp fell. He looked like a toppled chess piece. The same neat collar, the same well-trimmed hair, facedown in front of a nowhere fill-up, all those hours in the gym punishing a punching bag obviated . . .

"Run for your lives," the Indian yelled to those inside, his stutter gone.

He swung one leg up on the roof, yanked on his gun until the strap came free, then felt himself fall—pulled down.

The ground hit him, hard.

A flurry of legs and he rolled over. Still had the gun. Smelled blood, saw it leaking out of Casp.

Horror in the lot. Red ran out of the driver's compartment on the Transporter. Those fools . . .

The Indian and Red were throwing bundles into the back of his Pooter. His Pooter! They climbed in, pressed the starter.

Macon raised his gun, sighted. He'd blow their brains out and let a sanitation squad clean up the Pooter.

PKEW! the gun rocked sideways in his hand. It had never done anything like that before in his range practice. He lowered it, tried to work the ejector but it wouldn't slide.

Misfire—

No, the Indian had jammed something in the barrel. The gun's mechanism was jammed. Shit—this had never happened to him in the field before, he'd had classroom training.

The Pooter spun around in the parking lot. Macon rolled out of the way, but they weren't heading for him . . . they pulled up alongside the Transporter and the girl slammed a bag into the wheel well.

The bag hissed and smoked.

The Pooter kicked up pebbles as they roared out of the Wayside.

Panting, heart hammering as it had never beat before, Macon dropped the useless gun and rushed to the side of the truck. Expecting to be torn to shreds any second by the blast, he wrenched the charge free. Hurled the bag—odd shape for a demolition charge, and wet, must be some bathtub fertilizer mix in Kur-knows-what container. Had the presence of mind to hit the dirt between himself and the still-airborne explosive.

It landed on the road. He could see it from beneath the Transporter. The bag had split on impact.

The cigarette she'd stuck inside the bag had gone out. The sputtering hiss had been from a bottle of flavored soda that had sprung a leak as she crammed it against the wheel. It was the bag full of sandwiches he'd told the kid to gather.

Angry, angrier than he'd ever been—*who were these fuckers!*—Macon climbed into the cab and shoved the dead idiots to the side. The radio was smashed. How had that dolt Casp not heard the Transporter crew being killed? Why had the Reapers remained inside? The passenger-side body was grinning at the secret joke of their demise, a Bicycle brand card still in his hand and a vast hole in his throat, as though someone had pried out his windpipe.

He started the engine and pulled out after the Pooter. The rest of the Wayside occupants were fleeing to various compass points.

The Transporter was built like a tank. Nothing short of a cannon could stop it. True Georgia Control craftsmanship, superb in its simplicity. Solid tires behind automatic blinds. Self-sealing fuel tank. Explosive-channeling armored plate.

He drove as though demons had occupied the Pooter and he was an avenging angel. His charges pounded on the wall between the driver's cabin and their compartment. They were probably going crazy from the blood smell.

Still daylight. The Kurians had a hard time keeping connections with their avatars in daylight.

He couldn't wait to turn them loose on this pair. Regular Bonnie and Clyde.

"Shut up back there!" he yelled.

No radio, so the speaker system was voice only.

They didn't shut up back there. The banging increased.

"I'm saving our lives. It's still daylight."

Macon heard rivets pop. *What the hell were they doing back there?* Metal protested.

"For Kur's sake!" he shouted at the dimpled partition.

At last the banging slackened. Maybe they finally figured out he was doing the driving and the communicator was dead.

✝

The Pooter headed north into wilderness, pushing through brush like a rampaging bull, suddenly lifted its tail. A great fallen tree filled the road, with thick woods to either side. The Pooter might still be able to push through, but only at a pace a jogging man could maintain.

Macon slammed on the brakes as well, hard enough so he heard a thump in back. Well, the Reapers wouldn't mind a few bumps. Especially not after he turned them loose on Bonnie and Clod.

The pair rolled out of the transport. He saw heads bob briefly as they made their way to cover at the front.

Macon felt very alone, now. In his first anger, he'd pursued without thinking about what would happen if he caught up to them. The sweat running down his back had gone cold and his mouth dry.

He rolled down the window, heard nothing but the breeze rustling through leafy spring growth and the popping of hot metal from his engine.

He found himself staring at the back of the transport. It took a moment for him to see what he was already looking at.

Someone had looped a length of no-shit tow-chain around the handles, crisscrossing it several times. Those doors wouldn't open from the inside without being torn off, and some puckering at the hinges on one side showed that the Reapers inside had been trying to do just that.

Yes, the Control really knew how to build them. The air vent to the rear chamber was atop the vehicle, a little mushroomlike projection with a grid to keep out hand grenades. Even an expert shot with a good angle couldn't use the vent to shoot into the rear.

But the grid was stuffed with rags.

Macon swooned for a moment, realizing the implications. He dropped to his hands and knees and looked under the Transporter.

Someone had stuck a siphon hose in the Transporter's exhaust and fed it into the air vent beneath the compartment. With the top corked, the deadly gasses had nothing to do but concentrate.

The implications came—hard and fast. The sweat on his brow made itself felt at the same time—cold and greasy.

Reapers used oxygen like everyone else. Carbon monoxide would build up and kill them. Easier than bullets.

Especially with some fool in the driver's seat redlining the engine.

Just as well he couldn't see the mess inside. Three Reapers, paler than they'd ever been. He could imagine the blue lines in their faces, more distinct than ever. He wondered what those yellow, slit-pupil eyes looked like in death.

Macon understood how it had happened, but would the Green Prince? A new man on the team, a red-ribboned, gift-wrapped, perfumed fuckup like this, and the loss of three qualified lives to a pair of junkyard guerillas.

He'd be lucky to get a job processing corpses for what was left of the Green Prince's Reapers.

For a moment, Macon considered putting the barrel of the gun under his chin and pulling the trigger.

If you want to rise, do the difficult.

It took a long time to grow a new Reaper to useful size and learn to survive on its own during breaks in contact with its master Kurian. Maybe ten years or so, though that was only a guess. No one he knew could say for certain. Only a select few were involved in that process. Maybe he could achieve something that would allow the Green Prince to control Western Kentucky with however many Reapers he had left. Couldn't be more than nine or ten, he'd never heard of a Kurian who had more than a dozen or so.

He cocked the revolver and came around the Transporter, firing as he advanced. He made it to the driver's seat, put the transmission in reverse, and backed away from the Pooter.

The figures rose, watching him. The redhead made an obscene gesture. The Indian stared. Maybe he mouthed something.

John Macon pointed at them, then drew his finger across his throat. Silent promise.

The Indian didn't react.

This isn't over, zealots. If I have to crawl and beg, sleep in the rain, and dine on raw rat, I'll make it my mission in life to figure out who you two are. I'll find your holes or your family or your clan and bring the full forest-burning heat of the Georgia Control down on you like the fist of an angry god. Before this summer's over, I'll have you both skinned and made into an awning, drink Long Islands out of your skulls, and wash my ass with your scalps.

CHAPTER TWO

*S*ite Green, the Pennyroyal of Kentucky, February of the Fifty-sixth year of the Kurian Order: the violent winter, the worst in living memory for even the outdoorsy locals, has ebbed at last. Nothing that might be called spring warms the sky, rather, it is a quiet between-season pause, like the lassitude between the break in a life-threatening fever and actual recovery.

"Damn near as bad as '76–'7," would, in time, become the new standard for calamity of war or weather, depending on how the individual in question labeled it. Youngsters would later recall the onset of the winter blizzards followed hard by the terrible ravies virus outbreak that blossomed in screams and death. Flight, cold, hunger, fear—everything turned upside down in the deep snow.

While the disease strain was the deadliest yet unleashed on mankind, it did not have nearly the calamitous effect of the original appearance, in that dreadful summer of 2022 when the Kurians first appeared. Then, ravies struck like something dreamed up in an apocalyptic horror movie with terrible effect. The saviors-turned-soulstealers appeared in the wake of a perfect storm of natural disaster and disease, offering aid and comfort that soon transitioned to enslavement and death once *they had the half-starved, bewildered population properly under their control.*

But Kentucky of 2076 wasn't the civilized world of 2022. From the Bluegrass to the Jackson Purchase, a network of clans who ranched Kurian-introduced legworms—and yes, some horses as well—toughened by years of squabbles with each other and bitter fighting against those who tried to incorporate them into the Kurian Order grazed their herds and preserved their independence. Their wary, well-armed neutrality made this limestone-hilled country the Switzerland of the eastern half of the United States. Yes, they sold the Kurians legworm meat and allowed a few towers along the main rail arteries, but if a Kurian ventured outside the urban centers with their Reapers, they lost enough avatars to make "free-ranging" futile in the careful cost/benefit analysis of the Kurian Order.

When Kentucky dropped its guarded neutrality briefly enough to allow rebel forces to cross its territory with the aid of a few clans hungry for real freedom, Kur unleashed its fury—first with the murderous Moondagger fanatics and, when that failed, with a virus designed to wipe the slate clean.

There were losses, whole settlements and clans wiped out, but it was not the cleansing the Kurians had hoped for, especially in the rugged fastness of south-central Kentucky.

However, much of the Western Coal Fields and the axe-handle of Kentucky's Pennyroyal region were emptied as what was left of the locals fled to the protection of Kentucky's military in the heartland or the tiny bastion of Southern Command south of Evansville.

With frost and flurries still washing across the state on cold mornings, the Kurian Order seeks to take advantage of the emptiness. Nature abhors a vacuum, the unnature of the vampiric Kurian Order exploits one.

The Georgia Control, a manufacturing center for eastern North America, has the audacity and the organization to swallow such a huge bite of territory. Why the Western Tennessee Kurians, a looser organization called the Nashville Concordance, agreed to support the endeavor that would add so much to the Control's dominance in the region is a matter of some dispute. The various Kurian states are notorious for their plotting and backstabbing. Georgia either offered up a king's ransom in auras or the Concordance Kurians believed that where their northern brethren had bled and failed, southerners would do no better and a weakened Georgia Control would be much to their advantage.

There are other less likely guesses, of course, but those disputes are for the philosophers. Let us return to the beginning of the latest bid for Kentucky's rich hills and bottoms.

Signs that spring might be ready to appear are all around Central City, what used to be a little crossroads town near the old Green River Correctional Complex. Geese and ducks alight in the lakes and swamps northwest of town, drawn north by the warmth to their traditional nesting areas. Yellow coltsfoot blossoms—a local remedy for a lingering winter cough and sore throat—are beginning to open along the old roadsides, as if eager for the sun, though the roads are little better than broken-up streams of pavement filled with scrub growth and mudslide, a jeep trail at best.

The abandoned prison complex now houses birds, bats, and a multitude of hornets' nests at the top and everything from wild pigs to black bears on the bottom floors, with rats running between. For the Kurians, putting the stout concrete buildings in order and installing new glass and flooring can wait. The raccoons and owls will reign for a few weeks more everywhere but one office the engineers cleared in order to complete a survey of what needed to be done to restore the structure.

The future Kurian tower will need holding cells and forced-labor housing.

Noisy activity can be seen and heard around the clock at a construction site outside the defunct prison, on a patch of earth where the ground begins to rise between the prison and Central City. Two small signs identify it as SITE GREEN, one just off old state Route 277 and one off 602, both of which have been cleared of brush and tree growth by hungry-mouthed chippers for easier passage of equipment.

Two wire-fenced camps, one for the uniformed soldiers of elite Nashville Concordance Guard on temporary lease to the Georgia Control and police of the Clarksville Border Troop and another for the worksite proper, snuggle side by side like a pair of pellet-chewing rabbits, both covered by towers, zeroed-in mortars and machine guns and ever-vigilant guarded gates. The military camp is thick with green tents. The construction fencing guards what is currently a deep hole and a few mounds of construction materials and piles of steel reinforcing rods, with a cement-mixing facility blistered out of the side like a growth.

The race to fill the vacuum has begun. It would appear the Kurians were first off their marks.

As the sun set at Site Green on, appropriately enough, Valentine's Day, the other team joined the race. It seems an uneven contest. On the one side in this bit of empty are five companies of hired professional soldiers in the light butter color of Nashville khaki, their support staff and heavy weapons crews, police and reconnaissance auxiliaries, construction machinery, experts, technicians, strong-backed laborers, and a few cooks and cleaners and supervisors.

On the other is a single man lying as though nested in a patch of hairy vetch, watching the camps turn off and in for the night. He's dressed in a curious assortment of legworm leathers, insulating felt vest and gaiters, canvas trousers, and a nondescript green service jacket with rain hood missing its drawstring. One of the canny, nettle-scratched, and well-nigh uncatchable wild boars who root the nearby Green River marshes might recognize a kindred spirit if he came snout-to-nose with the man. Both know they're a potential meal if they're not careful, both have a dozen tricks to throw off trackers and hunters, or better yet, to avoid being observed in the first place. And both can be unbelievably fast and fierce when cornered.

Scarred on face and missing an earlobe, weathered, and with a few strands of gray in his still-thick black hair, he has an uneven set to his jaw that can look humorous or thoughtful. At the moment you might say thoughtful, thanks to the slow-moving piece of fresh grass shoot working at the right side of his mouth the way a cow absently chews her cud. He's not looking at the military camp. What's behind that wire and passing in and out of the tents has long since been observed, estimated, and recorded in a battered pocket notebook.

Instead he gazes at the mobile-homelike cluster of temporary housing for the most important members of the construction staff, especially the extra-wide one with the words Site Green Construction Supervisor V. Champers *stenciled next to the doorbell.*

†

They're not wasting any time, Valentine thought. Maybe he'd wasted too much, first in Tennessee trying to trace the traffic from the Georgia Control to its terminus, then observing the construction site for two days, slowly devouring his precious supplies—mostly canned WHAM! legworm meat, uninteresting unless you liked faintly barbecued-flavor chewing exercises—he'd brought.

After a long session of sassafrass tea–fueled negotiations with a shifty backwoods family of smuggled-goods dealers—he turned over the Pooter and its contents. He'd finally settled on a well-fitting pair of snake-proof military boots, two bottles of bonded bourbon, and a sum of Nashville cash he suspected was counterfeit. He kept only an Atlanta Youth Vanguard star-cluster leader key fob and a mobile file cabinet stuffed with papers and marked Asst. Staff Facilitator Macon.

He'd spent a lot of time reading, while watching the construction site and getting a feel for its rhythms.

He waited, reading and watching, lying like a snake in the tall grass on an old saddle-sheepskin so dirty the mottled brown passed for camouflage. Dirty or not, it still protected his belly from the cold earth. Beside him, in a protective deerskin sheath, his Atlanta-built Type Three, 7.62mm, four feet of match-barrel battle rifle, waited like a sleeping friend.

He hoped it would stay sheathed for the night.

When his hard-running Wolves had first reported the construction and military traffic—one of the long-range patrols had cut across a road leading back to Clarksville recently used and partially cleared and sensibly followed it north to the source—he'd taken the matter up with Colonel Lambert. Their bloodied-but-still-training companies of ex-Quislings, sort of a "Foreign Legion" grudgingly acknowledged by Southern Command but at the string-knotted end of the supply chain, now had something much more ominous to face than a few ravies-addled psychopaths starving in the woods.

The under-construction tower was like a sandglass being filled from the heavens above. Once it was up, the Kurians within would control everything within a fifty-mile or more radius.

Putting a monkey wrench in the Kurian gears was a job for the whole brigade, or maybe just a few men. Valentine shaved that down to one, then reluctantly accepted the company of a wolf messenger and Alessa Duvalier as far as the outskirts of Central City.

"One?" Lambert had asked, her usual brisk—some might say fussy, others attentive—manner shocked into immobility.

"I'm not going to fight. I'll go and have a talk with them," Valentine said.

That's still what he planned to do, go and have a talk, armed with information obtained from Macon's files. He checked the hilt of the fourteen-inch parang strapped to his thigh, the .45 automatic at his hip, and his quiet little silencer-threaded .22 tucked under his arm. The legworm pick was holding up some camouflage netting above his body.

One worry. There was at least one Reaper in the camp, and a man who left a Reaper out of his calculations could easily find himself dead and strung up like a weasel on a gamekeeper's gibbet.

Alessa Duvalier, a redheaded tangle of living razor wire who'd trained him as a Cat almost a decade ago, lurked somewhere alongside the road leading to the gates, ready to hunt the hunter should the Reaper venture outside the gate. While it could leap even the nine-foot-high fencing around the military camp, Reapers didn't like to exhibit their lethal prowess around their allies. It unsettled their underlings. They'd rather engage in quiet little murders in basements and abandoned barns.

Getting to the construction housing would be easy enough.

The trailers had nothing of value to protect. No valuable machine tools and construction equipment, no carefully guarded armories. Only a few hard hats and their laundry and some greasy baking foil.

Night fell early, cloudy and cold, and he waited for the guard change, slowly chewing the last of his canned WHAM! to convince his stomach he'd eaten more than he actually had. He gave the fresh guards another two hours to become not-so-fresh, marked the location of the lone dog patrol, and wiggled with his rifle down to the construction camp fence.

The smell of new spring green was everywhere. Some wild daffodils had opened, their yellow bluish in the dark. Their sweet aroma invigorated him.

He made it to the garbage pit behind the construction camp and waited out the dog patrol.

Thanks to the heavy equipment, they made a good job of it. The pit was ten full feet deep and much wider. Already it was littered with refuse, packaging, and bits from the construction already under way.

Valentine lay at the lip, pretending he didn't own a working nose.

The stuff these Georgia Control workers tossed out! There was foil everywhere, smelling of a better grade of barbecue sauce than the WHAM! he'd consumed. In the United Free Republics, the make-do populace would never toss out practically brand-new foil. It would be washed, flattened, and folded by whichever kid had reuse chores that week. Once holed and useless, it would be added to the mass of insulation around an icebox or root cellar or compost pile, if it didn't end up expanding the capacity of some old-timer's still.

The Control, one of the richest and best-organized Kurian Zones, encompassing as it did much of the old Carolinas, the civilized northern slice of Florida, and a good piece of Alabama and Tennessee besides, had resources the hardscrabble free territories couldn't dream of. Ports for trade, overseas air, the rich coastal waters to feed their population—

Then again, perhaps the Georgia Control had never fought a real war against determined humans choosing to die in battle instead of pierced by the tongues of the Kurian's Reapers. They could bite off pieces of their neighbors, but they might prove just an oversized band of vicious riot police. Everyone had thought the Moondaggers invincible until they fought real troops with real weapons.

The dog patrol passed, checking the overgrown ditches next to the road. Valentine saw a shape creeping behind, close to the brush, arms and legs splayed like a spider, wrists and ankles bent and fingers splayed in an unsettling manner

Reaper. Keeping watch over the dog and its handler.

This one scuttled more like a scorpion than in its usual biped locomotion, moving so it couldn't be easily observed.

Valentine pulled back into himself, imagining his consciousness a blue ball of energy he could shrink to a marble and place in his pocket. Reapers hunted mankind, seeking *lifesign*. It was an energy given off by sentient creatures in response to their size and mental development.

The Reapers had the usual senses, of course. No one knew how good they were, though Valentine had some idea they lay somewhere between the handler and his dog. He'd taken in an infant Reaper after escaping Ohio, and his "son" was growing up near

Saint Louis under the guidance of a woman who'd saved his life on Hispaniola.

The Reaper paused, rotated its head like a security camera, stared briefly at the garbage pit. Valentine, quiescent as a mushroom, saw a family of raccoons, a hefty mother leading her offspring, approach the ramp to the pit.

The Reaper cranked its head back to the forward position and scooted off after the dog and handler.

Valentine ceased relaxing. At last he could have his talk.

†

It was a homey little trailer, dark save for some light behind the bedroom blinds. The lock proved no more trouble than the polite gesture its manufacturer intended. One bedroom, a kitchen, and a cramped office in what he imagined was meant to be a spare bedroom at the other end. It smelled of pasta and vinegar salad dressing. The detritus on the counter showed everything but the bread and wine came out of a can, including the artichokes. There was a small bar buffet next to a comfortable chair with some ice melting in a cocktail shaker. Valentine picked up a yellow plastic ball and sniffed the lemon juice inside. That took the stench of garbage out of his nostrils.

Animal noises, the galumphing sounds and keening cries of lovemaking, pulsed out of the bedroom. Whatever was going on in there was vigorous enough to make the living room's main light fixture vibrate and one of the cheap kitchen cabinets swing open.

Valentine marked a little bouquet of plastic flowers.

These will have to do until the real ones appear in the spring, read the card.

He removed his new boots and waited in the dark, leafing through a digest of Kurian Zone newspapers by the floodlight coming in through the blinds. No sense spoiling everyone's fun.

A few strangled cries, a gasp, then a few murmurs. A dark-haired, pleasantly plump woman appeared nude in the hallway before shutting the bathroom door on Valentine.

He heard a shower curtain shut.

Her lingering sweat smelled like sex and verbena with a little bay rum.

Valentine picked up a plastic squeeze bottle of lemon juice on the bar and slipped into the bathroom. Moving fast—faster than an alert boxer could react, impossibly fast for a woman with soap in her eyes—he opened the shower curtain and grabbed the girl by her mouth and waist. She froze in shock.

"It's okay," he said, forcing the plastic lemon into her mouth. "It's okay."

"There's only a twenty-gallon tank for the hot water, Carrie," a male voice called from the bedroom as Valentine reached for the belt to a terrycloth robe.

Valentine bound her wrists with a strip of plastic, temporary restraints carried by every Kurian security man. She'd be able to chew through them once she worked the robe belt out from around her head and the plastic lemon out of her mouth.

"Don't signal for help while I'm here," Valentine whispered. "I'm not hurting anyone. I'm here to have a little chat with the construction supervisor."

He waved his brass ring under her eye. "I have powerful friends," he whispered above the shower. "Be quiet, now."

He left her tied to the toilet plumbing.

"What the hell," Champers gasped, sitting bolt upright as Valentine strode in, pointing his .22.

Champers seemed to Valentine more like an accountant than a construction hand. He had wizened eyes, a pale, angular body. He reached for some thick glasses.

"Don't be alarmed, Mr. Supervisor. I'm less your enemy than your bosses. Do you have any idea what your file says about you?"

"Carrie," Champers called.

"She's fine," Valentine said. "I didn't want her screaming out the window for help during our interview. It might help if you told her it's okay."

"That remains to be proved. So, what did I do this time?" Champers said.

Valentine sat down on an aluminum steamer trunk that smelled like mothballs. "I've no idea."

"Then why the midnight call? You make me think my time's up."

"That's not my department. I'm passing along some information I happened across. You've got below-acceptable evaluations in political activity and community service."

Champers swung his legs out of the bed, felt for slippers.

"Want some coffee?" he asked. Valentine stiffened as Champers's hand moved toward the bedside table, but he reached only for a pack of cigarettes and some matches.

Valentine had to admire the man's coolness, though he could still see a pulse going, fast and hard in Champers's temple. "Let's stay in here for the moment."

"Can I smoke?"

"It's your house."

"You with the Control?"

Valentine set the gun down on the trunk next to his thigh. "No."

Champers waited.

"Champers, you're going to have to come up with a reason to abandon these works. Go fifty miles west toward the Mississippi, go fifty miles east toward Lexington. Just don't build here."

"How do I—"

"That's not my problem. You're an expert. Say the ground's too soft for a tower of that height, or there's malaria in the river. You have men on your construction crew with malaria? Show them one. Hell, I heard the Control's mostly run by humans. Bypass this Kurian and take it up with the Control. Say Center City's a no go."

"You must be a Kentuckian. The rebels. You don't sound like one, you're more northern."

Valentine shrugged. "Doesn't matter. What does matter to me, very much, is that this tower never goes up. Now, we could stop it with a big fight, lots of explosives, God knows how many deaths. Or you could kill it with an engineering reason."

Champers cleaned his glasses with a corner of his sheet. "You really want this project stopped?"

"Yes."

"I can kill it. Permanent as a big air strike. But I need some help, and I need to get away. With my men. Every damn one of us, or the deal's off and you'll have to kill me and try your luck with the Control garrison."

Valentine felt control of the conversation slipping away. He'd intended to come in, bluff and talk round a powerful Quisling, and instead, purely by accident, learned a name of an engineer of top-rated technical competence but doubtful loyalty to the Kurian Order. A strange man to put in charge of a tower. He was either a Kurian agent under very deep cover or truly a brilliant misfit.

"Define help," Valentine said, smelling a bottle of bay rum aftershave on the dresser.

Champers adjusted his glasses. "You're with the resistance, right? Look, me and my crew's expendable. It's a bunch of men and women on their last legs with the Control. Records like blotting paper, all of us. They've put us out here on the spear tip because if we get sheared off, no loss, we're headed for the recycling bin anyway. Maybe once the tower's finished, we'll be the first official sacrifice. Just like the Control to save a tank of fuel bussing us back."

"I sat handcuffed in a recycling bin a couple years ago myself, Champers. I don't like to see others tossed into a black van."

The engineer's eyebrow went up. "The Control uses white."

"I didn't say it was in the Control. Why would they get rid of you? You look pretty healthy, except for your eyesight."

"I've got a reputation as a bit of an unmindful. I skip the Church and community stuff."

"Unmindful?" Valentine asked. Strange phrase, it reminded him of Orwell's *doubleplus ungood*. For a moment, he was back in Father Max's leaky one-classroom school in a forgotten stretch of Minnesota lake country.

"I don't toe the line. I've also kept my people out of the can. Not the easiest thing to manage. The Kurians are always getting rid of 'idle hands' in the building trades. *Idle* meaning not pulling a fifteen-hour day, six days a week."

He seemed a little too eager for a guy who'd just made love to his woman and had a man barge in on him as he was considering a postcoital cigarette. That or he was a man who felt increasingly trapped, and finally saw a way out.

Valentine hadn't stayed alive in the Kurian Zone so long by trusting, but something about this man was *sympatico*.

"Can you trust your woman?"

"Carrie's been my admin for six years. She's made all the right paperwork disappear. Could have turned me in for a nice promotion hundreds of times."

"It's your choice. Maybe we should all have that coffee and see about arranging a long-term retirement plan from the Control. *We* could certainly use some trained construction engineers in Kentucky."

✝

Champers had an engineer's mind. He adjusted to new factors quickly and settled on an efficient course of action. He'd argue for a new location for the tower's foundation. If they listened and switched, it would mean a week's delay or more. If they overrode him, he could arrange for an accident that would prove his original objection.

Meanwhile, Valentine would organize a breakout for the misfit construction camp.

With the woman named Carrie, he didn't seem so much the tanned accountant, more the attentive boyfriend. She needed it. Perhaps it was the strain of being assaulted in the shower and tied up showing, but she seemed terrified by the idea.

At the very least, Valentine decided, the works might be delayed until they could return with more forces. Then, if the Control put enough troops around Center City to meet an unknown threat, they'd have to weaken elsewhere. His companies or the Army of Kentucky could hit a weak spot then and really pour some fat into the fire.

Carrie had a hundred questions, but Valentine wasn't willing to answer any of them.

"He's trusting us on our end. We'll have to trust him on his," Champers said.

They worked out a dead letter drop, using a coffeepot in the garbage dump, shook hands, and wished each other luck.

"Honestly, how far can you set them back?" Valentine asked as he put his hand on the door.

The accountant look came back into his eyes. "Six weeks. Eight if they're careless with inspecting the heavy equipment after we've run."

Valentine wondered how much his battalion and the Army of Kentucky could accomplish in that time.

Well, he was but a major. The higher-ups would have to decide what to do about the Georgia Control.

He hurried away into the overcast night, around the garbage pit and under the wire fence, recovered rifle cradled in his arms. Just in case.

The light went on in the trailer's bedroom again. Maybe they were releasing nervous tension together.

"More power to you, hard hat," Valentine said, safe beyond the wire.

Of course, safe, anywhere near the Kurian Zone, was a relative term. Valentine's hair rose—a sure sign of a nearby Reaper.

He didn't know where he got the gift of sensing them. Perhaps he'd been born with it. Some of the other things he could do came from the Lifeweavers, humanity's extraterrestrial allies against their Kurian cousins. His night vision, sense of smell, reflexes, healing—there were others who had been enhanced better than he. But he'd never met another Wolf, or Cat, or Bear who could tell by a cold feeling at the back of the head that a Reaper was nearby.

It was up on the hill. Near where he was supposed to meet Duvalier.

He risked a run, hoping the guards in the towers weren't looking his way with night vision.

Panting and dragging his bad leg, he made it to the crest of the hill. The brush was lighter up here.

Duvalier approached, hands shoved in the pockets of her big duster, smiling. Her sword staff was tucked under her arm like a swagger stick.

He held up a clenched fist—danger!

Was she drunk? Crazy? She ignored him, still shuffling forward as though trying to make as much noise in the soggy leaves as possible.

A black figure exploded out of the trees, running for her.

Too late, Duvalier turned.

She screamed. Not her battle cry, half wildcat screech and half foxhunt yelp, this was a shriek of pure terror.

The Reaper put long pale fingers around Duvalier's arms. It lifted her. She kicked futilely at its kneecaps and crotch.

"Hey!" Valentine broke cover, waving his arms, anything to get it off Duvalier. "You! Over here!"

It opened its mouth. Duvalier managed to get a hand up to ward off the coming tongue—

The Reaper jerked back as though kicked in the head by a Grog. It fell with her, one arm still gripping skin so deeply blood welled up like a pitchfork thrust into rain-soaked soil.

Adrenals on fire in the small of his back he ran up, parang and .45 out, noise of the shots be damned, in time to see Duvalier sawing at the dead Reaper's forearm tendons with her own camp utility knife. Released from the death grip, she stood up and turned to meet him.

"You have your talk?" she panted, smiling.

Seeing red and needing a fight, he resisted an impulse to slap her. "What was that, letting a Reaper grab you?"

"Val, that was a hyperalert Reaper. I saw him come out of camp. He was feeling fine and ready for a night in the bush. His master must be somewhere nearby to have such a good connection. Hope he felt it wherever those squids keep their appetite. Just a sec—"

She vomited up watery bile. "That's better."

Duvalier had suffered for years from what she called a "delicate stomach." A combination of bad water and worse food while wandering the Great Plains meant that anything stronger than rice and stewed chicken gave her indigestion.

Valentine scanned the horizon three hundred sixty degrees, looking for something that might serve as a Kurian tower. "How did you kill it?"

She stuck the blade of her camp knife into its jaws, pried them open a little wider. The Reaper's stabbing tongue flopped sideways, like a broke-back snake smashed by a rock. With the jaws held open, Duvalier reached in and pulled out a blade about the size of a largish pen. It had a triangular base and narrowed to a fine point.

"Nasty little pigsticker Chieftain rigged for me." She rolled up her sleeve and showed the spring-loaded holder for a stiletto. "You have to hit a button. I'm glad he grabbed me by the upper arms instead of the wrists."

"I should think so," Valentine said, good and mad.

"Spit, the stick up your ass must like it there, I can hear it getting longer. I had it under control, Val. I've been hunting these dickless assholes longer than you. Stinkbait here thought I was easy pickins."

Valentine massaged his sore leg. "Thanks for the heart attack."

"Your heart! Ha. You're a little soft between the ears, and I can't speak for what's between your legs, never having been with you in the Biblical sense, but I think that heart of yours is unharmed and untouched as ever. You're all cold blood and hot steel, like those killer robots in the old whatchacallit we saw at the movie palace in New Orleans."

Valentine was examining the Reaper's dress. It wore a tight-fitting jumpsuit that reminded him of the padding a baseball umpire wore over his chest. It was almost stylized. The monk's robe look wasn't popular in Atlanta, it seemed.

"What's next, Val?" Duvalier asked.

"We strip your kill here. The material and the fangs will be worth something to the smugglers or the Kentuckians. Then we head back for Fort Seng and deliver the bad news. Georgia is on the march."

CHAPTER THREE

*O*dds and Sods: As it ages, any large institution develops quiet filtering areas where less useful or odd-fitting pieces wash up, to be either sluiced out of the prospector's pan or picked out for some more useful activity. In a well-run organization, these pools are managed so that those in them perform activity that's at least marginally useful.

In a more sclerotic bureaucracy, those who find themselves in such filter pockets may moulder away quietly until retirement, in happy or unhappy obscurity depending on temperament, devoting most of their time and talent to making a more comfortable barnacle shell for themselves.

Sometimes, out of a mixture of talent and boredom, an individual will energize the sluice.

Fort Seng, just south of Evansville, Indiana, in the early days of what soon would be the Kentucky Free Alliance, was that sort of place. Fort Seng was remarkable in its organizational gravity. It served as a swamp not for one such organization, but for three.

By designation, it was under control of Southern Command, the military arm of a welded-together federation of states resisting the Kurian Order called the United Free Republics. The UFR encompasses a region from Southern Missouri to Texas north of Houston, somewhat *protected by the vastness and emptiness of the plains to the west and the Mississippi River to the east. Southern Command's operations in Kentucky have received all the attention a butt-cheek boil would on a patient in the midst of coronary surgery.*

A fresh face and set of strategic outlooks in the form of Lieutenant-General Martinez has a large staff evaluating all of Southern Command's operations with an eye toward improving conditions, training, and chains of command. Martinez assumed overall command with a mandate from the newly elected president to prevent another in a series of expensive disasters that have dogged Southern Command since the mad dash through Texas at the birth of the UFR. Martinez has put Southern Command into a "defensive stance," devoting his energies to consolidating what has already been won and giving his forces much-needed time to refit and rest.

Commander-in-Chief Martinez has a few career graveyards for those who don't toe the new line. Fort Seng is one of them. It's too far away to be within his new, more defensible map of "chords and arcs." Withdrawal is not in the political cards, as the previous year's trek across Kentucky in an attempt to establish a new freehold in the Appalachians was a partial success, ending with a victory outside Evansville that inspired much of Kentucky's populace to rebel against the Kurians. With bodies of both Southern Command's soldiers and their legworm-riding allies scattered across last-year's battlefields, the United Free Republics aren't yet ready to forget about the smouldering embers of Operation Javelin that had lit a flame of revolt across Kentucky.

For the city of Evansville, a modest industrial town lately pried from the Kentucky Northwest Ordnance, Fort Seng is another sort of destination. The city has survived a dreadful shakeout. Kurian loyalists have fled elsewhere, and the factories and workshops fed by Ohio River traffic are short raw materials and components for their new duties in equipping Kentucky's forces in the field. Half the population has been reduced to survivalist farming in little garden and parkland plots, fish hatcheries in polluted water diverted from the Ohio, or keeping chickens and pigs in abandoned housing and the rest are underemployed and growing poorer and more ragged by the day. Some have "called quits" and crossed the river seeking work around Fort Seng, where even that trickle of funds and supplies General Martinez allows his Kentucky garrison is enough to attract the desperate.

Oddly enough, Southern Command scrip, the military currency disparaged throughout the United Free Republics and only accepted by most merchants at a highly disadvantageous exchange rate for macro- and microeconomic reasons that would make too lengthy a digression for our purposes, but which boil down to "can't buy jack in the here and now" is the common currency.

One might even say this stretch of Kentucky is a last chance for a few in the Kurian Zone as well. There are those who find escaping to Kentucky's Jackson Purchase easier than the long trek to the United Free Republics or the dangerous run across the Great Lakes for the deep north woods outside the Kurian Windsor-Toronto-Montreal Belt. They're valuable citizens, if they make it. Escaping across the Northwest Ordnance or through the military concentrations of the Nashville and Atlanta Kurians ensures that only the most careful, healthy, and intelligent make it. Once installed, they work hard to overcome the usual shortcomings of a Kurian Zone upbringing: near illiteracy, habits of blending in so as not to attract attention, and instinctive avoidance of authority figures.

It's also a destination for Quislings who worry their record supporting the Kurians will be used against them. Some are last-second "bolters" who've failed in some colossal manner and fear a visit from the Reapers. Others can no longer live with themselves as cogs in the dreadful system. Service with Southern Command's odd-lot battalion at Fort Seng for six years promises a new identity with an honorable military record. Those with grievous sins they wish to escape, forget, or expunge show up at Fort Seng, give their assumed name, take the oath, and are escorted to the showers and supply depots.

A few who support the Kurian Order even wash up somewhere between Evansville and Fort Seng. Kentucky was long a region of well-armed neutrality and there are those who would have it return to that condition. They would bring Kentucky back with tactics drawn from Shakespeare: "When lenity and cruelty play for a kingdom, the gentler gamester is the soonest winner." A missionary who ran a little one-man doughnut shop led the way. He had quickly become a fixture, not just because his doughnuts were tasty, but because of his zeal and friendliness with all who crossed his path. A few others have followed in his footsteps, unarmed and professing only peaceful intent, including a doctor and a dentist and a couple of teachers who provide services for little or no charge but pay for their necessities in silver and gold. Their offices are littered with Kurian tracts, their professional chatter full of careful probes and discreet offers. Not quite enough have arrived so that there's a "Kurian Quarter" in "Desperation Row" as the little strip outside Fort Seng is now called, but enough so that they too have a place in the remarkable collection gravitating to this corner of Vampire Earth.

†

Every time Valentine left Fort Seng, even for a few nights, the camp changed by the time he returned.

This time his return was from the south, mounted on a leg-worm, a sort of giant caterpillar introduced to the area by the Kurian allies in 2022. Atop the worm's back, riding at about the height of an old tractor-trailer driver and moving at a steady pace a little slower than a dog trotted—Valentine idly calculated it at nine miles per hour by dropping a weighted line and pacing the worm's back in a fashion not dissimilar from the way old sailing ships measured their speed—he could stretch out, sleep even, while the worm's driver prodded it along with pokes from a long hook.

The young worm and its driver were on loan from the Gunslinger Clan. The Kentucky legworm raisers were the closest allies of Southern Command's forces locally. He'd travelled with them, fought alongside them, saw victory and defeat beside them. They contributed a "troop" of legworm cavalry to support their allies at the base, with a few more available in a pinch. For now, they had five legworms providing slow, but all-terrain, transport and cargo haulage, and were training the fort's garrison to handle a dozen more. Southern Command's forces, which up to the Javelin operation had been only on the receiving end of legworm-mounted attacks, were learning fast—at least in Kentucky.

Back across the Mississippi, any species that had "appeared" since 2022 was considered suspect at the very least.

It was Colonel Lambert's doing of course. She liked her camp the way she liked her desk: neat, organized, everything in its place. Valentine had never actually seen her pencil drawer, but he suspected all her leads were sharp and facing the same direction.

Outside Fort Seng, there was a new sign up at the vast New Universal Church relief tent:

NO FOOD TODAY
SUPPLIES INTERCEPTED

Valentine had heard that once the sign claimed Southern Command had intercepted and confiscated their shipment. A few of the Bears visited the tent, tore it down, and bounced the churchmen on an improvised trampoline made out of the tent, explaining that if Southern Command had intercepted a food shipment, they'd be eating it.

Since being bounced almost high enough to see the Ohio River over the hills and trees, the missionaries had cut down on the specificity of their claims.

Always-hungry Bears had great noses for food.

He dismounted long enough to clear the legworm driver and Duvalier—a blanket-covered carbuncle on the mossy back of the worm—into the fort.

A block-and-log guardhouse stood at the gate now, along with an unmanned machine gun position. They were positioned well to cover each other. Valentine saw a couple of doughnuts resting on a sill, an easy reach through the window of the guardhouse.

"Crumbs on your uniform, son," he told the guard.

"Sorry, Major." The private brushed the crumbs off.

"Let's watch the eating on sentry duty. We don't want our friends across the highway thinking we're slack." He forced a smile.

Valentine scowled at the corporal standing at the guardhouse door. He didn't like this kind of petty officiousness, especially when he was riding into camp dirty, unshaven, and dressed in a collection of odds and ends that barely qualified as guerilla-wear. But a quiet word and a glare or two now were better than going to the man's captain, who'd roll it downhill to a lieutenant or sergeant, and the poor kid would hear about it tonight or the next day, with all that added momentum.

Once through the woods and to the fort proper, Valentine thanked the worm driver and checked off on a list of supplies he'd carry back to their Gunslinger allies. He woke Duvalier and sent her to the showers, then walked up to the great house that served as Fort Seng's impressive headquarters.

He noted new gravel on the athletic field and some log bleachers. Baseball and basketball were the traditional sports of Southern Command, but for some reason the men of Fort Seng loved kicking around soccer balls outside and Ping-Pong indoors. It had probably started because that was the only athletic gear at hand. They'd added some rule modifications of their own that brought it closer to rugby or football. Exciting stuff to watch, but Valentine hadn't had the chance to do much but goaltend during practices yet.

There were some new vegetable beds in on the mansion grounds as well. Time was, when a sergeant wanted to drill his platoon, he'd take them to "the field" or "the hill." There they'd crawl, run, walk, squat, and roll until he or she could smell the sweat. Colonel Lambert changed that. She preferred exercising the troops under her care by having them build or haul or dig, and if the fort didn't need gravel or lumber or rubble cleared away that week, well, the city of Evansville did.

Valentine approved—for the most part. He voiced a concern that Evansville had to look on their allies at Fort Seng as soldiers first, and a handy source of disciplined labor a long second. Evansville had to organize itself, the day might come when Lambert's battalion would move out and be gone for a year.

✝

No new faces at headquarters. Lambert was off at the big guns that watched over the river, so he reported to her acting adjutant, a former Quisling he'd trained up for the long march across Kentucky last year. She'd been promoted to captain and, next to his old top sergeant, Nilay Patel, was probably the best officer at Fort Seng. Captain Ediyak had proven her worth since day one as a Southern Command recruit, and Valentine was pleased to see her under Lambert's wing.

Through the doorway, Valentine saw an unfamiliar man wearing a major's cluster sitting in Lambert's office reading personnel files. He had the hard, glitzy look of a headquarters type, like polished chrome. He needed reading glasses but didn't put them on his nose. Instead he lounged there with one bow in his mouth, nibbling thoughtfully as he read through the lenses. Ediyak didn't mention him so Valentine didn't ask.

"Once you're cleaned up, there are a couple new faces you need to meet," Ediyak said. She always reminded Valentine of the models in the old magazines, big eyed, delicate, and thin. He knew the delicacy was only skin-deep. She was as strong as any woman at Fort Seng, just small boned from a youth on short rations. Her family had been nobodies in the Kurian Deep South, so as a little girl she probably hadn't seen a ham from one Thanksgiving to the next.

"Need, not want?" Valentine poured himself a glass of water from her office carafe—a nice piece of silver, the old mansion was full of flashy gewgaws its former Quisling owner had collected—and sat down. Ediyak knew him well enough to know that when he was off his feet protocols were relaxed and she could speak freely.

"Depends. We've had a couple more Bears come in. That makes five this month, I believe. These last two were busted out of their outfit for talking monkey about Martinez and his new 'defensive stance.' Or maybe they want to be where there's still fighting. One of them said something about your old unit, the Razorbacks."

Talking monkey was Southern Command slang for throwing feces, to put it politely. The Razorbacks were an ad hoc unit formed on the march into Texas, and had been disbanded a few years back after nearly being destroyed in the siege of Dallas.

"I never say no to Bears. Gamecock is good with discipline problems. We could use them. There's a Kurian tower being built about sixty miles southeast of here, more or less."

"The colonel will need to hear about that."

Valentine nodded.

"There's also someone the Miskatonic sent. Between us, I think Southern Command didn't know what to do with her, so she got shipped out here. She claims you're the only one that can appreciate her ideas."

Valentine noticed the major in the next room had been looking at the same page for the last minute without moving his eyes.

If headquarters wanted to spy, let them. Their officer would return and report that yes, Fort Seng is woefully short of Southern

Command's Interior Utility Gray paint and individual field toilet paper packs.

"A nut?"

Ediyak crinkled her nose and mouth into an expression half pucker, half smile. "More like a zookeeper—well, you'll just have to meet her. She's set up above the stables, so she can be near her little menagerie. I'd introduce you, but I've got the desk."

"I'll try and find her on my own."

"Ask for Victoria Pellwell. Tall. Hard to miss."

"Pellwell?"

"Victoria Pellwell."

"Sounds like a heroine in a Gothic romance," Valentine said. "Ailing father."

"Lots of windswept moors and a cozy hayloft."

He felt a gentle pang. He'd touched his first woman in a hayloft. Molly Carlson, who'd grown up in an agricultural Kurian Zone in Wisconsin.

"Don't forget the tin bathtub that the maid has to fill with a kettle." Valentine had baths on the mind. He disliked being dirty; personally, and professionally he didn't like wandering headquarters looking like roadkill, so he made his excuses to Ediyak and headed off to the big basement bathroom and sauna next to what had presumably once been an exercise room. There he used one of the luxurious, multihead showers to soap his collection of Tennessee and Kentucky dirt off and changed into clean fatigues. He handed his newly acquired boots to Bee for polishing.

Bee was a "gray" Grog, a member of a muscular, thick-skinned fighting race of near-human intelligence. Or maybe they were as smart as humans, with a different way of presenting and learning. Grogs possessed good instincts for machinery and weapons, tools and plants and animals, but they fell apart when put in front of a sketch board where two-dimensional icons represented the solid objects they understood. He'd known her previous companion, a stinky bounty hunter named Price, and had rescued her from a circus menagerie years later. She'd gained a few scars and lost vision in one eye serving him. Bee fretted when he was gone too long.

And the people around headquarters indulged her sweet tooth, affecting her digestion and making her fretting worse. She'd broken some furniture on blood-sugar rampages.

He tried to ignore Bee snuffling over his dirty clothes as he reduced his facial hair to sink litter and combed out.

Clean and feeling human again, he stopped by his desk, glanced at his in-box and the lone red flag on the Alert Map and decided everything could wait. He was curious about the new arrival at the stables.

"No mail in the diaper bag this time, Major?" asked a corporal with a tray of sandwiches and coffee on his way out.

"Afraid not. Came in from a different direction. Those sandwiches look good."

"They're for that spy Martinez sent. That major fella."

"I don't think we're supposed to know about that," Valentine said, turning down the path to the stables.

So, the new broom at Southern Command was finally doing some whisking in Kentucky, Valentine thought. Well, he's welcome to it. He won't be able to complain about their use of logistical supplies. Most of the arms they were issuing to recruits were captured, the uniforms and gear were made in Evansville workshops, and the good people of Kentucky were feeding them. About all the pack trains were bringing in were bullets and medical supplies.

He took a deep breath and pretended to forget about the bad blood with General Martinez. Enemies in the Kurian Zone prowling Western Kentucky were his business, not vindictive old snapping turtles two big rivers away back at headquarters.

He took a deeper breath when he saw the woman bending over a tack-cleaning table outside the stable feed-room door. Victoria Pellwell stood at least six three. She was one of the tallest women Valentine had ever seen.

She scooped grain, corn, and nuts out of assorted livestock feed sacks, filling a flour barrel. Her civilian attire was rather striking— sun-faded red denim from neck to ankle, short, lace-up riding boots, hair bound up in a yellow handkerchief.

"Victoria Pellwell of the Miskatonic, I presume," Valentine said.

She set down her scoop. "David Valentine. As I live and breathe."

Valentine was tall himself, but he found himself staring dead level, or perhaps a little up, into her eyes as they shook hands. Vigorously. Valentine felt as though his hand was attached to a pump head.

"I'm pleased," he said, hoping she'd relinquish his hand before shaking it out, "but not as pleased as you are, it seems. Can't account for it."

She was no beauty. She had an upturned nose and her steady, rarely blinking eyes were set at an almost uncanny distance from each other, but it was an appealing face you didn't mind looking at. Her teeth were well aligned and gloriously white; he hadn't seen such teeth on a woman since his brief affair with the Quisling obstetrician in Xanadu.

She freed his hand. Valentine fought the impulse to massage his knuckles. "Your papers are practically an archive all by themselves, Valentine. You've got a good eye for detail and you've met a rare level of exomorphs."

"The Miskatonic has been helpful to me on occasion too," Valentine said. He'd learned to grow suspicious of people eager to praise him within a few seconds of meeting. They usually wanted something.

"I'm hoping we'll be even more so," she said, knocking over her small barrel as she turned and put her hand up to her mouth. Valentine's arm flashed out, caught the barrel and righted it before she could whistle, or quack, or whatever the finger in her mouth was for.

Pellwell made a popping sound with her finger against tight-stretched cheek and stamped her foot.

A train of little brown creatures, nose to stumpy naked tail, trotted out of the stable. They had powerful rear legs and smaller, delicate forelimbs with widely spaced digits. The first stuck its snout in the air and sniffed the feed.

Ratbits.

He'd seen them in the wild, if "wild" applied to a creature at least as bright as a human child. The muscular haunches allowed them a good running pace, bouncing along as though on springs. Their front paws were gifted with opposable fingers and thumb and tough stumpy claws to dig; in their faces were sharp teeth capable of chewing through all manner of obstacles. Big, sensitive ears shifted this way and that. Though their faces were unlike either rats or rabbits, the eyes were set forward in the face rather in the manner of a weasel or raccoon.

Valentine had last encountered them in the Texas hill country. They were an experiment by the Kurian Order in a vast establishment called "the Ranch." The Ranch was in ruins by the time Valentine crossed it, abandoned to the ratbits, oversized rattlers the Kurians had developed to wipe out the ratbits, and other unpleasant fauna cooked up by the Kurian genetic tinkerers.

The Kurians had been looking for something that bred faster, and were hopefully more manageable, than humans. The experiment had produced the ratbits, who turned out to be so successfully enhanced in intelligence and social inclination they launched a revolt, since they were no more enamored of being bred to be eaten than humans.

When Valentine had met them, there was some misunderstanding that led to violence. Their squeaks and chirps were unintelligible to humans, and they communicated by spelling out words with Scrabble tiles, working the tiles with the quick-handed facility of a blackjack dealer.

This group looked a little better groomed than those he'd seen in Texas. They smelled faintly of pine chips. One had patchy-colored fur, and another had nearly black stripes running down its pewter-colored back. The others were in shades of brown to gray, with a mixture of lighter rings around their eyes, noses, and running up their ears.

"Are these from Texas?" Valentine asked.

"I met them there four years ago," she said. "I was a junior member of the Miskatonic team that went into the hill country to see what might be salvaged from the experimental station."

"The Ranch," Valentine said.

"The Ranch is an urban legend," she said. "Well, that there's one, and the Kurians do all their experiments there like a big Manhattan Project. If it exists, it's probably back on Kur, where they can all keep an eye on each other and what's being developed. The station in the Texas Hill Country is where they were experimenting with ratbits to test them in real Earth-wild conditions."

Valentine took a knee, and offered a finger. Each ratbit came up and first sniffed, then touched it in turn. They yeeked to each other. "What are you doing with them here?"

"I'm on Southern Command's rolls as a civilian consultant. Former Miskatonic associate, exozoology, if you want the full résumé."

"Exo—you mean Grogs," Valentine said.

The word Grog applied to pretty much any animal brought over from other worlds by the Kurians, though it was more precisely applied to the apelike bipeds of Bee's variety. Valentine didn't mind the inexactitude. You could tell from context whether the word was being used in its general or specific sense. He was part "Indian," to most folks, after all.

"Yes. The cognitives were my specialty. I'm more of a blackboard and bookshelf type than a bush researcher. Had my eye on a faculty chair. I was getting my field experience slot filled when I fell in love with your ratbits, Valentine."

Valentine didn't know much about the intellectual hierarchies of the Miskatonic, he knew interns were at the bottom and department chairs at the top, but where an associate came in between the two he couldn't say.

"They're hardly mine," Valentine said.

"You had the first description of them entered into the rolls. *Translagorodent Valentine,* they're labeled, in the latest edition of the *Guide.* Do you know scientific classification?"

"Never figured being in a book," Valentine said, hoping he wasn't blushing in pleasure. His face felt warm. So, his name would be remembered for a minor contribution to science. There were worse legacies. He could have been quietly hung as a war criminal, after all.

Valentine stood again. Pellwell picked up the patchy-colored one and stood, somewhat awkwardly, with it clinging to her shoulder like a big housecat. "You discovered and described them. It's an honor. I believe that they'd be a great help in the war."

The ratbits left on the ground whistled for attention and made chirping noises at the one on her shoulder. It wrinkled its nose at its companions.

"So these are—allies?"

"Of course," she said, pouring out a scoopful of her mix.

"That ratbit trail mix?"

"Some favorites. They'll eat about anything. Don't need much water either, they'll dig for roots. Though I've noticed that if they don't have drinking water, what little urine they do produce—pfew!"

Ratbits reminded Valentine of raccoons. They sat up to eat, using their paws to pick and discard. Pellwell clicked her tongue against the roof of her mouth, and the ratbits all nodded an affirmative.

"You can speak to them?" Valentine asked.

"A few basic words. I think they're exaggerating some of their sounds so I can understand them. Pidgin ratbit for humans only, if you will."

"Why did you bring them here?" Valentine asked. "Shouldn't they be running through mazes in a lab?"

"They've done all that already, both in Texas and at the lab in Pine Bluff. I want to make practical use of their abilities under real field conditions. I've an idea they could be of great help. Like dogs, only better."

"Plenty of opportunities for that in South Texas, I'd think."

She scowled. "Southern Command wouldn't even let me through the door. Ratbits are ideal for reconnaissance, surveillance, sabotage, they're even damn good thieves who can be trained to get electronic spares or medicines or whatnot that aren't easily accessible. I kept quoting your report, and your suggestions that they might be useful."

"At headquarters? I'm not a favorite of theirs."

"So I gathered. Honestly, I was expecting you to be a gilt-edged bastard. 'Let Valentine deal with them, he's such a grog-lover' they told me. And a few other things. But never mind. I found out where Fort Seng was, and decided I should look you up. Headquarters gave me transport docs to get rid of me, I think. I got myself attached to some volunteers heading out your way. I brought five I'd trained as a proof of concept."

We're collecting quite a menagerie in Kentucky, Valentine thought.

"Please tell me I haven't wasted my time," she said.

A visionary. Well, he'd been faulted more than once for following an ideal rather than military duty. Besides, another thinker around might give Brother Mark someone to latch on to on quiet evenings when Valentine would much rather be reading or enjoying one of Gamecock's raucous poker games.

"You want a chance to prove your concept? Get hard operational data?" Valentine asked, already bubbling with ideas. An animal about the same size as a cat, with sentient intelligence . . . It was her turn to blush. "Of course." Oh, God, what had they said about him at headquarters.

"When you say reconnaissance, what do you mean? What do you think their capabilities are?"

She gathered her thoughts. "Well, you can't just send them out and have them report what they see. They need specifics. They can count and identify some things. *How many trucks are in the warehouse.* That sort of thing."

"Map reading?" Valentine asked.

The teeth reduced their wattage. "Still working on that. You have to get them pretty near their objective. Surely you can see the potential."

So young. So eager. So bright.

He hoped he wouldn't have to bury her, the way he had Rand. His shy intelligence, those remarkable teeth. Of course, if she really were that smart she would have kept pursuing that comfy departmental chair, rather than trying to come up with a new way to beat the Kurians.

"You ever been in the KZ?"

"Kurian Zone? Not really. Only the trip to Texas. I did my first internship in Kansas and Missouri, though, with the Gray Ones."

Valentine felt a pang. His old friend Ahn-Kha had taught him that terminology. Apparently it had made it into the scientific vocabulary.

"We're going out on a task in a couple days," Valentine said.

"Lives will be at risk. We could certainly use you, but I want to see your team in action and interacting with our men. So let's try a test. If they do well, we'll bring you along for a real test under operational conditions."

"Thank you, Major Valentine."

"Most people call me Val when salutes aren't being tossed back and forth. Especially friends."

"I'd like that," she said, extending her hand.

Valentine hoped he didn't hesitate too much before gripping hers and submitting to another socket-rattling pumping of his arm.

"Thank you for the opportunity," she said.

Valentine needed time to think and plan and assemble his key officers. Perhaps coming along would be the best thing to ever happen to Miss Pellwell. She'd either be shocked into returning to her Miskatonic digs with renewed hopes of that chair, or she'd blossom into yet another oddly fitting cog in the Fort Seng machine.

†

Valentine had time for only a brief word or two with Colonel Lambert about what he'd discovered before he was thrust back into the affairs of training the battalion and improving Fort Seng.

He learned a little more about Pellwell. They chatted over tea during an after-dinner cards, charades, and chess session at headquarters.

The tea was out of a small supply left to him by a grateful mother. Most of the talk came from Pellwell.

Victoria Pellwell's grandfather was Southern Command's "very first Bear." The first to survive the transformation the Lifeweavers attempted on the volunteers, that is. She told him he was actually the third to go through the ordeal, which made him a very brave man indeed. Still, it was not a perfect case study. Her grandfather permanently lost the ability to speak, save for being able to bark out a word or two now and then that had nothing to do with the matter at hand.

For all that, he served twenty years as a Bear, surviving horrific wounds. As a child, she remembered him mostly pointing and grunting. He'd collected a formidable collection of Grog artifacts: weapons, tools, even a skull or two, and had a sort of dreadful candy bowl made out of a Gray One's oversized palm that he kept filled with butter toffee. "That's where I caught the exomorph bug, looking at his collection," Pellwell explained.

"Whatever happened to him?" Lieutenant Gamecock asked. The commander of Fort Seng's three Bear teams had been interested enough to leave a poker game and start lurking about the edges of their conversation. He made it very clear that he wasn't eavesdropping, only listening with interest and perhaps too shy or too sensitive to barge in until a decent gap appeared.

Pellwell seemed to welcome the question. Gamecock was handsome enough, with rugged features and a real fighting bird's brush of thick hair atop his head. That, combined with his old-fashioned South Carolina charm and cadences, made most of the women of Fort Seng lick their lips and throw their shoulders back when he approached. Perhaps he was just sniffing out the newest female addition in search of a fresh conquest.

"He was killed when Consul Solon came in, with our town's militia. At a little place called Viola, east of Mountain Home."

"Wait, you're Broadsword's granddaughter," Gamecock said, rubbing the back of his neck.

"Yes, Broadsword, that's what they called him. He had this patch like a sword where your names are usually stitched." She looked down at a spoon she'd been toying with, absently twisted it into a corkscrew while talking. Valentine watched her cover it and attempt to pull it straight.

"Honored, ma'am," Gamecock said. Valentine decided it wasn't an act. Like most Bears, it took a lot to impress him.

Maybe that's where she gets the strength, Valentine thought. The modifications the Lifeweavers had done to certain members of the human race, making them a better match for the Reapers and other tools of the Kurian Order, seemed to get passed down, sometimes in diluted or scrambled fashion, to their descendants. Bear blood was tough on women. None had ever survived the transformation. The genes didn't cross over to offspring, or if they did, it often ended in tragedy. From what he knew, most weren't even born alive. Valentine had known only one female Bear, a friend of his and Colonel Lambert's named Wildcard. She'd died helping the resistance in Alabama.

With that, Valentine went gloomy. He gulped his tea and made his excuses, leaving Gamecock to finish the evening with Miss Pellwell.

He found Duvalier softly snoring on his bed and quietly stripped to his underwear and crawled in beside her. She mumbled something about a mule in her sleep and pressed up tightly to him, back-to-back, without waking.

†

The next day, Brother Mark supervised the trials of the ratbits, per Valentine's two challenges.

Brother Mark was an odd sort of man. He had a loose-skinned, basset-hound face and the dog's permanently mournful expression. Though part of Southern Command, he wore black civilian clergy attire. He seemed condemned by life not to fit in anywhere. He'd been a churchman, a very high-ranking one, before undergoing his own personal awakening and fleeing the Kurian Order, taking a brain full of secrets and queer abilities with him.

There were rumors all over Fort Seng about him. Valentine had heard it said that Brother Mark slept on scrap wire and broken glass, that he ate only food that up to an hour ago had been living, and that he could read minds of men and Reapers alike. Valentine knew the truth about some of it.

As to the sleeping on glass and scraps, Brother Mark had taken up residence in an old tack room of Fort Seng's stables—once the residence of the pleasure horses of the wealthy and connected of Evansville. His mattress had been tossed down on a floor littered with odds and ends and he always slept in his clothes. "A habit of quick escapes," he'd once said.

As to the fresh food, Valentine knew from many shared meals that the churchman hated the smell of rotting food—fish turning particularly disgusted him, though he liked it better than anything if pulled fresh from the water and fried within the hour. Which reminded Valentine, he'd promised Brother Mark a morning's stream fishing, now that the winter had broken. Valentine preferred lake fishing, the mixture of crafty selection of site and bait taking into accounts variations on water, weather, and season appealed to the gamester in him.

That left the mind reading. Valentine had his doubts, but Brother Mark was like the bayous he'd explored in Louisiana. You never knew whether the next turn might bring you to a shotgun shack and still, a gator-choked mud-isle among a colonnade of bald cypress, or a graceful, five-column estate. One thing was certain—he had a power to sense the activity of Kurians and their mental connections with their Reaper avatars. Valentine had a bastardized, low-wattage ability along those lines. He'd evidently been born with it, but where his "tingles" were little more than an uneasy feeling or a spectral chill, Brother Mark's senses were as fine-tuned as an air-control radar.

Now the barn was home to a couple of riding horses, milk cows, a few stalwart oxen used mostly for hauling timber, and storage for the fort's sheep and goats and growing chicken coops. Plus the ratbits, who were already filching eggs. Brother Mark slept there, Valentine suspected, because it allowed him to be near headquarters and to camouflage his own lifesign. Perhaps Brother Mark emitted some special signal, like a high-power transmitter, that he wished to jam during the night hours when the Kurians were at the peak of their powers without sunlight to confuse their signals.

He'd counted Valentine his friend ever since the planning for Operation Javelin, when Valentine had been, rather unwillingly, paired up with the churchman. The upper ranks had been trying to forge a team, and it didn't look good to have someone always alone, never sharing a table at dinner, hovering at the perimeter of casual conversations.

Brother Mark had been pathetically eager for friendship. Still was, though he hid it better these days. Though he wasn't Valentine's favorite person, he felt a sympathy for him. In his younger days, Valentine had been a bit of a loner and an outsider, hungry for anyone to talk to, and overdoing it when someone actually did. Now Valentine relished his moments alone, when he had a few consecutive minutes to think, rather than constantly putting out fires while juggling the issues of a practically cut-off military mission.

The men didn't exactly go to Brother Mark for counsel, but he liked to work alongside them. He drew out even the most taciturn and started them talking. No confessional, no back and forth questioning, his methods were closer to psychiatric free association, only instead of a couch, they were often leaning on shovels together.

In any case, he was impartial, so Valentine's two tasks for the ratbits, by daylight and by night, gave Brother Mark a chance to work his magic with Valentine.

The first task involved the ratbits stealing a big bottle of aspirin from Captain Patel's quarters overnight. Patel, thanks to years of running Wolves back and forth across the old Ozark Free Territory, had bad knees and took aspirin morning and night to help with the pain. Patel didn't know the ratbits were coming, but if anyone could sense something creeping up on him, it was the canny old Wolf. His knees might be going, but his ears and nose were still sharp as ever. Patel used aspirin by the handful, and there was every chance some would be used and therefore all the more likely to rattle.

†

Valentine and Brother Mark were eating in the big garage of the estate house that had been converted into the dining hall. It wasn't nearly big enough to seat the whole battalion, but by eating in shifts and taking the food out to tents over a thousand men could be served in three hours.

The men were sitting at an inside table with a few other officers when Pellwell appeared. She was chewing a piece of bubble gum, and loudly snapped it as she set down a half-empty bottle of aspirin.

"Well, that's proof," Gamecock said.

"That Patel was sleeping soundly in his own bed in the middle of a fort," Valentine said.

Pellwell snapped her gum again. "Want to know what book was on his bedside table? They spelled the title with Scrabble pieces for me."

Knowing Patel, it was one of his wife's raunchy paperbacks. She was supposed to join him at the fort this spring.

He returned the bottle to Patel, eating with his company officers and NCOs two tables over.

"Sorry, Captain. You were part of the ratbit exercise," Valentine said.

"I thought I heard a rattle," Patel said, opening the bottle and taking out three tablets. "Slept with the window cracked. Never could stand stale air. I thought the breeze did it."

"Look for little tracks on the sill," Valentine said.

For the second test, Valentine let the target know the ratbits were coming. The ratbits were to somehow wreak havoc with the function of one of the artillery pieces, without causing permanent damage, of course.

So he stood at the observation post on the hillside that sheltered the three guns—Morganna, Igraine, and Guinevere—from Evansville and the Ohio River. Brother Mark stood beside, watching and waiting. The cannon-cockers were standing guard over their communications equipment, magazines, and stores, ready to spring into action when Valentine gave the signal.

"Wonder how she'll do it, if she hasn't done it already," Valentine said.

"I never like a woman who chews gum loudly," Brother Mark said. "What do you think, Major Valentine?"

Valentine shrugged. "I've never had trouble getting along with the Miskatonic people."

"Except where Blake is concerned," Brother Mark said.

Valentine took a breath. He'd seen a Reaper born alive into the world, carried by Post's wife, who he'd brought out of an Ohio hatchery called Xanadu. Named him Blake, after the poet. At first he'd let the Miskatonic people examine him—they'd never watched a Reaper develop before—but when they started using noise and light to test tolerances he reclaimed him and took him to old Narcisse, who lived on the bluffs outside of Saint Louis. They'd first met on Hispaniola during his trip to find a special kind of wood that killed Reapers. The gentle old soul had a way with Blake. It had been over a year since he'd seen them last.

"Well, rarely then," he admitted. "Usually all we do is swap stories. I've never tried to work with one in the field before."

"You think these creatures will be useful? Then why do you scowl so when you look at them."

"I was scowling? Well, they make me think about Texas. If I'd only been more careful."

Valentine had been bringing a load of Quickwood back from Haiti, crossing Texas's empty plains. Once back in Southern Command territory he'd let his guard down, only to discover the Ozarks had been overrun by Consul Solon's Transmississippi forces. He'd lost almost all of his precious cargo.

"Is that all? I've never known you to dwell on the past. Talk about it, yes. Learn from it, yes. But not lose yourself in misery over it."

You didn't know me in the years following my court martial, Valentine thought.

"I was with Ahn-Kha when we met them. He was with me on that trip. I've been wondering about him. Ever since that last radio transmission, when they said they were surrounded by the ravies in Virginia."

"You think he's dead?"

"You put it starkly, sir." Valentine brightened. A weight had passed away. "You know, I don't. I feel like he's still alive. But I'm anxious about it, for some reason."

Brother Mark stared levelly into his eyes in the manner of a doctor, as if evaluating the dilation of his pupils. Valentine wondered what he was looking for. "Is this your emotions, hoping against hope, or more of a realization?"

Valentine searched his features for expression, but the usual sad hound eyes revealed nothing beyond sorrow. "Do you know something I don't?"

"In the Church, there were those who became sensitives of one sort or another. I've been told that it's suddenly as though you've known something your whole life. Sister Gretchen is arriving this afternoon; you've always known Gretchen will arrive this afternoon."

Valentine believed in telepathy. He'd had Lifeweavers and Kurians alike, along with their agents, put thoughts in his head. Was someone feeding him information now? An enemy trying to tempt him into rashness? Or was one of nature's better angels planting suggestions, trying to move to come to the rescue of his old friend?

"Give the alert and practice coordinates, Corporal," Valentine told the Wolf of Frat's command he'd brought along to practice the artillery spotting.

The tanned young man studied the map one more time and started to read.

Fire control acknowledged, repeating back the coordinates.

"Communications are still up," Valentine said.

The loaders ran the trenches to the ready magazines.

Valentine looked down and saw confusion at Igraine. A sergeant hurried to the magazine.

"Uh-oh," Father Max said.

The spotter Wolf pushed his headset tighter against his ear.

"Major, Igraine is reporting someone stuck gum in the padlock on the magazine door," the Wolf said.

"What was that you were saying about gum-chewing women?" Valentine asked.

†

After getting his arm pumped off again congratulating Pellwell, Valentine presented his plan to Colonel Lambert. The mental diversion with the ratbits had allowed the operation to crystallize.

He sat in her office, so neat that the orders and papers and pens all seemed to cower in their allotted places.

Lambert in person was as severe and clean as her desk. She

didn't reveal her thoughts, but instead started firing questions. He answered them as best he could, then she moved on to options if the operation failed, and if it succeeded. "Valentine, I could use experienced construction staff, but we're having a hard enough time feeding the soldiers we have. How many more mouths are you planning to add?"

"Thirty or so," Valentine said.

"I'm glad spring's here. Fresh food's starting to flow again."

"I'm sure Evansville could use it," Valentine said. "They can't keep up with the refugees coming down the Ohio. Something awful must be happening in the Ordnance."

"I hear purges," Lambert said. "It might be nice to offer Evansville some tangible assistance. They're going a little wobbly on us."

"What do you mean?" Valentine asked.

"Do you want the good news, or the bad news?" Lambert asked, straightening a manila file on her desk that had somehow gone a couple of degrees out of alignment.

"Is there good news?" Valentine asked.

"Precious little."

"So far, it's still psychological warfare," Lambert said. "But damn effective psychological warfare. The Ordnance is floating bodies down the Ohio."

"Floating?"

"Rafting, sending them drifting. When there's a big pile they put them on pallets supported by plastic water bottles, Ping-Pong balls mostly. It looks like the usual Reaper victims. The sick, crippled, and old. Dead a few days, as best as we can tell."

"Cute. We get to dispose of their bodies."

"It's attracting the usual birds, rats, and flies. It's depressing for the fishermen and boatmen too. Nobody likes hauling up bodies. They've been burning them east of the city. Want to take a look?"

"Not really," Valentine said. He'd seen enough Reaper leftovers in the New Orleans bayou country, where the Kurian order left matters of corpse disposal to gars and crayfish.

"At least we've accumulated quite a supply of Ping-Pong balls. We can grind them up with some match heads and make smoke grenades. Have you met Major Grace yet? He's here from GHQ, 'estimating the situation.'"

Valentine leaned forward. "I think I saw him reading personnel files."

"He's on General Martinez's staff. I think he's here to decide whether to pull us out of Kentucky."

"They wouldn't," Valentine said. "We're the only success Southern Command has had since Archangel." Archangel was the operation that reclaimed the Ozark Free Territory from Consul Solon. The collapse was so quick and far reaching that Texas and parts of Oklahoma were added to the freehold, turning it into the United Free Republics.

Lambert leaned back in her chair. "You and I might think it's a success, but back across the Mississippi, it's being played in the newspapers as another failure. Though now that the wheel turned in the elections and Martinez is running the show, they'll be on the lookout for good news. Just a few successful small ops, written up and sent off by our friend Bolenitz and his magic pen, might win us a few more visits from the logistics commandos."

"Then I have the perfect op for you, sir. My extraction."

"I'll make you a deal, Valentine. You get Major Grace out of my hair for a few days by taking him along. Do your best to keep him alive and impressed with us, and I'll try and fit that Miskatonic egghead into the Fort's TOE."

"I can start working out the operational staff now, if you'll give the order."

She took a deep breath. "Very well, Valentine. If you want to put the future of matters in Kentucky on an operation to get a couple dozen hard hats away from the Georgia Control, I wish us all the luck in the world."

"More good news: I'm going to put Frat Carlson in charge of the extraction."

Lambert shifted in her chair. "You think he's ready?" Valentine thought she might as well have said *you trust him?*

"The whole camp is on eggshells about him," Valentine said. Frat Carlson had been responsible for the Ravies outbreak during the winter. While only the senior officers, and Brother Mark, knew he was a Kurian agent, the men knew that he'd done something *disastrous* for the Cause. They'd tried to keep the full story secret, not even reporting it to Southern Command. If the Kentuckians found out the whole story, they'd string Frat up and kick the entire Southern Command operation back across the Mississippi.

And there'd go a burgeoning alliance.

Perhaps they'd be right to do it.

"No such thing as secrets," Lambert said. "Well, if your op's a disaster, it'll be a well-rounded disaster. Maybe all the bad karma accumulated since last spring will get expunged in one bad night."

"Or we'll have a bit of luck and start to turn it around," Valentine said.

"Got a name for your op?"

"I was thinking 'Vendetta,'" Valentine said. He'd intentionally avoided anything that was evocative of destruction or a rescue. "Maybe it'll make a couple of Quislings nervous, if word gets out."

"Well, go make us some luck, Major," she said. She signed the order for Vendetta to go live and handed it to him.

†

Valentine decided to eat dinner in his room that night. The generously sized bedroom always made him feel a little guilty as a place to only sleep and get dressed, so he usually did some work at the old vanity table there as well.

Duvalier was cutting her toenails. She had gnarled, beaten-up feet thanks to the countless miles she'd walked in her exploits.

"How do you like this?" she said, holding up the clippers. "I think they're real gold."

"Good to be the big boss," Valentine said, removing his boots. He stuffed them with New Universal Church propaganda. Dry reading would absorb the sweat, and the odor would only be improved.

She heard a scratching above and looked up, her arm instinctively reaching to her side, grasping for a weapon.

A ratbit blinked down at her. It dropped a pack of gum onto Valentine's pillow and crawled back across the beamed ceiling to the door.

He heard a thump as it startled Bee on its scramble out.

"I think that's a thank-you," Valentine said, picking up the gum.

Duvalier dropped the mass of paper she was about to fling at the ratbit. "God, those things give me the creeps."

"What's that rolled up in your hand?" Valentine asked.

"I found all these great old magazines in the attic. You hardly ever see them like this, usually they're crinkled from being wet and dried."

"For toilet paper?"

"No. Too slick, unless you Minnesota types are fans of skid marks up to your spine. I like looking at the women in the pictures. So beautiful."

"Thinking of changing your hair?"

"I can read, you know," she said, wrinkling her nose at him. "The articles are fascinating. Look at this! *Fifteen ways to update your jeans.*"

"Only fifteen?"

"I only knew one. When they wear out, turn them into shorts. Then when those wear out, you have some patching material and an oil rag. Oh, mechanical dryer lint in a bottle of gasoline makes for a better Molotov cocktail, so I suppose that's two updates."

Valentine was deeply fond of Duvalier. She was like a sister to him, but there was a tiny frisson whenever they touched one wouldn't get from a sister. They'd been together so long, seen each other naked so often, the fact that they'd never made love had been made moot. They were partners on a level just as deep. Policemen who'd spent years together might understand. "That's my firebug. I thought you were going soft on me for a minute there."

"Never. I'm a good ol' rebel."

Valentine checked his teeth, went to work with brush and floss.

Some said he set the standard for field hygiene at Fort Seng, but he'd have a long way to go to meet her choppers.

Duvalier threw down her magazine. "Val, you give a shit about the Old World. They sure had a lot of stuff. It's like they spent all their time figuring out what to do with their clothes and hair."

"I suppose some did."

"Why don't the Kurians do that? In Kansas, we were always looking for a set of kitchen knives with matching handles or new shoe heels. Made you think that the Peedee knuckleheads didn't know what they were doing."

"Peedee?"

"Pee and Dee. Production and Distribution."

"You think the Kurians wanted shortages?" Valentine asked.

"No, I can't figure out why they don't string up the people running that end of it. You'd think if everyone was worrying about which of the fifteen ways to update their jeans, nobody would be questioning where Gramma went after her foot operation. Spending two hours a day working on your makeup doesn't leave much energy for guerilla activity."

Valentine shrugged. "The churchmen never were big on material things. You might say that if you're spending two hours a day scrounging for socks and underwear, you don't have much time to be a guerilla either. And not producing something is a heck of a lot easier to organize than producing it."

"Thank you, George Orwell."

Duvalier showed flashes, every now and then, of being much better read than her "simple and corny as a Kansas field" attitude that got her through sentry checkpoints let on. The thing is, he'd never seen her pick up a book, though Valentine had carried Orwell with him in a couple of their relocations. Maybe she snuck a book out to cushion her dynamite when she went out into the field.

"You in the mood to head back south to that construction site? Or do you have a pedicure scheduled?"

She kicked the magazine off the bed, checked to see that her sword stick was within reach. "I only need six on my back and two hot meals. It beats learning nine ways to make yourself part of his fantasies."

CHAPTER FOUR

The Rescuer and his Vendetta: If Major David Stuart Valentine has a reputation in Southern Command shared by both his subordinates and superiors, it is probably as a retrieval specialist.

On his first true command in the Kurian Zone, while trekking across Wisconsin, he and a wounded comrade were aided by the family of Molly Carlson. She ran afoul of a high-ranking Quisling and Valentine pursued her all the way to the living cesspool of the Zoo in Chicago to bring her back.

His first major mission for Southern Command involved bringing a legendary plant similar to an olive tree out from Hispaniola in the Caribbean. The tree, known as Quickwood, was lethal to the Reapers and caused a deadly catalytic reaction in their systems. Though his mission to return a large quantity failed because of Consul Solon's conquest of the Ozark Free Territory, he had a chance to have a say in the ownership of Arkansas at Big Rock Hill, where he and a handful stood against everything Solon could throw at them.

He found a friend's wife who'd vanished into the Kurian Order, at a medical facility where certain women who were immune to a physiological reaction were used for their wombs to create Reaper after Reaper.

He brought a pair of captured Lifeweavers back from the Pacific North-west. One of the reasons he was so eager to come along on Operation Javelin, the failed bid to establish a freehold linking the free territories in the Northeast with the Transmississippi, was that he had learned there was a large guerilla army operating in the Appalachians led by his old friend Ahn-Kha.

Now, in this grim spring, comes one more extraction of a couple of dozen tool-pushers. As it turned out, the rescue turned out to be a key event determining the future of Kentucky and its resistance against the powerful Georgia Control.

†

Tension throbbed from the back of his neck, up his skull, and over his ears to his temples. It was always the day before leaving that was the worst.

Valentine walked in the door of the little Evansville house, enjoying a minor dereliction of duty. He'd met Major Grace that morning and answered a series of questions. Hard to believe a man who wore a major's cluster with Southern Command's General Headquarters didn't understand that sometimes you went into the enemy's territory just to rumble, so to speak.

Valentine explained that a weaker force could be effective only if it could choose the time and place for a fight. Waiting until the enemy brings the fight to you might ensure that your men were well rested and fed, but livestock pens were full of animals both well rested and fed.

It was in a handy neighborhood, on a nice little rise close to the west side market and the riverfront, but the home itself badly needed paint, screens, and gutters. Plastic and bricks were keeping out the bugs in one window. Most of the nearby homes had similar improvised repairs. Wild dogs and a few desperate hookers wandered the fringe of the neighborhood, concentrating at a little pawnshop/bar/tinker's at the corner. It was a part of the city in constant flux, people who'd escaped other Kurian Zones tended to set up squats there. A few who found one way or another to rise a little in the city's social strata mostly moved out, but some stayed to aid, or prey on, the newcomers.

He was an hour late, he'd told Caral six thirty.

The house smelled like herbs. It always did. Apart from some poultry, Caral picked up a little money by making herb mixtures, labeling them in old Kurian pill bottles and selling them at Evansville's market days. Her house was always smelling of basil or oregano or garlic. With spring in full bloom there was a little extra in the air. Wildflowers that would go in iced tea in the summer were hanging upside down in masses from the ceiling over the big tiled living room that had been converted into her workroom.

"Home, babe," he called, dropping on her big wooden table a cloth sack of new potatoes and asparagus he'd picked up.

"You're late, hubbs," Caral said, emerging from her basement and removing her thick roasting apron. She'd appealed to Valentine from the first, shapely, using a few strategic dibs and dabs of makeup, but with a tomboy's taste in clothes.

Like now, for example. Beneath the apron, nothing but cutoff shorts and slippers made of old carpet. Her breasts had always intrigued him—she had the widest aureolas he'd ever seen. They were the size of a dessert plate.

She smelled like woodsmoke and accepted a kiss on the cheek.

"Thanks for taking a bath, David," she said in his ear. "My sweet, clean-living old man."

"Hot shower. Privileges of the headquarters building at Fort Seng."

She poked around in a nearly empty cupboard. Twentieth-century kitchens had overmuch room for late twenty-first century lifestyles, especially in a frontline city like Evansville.

"We missed your birthday."

"Subject to requirements of the service," Valentine quoted.

"Well, I made something just the same. Hope it hasn't gone stale. You said you'd be back Tuesday."

She practically went *en pointe* to reach in the cupboard. She probably knew exactly how attractive the strain made her legs and buttocks. "Here we are."

She walked over to him, holding a cupcake on her palm, offering it from a position midway between her eyeline and breasts.

"A cupcake?" Valentine said. "That's above and beyond, Caral."

"Tough part was the cake flour and confectioners' sugar," she said, lighting a little homemade candle with a wooden match. Valentine watched the twin pendulums of her heavy breasts sway as she did so. "It doesn't exist in Evansville. I had to go begging from the household cooks on Millionaire's Row. Sorry, the vanilla's that Kurian Zone crap. Might as well shop for a moon rock as a vanilla bean these days."

"Would you even know what a real vanilla bean looked like?"

"I've seen them in books," she said. "Your candle's drooping."

"Something else isn't," Valentine said, running a finger down her cheek. He blew out the flickering flame.

"Let's eat," she said.

†

He woke early, long before dawn, but luxuriated in the sound of her breathing and the tangy, animal smell she'd left on him.

If he'd lived a hundred years ago, and been reasonably lucky, he might have had this every day. Coffee with someone in the morning, making sure he used the right color toothbrush, a little pink-and-white razor by the tub. A messy head of hair on the pillow next to him and a clean, warm presence flowing across the sheets.

Of course, if he'd been born a hundred fifty years before that, he might have died as a child on the Trail of Tears. Life was a crap-shoot, but only in his bleaker moments did he think he'd rolled snake eyes. More like an eight the hard way, he supposed. Good or bad depending on the line and side bets.

Lovemaking was also more intense, when neither of you knew if it would be the last time. She'd sweated over him, working him with mouth, hands, breasts, and of course her voracious and trium-phant sex. The male might enjoy the role of penetrator, but the fe-male always overpowered and reduced it in the end, the way the soft and lapping surf eventually wears down the rock. Mark Twain had written something about the candleholder outlasting many candles, hadn't he?

He looked over at the cupcake wrapper. They'd shared it to the last crumb, only the candle was left.

After the lovemaking, they'd cooled together on the back porch, naked in the spring breeze, his head pillowed between those sunflower aureolas. They'd talked about household items that might be obtained in Evansville's workshops and markets. Evansville had a thriving brewery and a distillery or two now, and running alcohol into the Kurian Zone was making a few rich and a lot more able to afford to look for little luxuries.

"Nobody wants the Kurians back."

"No," Caral said. "A few want you soldiers out, though. There's some talk about Evansville being a 'Free City.' Or maybe an 'Open City'—depends who you're talking to."

Valentine turned toward her. He'd heard talk like that now and again in the Transmississippi—turning the Free Republics into neutral states that wouldn't accept the Kurian Order or oppose it. "That again. I wonder if there are some agents in town spreading that stuff."

Actually, he didn't wonder, he was close to certain. The organs of the Kurian Order, from the New Universal Church on down, regularly sent people in to the free territories to plant rumors and sow discord. They hadn't been very successful in the Free Republics because the region created enough argument, feud, rumor and discord much in the manner that a sheepdog grew hair, and the body politic had developed immunities. But Evansville was new to freedom.

"I would have saved you one of their flyers if I'd known you were interested. The Southern Command guys aren't going to bust up their meetings, I hope."

How quickly they forget. Just this last winter the troops in Fort Seng had saved them from being touched by the ravies outbreak. Perhaps they'd been a little too effective, and the Evansville citizenry assumed that because they hadn't suffered from the outbreak, they wouldn't have.

But politics soon bored Caral. She started talking about how

Evansville rivermen were passing Kurian cargoes up and down the Ohio, using their boats and tugs as a sort of portage across the Southern Command–controlled stretch of the Ohio. Often the barges didn't even uncouple their own tugs, the Evansville boat would simply nudge the rest of the mass up- or downriver.

"No human cargo, of course," she said. She was very sensitive to Valentine's feelings on the matter of Kurian aural fodder, and it had been a long time since she'd said of some female rival: *bitch isn't fit for a Reaper.* "Not that some of those suckling pigs wouldn't, between your boys with the inspection boats and our police, they can't get captives through. Still, they're making good money doing it, probably skimming a little off the manifests besides. Those rivermen are good customers."

He'd luxuriated in the domestic conversations and Caral showed every sign of enjoying them, but he didn't want to hear about her customers. "How's your tinker doing with the hot water heater for this place?"

"It's coming along," she said, and they launched into forty minutes' worth of plans for improvements to her house. Valentine gave advice only when asked, and soon they drifted off . . .

It was nice to get a little taste, play around in another generation's world, another man's life. Did those men, ordering their gourmet coffee on the way to work from an electrically operated car window, appreciate what they'd lucked into?

The man who'd raised him, Father Max, encouraged his interest in the Old World but had been determined to keep him from being lost in it. *Rome fell, but then a future Caesar couldn't imagine came to surpass it. One day, we'll know how to reach for the stars again, David.*

He sat up, suddenly a little guilty. Father Max would have a few choice words to say about his relationship with Caral. They'd met innocently enough on the ferry across the river. She'd been leafing through an old fashion magazine, he a dog-eared, glued-together copy of *National Geographic,* and they'd struck up a conversation about old magazines.

Valentine rose, located his things, and left her softly snoring. As he put on his shoes, he decided the cupcake deserved something extra. He added another fifty dollars of Southern Command scrip to the usual hundred in the envelope, and placed it carefully by the big vintage mirror. He noticed the mirror had an extra latch, so it could be extended to an angle where those who'd paid to be in her bed could look at themselves.

†

Valentine grabbed his first mosquito of the year. He knew better than to slap the little bloodsuckers, lest the sound carry.

They were outside the rising Kurian tower, near enough to see, through their binoculars, the power lines stringing from work light to work light.

Gamecock's Bears had departed for a crossroads blockhouse and communication center Valentine had marked on his exploration of the Kentucky/Tennessee border. It looked like exactly the sort of place, squat and thick and slit-windowed, for a secret cellar where a Reaper or two could wait out the sun. The Bears would take it on, and hopefully draw a large company of soldiers out of the camp.

The plan was that Gamecock's Bears would attack it, in a half effort, Kentucky guerilla fashion, and then retreat as soon as they started shooting back. That would hopefully draw out some of the troops from the construction camp, and maybe even a couple of Reapers. The Bears were the one military organization in all of Southern Command that relished a fight with the Reapers. When Gamecock found some advantageous ground, he'd turn on his pursuers, and the hunters would become the hunted.

He left Frat and crawled back into the thicker trees where Vendetta's operational headquarters had been set up. A limber Wolf had posted their antenna in a tree and the radio was manned.

It was a cold camp with colder food and no coffee. It would have to wait. They could celebrate success with a good fry-up and coffee boil.

Valentine would man operational HQ with the Wolves, in charge of the overall execution of Vendetta. So far, the most onerous part of being in command was the need to chat with Major Grace, who was making copious notes in a small pocket folder stuffed with papers and maps.

A third force had moved south with Vendetta. Six worms of the Gunslinger Clan rigged for cargo would be available to haul away wounded or valuables, depending on the outcome.

He looked up at the crest of the hill, where Frat sat against a tree stump, looking down at the rising Kurian tower through field glasses.

Frat Carlson still had the robust good looks that made Valentine think of Old World advertisements for colognes and watches. Except men in those ads never wore rather shaggy, shapeless deerskins over a pilled cotton shirt.

He'd changed since being revealed as a Kurian agent. The

whole camp more-or-less knew he'd been connected with the Kurians somehow and exposed, the details were still a matter of conjecture. Since many of the men at Fort Seng had their own Kurian Order skeletons, buried and unburied, Valentine had expected them to be more charitable toward the man they called "Tails."

He earned the nickname from his riding coat, a modified duster that resembled an old cutaway that he wore riding. Frat was good with horses; he'd grown up on a Wisconsin dairy farm that also raised working and riding horseflesh. The coat was a mix of heavy canvas, moleskin, and leather, and must have set him back a few months' pay or some scrounged valuables or technology. He'd worn it a lot more lately, Valentine had seen it only once before Frat had been exposed, now it was a regular feature of his wardrobe while in camp.

Frat had changed on the inside. Valentine wasn't sure what to make of him anymore. No longer needing to play the part of an enthusiastic, diligent young lieutenant, he'd gone cautious and thoughtful.

He still had everything that had attracted Valentine to him in the first place: energy, intelligence, a guarded tongue, which complemented a steadiness of nerve. Whoever the Kurian doctors and educators were that selected him at a very young age as raw material for their training, they'd known their business.

That was the frightening thing about the Kurian Order at its highest level of the human food chain. The men and women acting as intermediaries between the Reapers and their human cattle were frighteningly well trained, disciplined, and capable. Valentine had read histories of Nazis who were tireless in their efforts to rid Eu-

rope of Jews, or Maoists who could zealously destroy entire generations in the Great Leap Forward. To see such drive and talent used
in such a gut-wrenching manner . . .

Frat had been selected, trained, and released into Wisconsin to
penetrate the fabled, and no doubt part imaginary, Underground existing in the Kurian Zone. Valentine didn't know much about them,
save that there were small groups who met in highly secretive lodges.
How they received their orders was a mystery, but every now and
then a party of families would make it out of the Kurian Zone, or
a plane carrying some high-ranking Kurian would crash, or a city
would go dark long enough for some police prisons to burn.

Valentine had plucked Frat out of that Wisconsin farmland and,
joke of jokes, suggested that he join the Wolves. He'd written Southern Command a glowing letter, praising the boy's abilities. They'd
taken him in and trained him, and lo, the Kurians had an agent
among the Hunters. God knows what sort of damage he'd wreaked
while in the Wolves. Maybe he'd located and marked some Lifeweavers, or relayed information about scouting teams to Solon's army before its unusually well-organized and lucky blitz into the Ozarks.

Valentine decided Frat was simply a survivor. Perhaps part of
the doctor's selection was evidence of emotional detachment. Valentine could sympathize. He sometimes wondered if there wasn't
something wrong with him, deep down, to be able to have seen and
done *all that*. And still sleep like an untroubled child, pillowed by
some whore's fleshy breasts. What kind of a man was he? Was he
a destroyer of horrors or a horror himself? The Lifeweavers had
warned him, long ago, before he became a Wolf, that there was a
price for awakening these latent atavistic instincts.

Perhaps that's why, after all this, he still liked Frat Carlson, wanted him to take this chance and run with it. If Carlson could redeem himself, so could Valentine.

Valentine sometimes sweated out uncomfortable thoughts of what he might have become, had he been born in a well-run Kurian Zone rather than a Minnesota backwater. Would he have been selected as a toddler, taught and groomed and not so much brainwashed as brain-cultivated . . .

Carlson was also friendless. When he sat down to eat, others moved. People extinguished their cigarettes and picked up their shovels when he passed close and returned wordlessly to work, only to take up their conversations again after he had passed.

Valentine couldn't bring himself to either forgive or forget Frat's actions in central Kentucky, where he'd released a new form of the ravies virus that turned its victims into frothing psychotics with a madman's strength, able to tear doors off their hinges and break automobile glass without flinching.

Perhaps being freed of the Kurians had given him a new sense of honor, or a different perspective on life. Brother Mark was the judge of what was going on in a man's soul.

Valentine had bodies to look after.

Back with the Wolves, Major Grace sat primly on a natural stump. It even had a remnant of the trunk sticking up, forming an organic backrest.

Grace reminded Valentine of something his old friend Will Post had said, when they'd first served together on the *Thunderbolt*. The Kurian Gulf forces had had a new Inspector General come through, and he'd visited the *Thunderbolt*.

He'd removed the old captain and replaced him, and chewed out everyone from Valentine to the sailor peeling shrimp in the galley. He suggested a new color for the *Thunderbolt*'s upper decks, and as he left, finding fault with the perfect regulation and satisfactory manner in which the gunboat was tied to the wharf, Post muttered something about a *seagull visit*.

Seagull visits, Post had said. *They fly in, eat all your food, squawk every time someone makes a move, crap all over everyone and everything, and then depart.*

Expressing opinions like that had left Will Post an aging lieutenant in the Costal Marines. But the signs of both humor and what Champers had called an "unmindful" attitude had endeared him to Valentine.

†

Valentine tried to relax. It would be easier to be at the point of the spear, in a way. Gamecock knew exactly where he was and how things were going. Valentine's first excursion into the Kurian Zone as a junior Wolf lieutenant was on an operation very similar to the one he planned with Gamecock and Frat. Bears to create a diversion, Wolves to get some families out. After it was all over, when he trudged into camp after meeting some loosed ravies and a Reaper in combat, he'd wondered why the colonel back at rally base had looked as exhausted as he.

Now he knew. Waiting was bad. Waiting and not knowing was worse.

With the rest of the Wolves as a reserve, backing up Patel's A company and Glass's heavy weapons teams from the Seng battalion,

Valentine would attack the construction site in an effort to break out Champers's crew.

Valentine, Duvalier, Bee, and Brother Mark, plus some communications staff, would be the Operational HQ. Valentine felt guilty dragging Brother Mark into the country like this, but he had a sensitivity to Kurians that surpassed the indistinct tingle Valentine felt when Reapers were on the prowl nearby.

He'd done all he could, in his few days, to get the team ready. Using poles, clothesline, tentage, and some barbed wire, Valentine built a rough model of the construction site and two attendant camps based on his observations. He had the men run practice attacks, day and night.

The journey south went easily enough. They took pickups and trailers, fully half Fort Seng's motor pool, south along roads they were pretty sure to be safe. The last ten miles had to be covered on foot and legworm. Their vehicles retreated halfway to Fort Seng, where they waited for the pickup broadcast.

He passed the time by talking to Major Grace.

"If you don't mind me asking, sir, why all the note taking?"

"I'm The General's eyes and ears in Kentucky. He wants my opinion of you all. I want to make sure my eyes and ears have it right."

Grace's use of The General, with an intonation that suggested capitalization of the adjective, reminded Valentine of the man he always thought of as "The General," the leader of the Twisted Cross.

"Is this an opinion you can share with the subjects?"

Duvalier, having heard the beginning of the conversation, pulled her arms into the confines of her coat and settled down to sleep, pillowed by Valentine's pack.

"The General said he wants all the backwoods barons and per-fumed princes run out of Southern Command."

"Backwoods barons and perfumed princes?"

"By that he means," Grace said tiredly, as though he'd ex-plained this innumerable times to thickheaded subordinates, "that there won't be any more comfortable niches in Southern Command. For too long there have been officers who built themselves little do-mains, skimming what can be skimmed, tasting what can be tasted, and nobody dares challenge them because they're irreplaceable. No-body's irreplaceable, and The General's determined to prove it, or he expects to be replaced."

"Is that a direct quote, sir?"

Grace looked at him afresh through his glasses, held as though they were a magnifying glass. "As a matter of fact, it is."

"Have you found any barons or princes at Fort Seng?"

"You do live in style. I haven't seen so much silver barware in one place."

"We inherited it, it's not a collection. The last six months have been too busy to do much antiquing."

"But plenty of recruiting. Tell me, Major Valentine, how do you choose which volunteers to take? Your command could be easily in-filtrated this way."

"Could be," Valentine said. "Hope the infiltrators don't mind grading road and slapping some paint up, because that's what most of the men spend their time doing."

"You really expect to build a brigade out of a bunch of Quislings?"

"Not right away, we don't. It takes time to adapt to Free Terri-tory. Have you met Ediyak?"

"She's one of the brighter lights in your command. Good breeding. Springfield College ROTC?"

"You wouldn't have thought that two or three years ago. Fresh out of the Kurian Zone, scared to ever make a decision or sign her name to anything. She's been promoted twice in the last year."

Grace closed his book, tucked it into his camouflage fatigue coat.

"Poking sticks into a hornet's nest will keep one busy," Grace said.

"Or you might call it killing Kurians, but I'm equable. Six of one, half a dozen of the other . . ."

Grace's mouth tightened. "Did it occur to you that this may be a trap?"

"If it is, it's working perfectly," Valentine said. "There's no sign of a trap."

"Experience has shown the Kurians tempt us into rashness, throwing away our best and brightest on these wild ventures. They are like cats, luring the mice out of their holes where they can be swatted."

"Be sure to call Gamecock's Bears a bunch of mice, next time you see them," Valentine said. "But give me some warning, so I can watch."

"Now, Major," Brother Mark put in. "Rashness or boldness, by your definition, depends on the outcome."

"For two men who've left bodies from here to the Appalachians, you're both rather cocky," Grace said. "I'd expect a little more humility from people who'd killed off half a brigade."

"I notice you're still around, Grace," Valentine said. "Never made it on any of the lists for best and brightest?"

Grace purpled about the face. "That's a court-martial—"

"We run things a little different out here, Major. Anyone can talk about anything off their feet and out from beneath cover."

"I've never once seen you in a hat, on or off base," Grace said. "Seems very unmilitary."

"I've never seen you off base. Stealthy for a big guy."

"Sir," the communication tech reported. "Observation D reports two scout cars moving south on highway D. Georgia markings."

"D," Valentine said. That was the overgrown highway going back north, to their transport and the Gunslingers.

Duvalier was up and alert, Brother Mark puffing up behind.

"Well, they discovered us," Valentine said. "Just not when we wanted them to."

The radio chirped again.

"Handshake," said the communications corporal, giving a clear connection password. He listened.

"Sir, we've got word from transport hitch," the tech said. "They were spotted by some armored cars."

"That settles it," Valentine said. "This could work to our advantage. We've got to get our hands on those cars."

"Val, I can do it," Duvalier said.

"I'm coming with."

"With that bum leg of yours? And you're the shittiest driver under eighty I've ever seen."

"I'll land on the good one. I want to capture the car, not drive it."

"I'll take the first," Duvalier said. "That way, when you fall off, I won't have to hang on while they swerve to run you over."

"Do you let your civilians talk to you that way?"

Valentine turned over command of Vendetta to Frat. If things went south with the cars, the camp might very well turn out anyway to hunt the road. He gave a nod to Pellwell and reached to clap her on the shoulder. "Don't worry, your critters will get their chance, but not with these."

They hurried to the old highway. It was so overgrown it was practically a tunnel, but vehicles with toothy brush cutters had cleared the worst of it recently, exposing a broken-up roadbed like coral. The worst holes had been filled with sand and gravel.

They climbed trees with big branches hanging over the road, and waited.

They heard the armored cars long before they saw them.

The noise resolved itself into humps of metal kicking up the dust of crushed Kentucky limestone used for evening out the broken old highway.

Valentine brought up his binoculars.

They were a pair of armored cars—armored farm equipment, more like. They weren't designed like urban armored cars, built to rush to a trouble spot and survive the cinder blocks and kerosene of rioters. These were serious off-road brush-crushers, with wedgelike fronts and six fat tires. Towed trailers, a little higher than the armored cars, made them look like ants at a distance. Blue-black paint, chipped here and there, alternately caught and absorbed the sun.

The drivers were enjoying the spring weather. Their heads could be seen atop the vehicles.

"Drop on the gunner first," Valentine said. "Otherwise he'll sweep me off with the machine gun."

The first armored car looked rather festive, like a bull exhibited in a livestock parade. Young branches and flowering stems had been caught in mud guards, headlamp grilles, and the brush-cutting teeth at the front of the sloped armored nose, giving each a leafy, woody beard. The car behind had been turned a chalky pale yellow by road dust.

Duvalier dropped first. Valentine's request about dealing with the gunner quickly was solved by her hanging upside down by her linked ankles. Her blackened sword didn't flash in the sun, but descended clean and rose again from the slash bright red. A wet divot, possibly a hairy patch of neck.

The gunner's head dropped forward as though he'd fallen asleep. Blood had splattered on the bulletproof plastic that shielded the gunner.

Duvalier released her ankles, and managed to drop onto the first car. Valentine held his breath while she arrested herself with a single outflung hand, the other still around the sword hilt.

The first armored car passed under him. The gunner was watchful and alert, but looking down his machine-gun barrel at the road ahead. Valentine, concealed in the foliage ahead, timed a mental practice jump.

The second car approached. The driver had a big, creamy white cowboy hat with the high crown favored by some Texans. A pair of sunglasses and a scarf kept the dust off his face. Valentine would have to act quickly. All he had to do to remove himself from danger was duck down.

Valentine checked the wrist loop on his legworm pick, tightening it.

Five, four, three . . .

He dropped.

Landed on the good leg in a three-point stance, solid hickory in his right hand.

The gunner turned his head and got a brief look at his own death before the claw end of the legworm pick did its work.

The terrible exhilaration took over.

Valentine shoved the body aside with one hard pull. He scooted forward and tried to ignore the twitches of the dying man.

The driver turned, perhaps to point to Duvalier, hanging off the side of the front armored car's spotlight by one thin hand, the other unwilling to relinquish its grip on her sword hilt.

Valentine smashed him hard with the hammer end of the legworm pick. A reflex, perhaps, but the driver stood on the brakes. Valentine would have gone off without the claw end of the pick, which latched on to the driver's hatch.

He pushed the mess aside and sat in the driver's seat.

David Valentine wasn't comfortable behind any wheel. Machines bothered him, and the bigger and faster they were the more likely it seemed they'd get out from under his control and strike something. He pressed a pedal and the armored car slowed, another one sped it up.

The armored car slalomed as Valentine oversteered, heart pounding and the scent of blood in his nostrils.

His eye caught a reflected glint from the vehicle ahead. The driver there knew his job, and had set up some kind of safety mirror to keep an eye on the following vehicle.

He cranked his vehicle to the side of the road, into the thick brush. Duvalier was torn free as though by a dozen grasping hands.

Valentine found the brake and slowed the vehicle, but he still felt a thump as he struck Duvalier.

Heart pounding high and hard, Valentine halted the armored car and raised himself out of the seat.

Duvalier, her face a road map of scratches and wounds, grinned from behind a torn lip.

"You brake for redheads?" she asked.

"Thank God," Valentine managed.

"For inventing traction," Duvalier said.

Valentine pushed the vehicle into gear. "Get in the gunner—"

"No, I'll drive. You shoot."

"Catch up to him!" Valentine shouted, glancing through the armored glass. No wonder the driver was driving from the higher seat, the thin slits didn't give much visibility, and what there was had leaves and branches latticed across it.

Valentine went under to reach the gunner's seat in the armored car, noting that you could fit perhaps four men in the compartment between the driver and gunner positions. There were firing slots for them. Bags of gear were netted on the floor and against the ceiling.

Valentine saw a box of grenades and took a couple. He sat in the bloodstained seat and evaluated the weapon.

You pivoted it with a pair of pedals, and once pointed in the right direction, the gimbal allowed the gunner about a twenty-degree field of fire.

He saw the first vehicle with its dead gunner. Its driver was better than Duvalier; he was hurtling down the road, swerving around the bigger tree trunks, sending a constant hail of clipped-off branches back at the followers. He must be aware something awful was up.

Duvalier had to thump along in his wake as best as she could.

Valentine tried a burst, then a second. The bullets made a hole or two, but he could see no other effect.

Their quarry swerved and Duvalier struck a red oak trunk with a glancing blow, tearing off a sheet-sized piece of bark and knocking Valentine out of the seat. The Georgia driver had waited to the last second to swerve around it and only Duvalier's keyed-up reflexes prevented them from crashing into it.

No good throwing grenades in this mess. Valentine climbed out of the cupola, flexed his fingers and tested the skin on his hands for machine oil.

He crouched next to Duvalier.

"Get right up behind him!" he shouted in her ear.

She hit the gas, edged closer in the green tunnel.

Valentine crawled across the top of the armored car, the little cylinder of the grenade held carefully in his lips and teeth, like an oversized cigar butt. Overgrowth ticked off his legworm leathers.

Weirdly, he thought of the saunas he sometimes took in the winter up in Minnesota. The locals up there liked to hit each other with birch branches, claimed it brought the blood up to the skin and was good for the circulation. A bunch of naked men flogging away at each other in a stone-heated room made an impression on him as a preteen, and he'd tried a branch on his arm. It felt like this thresher of a green tunnel.

He tapped Duvalier, pointed at the forward armored car. She nodded, pulled up close enough for him to see the hinges on the forged steel grids over the rear lights.

Valentine waited for a gap in the growth above—he didn't want to be knocked by a tree limb under Duvalier's wheels—and leaped.

He landed hard, and badly, with the wind knocked out of him and the grenade rolling away. He somehow ignored the instinct to hold on with both hands and tried to retrieve it, and missed. It rolled up against the gunner's ring, wobbled there as though deciding which way to go, and he picked it up this time.

Ring out, lever off—he got around the gunner Duvalier had nearly decapitated and underhanded the grenade toward the end of the driver's compartment.

"Grenade!" he heard someone shout within. So there was a third man in this car.

The driver looked over his shoulder.

Valentine showed him the grenade ring.

The driver got one arm out, then the explosion launched him like a champagne cork.

Valentine found himself atop a careening armored car. It bounced off a tree root.

Duvalier was braking, hard.

The world tipped on its side and Valentine felt momentarily weightless, before he landed, painfully and like tricky old Br'er Rabbit, in a thorny tangle.

When he regained his bearings he felt the warm sensation that meant the pain would come in a minute or two. He cautiously moved each limb and looked down at his body. He felt like Scarecrow after the monkeys had finished tearing the straw out of him.

Duvalier appeared, smiled through a mask of drying blood, and held out a hand.

"I think we're each down one of our lives," she said. She helped him to his feet.

They sure build these things tough, Valentine thought. *Typical Control quality.*

They found the driver of the first armored car, bleeding and unconscious. She drew her skinning knife.

"No. We can take him with us as a prisoner. He's good, and he's lucky. I've never seen someone blown out of a vehicle like that still living."

They spent ten minutes working on the driver's injuries—abrasions and contusions, luckily for him—and secured him with a plastic restraint. Then they took a look at the vehicles.

He learned why they were hustling back to the camp so quickly to tell their news. The vehicle on its side was rigged for long-range radio. The antenna, designed to lie flat atop the armored car, had been torn away somewhere or other.

"The base still doesn't know about us," Valentine said.

"Unless there's a Reaper prowling around," Duvalier said. "I checked out the interior of ours. Either the previous users had really big feet or the car carried a Reaper recently. Long, pointed boots with the climbing toe."

The Wolves, pounding down the road in a double line, caught up to them.

"Lieutenant Carlson says a couple of platoons left camp in trucks and a command car, sir," the sergeant in charge reported.

The dead driver from Valentine's car looked clownish now, in that big white hat and gold-rimmed aviator glasses. Like Carlson, he was black. Valentine had an idea.

With tow cables, a stout tree, and some judicious driving by one of the Wolves, they managed to right the tipped armored car. They drove back to headquarters at a much more cautious pace, with Valentine and Duvalier tucked inside the front one, tending to each other's scrapes and cuts.

"Lieutenant," Valentine said, upon their return. "Do me a favor. See if that hat fits." He handed Carlson the hat and sunglasses.

"The glasses are prescription, but I can manage," Carlson said.

Valentine took a cautious look at the camp. "They're expecting these armored cars, right? Let's have 'em drive right up to the gate."

They had hidden the damage somewhat by hanging packs and ponchos over the bullet holes. It looked sloppy, but if the plan went right the Georgia Control sergeants would have graver concerns than chewing Frat out about the gear exposed to roadside growth.

Valentine filled both armored cars with Wolves, and distributed the grenades.

Carlson drove up to the gate, and in an inspired move, sounded the Klaxon and flashed his lights. He took off his hat and waved it.

The Wolves, before opening fire, whipped off their Georgia Control helmets and jackets. Valentine himself had done plenty of damage wearing the enemies' uniform, but Carlson had told his platoon differently.

The armored cars tore through the camp's temporary structures, pouring fire into machine gun positions and the camp's watchtower. Grenades exploded all around like fireworks, adding a sharper *krack!* echo to the popping noise of the machine guns.

Valentine surveyed the action with his binoculars, hurting all over. He served as Bee's spotter as she employed her heavy, big-game rifle. One of Fort Seng's armorers, remembering how she probably saved his life by taking down a plane as it started a strafing run, did her loads by hand, testing each production run himself with her rifle on the camp's range. She eliminated a machine gun crew with three quick shots before they could ready their weapon.

She didn't even have two good eyes. Remarkable shooting.

With the wheeling armored cars causing chaos within, Valentine watched the Wolves hit the wire like a tornado. They tore through the posts and wire like a scythe through dry straw.

The shooting died off to a trickle, like the clamor of a noisy party winding down as the guests left.

"Carlson signals he's starting the mop-up," the coms tech said. "Fourteen prisoners so far."

†

Champers's engineers, an assortment of men and women, mostly over forty-five, Valentine suspected, seemed a strong, capable lot. They and their rescuers eyed each other, misfit to misfit.

Duvalier had gone in to the engineer's camp before the Wolves hit to poke around, and found a frightened, confused Reaper snarling in the explosives dugout. She quickly locked it within, and the engineers parked a bulldozer across the door. Campers kept everyone well away from the dugout.

"His master's probably running for Tennessee as hard as he can," Valentine said.

"Be nice if we could take it alive," Pellwell said. "The Miskatonic has wanted a living Reaper forever. Especially one bred to be controlled by a Kurian."

"You're welcome to try, shanks," Duvalier said.

Sooner or later it would get hungry and dig its way out. Champers volunteered to try setting off the explosives, but Valentine declined.

"The Control will move back into Site Green sooner or later," Valentine said. "Having a wild, hungry Reaper lurking in the area will add some excitement to their return."

Valentine gave the usual speech to the military prisoners, promising them freedom. Anyone trusted with a gun in the Kurian Zone had probably left a hostage or two behind.

"You know what's in those cells, Major," Frat said. "Human litter. Petty criminals, terminally ill. They'll slow us up."

Valentine thought back on his own days as a Wolf lieutenant, when he'd been upbraided for what his old captain called "rounding up strays." *More trouble than they're worth, Valentine.*

"Denial of resources, Lieutenant," Valentine said. "The Kurian wants them. That's enough of a reason for us to try to take them away."

"Perhaps," Major Grace began, "perhaps we could do our part by just setting them loose."

"For the Reapers to hunt down?"

"If it keeps them off us," Grace said.

"You ever heard the expression 'Whoever saves one life, saves a world entire'?" Valentine asked.

"I'm not sure. Is that some maxim of that Quisling churchman?"

"Older than that. How about 'Go fuck yourself'?"

"That's insubordination!"

"I was only asking if you'd heard it," Valentine said.

Valentine noticed lights on in the old prison. Had the Kurian Lord already begun gathering an aura supply?

He might even have slipped in, but finding him, let alone killing him, in such a large complex would be difficult without surrounding the prison with flamethrowers and having the men burn their way to the center.

For all he knew, there wasn't anyone in there except a couple of Control soldiers cleaning out the animal and plant infestations that had no doubt built up over the years.

"Leave it alone, Val," Duvalier said. "Look at that place. I doubt anyone's in there who isn't fixing a toilet. It would take us two hours, probably, to get there, check the whole place out, and get back. Plus, probably more killing. Now me, I'd go there just to knife a sentry and set fire to it, but I know you'd want to bring out some one-legged senior citizen who lost the last round of musical chairs at the post office."

"Maybe I'll go over and peek in a few windows," Valentine said quietly. "Or not," he said, looking at his radioman, who was working a scrambler radio taken from the armored car that should be able to pick up Georgia Control communications.

"Major Valentine, may I—" Pellwell said.

"Cool your engine, college girl," Duvalier said.

Pellwell drew herself up and ignored the interruption. "You could let me send in the ratbits. They could cover that building in half an hour. If it's in as bad a shape as it looks, they'd have no problem getting in or getting around."

Valentine looked at her charges. They'd found a greasy wrapper caught in a bush, probably blown from the construction landfill, and were sniffing stains.

One looked up at Pellwell and chittered.

"Yes, food soon."

"Do they understand what a uniform is?"

"They know how to tell an armed man from an unarmed one."

"You send them into that building, and if they find any prisoners and count them accurately, I'll buy them a steak dinner. Or whatever their favorite treat is."

She squatted, looking like a grasshopper thanks to her long limbs, and lifted up the biggest ratbit, the one Valentine was calling Patches. She pointed. "That building. Count men. Count soldiers. Very quiet. No steal. No wreck."

Valentine heard it yeek back. She handed out a piece of bacon to each from one of her big leg pouches. The ratbits stuffed them into cheek pouches as Patches chittered at the others.

They bounced off on their oversized hind legs, making Valentine think of a kangaroo he'd seen on a TV documentary in his time with the Coastal Marines.

Pellwell looked anxiously at the sloping ground between the hill and the old prison.

"Worried they'll screw up?" Duvalier asked.

"Not so much that," she said, blinking fast. "They know what to do. Before, it was all play in old warehouses and apartments and school offices. One of them gets caught down there, it isn't just a loud no and a spell in isolation. They'll get stomped on and scraped out into the garbage."

Valentine had his own anxieties. He'd heard nothing from Gamecock's Bears.

The only blemish on the operation was that they couldn't destroy the foundation of the Kurian tower. No one wanted to venture in to get the explosives and face the fangs of that locked-up, anxious Reaper.

†

Valentine nearly had the prisoners organized for the ride back. Thanks to the armored cars, some utility trucks, and a personnel transport bus, everyone would be able to ride.

As dawn came up, Valentine thought he heard gunfire in the distance, but he couldn't be sure. His ears sometimes played tricks on him when he pressed them.

A Bear messenger rumbled in on a captured motorcycle. He reported that Gamecock's radio had "crapped out" before they even hit the crossroads blockhouse, and the Bears had successfully executed their ambush. Gamecock would pursue the Georgia Control Company south for an hour or so to "keep up the skeer" and then turn back north and head for the rendezvous.

The Gunslingers came in on their legworms and picked through the camp. Valentine was giving them advice on keeping well clear of the explosives dump when Pellwell returned. She gave him a salute.

"You don't have to do that, you're a civilian."

"Oh, sorry . . . I was excited. Major Valentine, my guys are back from the prison. They searched the whole thing. They counted three soldiers there, four other men total, one other."

"One other what?"

"They're not sure. *Big like her*, they say."

"Like Bee?" Valentine asked. "You sure they didn't mean scared of them or something like that, but 'big'?"

"I think they might mean even bigger."

"You think they mean a legworm? What's bigger than Bee?" Frat asked.

"We're going down there to find out," Valentine said.

†

As the Wolves came in the front the guards ran out the back. Valentine decided to let them go. They were ordinary security types, by the look of them, not soldiers. None ran off with anything larger than a pistol. They wouldn't even give the Gunslingers any trouble if they decided to turn and fight.

The prison had only one wing cleared for human habitation, the rest still had much of its moldering infestation, with thick slimes growing in all the drainage fixtures, revived by the recently repaired water system.

A few of the cells were occupied with backwoods Kentucky folk, probably rounded up by patrols while hunting for their families. Valentine felt a wash of achievement. There was nothing like the look on a man's face when he stepped out of a cage.

The "other" was not in a cell. In fact, he startled Bee into an excited yelp as he emerged from a dank stairwell.

Seven feet tall without even drawing himself up to his full height. Golden faun-colored fur, darker on the back and lighter toward the belly and beneath his manhole-cover pectorals. Well-scarred, crudely stitched, missing a piece of ear, with fur patchy over his wounds and fresh blood, sticky and spiky, about his muzzle.

He carried a short aluminum pole threaded to take a variety of tools. In this case, the handle was capped by a small shovel blade, bright at the edges where it had been recently sharpened and so bloody and covered in dripping shards of viscera it looked as though it had been used to stir a vat of grue.

"Well, my David," Ahn-Kha said. "This saves much explaining in both directions. Could you offer me a detachment? A few skulkers fled into the woods, and there may be one or two more in the basements. I might need some assistance in rounding them up."

CHAPTER FIVE

*T*he Cutthroat's Room, Fort Seng: It would appear that once Valentine's bedroom suite in the old mansion house belonged to someone named Cuthbert. THE CUTHBERT ROOM is carved in elegant letters on the door lintel.

Southern Command's soldiers, being who they are, defaced the beautiful woodwork in such a way that it now reads THE CUTTHROAT ROOM.

Many of Fort Seng's soldiers are better at fighting than spelling, it seems.

His quarters are sparse but not quite Spartan. Military billets were the only home he'd known since leaving the Northwoods at seventeen. He's done what he can to make this unusually lavish room his own.

Apart from the gun rack with his ready weapons, that mean-looking type three Atlanta Gunworks battle rifle and an unusually elegant 1911 Model .45, plus his blade and pick, legworm leathers, issue helmet, and combat harness.

A neat little .22 isn't visible, just as it is when he wears it. But it's in easy reach between the mattress and box spring.

Sketchwork covers the walls, picturesque ruins of old public build-

ings and burned brick structures around Evansville and Owensboro with new growth in the windows and feral cats lounging. They're not his art, they're the work of his Bear chief, the Carolinian named Gamecock.

There are also photos. A surprising number decorate the room on a byway of a big bulletin board salvaged from some office. To those who do not know him well, the little collection of pictures hung in protective plastic baggies—the experienced might recognize the plastic polymer as Ordnance ID sleeves—might seem bewildering. It's hard to gauge who those depicted are and how old Valentine was when he met them because he's featured in so few of the shots.

You can hardly see a young, sunburned, shorn young Valentine standing, holding a shovel comically at "present arms" with a group dressed in Labor Battalion overalls outside of a fortified enclave gate reading Weening. A young Asian girl standing beside him makes a classic two-finger addition to his hairline. There's a shot of a group of soldiers in Wolf leathers showing a mixed group of men and Grogs how to use a Southern Command machine gun, and a picture of a smiling family cutting the ribbon on a prefabricated pole-barn gate, two pretty blond daughters each holding half the shears. A gangly black youth holds two cows ready for entry into their new home.

There's a shot of Ahn-Kha digging up a massive heartroot—a Golden One staple—for a group of interested farmers and uniformed people. There's also a picture of a ship with a big gun on the bow and armoring around the bridge and weapon points tied up at a coastal wharf. A photo of a lithe little girl, black hair flying as she chases some seagulls on a sunny beach, shows signs of having been trimmed with a scissors. A newspaper clipping of someone named "Hank Smalls" smiling and holding a game ball after pitching a no-hitter in game one of the Transmississippi All-School pennant occupies a prominent place.

There's a picture of a salt-and-pepper-haired man in a wheelchair flying down a hill as a woman on his lap hangs on for dear life. Another one shows Valentine at the very back of a serious-looking crowd of bearded men who might be Mennonites standing in front of a massive rock etched with letters.

A photo stamped SOUTHERN COMMAND VERIFIED RELEASE *depicts a group of soldiers climbing off a riverbank boat, all wearing shiny, tinfoil skullcaps. A brand-new shot of a commanding-looking woman standing in front of some off-road vehicles with an assortment of hirelings soldiers is a new addition, as the shot is a professionally printed eight-by-ten and Valentine is clearly having trouble finding a protective frame. Her aged-but-still-handsome features and almost prim appearance contrast nicely with the armed men behind. Only Bears wear their atavistic garb of bones and teeth dangling off or pinning together captured Reaper robes with such lethal aplomb.*

There's one newspaper clipping of himself, a shot that made it into Southern Command's war museum, in fact, of David Valentine sitting mud-splattered in a command car next to the big golden Grog who now slumbers on the floor of his room.

†

David Valentine had forgotten how much the smell and sound of Ahn-Kha comforted him. The Golden One's vast presence was like having your old family dog sleeping nearby. Only better. The old family dog can't knock a Reaper off its feet with one swing of its fist.

As Ahn-Kha slept, bleeding heat like a cooling potbellied stove,

Valentine read by a tiny shake-and-glow clip light. The light began to dim, and Valentine picked up the light, shook it vigorously until it visibly brightened, and then returned it to its magnetic cradle.

Every time he did this routine, he marveled at the wonders the world used to produce. To only know the pre-22 world from New Universal Church propaganda, you'd think the old United States produced nothing but pollution, illness, and hunger. But still they made lights like this, still going strong almost a lifetime later.

Not quite as good as those Lifeweaver crystals, of course, which would shine brightly all night if left in the sun for an hour or so. He'd once had one, lost it in Nebraska when he was captured by the Twisted Cross.

With difficulty and care, he turned a page of the spineless mass of print he was reading.

Valentine had never seen a document composed entirely of wastepaper repurposed as manuscript pages. Two great wads of it, rolled up and filling a plastic-lined leather map tube that Ahn-Kha had evidently stitched together and sealed against the elements. Ahn-Kha had written mostly in English but here and there in his own language—the printing looked like a cross between Viking runes and mathematical formulas. Every now and then there were little pyramids of writing with horizontal lines between.

"What are those?" he'd asked the Grog while he was still awake.

"Names. In my language. In case it fell into the wrong hands."

"Didn't they ever find it?"

Ahn-Kha had been around humans enough to imitate a shrug. "It was my pillow. It looked like a big roll of wastepaper wrapped up in a towel. Remember, my David, they didn't know I could write."

"I had no idea you were such a diarist."

Valentine fell asleep reading about a mine revolt in Kentucky, marveling at his friend's eye for detail.

He brought it up over breakfast, where Ahn-Kha was taking up two seats and three-quarters of the table. At the rate his friend was eating well-salted hard-boiled eggs, they'd have to add a few more chicken coops.

"If I didn't know better, old horse, I'd think you were thinking about publishing your memoir. Some of your descriptions get a little rich for a military report."

Ahn-Kha bit his hard-boiled egg, shell and all, and salted the remaining half before popping it like a pill.

"My David, like many of my kind, I have a poor memory for that which I don't see, smell, do, and touch every day, or has been taught to me in song or rhyme. Set the letter 'V' of your dictionary to music, and I should improve my skills in your language for the rest of my days—but to look something up once and then remember it, that is very hard for me. I remember the manner in which we were—what was your word—de—"

"Debriefed."

"Debriefed, yes. I remember the manner in which we were debriefed. The volume of information and detail we were expected to provide on that which we'd seen once, and briefly—I started taking notes early on."

"I remember you writing on some old kid's tablets during the drive on Dallas. But to keep a diary when the Kurian Order's sending you underground in chains—that takes dedication."

"The practice kept despair at bay at first. Later, once the practice had worn down and rutted deep into habit, it became a way of clearing my head for sleep at night. Whatever my problem, if it had been put down on paper, it could be reread and rethought with the dawn. Never underestimate the power of a good night's sleep."

"Depends on what you're dreaming about," Valentine said. Valentine rarely slept really well, being troubled by dreams. Alcohol drove away the dreams, but he didn't care for the other side effects. Sex brought an emotional purge and exhausted oblivion, but it seemed doubtful that he'd see Caral again anytime soon. Or Tikka, who was leading the Army of Kentucky. With the Ordnance still looking for a way to reclaim Kentucky from the north and Atlanta probing at their southern flanks and the AOK healing the wounds inflicted by the ravies outbreak, she had better things to do than recreational lovemaking.

†

Valentine cleared his desk and spent the day touring Fort Seng with Ahn-Kha, introducing him to the NCOs and as many of the troops as possible. Golden Ones were gifted engineers, and Ahn-Kha quietly offered suggestions for a second river landing and a new road linking the artillery positions with the motor pool.

The motor pool had grown since Valentine last inspected all the vehicles. They'd captured some light armor from the Northwest Ordnance when they moved in on the winter offensive in the wake of the ravies outbreak and were working on refits using bits and bobs scavenged from Evansville.

A messenger found them atop one of the scout cars, testing the rotating ring for a machine gun. Both had oil on skin and fur.

"Colonel Lambert requests the Major's company at a working dinner, sir," the recruit relayed.

Valentine didn't recognize the boy. New recruits, most from the Kentucky backwoods desperate for new clothes, a bed, and chances of pay started out as messengers so they could learn the location of the companies and the officers and NCOs of the base. The best Lambert kept, the others went across the river to join Evansville's home guard regiment now training under Fort Seng's supervision.

Valentine acknowledged the request and fought off a groan. Lambert and her working dinners.

†

The outer office was empty by the time he'd showered and changed his shirt. Valentine heard voices from the base com center across the hall.

He knocked and was invited in. The air was so thick with smoke it formed its own weather system. He saluted and sat at the usual polite invitation, slouching a little to get his head below the worst of the fog bank.

Valentine admired Lambert, for all her taste for cold sandwiches and milk surrounded by baskets of flimsies.

If the weight of keeping over a thousand fighting men of ad hoc backgrounds and muchly inclined to killing each other a few short months ago fed, sheltered, healthy, all the while improving their integration and skills, she didn't show it. Her eyes looked bright and alert, not a hair out of place, and her blotchy gray-green uniform could have been photographed and used as an example in an officer's reference manual.

She was a skilled officer when it came to keeping the brigade's rolling stock on the rails. She was also a by-the-book officer in her thinking. To Lambert's indisputably agile mind, better and more experienced heads than hers had laid down the tracks the military machine ran on—her job was to keep everything in repair and on schedule. Her one big attempt to lay down some new tracks had ended in near-disaster last year, a year of almost uninterrupted failure for the forces of freedom. Since assuming command of the tired, whittled-down remains of Operation Javelin in Fort Seng last year, she'd been even more of a stickler than she'd been in her days running the War College's administration, when everyone had called her "Dots" because of her thoroughness at dotting i's and crossing t's.

She gestured to an elegant carafe and went back to rapidly filling out a Southern Command report in neat block letters.

A year or two younger than he, Valentine had first met her as a newly promoted lieutenant attending the old war college in Pine Bluff.

Lambert lifted her short churchwarden pipe, relit, and took another puff.

"Tobacco is my vice," Lambert said.

Valentine's shock was authentic. "You admit to a vice, sir?"

She smiled. "Purely privately, Valentine. If you go public, I'll say I only smoke to cover the B.O. from the Bears."

"Good stuff," Valentine said, sniffing the air. It wasn't the usual mix of tar and bark, sometimes blended with a little hemp, one smelled when the real tobacco ran out.

"Gamecock has some connection in Lexington who knows another Carolina boy who knows someone else in Chattanooga and so on all the way back to the Cooper and Santee. They keep me supplied. It comes in with the Army of Kentucky mail."

Valentine sipped his water and took a bite of a sandwich. The bread needed salt and the shredded legworm meat tasted like it had just come from the smokehouse.

"Read your report on finding your big friend and your notes on those Texas-sized rodents our friend Pellwell trains. Anything you want to add off-paper?"

"No. But I'd like to keep Pellwell and her ratbits, if she'll stay."

"She'd stay at the mouth of hell if she can have her hairy band with her doing mischief, I suspect," Lambert said. "The Kurians will come up with a countermeasure, they always do. They'll probably come up with something that eats them or a bug that kills them. I'm sure we're only waiting on a batch of Reapers immune to Quickwood. They ought to show up right about the time we go into full production on the Quickwood bullets."

"We'll still kill a batch in the meantime, sir," Valentine said.

Lambert took another long, slow puff at her pipe. "That's what makes you unique, Val."

"Excuse me, sir?"

"Back when Stoyachowski and I were running our special operations department, we had her collection of 'Wild Cards.' Yeah, we took the name from her 'Bear' handle. We both knew you were one for the books."

Lambert wasn't free with compliments beyond the usual polite phrases. Of course, "one for the books" might not be a compliment.

"Could you explain, sir?"

"The hunters should be our best and toughest. They are, but

they never last. Take the Cats—most quit after one trip in country. The rest—two, three, four outs and they were finished. Some go out again and never come back, others quit. The Bears are even worse. Like someone had planted rotten seeds in them, they sprouted differently, but it was always ugly. Some had the sense to request a transfer, others started in on drink and drugs and took themselves out of the TOE that way."

"I saw it in the Wolves, sir," Valentine said, wondering where this was headed. "My first hitch, with LeHavre, the senior lieutenant drank his way to a quiet desk job. Some go into the logistics commandos when they can't take the strain anymore."

"The Wolves wear out, the Cats disappear, and the Bears die violently. So what's your secret, Valentine? Do the seeds of self-destruction get in but never germinate?"

Valentine didn't know if he could tell her the truth—that he liked it. That truth was still something he was coming to grips with. The shadow inside, nibbling away at his soul every time he killed. In his darker moments, he wondered if he didn't thrive on blood in the manner of the Kurians and their Reaper avatars.

He thought it best to shift the subject.

"Actually, I wanted to talk to you about that, sir. Duvalier may be due for a rest. A year or two back in the Ozarks with good food—"

"My permission isn't the problem. She's not about to leave you any more than Bee. Nice dodge on that question, by the way."

He sat in silence, hoping she wouldn't take it for dumb insolence. Lambert neither liked him nor disliked him when they were both on duty. When she looked at him she might have been examining a rack full of tires for wear.

"No one knows what to make of you, Valentine. You're capable of looking someone right in the eyes and sticking the knife in, but you've half killed yourself fighting for people you didn't know ten minutes earlier."

"It's in the Southern Command oath, sir. *Render aid and comfort to our people.*"

"You're open-ended in your definition of 'our people.' Kurian Zone folks, Grogs . . ."

"I reckon it only makes sense if you go through life looking for friends or looking for enemies, sir," Valentine said. "I picked friends."

"In any case, I'm glad to have you. The Valentine fame adds a touch of dangerous glamour to this endeavor. We had two more recruits join while you were out, brothers who shared a cousin who served with you in the old Razorbacks. I hope you'll keep taking those trips into KZ country."

"Duty, honor, country," Valentine said. "I think they're in that order for a reason, sir."

"And coming back," Lambert said. "I like it when you head out. I love it when you come back." She went to work with a bent paper clip on the burnt-out plug in her pipe.

Odd phrase coming from someone as squared away and get-to-the-point as Colonel Lambert. Well, they did go back a long way. Come to think of it, she was his oldest friend in the service, he'd known her longer than even Captain Patel, who'd been his sergeant in the Wolves, trying to keep the young, fresh-from-the-mint lieutenant he'd been from killing his platoon.

He'd learned to exult in surviving. Every time he passed through the jaws of the bureaucratized temple of Moloch that was the Kurian Order, he felt reborn and relished birdsong, a quiet hour with a book under the shade of a tree, or the feel of clean skin after a good shave, lather, and rinse. The person who knifed sentries and sniped from cover was the entity Southern Command and the Lifeweavers had created to do the dirty work of cleaning the Earth of the Kurian stain. The man who checked up his nostrils while he shaved liked to read and observe and fish quiet lakes and poke around for telling remainders of the early twenty-first century. That man was strangely untroubled by all the bodies left in the wake of the Other.

She was wrong about one thing, though. He did feel worn down. He wasn't that old, barely past thirty.

"I'll see about forcing a leave on Duvalier. As to the other member of the old Thunderbolt Triumvirate, I have to warn you about Uncle—or Ahn-Kha. I hate to part you two again so soon after the happy reunion, but he's needed in Missouri."

"I'd heard they were hard-pressed in Omaha, sir."

"Yet another front in the war where it could be going a lot better. I understand they've been forced out of Omaha. Southern Command will probably try to form what's left into a guerilla band."

"Guerilla band? That's like saying 'form Dallas into a guerilla band.' It's a town, there are the old, the sick, the young. Pregnant females."

"I didn't think they hatched from a turtle hole, Major."

"Of course, sir."

"Let's get on with the work," she said, taking up one of the smoke-dried sandwiches. "I wanted your opinion on some NCOs for the 'A' Company Patel thinks we should form . . ."

†

Valentine spent much of the night finishing Ahn-Kha's notes. He dropped exhausted into an untroubled sleep.

Ahn-Kha had his hard-boiled eggs soaking in salt water the next morning. He reached into them while drinking his pomegranate-colored juiceless "juice."

"I'm almost done with your diary," Valentine said. "There's not much at the end, once the ravies overran everything."

"We broke out. It was fairly simple. Each man wired himself with a bomb timed to go off in twenty-four hours. Fairly easy to deactivate, if in full possession of your faculties."

"But if not?"

Ahn-Kha spread his fingers wide.

"That's harsh," Valentine said.

"None of them much wanted to stagger around the woods until they starved to death or ran down a child."

"Not much of an end for . . . what did you call it . . . 'the gallant rebellion'?"

"One cannot see the future," Ahn-Kha said. "I'd heard of bridges burning, maintenance garages burnt down. Not our doing. I think the Virginias people wound up the courage to do what we'd been doing, thinking that it would get blamed on the mine revolt. It may continue."

Ediyak and Duvalier set down their trays and Ahn-Kha tucked in his elbows. He was relieved to see Duvalier. She'd gone south again with the Wolves to see what the Kurians were doing with that tower.

"I dropped by Cutthroat Room last night," Duvalier said. "It reeked of his hairness's Grog farts, so I didn't knock."

"Any news?" Valentine asked.

Valentine dragged himself back to the present. "They've still got the ground occupied. I didn't see any work. I grabbed some mail I found on a car seat, nothing but the usual Atlanta snow shower of forms. DFSs and PCQs and RMVTs, whatever all those are."

"Ediyak, you were in the Georgia Control, right?"

"Sounds like personnel forms, sir. Everyone has a thick file. Health, work, and personal assessments."

"Assessments," Duvalier said. "Make an ass out of men, or something like that."

"Tell me more," Valentine said. He pushed his meat ration onto Duvalier's tray—she looked like she needed it. He wanted to force her to eat out of sheer boredom, so he'd keep Ediyak talking about paperwork if he had to.

"First, there's your HSA—Health Status Assessment. That happens every three years for twenty-to-forties, every two years for forty-to-fifties, and every year after. I'm not so hot on that—stress. My blood pressure's up. Normally, what would save me is my PQW—Performance Quality Workload. But I've been out here in the north of beyond for the last six months, so my CRI—Community Responsibility Index—is shot to shit. They don't make allowances for being a hundred and fifty miles from the nearest VETAMIN—that's a Volunteer Effort Task Association Municipal Infrastructure Node, for those of you who don't know Atlanta acronyms."

Ahn-Kha crunched on eggshells. "It gives me a headache. The poor people who keep track of all that nonsense."

"What do you think of all that, Ali?"

She swallowed the mouthful she'd been idly chewing, winced as it hit her stomach. "They left a couple letters out by oversight. Typical Atlanta spreadshit. Back in Kansas once a year the doc just stuck a piece of wood on your tongue, a finger up your ass, and some salad tongs piloting the oyster bed. If you passed for female, that is."

"Oyster bed?" Ediyak said, puckering her tiny nose.

"Slang Val and I picked up when we were on the Gulf Coast, passing for married. Not that mine's been much explored lately. Hey, Fuzzy, want to go pearl diving later?"

"Only for these," Ahn-Kha said, pulling another egg from the salt water.

"One thing, though, Val," Duvalier said, turning serious. "The Control's stepped up their patrols. Some planes were buzzing around too. I heard engines overhead day and night. They don't want any more raids."

"Do the engines circle over the tower?"

Duvalier switched from the alleged sausages to more reliable—and digestible—toast. "No, they went off and came back."

"Could be they're getting ready for a raid of their own. I think we'd better see if Gamecock can send half his Bears to back up the Wolves," Valentine said. He had better report this to Lambert right after breakfast.

When the women finished their food and left, Valentine told Ahn-Kha about his people.

†

Lambert held an officer's call over dinner that night. She passed the word that she wanted to talk about the threat from the Georgia Control.

They use the old formal dining room of the mansion. The woodwork here was left untouched by Southern Command whittlers, probably because all the ornate decor reminded them of a funeral parlor.

Ahn-Kha came along and brought an appetite, but couldn't fit his legs under the table, so he sat on a window bench and looked out over the east lawn of the mansion. A headquarters rooster led his hens in an exploration of the terraced landscape.

The lamb and spring potatoes with rosemary were good. For dessert, they had hand-cranked ice cream. Valentine avoided the wine and had a stainless tumbler full of milk.

"I find," Lambert said, when the dessert and small talk over coffee began to drag, "that it's easier to solve a problem if you can define it. Anyone want to take a shot at defining the problem?"

By tradition, heads turned toward the junior officer, who was usually allowed to speak first. Valentine suspected that the tradition predated Southern Command. It prevented the lower ranks from keeping silent during a meeting and just agreeing with the superiors.

Glass, now the Sergeant Major for the entire battalion, attended the officer's call for reasons of courtesy and efficiency.

"Atlanta's moving in on Kentucky," Ediyak said, speaking as the junior.

"Anyone heard otherwise?" Lambert asked.

The staff sat silent.

"Okay, the buildup isn't a feint so they can take over Nashville and Memphis. But why do they think they can move on us?" Lambert asked.

"The Army of Kentucky's still putting itself back together after that ravies outbreak," Captain Patel said. "The legworm ranchers are tough enough when they have to be, but they've got communities and families to think about. They can only play guerilla part of the year."

Valentine remained silent. He had an oddly defined role at the fort—on Southern Command's paperwork he was a corporal of the militia, but in practice he was the executive officer for operations. Everyone called him "Major" and kept up the appearances, despite the fact that his career had been permanently broken by a court-martial verdict years ago. He had some ideas of where Lambert and Ediyak were taking this meeting—they'd quietly consulted his opinion—but while he had an idea of the strategy, the tactics to be employed were still a mystery to him.

Still, he had a role to play. They hadn't exactly fed him his line, but it was time to put in his discussional ante.

"What keeps the Kurians from doing the same thing in Arkansas or Texas?" Valentine asked.

"Southern Command," Patel said.

"More than that," Valentine said. "The populace living there. Every village has some sort of militia. They're armed and the guards have special dedicated support units to show up with the mortars and machine guns. It keeps the Kurians from doing anything beyond small terror raids. In the Kurian Zone, the poor bastards are subject peoples, as likely to help enemies as inform on them. In the Republic, the locals will break out the machine guns and dynamite if they think there's a Reaper in the neighborhood."

Which can be bad enough. Valentine's first blood in the Free Territories had been in such an incident, in the little town of Weening.

"Why hasn't the Ordnance moved against Evansville? Because there are ten thousand adults there being organized to fight if they have to. The Ordnance lost the Moondaggers to us, some good assault troops to that ravies outbreak, and their garrisons don't dare concentrate too much or they might lose land to a rival Kurian. They can't arm their people in the same ratio that we can, or they'll risk a revolt. The Grogs are sick of dying for them, except for the ones that can be trained like dogs and a few elite units under close supervision."

"What we need is an instant population," Lambert said.

Valentine thought of an old Warner Bros. cartoon he'd seen at the theater in Pine Bluff. A little alien had run around sprinkling seeds with water, growing big bird creatures. He once thought that the Kurians probably had a similar system for growing Reapers, but he'd learned in his search for Gail Post that they used human females who possessed some kind of special genetic marker.

"Ex-soldiers from Southern Command would be my choice," Patel said, after swallowing his usual after-dinner tablets of aspirin. He had bad knees, and popped the white caplets morning, noon, and night. "Some guard vet, has his twenty years and five hundred acres—or better yet an ex-Wolf. I could put the word out."

"There aren't enough ex-Wolves in all of the Free Republics, even if they all moved," Lambert said.

"What would it take to occupy the lands between here and the Tennessee?" Ediyak asked. "Maybe Southern Command can offer some kind of bonus for settlers. I know the people in the refugee camp they put me in would jump at the chance to get their own land."

"We need something like ten thousand," Lambert said. "At best, there are a thousand Kentuckians from the Gunslinger Clan there now, and that's counting all the kids and grandparents."

Glass snorted.

"You have something to add, Sergeant Major?" Lambert asked.

"No, sir," Glass said.

"I expect he nasalized what we were all thinking," Valentine said. "Getting ten thousand people to leave the relative safety of the Free Republics and move into Kentucky."

"The papers haven't had much good to say about our performance here," Lambert said. "Kentucky—chaotic, dirty, disease-ridden, nothing but legworm meat to eat. The Four Horsemen of the Apocalypse riding back and forth across the state with some obnoxious cousins following behind."

"Maybe we should give it back," Patel said, eliciting a few chuckles.

"May I offer a suggestion?" Ahn-Kha said. They'd spent long hours the previous night, looking at each other in the blue darkness talking about his suggestion.

"Of course," Lambert said. "Err—Valentine, does he have a rank with Southern Command?"

"When I last appeared on the lists, I was a Colonel of Auxiliaries, sir," Ahn-Kha said. "So even a Southern Command corporal outranks me in combat zones. But I fear my commission is defunct since the unpleasantness following Major Valentine's legal trouble."

"You still have your old gift for understatement," Valentine said. "Just call him Uncle."

"Your suggestion, Uncle?" Lambert said.

"Two generations ago in my people's history, we were promised green lands and good stone by the Kurians, once you difficult humans were under control. The Kurians gave us a ruined city poisoned by sun weapons and dry prairie. I've seen the limestone all around here and the richness of the land speaks for itself. If you would have my people here, they would gladly come."

"The Golden Ones," Lambert said. "I don't remember how many you had in Omaha."

"It was some thousands when I left," Ahn-Kha said. "Fifteen or so."

"Moving them would be tough," Patel said. "That's six hundred miles or thereabouts, most of it covered in Grogs. We don't have any friends in Missouri or Southern Illinois."

"Excuse me, sir," Glass said. "I was involved in the offensive that was supposed to relieve them Groggies. Never got off the ground what with the setbacks in Kansas. They said there were upwards of twenty thousand in the city alone, something like another two thousand outside it."

"I've been told the Iowans finally took Omaha back," Valentine said.

"I'll look into it," Lambert said. "They're an awful long way from here, and there's no direct route across friendly country."

"What about the Kentuckians?" Patel asked. "How would they feel about nonhuman neighbors setting up? Nothing against you personally, of course, you're a rare Grog. Most of 'em are unneighborly. Having a colony just around the bend of the river could cause bad blood, between the head-hunting and cattle raids."

Ahn-Kha's ears flattened. "Golden Ones don't rise by being thieves or trophyteers, Mr. Patel. I would not judge you by the behavior of a silverback gorilla."

"Brother Mark and Major Valentine have the best connections with the Army of Kentucky," Lambert said, smothering the incipient argument. "What's your assessment?"

All eyes turned to Valentine. "Hard to say," he finally said. "I think they'd welcome any allies. They're a flexible bunch. I think they'd adapt. Out of all of North America, as far as I know, they're the only ones who made use of legworms. Built a whole culture around them over the years. The Golden Ones are smart, tough, and reasonable—sorry to distill your people into a few words, old horse, but there it is—I think the Kantuck would want 'em."

"I doubt the Missouri Grogs or the Iowans would appreciate us marching a host of Uncle's relations through their lands," Glass said.

"If you could hurry me back to my people, I could sound them out on the matter," Ahn-Kha said. "I would be eager to be among my own kind again. It's been many years, and if they are in distress, I should be with them."

"Let's at least explore the idea. Major Valentine, you and Ahn-Kha and Ediyak come up with a plan, based on moving twenty thousand civilians. Make it twenty-five—Grogs eat a lot."

"That's a college stadium," Patel said. "Lots of food and water. We're talking divisional support."

"We're wasting our time talking about it, sir," Glass said to Lambert, though whether he objected to exploring the idea or further chatter was hard to say. Glass was notoriously asocial for such a popular NCO. "Not a whole population. No way we can take that many cross country without killing half of them."

"I agree. There's simply no way to move that many civilians," Patel said. "Not through hostile country."

"Be easy to do on the river, if we controlled those waters," Valentine said. "The river takes care of water and sanitation. You could fit a lot of Golden Ones in a barge, for a few days anyway."

"You might as well have suggested an airlift, sir," Patel said. "We don't own any part of the Mississippi, at least not on a permanent basis. The skeeter fleet is strictly hit-and-run. That's why our supplies and mail, what little we get of it, has to come overland."

"We need a brown-water navy," Lambert said.

"Then the question for us is—lease or buy?" Valentine said.

CHAPTER SIX

*T*he Logistics Commandos: What the Ozark Free Republics can't make, they take. Southern Command has turned scavenging, black market trade, and outright theft into a science. Oftentimes, their toughest veterans retire into the freewheeling Logistics Commandos rather than retire to their allotted acreage and meager pension. Former Wolves and Cats often make the best LCs—they know the Nomansland terrain and the surrounding Kurian Zones and usually have a network of contacts.

In the field, the Logistics Commandos are wild cards, the last reserve of every commander. They'll follow behind a successful attack, grabbing everything from prisoners and intelligence and truck batteries to dropped weapons, always sorting, always prioritizing. On a retreat, they decide what can be saved and what must be sacrificed. Because nearly all of them are long-service veterans with combat experience, they can fill almost any role in a fight from artillery to signals.

Of course they can be difficult. They have an old soldier's nose for food and comfort, and the other forces of Southern Command often complain—with justification—that the Logistics Commandos grab all the best beds and let only their scraps of their ample tables and second-rate luxuries reach the rawer hands and newer heels at the front.

†

"These are the boats?" Lambert said.

"Everything that floats," Valentine said. He and Ediyak were taking the colonel on a tour of Evansville's waterfront with the commander of Evansville's River Guard, an ex–river patroller named Jackson.

Jackson was a very *what you see is what you get* fellow. He had no office, only a fast, heavy boat with twin machine guns set up on a mount that probably was supposed to be used for sportfishing. He took them on a waterborne tour of the three miles or so of Ohio River that unequivocally belonged to Evansville. The locals had many less-lethal boats, mostly used for ferrying people across the river or east-west travel between a southward loop known as the "west hill" and the heart of the old city to the east. Like many old river towns, its biggest vessel was a derelict casino barge, hollowed of all but the ceiling glitz, now used for sheltering livestock—mostly chickens and pigs—traded to the river traffic.

They had a few barges, coal and corn vessels for the most part, still held together as a city storage reserve. One was even rigged to hold freshwater. A single decrepit tugboat was still in service for pushing them around, if necessary, but by the look of the engine and the part-time crew, it wasn't up to the job of even getting a single barge to the Mississippi, let alone up it. There was also a smaller tug designed for firefighting. It could, Valentine supposed, be pressed into duty as a barge pusher, but it would need some modifications for tying itself on to a barge train.

There were plenty of men in Evansville with riverboat experience, according to Jackson. Most had fled the Kurian Zone once

Evansville became known as a haven, so getting them back on the river and in hostile territory might call for an old-fashioned press-gang. Valentine didn't like the idea, but it might be their only option.

Jackson gunned his engines and weaved around a sunken wreck of a tug, sending his passengers lurching into each other. The wreck was rather picturesque, if you liked rotting wood and rusty metal. Waterfowl nests covered the wheelhouse roof. In the slack water next to it, the Evansville River Guard's other battle-ready boat sat, holding on to the wrecked tug with a boat hook, ready to dash out downriver.

A tiny brown-water navy was being put together by the city, mostly to help defend the booms and check approaching barges for enemies. Evansville's leaders decided their best chance for survival was to allow river traffic up and down the Ohio, provided it wasn't military supplies or fodder for the Reapers. Corn and coal and dry goods could pass after being checked.

The Kurians were putting extra troops on the "peace marked" barges to discourage deserters.

Valentine wasn't a fan of "hostile neutrality" or whatever the Evansville town fathers were calling their attitude about river traffic these days, but Southern Command had no business telling civilians how to run their affairs unless bullets were flying.

"Men aren't the problem," Jackson said, when they asked him what his capability was to get to the Mississippi junction. For now, grander plans weren't being discussed, even with someone in the Evansville armed service. "Machinery is. You get me the boats, I could fill them with hands."

"Can you build them?" Lambert asked.

"Marine motors are the real problem, okay. They have to be

tough and reliable. What we have is cannibalized, fifty-year-old gear for the most part. We have plenty of people in Evansville who can steer a boat, read the river, fix an engine. The weapons and combat stuff, on the other hand—"

"Well, we have a lot of men who can do that," Valentine said.

"River fighting is a little different than on land," Jackson said. "It starts and finishes very quick. You need men who can put a lot of shit on target—begging your pardon ladies—fast and I mean fast, or you lose boats and the next thing you know you're swimming in an oil slick."

†

Lambert sat with them on an airy, upper-floor balcony of the mansion, resting in the quiet after their day on the river. Her bedroom connected with it. It had a nice view to the north.

Duvalier and Frat had joined them for the very informal meeting, as they were talking about the Kurian River Patrol on the Tennessee, who had the nearest brown-water combat craft.

Lambert started off: "Okay, to sum up, crews will be difficult but doable. It's motors and hulls that are the problem. We can't build boats, at least not in time, and we can't buy them and Southern Command, when I asked, said that all forces were allocated."

"Then we'll have to steal them," Valentine said.

Duvalier and Frat's Wolves knew the ground along the Tennessee best. Ediyak had already assembled their observations into a concise report.

"There's a cute little rest stop on the river right off the Cadiz inlet," Duvalier said.

"I think it used to be a training base, before they moved it up-river to Tennessee," Ediyak said. "According to this week-old Wolf report, there's a couple of dry-dock ships, a machine tool work-shop, a little dispensary still in operation. Respite Point, they call it now. There's a couple of bars and a brothel in the old base. Very popular with the River Patrol. Not big enough for a Kurian and plenty of fun for the crew while their boats are out of the water being refitted."

"Hulls, engines, weaponry, that sort of thing?" Valentine asked.

"You bet," Frat said.

"Garrison?"

"Platoon strength, not even," Frat said. "Plus whatever of the River Patrol is in camp. The locals are very friendly to the River Patrol and would give warning of a large force."

"But a small team could make it."

"Maybe, sir. Doubt if they could hold it for long, though. Re-spite Point is well guarded," Frat said. "Upriver, near the Tennessee border, there's a big River Patrol base. Even if we were able to sur-prise them and hit it, I doubt we'd get many boats, as they'd scream off into the water as soon as the attack got rolling. Then, even nearer downriver, there's a big gun fort supporting Cadiz on the other side. Lots of mean ordnance sighted on the river, and three booms you have to weave around. The cables to pull them out of the way lead right into the fort."

"Still," Valentine said. "Might be worth a closer look. I wonder if the joyhouse lets in Kentucky men, or if they're river rat only."

Valentine noticed a ring of expectant faces. "What, you don't know?" Lambert asked.

"Why are you all looking at me? Am I supposed to be an expert on brothels?"

"You keep finding your way into them," Duvalier said. "I thought you might have patronized it. Just once I'd like to hear that you met this contact or that one at a dentist's, or a smokehouse. No, you're always emerging from a brothel, beat and bloody."

"Still, it's a possible excuse to bring a small team in. Even Bears carrying wrenches from toolboxes could probably take that place."

"There's a flaw in your plan, Val," Lambert said. "I've looked at that same location. Sure, that depot is lightly guarded. But even if we seize some boats, we'd never get them downriver. The River Patrol has a fort at Gilbertsville—a fort they've reinforced, lately, by the way, to try and cut off the Western Kentucky trails. There's a boom blocking the Tennessee at the old interstate pylons. A double boom everywhere but the gate as a matter of fact. Plus wire to stop hotshots in speedboats from doing any fancy jumps.

"It would take the whole Army of Kentucky to take that fort," Lambert continued. "And we'd probably have to haul our guns to support, and I'm not sure we have enough shells left to wreck the boom or rubble the fort."

"Do we have a sketch of the place?" Valentine asked.

"Pretty good one," Frat said.

"Put some coffee on," Valentine said. "Let's have a look."

†

Getting into the River Patrol base had been simple enough. It wasn't really a base. There were two lookout points and fencing built more for livestock than keeping people out. A dog patrol wandered the fence.

After spotting the dog, Valentine pulled Gamecock and his six Bears back another hundred yards.

He exhibited ID and a broken, chain-free bicycle, claimed to be a hungry communications "local support" staff working the lines running south from Cadiz, looking for a hot meal and somewhere out of the woods to sleep. And hopefully a new chain for his bike.

"Don't get your hopes up," the corporal patting him down said.

They found no weapons. They let him keep the tool belt after flashing their lights in all his pouches and feeling around. They even opened the battery shaft on his flashlight and inspected the cells within.

"You're under River Patrol jurisdiction on base," he warned Valentine. "Cause any trouble, try to steal, and we'll weigh you down with scrap and sink you in the Tennessee mud."

"Understood," Valentine said. His stomach gave a fortuitous growl.

The serious part of the security was at the dock itself, where a pair of barges were tied up next to a long dock branching out like plant roots into the river from some broken concrete steps down to the Tennessee. Above the concrete steps was a nest of fencing and barbed wire, with alert-looking RPs on anchor watch at their riverine weapons. A few more stood at the gap of the wire, smoking and talking to a sentry. A squat emplacement on the highest point of the bank with a two-barrelled antiaircraft cannon had a commanding view of all. Odd that there wasn't someone at the gun; it was in a great position to cover the river.

Have to do something about that gun.

Valentine smelled gasoline and followed it to a sort of wharf a little way downstream with a pump under a lonely light. From one of the barges he heard a machine tool whirring away and metal-on-metal tamping, with the occasional rustle of chains being shifted.

The spring flow of the Tennessee filled the riverbed bank to bank, covering the usual washup of garbage and driftwood.

Lovely night. Valentine felt oddly relaxed, now that he was finally here. He had a bit of a headache from hunger, but it sharpened his already tuned-up senses.

Presumably, if they were attacked, the River Patrol could fire up their engines and escape. But the craft could throw a tremendous amount of what Jackson had called "shit on target" in the form of machine gun bullets and cannon—anyone wanting to take the docks would pay a heavy price.

Valentine wandered through the corpse of the older, larger base. Everything of value had obviously been moved into the barges. A few heavy old engine blocks remained, well chewed by rust, and the black-rimmed doorways smelled of rats and cats.

Rats and cats. Something to think about.

Typical Kurian disorganization. A partially shut-down base, but still functioning as a service point for river sailors coming off of their weeklong patrols. Too small for a Kurian to take up residence, too big for a couple of locals to slit any throats. Up the estuary in Cadiz, a ruin of a town with some Kentuckians scraping a living one way or another, smuggling, trading, repairing, laundering—in a way it wasn't that different from the townlet growing up outside Fort Seng's gates. Men off duty liked short travel times to their services, rest, and recreation.

He evaluated the anchor watches as he walked his bike in. At least two men in each armed river patrol craft. A few more unarmed craft, probably for ferrying men and supplies. A permanent garrison at the supply barges of technical and support staff. Maybe sixty uniformed River Patrol soldiers, plus a few older men making themselves useful while hiding from both river duty and the Reapers.

About the right size to support a decent bar, eatery, and brothel, as long as the nomadic nature of the River Patrol meant they didn't get too sick of the taste of the old grease in the fryers.

The Inlet the sign read. Sort of. It was illuminated by three orangeish LED spotlights, one of which had been stolen—unfortunately the center, so Valentine played with the idea that it was "To let" or perhaps named "The Toilet."

The bar was half built up on pylons, set into the side of the hill sloping down to the river, about the size of a ranch home. A roomy second floor above. Chain-link fence guarded storage beneath. A cross between a porch and a patio was empty, even in the easy air of the night.

Valentine parked his bicycle. Despite its nonfunctional condition, he chained it to an old water meter.

He walked up the short flight of steps, tried the door. It was locked.

He rapped on the door.

After a moment, a scratchy woman's voice shouted, "Yeah?"

"You open?" Valentine called.

"This is a private club. You know the password?"

"I'm hungry, thirsty, and lonely."

The door opened. A squat woman, who might be a New Universal Church informative poster on the danger of too much fried food, smiled. She had impossibly blue-black hair piled high atop her head, not really making up for her four-feet-eleven. "That ain't the password, but I've got a soft spot for anyone that broke-dick."

"Thanks. I'm Rice."

"My name's Dirty Nel. This is my establishment. My job's to make sure you have a really good time, at least until I have most of your money. You okay with that?"

Valentine glanced inside. Bright red shag carpet, gleaming pine paneling, and brassy nautical gewgaws pounded themselves into his eyeballs.

"Great," he said, entering.

The interior was a long, low-ceilinged, shaggy red bar, dimly lit, and hung with fishnets and twinkle lights. A bar with a kitchen behind communicated through the usual order window of stained stainless. The nets seemed to press down from the ceiling, anyone over six three would have to watch himself. He felt like he was inside a giant whale that had swallowed the *Pequod* with a strip club chaser.

Meaty, tired-looking blondes arranged their lips into imitation smiles. One blew him a kiss.

Judging from the smells coming from behind the kitchen door, he'd better keep to liquids.

"Bottle of beer?" he told the girl behind the bar. She was dressed like the working girls, only her choice of animal print varied. Perhaps she filled in if they became busy.

"Sure thing, brown eyes," she said, showing a nice set of what were probably false teeth.

"Want to bump that up?" Nel asked. "Kentucky bourbon. Only two dollars extra, Nashville, or three bucks Ordnance."

"I've got Control bucks," Valentine said.

"Then it's one lonely dollar, my friend," Nel said. "Control's scrip is really worth something."

Valentine tapped the bar and the bartender poured him something from a Maker's Mark bottle. It tasted like nitric acid.

He wondered what The Inlet had been, formerly. Perhaps an officers' housing complex with the diner and lounge conveniently attached. The River Patrol was famous for its accommodations for boat captains and their lieutenants—probably to keep the lower ranks serving in hopes of promotion to an officer's splendor, and to prevent the officers themselves from simply steering their craft to a much less luxurious lifestyle up an enemy river.

The only customers were two river patrolmen playing cards, separated by a hedge of amber Nashville's Best empties and a petty officer reading his *Bulletin*. Valentine wondered if he was sending away for any merchandise.

"My name's Randy. Want to go upstairs?" one of the blondes asked. She had a painted-on dimple, a practice Valentine never understood.

"My thought precisely," Valentine said.

"What do you have in mind?"

"I was just thinking you had a very nicely shaped mouth."

"Thirty, if it's Control," Randy said.

Valentine showed the cash.

"Pay Nel," she said, flashing a hand signal to the madam.

Valentine handed over the captured bills and took her callused hand—did Nel put all her girls to scrubbing the floors every morning?—and led her up the world's shortest staircase.

"Watch it, man, that's the loosest slip on the Tennessee you're going into there!" one of the card players guffawed.

"Check for crabs, meat!" his partner said.

"Don't worry about crabs," Randy said. "Or anything else. I'm clean. I get to the doc in Cadiz really regular. He fucks me too, so I know he's not lying."

The room smelled like someone had spilled a gallon of perfume and tried to clean it up with pine cleanser. It depressed Valentine that she entertained in her own living quarters, but since everything else in this hair trap was cheap and functional, the girls' business rooms would be too.

It had a window big enough to climb through—unusual for a brothel. He tested the locks holding it on.

"Mind turning off the light?"

She flicked a switch at her bedside. A soft red night-light went on, tucked somewhere behind her slat headboard.

"So, you want to listen to some music, have a little massage first, or—hey, careful with those screens, bugs'll get in."

Valentine carefully set the screen next to the window.

"You ever do it on a rooftop?" Valentine asked.

"What, are you kidding?"

He squeezed out her window, felt for the edge of the roof, tested his grip. He got a leg up, and briefly hung head down, looking in on her room.

"You aren't paying me enough for this!" she said.

"Just having a smoke. I'll be right back in."

Valentine shucked the handle so the reflector went wide, flicked off three flashes, then three again, then a final three toward the woods where Gamecock waited.

A brief red flicker answered.

The Bears wouldn't attack yet, but the signal would get them close enough to the fencing for the dog to smell. Valentine would send up a flare, or they'd go in when the shooting started.

"Yeah, they're out there," Valentine said, coming back through the window.

"Maybe you should leave," Randy said. "Wait. What do you mean, *they're* out there?"

"I work in a competitive field," Valentine said. "High skill, lots of pay, not many openings. You need to be trustworthy. I'm gay, and that's a big black mark. There's a man who wants my job, and he's paying a couple of stiffs to follow me and get evidence."

"What are you paying me for, then?"

"Oh, a little camouflage. My boyfriend's in the River Patrol. I'm trying to kill two birds with one stone here—I want you to act like you had a good time with me, while I nip out and see him."

"Don't I know it. Odd trade on the river. Which boat's he on, *Red Forty-Five?*"

"Best not to spread gossip," Valentine said. He checked the drop to the ground. "I'm going to leave a little safety line. You relax. I'll be back in less than an hour. If you look a little exhausted when you go back downstairs, there's an extra hundred in it for you."

"What I do ain't usually that exhausting. I save that for my boyfriend."

"Speaking of boyfriends . . ." Valentine said.

"Hey, have fun. I'll make sure no one comes through that door until you get back. It's a slow night, Nel won't mind."

"You're sweet," Valentine said, dropping out the window.

†

Valentine slipped off his shoes and tied the laces together.

He looked up at the sky. It was a night of danger. This was always both the best and the worst moment, right before you started. The best, because everything came alive. You could swear you could feel your toenails growing. The air was suddenly full of life, not only the smell of diesel oil and river rot.

Working quickly in the shadows, Valentine marveled at how easily this forgotten corner of the Kurian Zone could be defanged. Working quickly, he wedged every door he could find, and cut the wires to the radio antenna. He would have had a harder time with a fueling station in Little Rock. The employees guarding gas pumps were armed to the teeth and alert as Dobermans.

Evidently the "neutrality" of the Kentucky locals here, neither supporting nor resisting the Kurian Order, was still intact. The few personnel on base must have figured that the legworm ranchers wouldn't have need for riverboats anyway. And they were largely right. A legworm could go anywhere, a boat had to stick to easily choked-off river routes.

Valentine turned his collar up and pulled his cap down low. He dug around in his tool kit, came up with two cylinders. He dumped the screws inside out, made sure the heavy-duty spring inside was clean. Then he cut open the lining at the bottom of his tool kit, and took out two razor-tipped darts.

The dart launchers belonged to one of Gamecock's Bears. Valentine had experimented with them. They could bury the dart halfway into an oak tree from twenty feet. The problem was aiming them. You needed to be very close, or very lucky against a man-sized target, especially if he was moving.

Valentine had yet another weapon, a plain old pipe wrench. Five pounds of cast iron, properly swung, was as deadly as his old parang.

He slipped into a gun emplacement covering the river and docks, carefully unrolled the waterproofed canvas covering the 20mm cannons there.

He almost tsk-tsk'ed. There was visible rust on the action. It would be more of a threat to the firer than anyone in its sights. He might as well take one of the guns out of its mount and use it as a club.

He evaluated the anchor watches on the river patrol craft: two men in each of the long cabin cruisers, with guns at the stern and on the flying bridge, one on watch while the other rested. Each boat had one gun ready for action, a machine gun with an armored shield at the back of the boat where it had the widest field of fire. The River Patrol had followed procedure and parked their boats like two horses in a field facing opposite directions, so each one's tail could swat the other's flies.

Nothing to do but start it.

Mouth dry, he walked down to the docks, a spring-loaded dart in each coat sleeve. As he approached the boat, he tapped his utility-worker's hat.

"Dumbledore watermelon hopscotch juice on?" Valentine

called, stomping hard on the weather-beaten old boards of the river dock.

"Pfwat's that?" one of the men at the guns said, coming awake.

Valentine shined his flashlight right in the other's face.

"Hey!" he shouted.

Valentine knelt and fired his first dart. He heard a clatter. The second twanged off toward the gunner, and he heard a wet impact.

The man let out an awful sucking sound.

He dropped the now-empty tubes and grabbed for the wrench in his pocket. Naturally, it decided to catch as he ran.

Valentine took one long stride and launched off his good leg, giving up on the wrench for now. He went over the gun and managed a head tackle, spilling them both into the boat to the sound of cartilage snapping.

"What the hell," the other anchor watch said, from the dim light of the armored wheelhouse.

Valentine managed to free the wrench, rose, and struck as the other drew his pistol.

And struck again. This one was even wetter.

Now he had a bloody wrench and a Browning-model 9mm automatic.

The anchor watch at the stern gun was being held up by the machine gun's steel harness. "Fuuuck! I'm—yak! I'm hit, Grantski," he wretched. "Somebod—yak! Put an arrow in m*yak!*"

Valentine heard shooting up the riverbank. Gamecock's Bears must be at the wire.

Red, white, and blue lights flashed on the attention bar of the patrol craft. A siren sounded.

Valentine saw the other anchor watch peering from the armored cabin. He didn't want to chance running out for the stern mount, it seemed, not with his fellow sailor screaming out his bloody death throes.

"Better hit the river, you," Valentine called to the other boat. "That's Southern Command come calling."

The man he'd knocked out of the gun groaned and moved. Valentine tested the Browning model on him. It worked.

The anchor watch at the other boat's gun slumped out of his harness. Valentine saw two dark patches on his white shirt. He hadn't missed after all.

"Don't you shoot, I'm leaving," the man in the wheelhouse said. He scuttled up a ladder to the flying bridge, butt and head tucked, and used the first two rungs to throw himself into the river.

Lights appeared around the bend in the downstream Tennessee. Another River Patrol craft was coming in, hot and ready for action.

Valentine went to the wheelhouse of the vacated boat, the one with the lights flashing. It was a smaller boat approaching, no flying bridge but what looked like a big damn multibarreled gun in front of the wheelhouse. Two oval ammo drums hung off it like testicles.

Probably a crew of three.

Valentine waited. It approached the dock, slowing, those gun barrels aimed up the riverbank, where Valentine saw scattered gun flashes. The Bears were sensibly using single shots. Nothing drew fire like long bursts of automatic.

Valentine was busy looking at the boat's spotlight. Seemed simple to operate, a smaller version of the cannon he'd known on the old *Thunderbolt* in the Gulf.

"For fuck's sake, they're in the gun emplacement on the hill," he shouted to the other boat. "Lay down some fire on it or they'll blow you out of the water."

That didn't work. The gunner wouldn't be goaded into firing.

He lit up the other boat, zeroed the spotlight in on the gunner. A face gleamed whitely before it threw up an arm to ward off the blinding light. Valentine tightened the spotlight beam as best as he could and then ran to the gun mount. He was chambering the first round of the belt when another spotlight struck, blinding him and shooting white pain through his head.

Here it comes.

Blindly, Valentine fell backward out of the boat and into the Tennessee. Bullets ripped up the cabin of the craft, killing the spotlight, then clanging off and through the armored shield on the rear mount.

His head broke water behind the bulk of the tied-up boat.

Fire poured down from the gun emplacement. Valentine saw two of Gamecock's Bears, faces full of war paint and toothy helmets on, lighting the night with tracer from their miniguns. He could see the brass casings dancing off into the night.

The boat swerved, headed for shore, the man at the wheel dead.

Valentine raised the Browning knockoff, pointed it at a bleeding crewman who was attempting to return to his feet.

"Okay, riverman, this is either the luckiest day of your life or the unluckiest. Take your pick."

†

The scuffed-up river patroller decided to be lucky.

"That's why I'm on the water. Can't stand them hissing no-dicks," he said, cheerfully taking the oath that would swear him into the battalion after hearing the terms.

"Likewise," a suspicious Bear agreed.

"Can't get away from 'em," the sailor said. "Even when I'm up-river, still show up in bad dreams. Yellow-eyed bastards." Valentine's two Bears herded the survivors, hands clasped atop their heads, into the beer cooler.

"Have a drink on us," Gamecock suggested.

"It's safe-locked," Dirty Nel said. "You can unscrew the latch from inside—even if we put a padlock on it."

Valentine reached into his tool belt and extracted some plastic triangles and began to shove them into the gap around the lock. He was the proud owner of a migraine, thanks to that damn spotlight running up his optic nerve like a gas flame.

Dirty Nel looked at the wedge. "Where'd you get these? Looks like a kid's toy."

"Evansville security services. They're just wedges with a little quick glue on them. They'd use them when conducting a raid, or temporarily keeping those detained in an improvised secure location. Jam a couple of these into a door or window frame, and no one's getting through without busting it down and making a lot of noise. Soft enough to jam in from either direction and stick."

"How do you get rid of them?"

"Easy enough to dissolve, paint thinner and other acetates work. Nail polish remover."

"Oh, I always keep some of that around," Dirty Nel said, rolling her eyes.

"We don't have to worry about opening them for now."

"Why do they call you Dirty Nel?"

"You know, everyone asks me that within five minutes of meeting me," she said, as slow smile on her face. "The men, anyways. Well, some women. Problem is, the real answer isn't very interesting. So I keep silent. Whatever they come up with in they's own heads, it's better than the truth."

†

Seeing properly handled legworms in action still took Valentine's breath away. With modified cargo saddles mounting a sort of oarlock, old suspension cables were run and crossed in such a manner that the network of blocks and tackles could first hoist and then secure the emptied-out boat hulls. Then the paired legworms, with the hull between them like some kind of land-going catamaran, headed up the hill for the overland trip back to Evansville. The legworms moved as though they didn't even know they were carrying a load—which, considering the tiny mass of nerve ganglia that passed for a brain in their midsection, was very probably true.

The men had worked like furies. Everything that could possibly be done to lighten the hulls was tried. Weapons and armor were stripped; precious gasoline out of fuel tanks and into mobile trailer tanks pulled by the patient legworms; cordage, supplies, even portable stoves and the boat generators were unbolted and fixed to the tops of the worms. Engines were even taken out and put on boat trailers.

In fact, the weapons and engines were more valuable than the hulls. Evansville had plenty of river-worthy hulls, what they lacked were arms and engines.

Valentine gauged their progress to the sound of winter-dry grass crunching under hundreds of clawlike feet, a sound that reminded him of a covered cauldron of popcorn popping. "How long to get them back to the Ohio?" he asked the Gunslinger legworm drover.

Another legworm passed, this one hauling a smaller boat on an old-fashioned trailer with oversized wheels. Despite the wheels, the drovers called the contraptions "sleds." Other sleds carried engines, armor plating, light cannon on the river-craft mounts, and booty from the warehouses too heavy to risk mounting on the back of one of the worms. Put too heavy a load in one particular spot, and the shaggy skin tended to simply slide off in a big, wet, mattress-sized piece.

"A damn long day, I expect. You boys do your end, we'll do ours."

†

They had one scrape with a column of light armor out of Cadiz that resulted in a night action.

Frat's Wolves gave them plenty of warning as to size and route.

Gamecock's Bears, eager to use their new weapons, hustled off to set up machine guns and light cannon. Valentine, restricted to an observation point coordinating the attacks of the Bears and Wolves, saw only the night action from a distance.

The captured ordnance of the River Patrol used an interesting mix of tracer—blues, greens, and reds. Perhaps the distinctive rainbow tracers helped the River Patrol distinguish friendly from enemy craft. Valentine filed the knowledge away, might come in handy at some future point.

Meanwhile, he had boats to drag to the Ohio.

†

"Well done, Valentine," Colonel Lambert said, looking over the boats.

"But what's with all the aphrodisiacs? Is there something in the works I should know about?"

"Yeah, Val, big weekend planned?"

"I'm not sure—," Valentine said.

"We have twelve cases of Kurian Zone sexual stimulant under a couple of names."

"That was me, suh," Gamecock said. "I made sure they brought it along. Not for us, now, but I thought it might be useful for trade. The Grogs love it. Gets them high as kites and horny as hell."

It was the sort of fuzzy case high-priced jewelry used to come in, a purple so deep it could pass for black in all but the best light.

Valentine opened the presentation case. A shiny old piece of plastic lay inside, a cheap mockery of a police badge.

BROTHEL INSPECTOR

it read.

"I found it last summer in the ruins of a dollar store," Duvalier said. "I've been carrying the stupid thing around ever since, waiting for the right opportunity."

156

"Hilarious," Valentine said.

"You should go over to Orfordville and break it in," Frat said. "The Wolves say there are a couple of nice houses there. The Ordnance patrols west of Louisville sometimes de-uniform and sneak over."

"They're true Kentucky as bourbon. We get regular reports about any loose tongues."

The party chuckled.

Ahn-Kha's uneven ears were up and forward. "I do not understand."

Duvalier, boosting herself up with his axe-handle shoulder like a gymnast mounting a pommel horse, whispered something in his ear.

"Humans," he muttered, shaking his head.

CHAPTER SEVEN

*B*anquets: *Southern Command is famous for holding feasts at the drop of a hat. There are always a few volunteers ready to drop a hat themselves, if a better reason isn't on the calendar or out-box.*

Word of a "feed" passes quickly, even before the barbecue smoke rises. In this case, the smoke was from one of the winter hogs raised on camp food waste and the inevitable spoiled food brought in on the ir-regular supply runs up the Ohio River by Southern Command's "Mos-quito Fleet."

Fort Seng's were never as resourceful as Southern Command regu-lars at scrounging "grits, grease, and gluss"—the first two being traditional Transmississippi staples, the third liquor mashed, heated, and dripped out of any stray carbohydrates at hand. Gluss, another of the many names for army busthead, was a variant on Mosquito Fleet acronym General Liquor Unspecified, Standard Ration. Southern Command's boatmen were legendary in the aptitude for acquiring alcohol—strictly for purify-ing questionable river water, of course—and, to cut down on the cases of ethanol poisoning, their captains took to issuing a small daily ration unit.

†

The captured boats were returned briefly to the Ohio, but only to be taken up a short length of river to Evansville, where they were again hauled up out of the water and brought into riverside workshops. One boat, kept fully intact and armed in its drag across Western Kentucky, was tied up next to the old casino, to be used for training.

The battalion was in the best spirits Valentine had ever seen. Upon returning from the operation, the companies that had gone out to get the boats immediately set to laundering and cleaning and polishing their bodies, uniforms, and equipment as though they couldn't wait to be sent out again.

They'd proved themselves before, certainly, in the fight against the ravies outbreak of the winter. But that had been purely reactive. The raids on Site Green and Respite Point were their idea, successfully carried out by the battalion.

Colonel Lambert decided they needed a reward. The first of the spring vegetables were in, along with a bountiful amount of strawberries, so she decided to sacrifice a few head of cattle for a big steak fry.

They used the big open field to the south where the brigade's horses grazed. It was the largest stretch of flat, open ground in the confines of the fort. With the horses cleared away, it served as an athletic field for football, soccer, and baseball—and conditioning sprints, of course.

Glass volunteered to miss the festivities—he was no social animal, and stayed with Ford and Chevy, his heavy-weapons Grogs, and the company left on security. Especially at a celebration like this the Grogs sometimes caused trouble. They believed the greatest warrior ate first and most and had trouble with the human tendency to share out by the plateful.

Lambert skipped it as well, though she gave Ediyak the night off. Valentine filled a tray with steak and sauce, strawberries and clotted cream, and some tender spring vegetables (asparagus was early and plentiful in Kentucky, leaving the fort's latrines more pungent than usual) and brought it up to her. Even if the ascetic workaholic in her was currently reining in her appetite, he could eat both their shares. He could still smell the grill on the steaks and his mouth watered at the hot, fatty smell.

"I've been studying this map of the Eastern United States," Lambert said as he set down the tray on an empty chair. Lambert's desk was unusually cluttered with notes and colored grease pencils for writing on the plastic overlays that lay on the maps.

The bright light of her desk lamp reflecting off the map hurt Valentine's eyes and gave him the beginnings of one of his headaches.

Valentine glanced over it. Old maps were interesting but of limited use. Most of the roads were overgrown and broken up and the towns run back to kudzu and scrub oak.

"If we only had something comprehensive and up-to-date," Lambert said.

"I know, sir," Valentine said. "Someone really needs to make some new maps," Valentine said. "The Kurians have good local ones, but beyond their regions—"

"Here be dragons," Lambert said.

"Basically, sir."

"Maybe we can team up with the Kentuckians and get something accurate of at least the zones surrounding us. If the Georgia Control is going to come after us, it would help to know what roads and rail lines they still have up and running. What bits are full of bad guys and where the hostile neutrals and Grog tribes are. But the rivers are still the same."

"Yes, sir," Valentine said.

She placed her palm over an area covering Western Kentucky, the southern arrow tip of Illinois, southeastern Missouri, and a corner of Tennessee.

"Whoever controls these waterways has the Ohio, the Tennessee, the Missouri, and most importantly, the Mississippi."

"I see, sir," Valentine said.

"It reminds me of something Shelby Foote said about Gettysburg," Lambert said. "Gettysburg was at a nexus of roads, so when the Army of Northern Virginia and the Army of the Potomac were chasing around up through Maryland and into Pennsylvania, Gettysburg turned into a place where both armies could concentrate quickly. He called it a spiderweb or something."

Valentine was a bit of a Civil War buff as well and vaguely remembered that quote, and nodded.

"Back in de Tocqueville's day, in the early days of rail, there was some contention over whether river or rail traffic would win out. Rail won, of course, but there's still a lot to be said for barges."

Valentine, who'd learned his service in the hard school of foot-soldiering with the Wolves, couldn't agree more. In his days with the Coastal Marines, while serving in the Kurian Order working his way into a slot in the *Thunderbolt*, had marveled at how easily tonnage could be moved by water.

"What Southern Command should do is put all its efforts into controlling the river between Arkansas and here," Lambert said.

"Against the River Patrol, sir?" Valentine asked.

"It would be a matter of choking off a few big bases of theirs. Vicksburg to the south, and the one on the Tennessee-Kentucky Border, and the Iowa fortress. We've got the Ohio choked off here. Now we've got the boats to contest the Ohio, and the mouth of the Tennessee. Maybe even all the way to the Mississippi."

"For now, sir," Valentine said. "They'll get sick of us at some point. I'm not sure I like our chances for holding them off without a lot more support from Southern Command. With Martinez in charge—"

Lambert held up her hand. "I envy you in a way, Valentine."

"Excuse me, sir?"

"Your career. It's dead, just not buried. Gives you a great deal of leeway. You're a free man. You can say what you like."

"Sorry, sir, if I've been too free with my opinions."

"Don't worry about it, Valentine. I'd rather have you letting off steam to me in here than in front of the men. I'm not in a position to stop you."

Like her uniform, Lambert rarely showed anything other than her usual efficient mind-set. Valentine wasn't sure how to handle a colonel suddenly turned prosaic. "Odd thing to say about someone in uniform, sir. You can order me to hopscotch to your door and back, bad leg and all."

"In return you can bleat, 'Up yours, *L-a-a-a-mbert*,' the way they used to in elementary school. Not a heck of a lot I can threaten you with in return, except maybe to kick you off base."

"With great freedom goes great responsibility. Or that's how it should work," Valentine said.

"Didn't some movie character say that?" Lambert asked.

"I think that might have been Spider-Man," Valentine said. "Frankly, sir, I'm not used to hearing you talk this way."

She nibbled at one of the asparagus spears, stood up and started to pace her office. "The Respite Point raid has me hoping again. Those boats might give us some real mobility. I'd like that freedom. I feel trapped in this headquarters, sometimes." She ran a finger across a heavy wooden mantel. "Even if it is a comfortable prison."

"You're the base commander, sir. The KZ types or people who aren't in the service might think you're the freest one here, since you're at the top of the rank table, but most know better. If I could give you one piece of advice—it's okay to dig your heels in when you're right and upchannel to HQ is wrong. You're here and they're not."

"Now you're being philosophical. That's a recipe for not getting anything done at all. Better go back out and get the music going."

"Yes, sir."

"Make sure not too much liquor is being smuggled into the party."

"Of course, sir."

He headed for the back entrance. The musicians were assembling on the back patio in the lights.

Valentine looked out into the darkened fields at the big tents in the athletic field, lit up like New Year's was celebrating Christmas's birthday. The barbecues glowed warm and the smells—Valentine's nose could smell food farther off than he could smell blood—were warm and inviting.

His stomach growled.

Pellwell was taking the steps up from the gardens two at a time.

"Valentine," she called.

Her usual composure had deteriorated into twitchy agitation. The ratbit on her shoulder had its head buried in her hair.

"Yes, Pellwell?"

"It's the guys," she said, referring to her intelligent menagerie. "They say something bad's coming. They can hear it."

Valentine switched to his "hard" ears, concentrating on the night air. All he heard were the sounds of musical instruments and dishes being washed up and stacked. Someone was making love rather frantically in the woods above the artillery lot above them.

"I don't hear anything."

"You wouldn't. They can hear outside our range."

Valentine didn't wait for her to elaborate. He dashed for the door to headquarters.

"This is Valentine," he shouted, loud and clear at the com center. "Full alert. No drill."

The dispirited corporal stood up so fast his plate of congealing beef and french fries hit the ground.

"Kill the lights," Valentine ran to Operations, the siren sounding.

"Kill the lights," he repeated, but the men in the operations room had anticipated him. The lights died in the headquarters, dim red battery-operated hand LEDs flickering on at the hallway outlets. Cheap Kurian Zone junk used in their cities during the routine power brownouts, but they worked admirably for a couple of hours.

Now he heard them too. Engines, in the sky. There was a deeper thumping sound, lower and farther to the south. Helicopters.

Air raid.

Valentine had seen this horror before.

The electricity might have died, but the fires were still burning bright out at the barbecue.

Explosions ripped up the barbecue pits as rockets struck. Valentine heard engines roar overhead, caught a quick glimpse of flashing red and green at the wing tips of the propeller craft.

Following the rocket attack, a pair of biplanes, probably converted crop dusters, came in low. They lifted their noses and slowed as they pancaked through the air. Two figures dropped from each plane, off the wings, where they'd been riding like stunting barnstormers.

They hit the ground and rolled, then came up on long legs.

Reapers!

Valentine sidestepped to his woodpile behind headquarters, grabbed the axe he used to split wholes into halves and halves into quarters. The familiar feel of the polished hickory calmed him. With death running loose on the lawn, a piece of sharpened avativism comforted.

He remembered the night on Big Rock Hill when Reapers fell from the sky. They'd been wild ones, deadly to whoever was nearest to where they landed, but vulnerable to skilled hunters once they'd fed on their victim.

But these Reapers moved with purpose. Before, they mindlessly fell on the nearest beating heart. These struck with hands and feet, breaking and ripping without stopping to feed.

The former Quisling troops, who'd had fear of the Reapers put into them along with their mother's milk, fell into absolute panic. Valentine ran forward.

"Get guns, knives, anything!" he called, keeping some fleeing men off the steps up to headquarters with the handle of the axe. "Swarm 'em! Douse them with gasoline! Anything!"

Valentine had flashbacks to the night the Twisted Cross came for the Eagle Brand in Nebraska. But these avatars didn't fight like professional soldiers were operating them. They put weapons to their shoulders, strange contraptions that reminded Valentine of small I-beams with a handle and shoulder pad welded to the bottom. Atop the back of the device was a V-shaped rack filled with tubes the size of a household conduit pipe.

One turned his in the direction of Valentine, still trying to reach the action and turn the panicked men back into soldiers.

Even the Reaper with the weapon, pound-for-pound one of the strongest creatures on earth, braced itself as it aimed at the vehicle shop.

"Rockets! Down, down!" Valentine shouted, flinging himself forward.

F-whoooosh f-whoooosh f-whooosh spat the rocket rifle.

The vehicle shop erupted into orange flame, the roof rising and spinning into the air like a Harryhausen flying saucer.

A Bear exploded out of the darkness, driving a shattered tent pole through one of the Reapers as it aimed. It was Chieftain, the most experienced of Gamecock's Bears. He hoisted the convulsing creature as though raising a tar-dripping flag. Another Reaper, suddenly and unaccountably headless, took a few wayward steps before crashing on its side. Alessa Duvalier rose and ran a few steps and dropped again, her oversized coat looking like a forgotten rag blown from a laundry line as it covered her, lying in the culvert next to one of the macadamized camp utility roads.

Ahn-Kha stormed up from the stables, one arm full of shotguns, the other wrapped in bandoliers. He handed out weapons and ammunition to any hands willing to take them.

The grass-pounding beat of a helicopter sounded, suddenly overwhelming the gunfire with its air-cutting anger.

Three helicopters, a fat one in the center flanked by two smaller maintaining a jostling, zigzagging formation like a queen bee in the air with two suitors, thundered up from the south.

Ahn-Kha picked up a smooth landscaping stone the size of a softball. Running forward, he made a swooping overhand throw.

A picture flashed in Valentine's mind—probably one of the old volumes in Father Max's library where he whiled away the long Minnesota winters after his parents died—of a cricket bowler. Ahn-Kha echoed the motion.

The stone, hurled with such force it described an almost straight-line trajectory, struck the windscreen of the big central helicopter. Valentine saw it strike sparks as it passed through and impacted the pilot and his instrumentation.

The helicopter went nose-down, and the big rotors threw up high-flying divots of earth as the craft nose-tipped in.

The other two craft, unsure of what had brought down the big one, pulled high, both banking right and just missing each other's blades.

Three monstrous forms—at first Valentine thought they were an exotic creature like a hippopotamus or a rhinoceros—jumped out, apparently unhurt by the crash.

They were hulking, a third again as big as a typically oversized Grog. Ahn-Kha, drawn up to his full height, would come up to the shoulder line of the beasts, leaning out over their pier-sized forelimbs like gorillas.

Valentine had never seen anything like them. Pale-skinned, like the Reapers.

He rushed forward with his axe, Ahn-Kha falling in behind.

One of the men Ahn-Kha had armed with a shotgun fired right into one of the giant Grog's faces. It turned away, threw out an arm and punched the man into red-topped mush.

Another was crushed beneath a stomping foot the size of a wheelbarrow.

Ford and Chevy, the core of Valentine's old heavy-weapons group, each carried a vehicular machine gun in a harness. They held their guns high so as not to hit any of their allied, and scattered bursts at the monsters. Valentine saw bullets strike, tearing out chunks of hide, but the beasts showed no more sign of feeling it than the armored car Valentine had shot some weeks before.

Valentine froze. The giant Grogs had yellow eyes with slit pupils.

One opened a cavernous mouth as though to bellow in his face. Instead, a stabbing, barbed tongue the size of a harpoon shot toward Valentine's chest.

He ducked under both tongue and chin, swung the axe with every iota of strength he could summon. The blade buried itself deep in the beast's neck. It let out a startled cry and reared, dragging the axe handle out of Valentine's hands.

Its tongue was limp and flopping. Valentine must have severed some nerve, or the trunk of the tongue itself.

Weaponless, Valentine froze. The creature stepped forward

and put a wide foot on its own tongue. It crashed down, threatening to bury Valentine, but a powerful arm hauled him back.

Ahn-Kha blasted another of the beasts in the eye with his shotgun, wielding it with the quick ease of an experienced gunfighter with a pistol.

"We must run, my David. Explosives are needed!" Ahn-Kha said.

The creature Valentine had struck in the neck fell dead at last.

One of the Grog-reapers had picked up a tent pole and swung it this way and that, knocking soldiers about like a man killing rats with a club.

It was Bee who finally turned them back. She rushed forward with a white tank resembling a field soup pot in one hand and a burning rag on a stick in the other.

She hurled the tank, tearing the valve free with her toe. Valentine heard it hissing as it flew. She followed it with the brand, then threw herself on her face.

"Good thinking, Bee," Valentine said.

She said something in return. Valentine recognized the Grog word for "fire."

"She heard you say that they needed to be killed with fire," Ahn-Kha said. "A propane tank makes the most fire she's ever seen."

†

"Well, they sure blew the hell out of that barbecue, suh," Gamecock said, surveying the smoldering ruin of cookout, helicopter, and giant Reaper the next morning.

The salvage teams crawled over the corpses of the helicopters, uniformed ants on mechanical carcasses wielding wrenches, tin snips, and screwdrivers.

Pellwell, meanwhile, had forgotten her ratbits for a moment. Or if not forgotten, was at least ignoring them in her haste to examine the beastly mega-Reapers. She'd scared up a camera from somewhere and was taking pictures and writing notes with each frame.

"Hey, they did us a favor. Maybe we can fill the craters with wood and roast a couple pigs."

"Dangers of a night attack. There might be confusion."

Valentine shook his head, wondering. "I'll give this to Atlanta. They learned who hit them. They struck back, and meant it. Both had some bad luck tonight. They attacked a barbecue rather than our main buildings. We lost months' worth of work."

"Let's hear from observation points. North, south, east and west. All of them, and send out patrols. The air raid might have been a setup for the finish."

"If they want us out of Fort Seng," Valentine said. "I wonder if it might be best to accommodate them."

CHAPTER EIGHT

T

he Trails: North America is once again a land of trails. With so much wartime destruction and neglect to land corridors, outside of an individual Kurian Zone or the free territories, getting from here to there proceeds mostly in fits and starts. One makes a fast, exhausting dash of long days of travel to the next safe area, where packs can be refilled, animals rested and exchanged, fuel and munitions purchased—if they're available, that is. Complex does not even begin to describe it.

It's possible to carve out a new trail, of course. One just needs the manpower to establish waypoint bases for rest and resupply. There's already a well-established trail between Southern Command and Fort Seng; the only thing that changes are the river crossing points on the Mississippi and the Tennessee. Escapees from the Kurian Zone flow one way, a trickle of replacements and supplies travels the other.

What Valentine and company propose to do has not been tried before on this scale. Their plan involves establishing a one-shot "river trail" from the Mississippi bank north of Saint Louis to Evansville. There are no substantial Kurian forts on the river between the two points, as the area largely belongs to the Grogs. While the land route would be much shorter in miles, the river will allow speed, which could prove vital for transferring a stadium full of Golden Ones without it turning into a late twenty-first-century trail of tears.

✝

"You know, David," Brother Mark said, "there's a fine old saying ripened by the distinction of years. Doing the same thing over and over expecting a different result is one definition of insanity. Which is how establishing a new freehold in the mid-South is beginning to look to these weary eyes."

The old renegade churchman smelled like mothballs and spiced aftershave to Valentine. It was an oddly comforting mixture, suggesting generations of familial secrets. He was bone tired from putting the fort back together after the air raid, seeing the worst of the wounded into the Evansville hospital, and finishing the plan with Ediyak. "I think *'if at first you don't succeed, try, try again'* is even older."

The battalion officers sat in the big entrance hall to headquarters, overstuffed chairs pulled into a circle and sentries posted at the doors and windows. Lambert had finished presenting the plan she, Ediyak, and Valentine had worked out for moving whatever Golden Ones wanted to come to Kentucky.

"It might be wiser to pull back down the Ohio to the other side of the Mississippi," Brother Mark said.

Ediyak gulped and grew wide-eyed. She'd spent much of her life in the Kurian Zone, and when a churchman spoke, you listened and complied.

"The new freehold was your idea," Lambert said. "We military types, once we get hold of something, crack our heads against it until one gives way."

"Can't stop now. The Kentuckians have thrown in with us," Valentine said.

"Nobly spoken," Brother Mark said. "But we've brought with us all four horsemen, and they've had a run of the land. The Western Coal fields and much of the Pennyroyal is empty, thanks to the ravies virus."

"Depends on how you define empty," Devlin said, attending to represent their nearest allies, the Gunslinger Clan. "There are still a lot of legworm herds. We had a good spring for legworm leather. Maybe the cold kept parasites and rats out of the eggs, I dunno, but there's a record number of young legworms crawling. Those Wolves of yours make good hands for herding once they learn which end is which and how to move 'em along."

"They should be patrolling," Lambert grumbled. "I'll talk to Carlson about it."

"We're letting them keep some of the legworm leather from the eggs for their help. It's good for trade with just about anyone."

"We're getting away from the point. Ahn-Kha, how quickly can your people get set up here?"

"Two generations ago the Kurians promised us a rich, green land with good rock for building. I've never seen such limestone as is in the hills here. Rich deposits of silver sand, err, what is your word—"

"Mica," Lambert said. "Used for some glasses, drywall, electrical insulation, and so on," Lambert said. "Evansville's still doing a little of that on a shoestring."

"Mica. Thank you, my colonel," Ahn-Kha said. "This is good land. Very good. Certainly a milder climate than shivering Omaha.

One season of growing, another of building, and we will have the beginnings of roots."

"The whole history of Kentucky is nothing but immigrants," Devlin said. "We're flexible, as long as you let us be. We adapted to using the legworms pretty darn quick. We'd rather have big fellas like Uncle here than the Kurians."

"Still, I'd better touch base with the provisional government and the Army of Kentucky," Lambert said. "Brother Mark, are you up for the trip?"

"My spirit never objects to seeing old friends again. My hips and shoulders, however . . ."

"The hard part will be getting them to Saint Louis," Valentine said. "From there, we can use the Mississippi."

Over the next three days they finalized the plan. Valentine found himself in awe, yet again, at Lambert's command of detail. And the sheer amount of work she and her two assistants—camp scuttlebutt said she worked one until he keeled over, by which time the other had usually revived from his own marathon session. The three of them plus a secretary clerk for typing orders, produced a working plan.

Still, more had been left to chance than Lambert liked. Valentine had learned to trust luck backed up by tactical flexibility to see himself through difficulties, which would come one way or another.

Control of the river would make so many of these issues simply vanish. The Kurians had held the great rivers of the North American middle—what Lambert had compared to the central arteries of the circulatory system—for so long, both sides had grown accustomed to taking that as a given, like weather or seasons or growing cycles. Certainly, a talented smuggler like Captain Mantilla could get through with his anonymous and ever-reconfigured and re-painted boat, but the barges of supplies that would make operating in Kentucky or Missouri or into the rusted-out cities along the Ohio would never pass without notice.

When was the last time anyone tried? Valentine wondered.

Any way they looked at it, use of the rivers would simplify matters. The tonnage requirements of moving such a population was nothing to a string of barges.

Still, their alternative was workable. Not without risk, but workable.

He and Lambert planned to divide the camp in two very unequal forces, minus those unfit or unable to make the trip, who would remain at Fort Seng.

Lambert would be in charge of "Force Heavy." Driving every young legworm they could gather, they'd cut across Western Kentucky two waypoints, one on the Ohio of the proposed riverine route, another overland. East of the Tennessee, Kentucky was dangerous ground filled with bounty hunters, legworm ranchers who hadn't joined, and patrols and troops from Memphis. They could buy stores of food from the locals with packaged and processed legworm flesh, hides, and some captured Moondagger weaponry and whatever footwear and metal cooking pots they could scrape together from Evansville's market.

A threat to sell derelicts to the Amazons might even improve march discipline. Certainly there wouldn't be any stragglers.

Captain Patel had put in two years as a corporal running reconnaissance in that region, and Valentine had been across it off and on ever since Operation Javelin was in the planning stages. Between Lambert's sensible orders and her subordinate's experience they should be able to cross in peace. If not, they had the guns to fight the underequipped natives. The Amazons considered Southern Command's forces minor enemies, territory for an occasional raid, compared to the major enemies in the northern part of Illinois or the gray Grogs across the river in Missouri. Attempted genocide tended to leave an impression on the genocidees.

But all that would take time. Lambert expected the hundred-fifty-mile march from New Harmony to take two weeks without fighting, and double or triple that if the Amazons proved hostile.

They'd have to live on WHAM!, flatbread, and Kentucky molasses, and possibly a culled legworm or two, but with a little luck spring vegetables could be found.

Valentine would take Ahn-Kha and a handful of others as part of "Force Light." They would go ahead and, using Dizzy Bee, the sole operational airplane at Evansville's former International Airport, and fly to a small Southern Command field Lambert had used when she forcibly "recruited" Valentine into her Special Operations force three years ago.

He could stay up all night counting the miles he'd travelled since reconnecting with his old schoolmate across that conference table.

Valentine would gather those Golden Ones willing to take a chance and move east across Missouri. There was a wide swath of no-man's-land there, patrolled by the Iowans and Grog tribes. Southern Command should be able to start them off well supplied, Lambert had already requested the rice and beans, and the Golden Ones had their own stores and herds, he imagined.

As the days to departure ticked off, Valentine looked forward to the relief of being in country. The endless details and questions coming at all but the night watch hours—he volunteered to pull duty at the base security and communication center so he could get caught up on his paperwork—maddened and exhausted.

Ex-Quislings were terrified of taking initiative. Even the small force remaining at the base had been thrown into a panic by the thought of being abandoned by Duvalier, Patel, and Valentine.

He squeezed himself, Ahn-Kha and Bee, Frat, and a trio of Wolves, two with communications ratings, Chieftain the Bear, and their assorted gear into the cabin along with Pellwell and her ratbits in their two big carriers.

Duvalier had come too, a slight figure wrapped in her coat at the very back of the plane, riding next to a seat carrying a duffel bag filled with Chieftain's guns, Valentine's Type Three strapped in between the two like a thin commuter making room. Valentine had lost the struggle with her, she told him in private that she'd simply tag along around Force Heavy somewhere.

Valentine knew luck figured into everything. Every time he'd had Duvalier along, somehow they'd found their way through to some mixture of survival and success and satisfaction. They combined, despite their differences, on some basic level like salt and pepper.

Bee, with her one eye full of fierce devotion, would pine like a loyal bluetick left home while the rest of the men and dogs went out for a hunt.

At least if she were under his eye he could make sure she slept and ate.

"You won't blow it for lack of muscle," Lambert said to him as she hung on the door. Outside the pilot walked around the plane with his mechanic, doing a final check. The wind sock showed a stiff breeze straight out of the west.

Valentine relished his role of navigator, even if the grizzled Evansville pilot gave him the controls in order to pour a cup of coffee from a red Thermos.

Valentine had learned to fly during a brief spell with Pyp's Flying Circus in the Southwest, and this was his first opportunity to be in the air since he'd left his autogyro, a parting gift from the officer whose life he'd saved, outside Seattle. The Evansville pilot, who went by the handle "Wizard," mostly told stories about all the fun he'd had shuttling higher-level Quislings around the Northwest Ordnance. The only interesting passages in three hours' worth of remembrances of liquor and ladies of his glory days were a few details about the Quisling who used to own the great Audubon Estate, now the almost garishly lavish headquarters of the Legion.

"Old man Cass made his money in coal and timber from the knobs. Plus he was one of the partners who originally developed WHAM! After his plant opened up in E-ville, he fixed up his piece of Henderson and set up with the nicest ass he could find between here and Pennsylvania. She popped out a few kids to keep up appearances and stay in the good graces of the Church, but none of them grew up worth anything. That's how it usually is with those captains of industry."

"You wouldn't know where he is now?" Valentine asked.

"Would I? I flew him out personally. He's up on the Michigan shore now living on some other industrialist's charity. Pisses him off that one of his kids is probably sweeping your floors."

"I thought they all fled?"

"Slim Jim Cass was one of the Evansville club-spinners. Of course, even when on duty, the spinning was at the local strip joint off River Row. He joined up with you guys to keep from getting hung."

Valentine didn't remember anyone named Cass in the command. He wouldn't be surprised if the Quisling had taken the name of a dead comrade or made something up. Still, the factoid troubled him. He took out his order book and made a note to contact Lambert about it.

Dizzy Bee struck weather over the Mississippi, making Valentine glad he wasn't at the controls. The pilot looked at the approaching cloud line, gave a verdict: "Not that bad," and altered course a little south in hopes of either sliding along the front or getting a little more distance should they be forced to set down.

In the end, the pilot picked a spot and plunged through. Valentine had a few bad minutes, wondering if his bumpy career would come to an even bumpier end.

Ahn-Kha made a terrifying howl, followed by a long wretch, followed by an even more terrifying smell. Valentine had forgotten to tell his friend to breakfast off something that wouldn't smell too bad should it come back up.

Suddenly the whole plane went wet with a loud smack of rain and the air steadied.

"Yeah," the pilot commented. "We'll be fine."

Valentine noted that aircraft pilots thought it wise not to tell their passengers if they thought it wouldn't be fine.

The little Southern Command airstrip was as much as Valentine remembered it from his brief visit before. A small Southern

Command flag on a pole, a big wind sock on an even taller one—practicality forcing military pride to bend.

"Didn't anyone tell you? Sure the big fuzzies are under the protection of another Grog tribe. Only problem is, it's Deathring Tribe."

"Deathring?" Valentine asked. He'd heard the name somewhere or other back in the blurry memories of before he became a Wolf.

"They're the pet tribe of the Iowa Guard," Ahn-Kha said. "You and I encountered a few of their kind shortly after we met the Wrist-Ring Clan. Brass or bronze loops worn about the ear, neck, wrist, ankle, depends on the clan."

"You forgot mean as a gutshot wolverine," the sergeant put in. "Yeah, the poor Big Fuzzies—"

"Golden Ones is the correct term, Sergeant," Valentine said.

"The Big Fuzzies," the sergeant continued, "didn't have much of a choice."

"Sergeant, the Golden Ones saved my life. Call them Big Fuzzies one more time and I'll be very angry," Valentine said.

"General Martinez himself—"

"Isn't here," Valentine said. "But I'll send him whatever part of you I chew off if you don't start calling them Golden Ones."

"Hey, Sergeant, he's right," a Wolf corporal said. "They did plenty of bleeding 'gainst those Iowa brownrings. Show them some respect."

"Golden Ones, sir," Sergeant Durndel said. "They got pinned against the Missouri. A couple swam for it, we have one here on the base cutting kindling and scrubbing pots and pans, matter-of-fact. We got orders to get rid of 'em, but we hide the Bi—Golden Ones when brass shows up."

"What's your name, Corporal?" Valentine said, turning to the other.

"James, sir. LaPorte T. Portly, to anyone who used to wear the deerskin. I mean yourself, sir."

He was anything but portly, underneath a thick mane of dreadlocks he looked as lean as a cheetah.

"Sorry, have we met?"

"No, but an old lieutenant of yours, Finner, he's a captain now and he trained me. Told me about you and Big Rock Hill and all that. I'm proud to meet you."

Big Rock Hill seemed an awful long time ago, especially when talking to a man who must have been shaving his first and only whisker when it happened.

"Thank you, Corporal James. If you're in the mood to get out from under Sergeant Durndel's eye for a week or two, you could take us up north."

"Your friend there want to look up a relative?"

"Something like that."

"Well, if it involves hunting a Reaper or knocking the Iowa Guard back to their corn silos, I'll grab my clean underwear and rifle, sir. This gin rummy playacting war is for the legworms, if you know what I mean."

†

Valentine didn't know what Corporal James meant, but he soon found out over a plate of salted pork and some unusually decent carrot soup.

"Don't get me wrong, I'm not a malcontent or an insubordinate," James said. "But since Martinez started running the show, the only time our rifles are out of their sheaths is for inspection, Major. The shoe leather and coats are better these days, and the food's improved so much you might think we're back home with Mama. I'll give him this. General Martinez is crazy about food quality, he has every cook between Jasper and the Rio Grande shaking in his apron when his staff blows in. It's better. No more runnin' and gropin'."

Valentine recognized the old Wolf slang for running for a bush and groping for something to wipe with.

"You can call me Val, James. When I'm off my feet, we can drop the formalities."

"Well, there's someone came in special to meet you, sir. Major Brostoff. Said he used to serve with you under LeHavre in Zulu Company. He'll dock my ears if I keep you any longer, he's looking forward to sitting down with a drink or six with you."

CHAPTER NINE

Northern Missouri: The Iowa Kurians and Brass Rings, mindful of the importance of their fertile land and rail corridors, cannot put any more physical distance between themselves and Southern Command's forces in the Ozarks, so they do the next best thing. They put difficulties in the path of any move north and do all they can to add to the psychological distance.

The first layer of their defense is the free Grogs. While a few clans have been subverted by Kurian agents to launch raids and counterraids against Southern Command's forces—David Valentine experienced one in his last year as a Wolf—in order to keep bad blood between man and Gray One, most are doing what tribal communities always do. They tend their herds, gather their crops wild and planted, and guard their territory from all comers as fiercely as needs must.

The Iowans keep these Grogs well supplied with weapons matching their formidable size and voracious appetite for heads taken in battle, accepting surplus legworm and mutton (the Gray Ones are fond of sheep and lamb for their meat and wool) and the wood and leather gewgaws the females and youngsters produce at a great disadvantage. But if the Gray One traders cackle over the canniness of their trades, they are obliv-

ious to the manner in which their lives are being sold cheaply in skir-mishes with Southern Command.

The next layer of defense is the Missouri River. The wide-ranging River Patrol with their fast, shallow-draft boats traveling between the kudzu-chocked banks, backed up by artillery barges towed into posi-tion when and where necessary, make life miserable for any incursion in strength. With every bridge demolished and the riverbanks full of hostile Gray Ones, keeping a large supply of boats for crossings or rebuilding a bridge becomes a near impossible object.

Between the Missouri River and the Iowa heartland is the brush-filled expanse of Northern Missouri. This is the realm of the Gray Baron.

It's hard to say why men choose service as military advisors to the Grogs. Freedom from the strictures and Reapers of the Kurian towers, the Universal Church lectures, and the endless "volunteering" for time-wasting make-work projects can be found in the brush as an Officer of Nonhuman Forces. The capricious Gray Ones are good friends in vic-tory, but after a defeat are likely to place the blame on allies and assuage the sting of humiliation with the ONF scapegoat's brain-basted liver. The Gray Baron is unusually adept at keeping his allied Grogs in line, perhaps because his savagery matches their own.

His Grogs roam the lands between Omaha and the Mississippi, running their own railroad (the "Grog Express" runs the chord of his protective arc between Saint Joseph and Hannibal). They provide a backstop for any in-strength incursions from Southern Command and do what they can to stop the raiders and cattle thieves of the free Grogs south of the Missouri River.

Finally, there is the formidable military organization of the Iowa Guard. Able to draw on the sons and daughters from Kur's most privi-

leged Quislings, the wearers of the coveted Brass Ring, these scions of aristocracy get to "prove their brass" in keeping Iowa fat and contented. When the Grogs in Omaha cut the key rail line running to the west, they started a long, hard-fought campaign to evict the rebel Golden Ones. After a costly frontal-assault disaster and an even bloodier attempt at an envelopment, they settled into a siege that eventually broke the Golden Ones with heavy artillery and fearsome flame-spewing vehicles.

The Golden Ones still refused to surrender, and fled into the wild tangles of Northern Missouri for shelter. There they were eventually run to earth by the Gray Baron and bargained for what autonomy they could in exchange for giving up the fight.

Picking up with the rest of their unhappy history in this fateful year begins with the Force Light team's venture into the Missouri brush from the Wolf outpost.

†

Brostoff's airy tent still smelled of leather and rank sweat, the old odor Valentine was all too familiar with from his days in the Wolves.

Long ago, Valentine had served with Brostoff as a lieutenant. He was still obnoxious but a decent enough man when sober, who looked after his Wolves as though they were his own sons. Carefully guarding their health and blood, he made sure each of his team was equipped and ready before sending them out into the brush.

Still, it struck Valentine as odd that he'd made major. Especially major in a forward area. Southern Command kept all but the most secretive drunks in quieter areas until they either sobered up or their health gave out.

"We supply ourselves by trading with the Groggies," Brostoff said. "There's a good supply of root beer mix, always ready to send north. As long as we don't shoot at each other, root beer flows north and lamb chops, 'shrooms, and spuds come south."

Valentine sipped his root beer—the old Southern Command syrup, a legacy of some boggy old general who believed that the men built stills to brew alcohol because there were no quality soft drinks available. Brostoff drank artificial lemonade, a popular Kurian Zone beverage that Valentine suspected was generously seasoned with bad vodka. At least he tossed it down as if in a hurry to have it hit his stomach in the same manner he'd used as a younger man in Zulu company. Though in those days his hand didn't shake when he set the glass back down again.

"My team needs to get to wherever those Golden Ones have been taken, sir. The sooner the better," Valentine said.

"Wish I had a couple of scout cars or a good truck, but all our wheels have been put into reserve," Brostoff said, topping off his glass. "You know, they used to have a plane at this post, back in the day, after we captured Dallas and those airfields in North Texas. I looked it up on the old base TOEs. There was talk of flying out to Colorado for talks with the Legendaires—the 4th Division. See if we could meet up mid-Kansas. I would have liked to have seen that. Now the 4th could be in Kansas City, Kansas, calling for help, and I'd have to sit on my hands and patrol the security zone. *Defensive stance* my right nut."

"How about a guide?"

Brostoff downed his tumbler and belched. He winked at Valentine. "I can do better than that, Val. I'll get you a couple of Cats to take you there. Cats don't pay no attention to the Defensive Stance any more than the Bears do."

†

Scheier and Jarvis were both impossibly young for Cats, to Valentine's eyes.

Scheier, small and dark and pinched, looked to be older by a year or two and talked as though she were vastly senior to Jarvis, though Valentine doubted there was more than a year's difference between them. Perhaps the extra attitude made up for the fact that Jarvis was a full head higher. Jarvis reminded him of the big, strong milk-fed farm girls of Wisconsin. She even bound her head in a red handkerchief like a teen setting off to do the morning milking.

Being Cats, they both wore civilian attire, or at least what a sensible civilian moving among the Grogs might wear. Heavy canvas, layers of flannel, and some discreet padding at the knees, elbows, and shoulders offered a little protection under vented leather jackets.

They took Valentine's team north in a series of careful quick-marches. Sometimes they moved by day, others by night. Valentine approved of the care they took in open country, careful to never skyline themselves and keeping well in the trees whenever possible.

The march was tough on Pellwell, however. She was still basically a civilian, and for all the power in her wiry body, she exhausted easily and finished her meals too quickly.

"The shorter the rations, the longer you chew," Chieftain suggested during a morning meal of a toasted, doughy paste and some young heartroot Ahn-Kha had dug up from an old Grog campsite.

He rarely saw their two guides together. One always remained behind "babysitting" as he heard them whisper, while the other scouted, scrounged, foraged, explored, or picked out the next four-hour dash for safety.

Valentine had killed his first Reaper when their guides were practicing their handwriting on a blackboard. Babysitting, indeed.

Valentine discreetly inquired of Duvalier whether she knew anything about the pair.

"They came up after me," Duvalier said. "I'm pretty sure they're both second-generation true breeds."

"Second—"

"Daughters of other Cats, trained by Cats. When the Lifeweavers hid themselves when the Free Territory was overrun, we had to make do. Maybe they don't quite have our skills, but youth and confidence is still on their side. When more Lifeweavers come, I hope the first thing we do is train more Cats. You should start looking around the command and see who you want to bring in to the family."

Duvalier had faith that the Lifeweavers were off starting another freehold and would return at the first opportunity. She believed in their return like some Christians expected the Second Coming to sweep away the Kurian Order.

"If you're a human who wants to get up Iowa way, you need to know the Scrubmen."

"Scrubmen?" Valentine asked.

"They're mostly kids of slaves from the Groglands. A Grog chief can't keep or sell a slave his clan hasn't captured, and most of 'em know better than to bury the newborn like what happens to deformed little baby Groggies. Poor things. If the child's really lucky he gets turned over to the missionaries in Saint Louis, otherwise once he's weaned he gets set loose. Groggies don't know that just because you're off the teat you can't take care of yourself the way a little Grog can, naturally rooting around and hunting."

"I've never run across them. I've been across northern Iowa several times."

"You probably stayed close to the river," Scheier said.

"Yes."

"What do you think of Brostoff?"

Scheier and Jarvis exchanged a look.

"Durndel said you knew him back a whiles," Scheier said. "You tell us if he's changed."

"More whiskey lines," Valentine said.

"We can't figure it," Scheier said. "Last year, they had a decent C.O. Captain Finner. He knew Missouri like the back of his hand; been from Iowa to the Ozarks more times than I've been issued shoes. His men were ragged and patched, sure, what Wolf Unit in the bush doesn't look that way?"

"Good man," Jarvis echoed. "Made a speciality out of blowing the crap out of the River Patrol, only he used Grog guns for it so they'd hit back at the wrong target. One time he made it look like the Red Scalps Clan did it—scalped a boat captain with red hair—and started a big feud between the River Patrol and Red Scalps."

"Then one of Martinez's inspector generals comes in, and suddenly no more Finner. Sent back to supervise a depot full of blankets and winter socks."

"I'm no fan of General Martinez," Valentine said. "The way he runs things, I'm not sure the Kurians would do much different if they were giving the orders instead of him." He was breaking military protocol fifty ways from Mountain Home, but one more charge on his long list of sins wouldn't make a difference now.

With the cautious ice broken, Scheier continued.

"I don't know about Martinez. Sure, he's made improvements. Lots more supply getting to us now. Mail's better. But then his staff goes and puts a guy like Brostoff in charge of the Missouri Wolves. *Force conservation. Avoid areas of possible conflict. Observe and report, under no circumstances engage.* Don't make sense."

"All they do is eat, clean their guns, and then wait to rotate back to the home areas," Jarvis said. "What kind of formula is that for winning anything?"

"Those poor Grogs in Omaha kept expecting us. It was building, too. Bear Teams. Jarvis and I had set up a chain of supply caches with some of the Golden—the Bears and a bunch of Wolf heavy weapons trainers teams backed up with regulars and special forces were going to go hit Iowa on the supply lines for their siege. Soon as Martinez came in, that whole op got canceled on us."

Ahn-Kha planted his feet wide and set his pylonlike arms so he leaned in over the Cats.

"Tell me the truth. My people were promised warriors in a fight, and they did not even attempt to come?"

Scheier and Jarvis, both a little wide-eyed with Ahn-Kha looming over them, shrank into each other.

"No," Scheier said. "Or rather, yes. What I'm saying: the whole thing got scrubbed as soon as Martinez got in with all that talk about a 'respite' at the last election."

"That's what happened all right," Jarvis said. "No wormshit."

"Martinez don't think too much of Grogs. Said whole lot of 'em wasn't worth 'one son of Texas'—I think that's how he said it. It was in a speech he gave at the war college. Got reprinted and distributed, like all his speeches."

"He loves giving speeches and sending bulletins," Jarvis said. "Keeps us in writing paper and asswipes every month."

"They all begin 'Soldiers!' With the exclamation point, like the soldiers are all excited."

"Now he's made an enemy of one," Valentine said.

"My David, you will do me the honor of hearing this oath." Ahn-Kha drew his utility knife, and taking great handfuls of his Golden Mane, began to trim it down to stubble, with a good deal of nicks and cuts in the process.

He threw his head back and made a high wailing call as he cut his hair.

"For your benefit, my David, I will translate. 'Hear me, souls of the fathers in Paradise. Before I join you, I will take my fallen brother's revenge from General Martinez.'"

"I've never wanted to do a Grog before, but I'd consider it with that one," Scheier whispered to Jarvis.

"Ouch," Jarvis said. "That's not a team change, that's a different league."

"You'll have to wait in line behind me, old horse," Valentine said, after a moment to let Ahn-Kha collect himself.

"You take my words lightly?" Ahn-Kha growled.

Valentine felt a stab. He'd never had so much as a harsh word from the gentle giant. Ahn-Kha laughed at misfortune and bore hunger and discomfort with the same equanimity as he accepted sirloins and featherbeds.

"I'm sorry, my friend. If we survive this, I'll say good-bye to Colonel Lambert and follow you right to Martinez's headquarters, if that's what you want to do. What we have to do now is find your people and see if there's anything that can be done to help them."

Ahn-Kha tweaked both of Valentine's ears and flicked his own forward. "I forget, sometimes, my David, that you are not my people. You are only human, as you humans most accurately say."

Valentine wondered if he was blushing. He'd seen mother Grogs take their offspring's ears in this manner to chide them. He tweaked Ahn-Kha's snout.

"Did we just see a moment, here?" Jarvis said.

"Kiss already!" Scheier laughed.

Valentine had been among his squared-away-and-zipped-tight KZ refugees too long. He'd forgotten how free and easy the Southern Command's men and women were, especially when out cutting bush and chewing jerky.

"My friend is right," Ahn-Kha said. "I must see to my people before indulging in matters of old wrongs, no matter how grievous. Let us not waste time in getting me to them."

"To do that, you're going to have to go into the Gray Baron's stronghold. That's where he's got them now. They're digging holes and setting up building frames."

"We keep tabs on him," Jarvis said. "The Gray Baron's forces are the toughest between here and the Rio Grande. They get plenty of practice against the Missouri Grogs, and us, now and then. He's really dangerous."

"Wish we could still say the same about Southern Command," Valentine said.

†

They left the rolling hills of Southern Missouri behind when they crossed the Missouri west of Columbia and cut into prairie country.

Valentine had been nervous about the crossing, but the old interstate bridge was still intact. Scheier floated an old boat chair across and explored the other side in the predawn gloom and pronounced it safe. She'd scared off a couple of Grogs by stomping around their camp, breaking twigs and making hissing noises through her teeth.

The river, at least here along the small length Valentine had seen, would be difficult to navigate. While the Mississippi still had a few channel markers in difficult areas and the odd lock and dam working, the Missouri had run totally wild. Unless they could find enough bass boats to float Ahn-Kha's people to Saint Louis, travel by river would be impossible.

The open prairie presented its own challenges. Water wasn't difficult thanks to the spring—rains had filled every brook and pond.

The land, dotted with the blues, whites, and yellows of the tiny spring blossoms, harbored its own host of dangers. To those who haven't experienced it, prairie country is flat with horizon-spanning views.

But in this stretch of Missouri, prairie grasses and brush grow head height or higher between the deep-rooted oaks, widely spaced in their competition for midsummer water. There are many paths and game trails, but there's every chance of meeting a hunting—or worse, raiding—party of Grogs.

Valentine knew enough about legworms now to prefer running

into them. Their snap-crackle-popping sounds of feeding and move-ment carried far across flat country. Grogs on legworms could be avoided, provided care was taken.

So, in a sweaty single file, with Duvalier at the front of the col-umn and Ahn-Kha at the rear—where he could keep an eye on the flagging Victoria Pellwell and her ratbits—they entered prairie country under brushstroke clouds.

Valentine would stop at times and observe the column as they trudged past, making up some excuse to check in with Ahn-Kha. Duvalier, steady as always and traveling light with her loose-limbed stride, a teenager's purposeless shamble that looked busy without drawing attention to itself. Bee followed in her usual spot alter-nately trailing or leading Valentine like a hunting dog. She wore her sawed-off shotguns in hip holsters, and had a modified Kalash-nikov across her chest and a big-game rifle with an extra-long stock in her hand. She'd already brought down one deer yesterday with a single, well-placed shot through the ears and was eager for another. They wouldn't go short of meat if she had anything to say about it. Valentine gave her an encouraging lift of the chin. Bee liked being acknowledged.

Her nostrils flared and the mountain of she-Grog muscle moved on.

Then came Frat and his Wolves in their traditional leathers, camouflage ponchos thrown over their shoulders like capes. Frat seemed at ease in the prairie country, with eyes up and moving. The Wolves, burdened with carbines and communication gear and sup-plies, bore their loads with the familiar patience of oxen.

Chieftain followed them, wearing the Bear nonuniform of a

mix of Reaper robe, legworm leather, Southern Command camo, and an old felt hat with a single nostalgic eagle feather stuck into it. Duvalier had cracked a joke that he'd molted over the winter, but the fact of the matter was he was still mourning Silvertip. He had his usual close-in weapons, twin forged-steel tomahawks. He'd add some support fire to the group with an old-fashioned 40mm grenade launcher that could either fire grenades or a sort of enormous shotgun cartridge of razor-edged fléchettes that one of Fort Seng's gunsmiths customized. Rippers, he called them.

Pellwell followed with her ratbits. She carried one, the other two scampered, sniffing at the unique scent of Chieftain (he weatherproofed his uniform with a gummy concoction based on Reaper blood, or so he claimed).

Pellwell was his big worry on the march, though she'd carried her own weight so far. Field researcher or no, she wasn't used to the tired, stinky, hungry life of a soldier in the field. Dealing with the dirt and uncomfortable overnights took a mental toll on some, and Valentine looked for signs of mental stress in Pellwell. But apart from her usual clumsiness—she tended to stumble but not fall—she appeared to be bearing up. Valentine decided he'd have his next meal with her and chat for a while.

And last came Ahn-Kha, serene as a drifting cloud. He carried a support machine gun usually found mounted on a vehicle, a squat little death dealer fed by a belt-in-a-box. It was known as a "Heater" in Southern Command. A revolver big enough to bring down a grizzly hung under one vast arm, and he slung a sharpened shovel that came in handy for scratching out a toilet pit and a long hunting knife known as an Arkansas toothpick.

"What's with the shovel?" Valentine had asked him.

"A memory of my time in the coal mines," Ahn-Kha replied. "When we had no other weapon, we fought with our shovels."

Valentine remembered some of the grisly scenes described in Ahn-Kha's collection of diaries and shuddered.

†

The second day out from the Missouri crossing, Scheier returned out of breath at lunch.

"Jarvis and I saw signs of Scrubmen, a large party."

"Are they a threat?" Valentine asked.

"Can't say. We found a recent camp. Lots of them, forty or more."

"What would you do if it was only you and Jarvis?" Valentine asked.

"Get a feel for their trail. Moving fast or slow, and with what. If they're hunting, we'd find a place to hide and be ready to backtrack if they approached. They're tricky on the move when hunting, they'll backtrack, parallel themselves, send scouts back along their trail . . . Otherwise just observe."

Valentine considered the delay in backing off and moving north along another trail.

"Is there any good news?" he asked.

"There probably aren't Grogs around."

"Where's Jarvis?"

"Keeping an eye on the camp and the trail they left, to see if they reverse course."

"Let's try to swing round in their wake," Valentine decided.

"They're nothing to mess with, sir," Scheier said. "Don't let the spears and arrowheads fool you."

†

After it was all over, Jarvis tried to make Valentine feel better by telling him that the Scrubmen had probably spotted their party the day before and overnight, and left the cold camp in their path to gauge their reaction. The only way they might have frightened them off was to take off headlong along the trail like a pack of wolves. The Scrubmen might have assumed they were an advance party for a larger force that way and avoided contact.

As it was, Valentine's decision to dodge them solidified whatever ideas the Scrubman chief had been making.

They executed the ambush admirably, rising out of an open field at the shrill imitated cry of a Cooper's hawk as the file passed through a horseshoe-shaped bowl in the land.

A hedge of spears and drawn slingshots appeared all around. Valentine heard the creaking sound of bows being drawn from the brush. Valentine didn't count spear points, his brain guessed thirty and left it at that. They were well-made, simple weapons, their brutal effect proven since men were slaying each other with jawbones.

Valentine edged closer to Pellwell. "When the fighting starts," he said out of the side of his mouth, "drop. Get behind one of the Wolves and don't get up unless you see the rest of us running."

The Scrubmen dripped with mud and willow tresses. Valentine had seen some atavistic figures before, but the Scrubmen were like something out of early human history. They wore bits and bobs of Grog jewelry—probably tokens of friendship with certain tribes—

shell casing necklaces, dog tails, and in one potbellied oldster's case, an old Kevlar army helmet.

It was their eyes that interested Valentine. Tough, hungry eyes, looking this way and that, these men were of, by, and for their pack. All it would take would be a nose twitch for spears and arrows to start flying.

"Yours guns, nows," the helmeted leader said.

"Gets good prices, yesses? Sweets-likkers-juices!"

Valentine called out: "Everybody, keep calm now."

"Guns! Down!"

Ahn-Kha dropped his machine gun directly in front of his long-toed feet, raised his arms in surrender. The Scrubmen had picked the wrong day to point a weapon at Ahn-Kha. The Golden One didn't let out a battle roar, he simply brought both mighty fists down on the spears in front of him. Wood shattered, knife tips dug into dirt. With his fists planted, he swung out with both long-toed feet and kicked the two Scrubmen facing him toward Iowa.

In later years it was said that they fell just short of Burlington.

Valentine drew his legworm pick and borrowed parang. He jumped back from the extended spears, heard a pellet buzz by. His enemies, off-balance and overextended in their lunge, turned it into a charge.

Valentine heard motion behind and dropped to the ground, rolling. Two ranks of spears clattered against each other. Valentine heard the *snick* of a blade sinking home as the Scrubmen met.

He lashed out at an ankle with his parang, pinned a foot to the turf with his pick, let it lie and rose, lifting and twisting a spear.

"Looksee!" "Watch hims!"

A four-armed blur. The Brushmen had never fought Cats before.

He saw a Scrubman go down, weighted by ratbits biting at the tender flesh behind his knee and on the inner thigh. The scratching, pulling furies came away with tendon and other terrible trophies clamped between paired front incisors.

Valentine had read somewhere or other that, given time, rats could gnaw through concrete and some thinner types of conduit. These were a good deal larger and had obviously learned exactly where a man was vulnerable.

The Scrubmen valued survival rather than honor. They took to the brush with alacrity, sending pellets whizzing overhead to cover their retreat.

†

What the Wolves did with the wounded, Valentine didn't know and didn't want to know. The cries were brief, and for that he was thankful.

Frat's head appeared at the top of the crest of the horseshoe.

"Major, looks like they left a few things behind," Frat called.

Valentine trotted up to Frat's position with Ahn-Kha parting prairie grasses like a living snowplow.

Frat led him to a four-foot-deep ripple in the earth, closed over by oak and grasses into a shady tunnel. A line of people, anchored by a Gray One at each end, were linked by neck collars and six-foot wooden poles.

Valentine had rarely seen such ghastly restraints. The leather was filthy and rotted, with flies buzzing around dried blood caked and recaked at the edges.

"Free those people."

They looked thin and bruised. Valentine guessed the Scrubmen had kept their captives moving with lashes from thin tree limbs and yanks on the collar chain.

"Can you get anything from the Grogs?" Valentine asked.

Ahn-Kha spoke to the pair.

"They say they're on their way north," Ahn-Kha translated. "Those two, they're deserters from the Two-Mouth's army."

"Who is Two-Mouth?"

"A great man. Killer of Red-Blanket, chieftain of the Death-ring Tribe. Conqueror of the Golden Ones. Ruler of Rails-between-the-Rivers."

"The Gray Baron," Valentine said.

"In too many words," Ahn-Kha said. "But when the Gray Ones get around to talking, talk they will."

"Why did they desert?"

More burbling words and emphatic gestures.

"They were part of a rail crew. They thought they were supposed to fight, not lay ties and iron," Ahn-Kha said. "They're young warrior Grogs, they want a tally of enemies, not a record of track laid. Since they couldn't fight, they fled. But Two-Mouth has a standing reward for deserters and any and all humans."

Valentine questioned the humans himself. They were two groups that had met up while fleeing the Great Plains Gulag. They'd struck the Missouri River and followed it southeast, and were planning to turn due south and head for Southern Command's forces once they dried and smoked some of the Missouri's famously oversized catfish. But the Scrubmen had smelled the drying fish and taken them prisoner.

"So, the Gray Baron has a taste for human prisoners," Valentine said.

"We must endeavor to bring him some," Ahn-Kha said.

"Like the first time we went into Omaha," Valentine said.

"Only this time, you get the cuffs."

"You'll need a woman along," Duvalier said. "I'm still young enough that they won't put me to digging ditches."

†

"We'll establish two camps," Valentine said. "A far one and a close one. Frat, you'll be in command of the far camp. We'll probably need to stockpile Grog trade goods to ease the journey across Missouri. Like the Scrubmen said: sweets, liquor, weapons. Some fireworks and matches might not go amiss, either. Grogs love fireworks at their celebrations. A chief that can put on a good fire show has many friends."

Frat nodded. "Yes, sir."

He turned to Duvalier. "Ali, I want you to set up a close-camp. Hopefully Ahn-Kha will be free to do a little roaming. Make contact with him and set up a communication chain back to Frat."

"Sure."

"Keep Pellwell and the ratbits with you. I may need them," Valentine said.

She made the same face she made when he had a bad case of morning gas. "You're kidding, right? Her? She'll get us both killed."

"You've had it in for me from the first, Red. What's that all about?"

"You big-idea college fucks get people like me killed, that's why. Running down rumors, looking for docs that don't exist, counting baby legworms when we should be setting charges."

Ahn-Kha, with his shorn hair and wounds from the fight with the Scrubmen, looked the part of a Grog trader. He wore a pair of saddlebags on each vast shoulder with his most valuable "merchandise." Valentine, weighted down with simple trade goods on a carrying pole and wearing filthy rags taken from dead Scrubmen, followed. As a token of belonging to Ahn-Kha, Valentine wore an old license plate painted white and hanging from his head vertically. Ahn-Kha had made himself a leather wristband with the letters and numbers burned into it.

"Good to be working with you again, old horse."

"I could say the same, my David."

"If this goes to shit, you beat out of here, okay?"

"I'll run with you on my back to the Missouri River if that happens."

At first, Valentine thought the distant smear might be a legworm. Then he saw heads bobbing among the brush, appearing and disappearing through the gaps like targets in a carnival shooting gallery.

"Our Baron's guys, do you think?" Valentine asked.

"Almost certainly," Ahn-Kha said. "A band of Gray Ones would not stay so tightly in line."

Valentine watched the bobbing heads for a few more minutes. There were men at the front and the rear of the column, it looked to be no more than two or three, with a hundred Grogs or more in between. Two of the men, presumably the officers, rode horses. Valentine couldn't tell the breed with certainty at this distance, but they looked like tough, squat mustangs.

The men wore a vertical-striped camouflage, ranging from a buttery tone at the lightest to a rabbitty brown. He'd seen the pattern a few times on his previous trips into Iowa, when he'd wandered as a rather vengeful exile shortly after Blake had been born and relocated to Missouri. It was equally effective in light woods as prairie. Instead of helmets, gray kepis with another band of the camouflage material running around the brim sat on their heads.

The Grogs wore smocks or vests made out of the camouflage as well, probably ponchos or tenting repurposed for oversized Gray Ones' heads and shoulders. Big, bolt action rifles proportioned like Kentucky squirrel guns with oversized stocks hung by short straps around their necks in the human stock-up, muzzle-down fashion, allowing the Gray Ones to use all fours on the march.

Valentine noted that their rifles had some kind of latch attachment and rest so they didn't bump and chafe on the march. Good officers, these.

"At least this Baron grants them their stride," Ahn-Kha said. "Remember in New Orleans, the way men were always trying to make them walk upright when marching? They can do it, but it is not a natural gait and is fatiguing."

"They cover more ground per minute this way. Those officers are really puffing to keep up. The Baron should put his men on bikes."

"Perhaps you can suggest that when you meet him," Ahn-Kha said.

"If we're lucky, he won't ever notice us," Valentine said. "Your call, old horse."

"I see no signs of wounds or fighting," Ahn-Kha said. "They seem well fed and well rested. Dirty, looks like. See the pollen crusted into the sweat stains. I would say they have been out a few days. Perhaps they are on their way back in any case."

That was the real danger in contacting opposing forces. Valentine had heard stories of surrendering men being shot outright, if the opposition didn't feel like taking the trouble to secure, feed, and transport prisoners.

Ahn-Kha checked his weapons, squatted and stretched, and cleaned each ear with his tiny end finger. "My teeth clean?" he asked Valentine, showing his prominent near-tusks of a well-matured Golden One.

"I remember the dentist visiting the old Razorbacks and saying he needed machine tools to do you," Valentine said. Ahn-Kha rinsed his mouth with wet sand morning and night, if he could find it, and used baking soda and a brush when it could be had. "Yeah, they look great."

"Nothing puts my Gray Cousins off like a bad set of teeth," Ahn-Kha said. "Let us empty tracks."

"Make tracks," Valentine corrected. Ahn-Kha was more nervous than he let on, he only flubbed his English when preoccupied.

Ahn-Kha hailed them.

Valentine wondered what they would think. A scarred, bitten Golden One with shorn hair leading an equally scarred human dressed in Scrubman rags.

"Peace, peace, I call peace," Ahn-Kha said, approaching the soldiers. He carried his rifle by the barrel so that the butt faced the troops, a friendly gesture to Grog eyes.

Valentine waited for the order to deploy or ready weapons, nerving himself for a wild flight, but it didn't come.

The officer turned up the corner of his mouth under his kepi brim and Valentine relaxed. A little. Perhaps the officer found this an interesting diversion in a dull patrol. Valentine noticed that both he and his sub-officer, and the two human NCOs, all had full beards or mustaches. Strange for Kurian Zone troops. They were usually fit and trim and cleanly cut as a recruiting poster.

Now that he could get a better look at the horses, he decided the duns were Kiger Mustangs, a tough breed, surefooted, agile, and durable. After 2022, a good many horses had gone feral and multiplied on the plains, and over the generations the cream of those rebroken to saddles were called "Kigers."

"I don't know you," the officer said, from under an impressive walrus mustache. "But come in peace."

"A rhapsody in your name, chief," Ahn-Kha said. "I have been years south of the Missouri River and in S'taint Lewee. I hear my relatives now live under the protection of the one called the Gray Baron."

"Your English is excellent, civilized one," the officer returned.

"Thank you, chief. You call the Gray Baron your chief?"

"I do."

"I understand there has been fighting. I wish to be among my kind and see if any of my family still live. Will you allow me footpass upon your lands?"

"Fortune blesses you, civilized one," the officer said. "We're on our return trip. Feel free to follow."

"Another stanza to your rhapsody, my chief," Ahn-Kha said, pawing the earth in front of the officer's horse to clear his way.

"One request, however," he said. "No shooting. Makes the geros nervous."

"I'm sorry my chief, what is this word, 'geros.' Your warriors?"

"Yes, them. Oh, what's the word in your language? Gray Ones."

"Of course. Geros. I shall remember that, chief. If we do see game—"

"This is a patrol, not a hunting party. Leave it be. Discipline, civilized one."

Ahn-Kha flashed his teeth. "No shooting, chief."

"That slave armed?" the other officer asked.

"He has a small knife. He can be trusted."

"Don't cuff him about where the geros can see. In the Baron's command, no one is struck except by punishment after trial. Understand?"

Ahn-Kha nodded.

"Follow on, then. The man in charge of the tail is Sergeant Stock. If you have trouble, go to him."

They let the column pass, then fell in about twenty feet behind Sergeant Stock.

Valentine took a second look at the NCO as they passed, keeping his head down and some hair in his face. He had seen the sergeant's face before. Something about the heavyset brow and cool eyes.

Stock . . . Stock.

Stockard. Graf—a lieutenant in the old Free Territory Guard. Molly's husband, the father of her child.

Valentine hardly noticed the miles passing as he stared at the man's back. He'd never met him, just seen a picture or two when he visited Molly a few years back while hunting down Gail Post. He'd been missing in action since Solon's takeover, presumed dead. Molly was collecting a tiny widow's stipend of money, and since there was a child, food and housing benefits.

†

The Gray Baron's stronghold impressed Valentine, even as a work in progress.

Stronghold was the only word for it. It was larger than a stockade, but not quite a city. The old maps would have put it west of Kirksville in northern Missouri, but this stretch of country was one of the wildest in the nation, and the old infrastructure could only be traces between burnt farmsteads and overgrown towns.

The stronghold was nestled against a protective line of heavily wooded hills with the broken rooftops of a ruined town to the north. Dust rose from some workplace in the ruins and faint mechanical sounds carried in the dry prairie air.

Valentine thought the architectural style might be called "firebase in skulls, with church behind."

A vast killing ground of a thousand yards or more yawned in front of a network of log bunkers and weapon pits covering a low rise of earth surrounded the complex of towers, buildings, water tanks, and chimneys the Grog column approached. A high, nearly bare tree with an observation post like an eagle's nest looked out over the road approach to the south, a sawed-off church steeple with a blockhouse of railroad ties and sandbags watched the land to the north. Valentine could only presume there were other pickets in the hills behind.

"No barbed wire?" Valentine wondered.

207

Ahn-Kha, who'd been talking to the Grogs at meals and breaks, gestured with an ear, sweeping the front of the stronghold: "There are hidden pits all along in front of the battlements. They might seem to give cover, but many have false bottoms. Tunnels lead back to the entrenchments. Warriors sneak down under any enemy caught or sheltering in the pits and stab up. Or they're built to be flooded with gasoline and set ablaze. They have many explosives to drive off legworms, or so they claim."

They fell silent as they passed through the "gate"—a wrought-iron trellis rigged for electricity. The officer leading their column paused to say a few words with a lieutenant who stepped forward. Presumably, anyone coming in at night was searched under the hundreds of LED spotlights. Valentine made a show of hesitating to pass under—as an ignorant Scrubman might—and Ahn-Kha sent him sprawling with a shove.

"Grog hittin' a man," a sentry said.

"Ain't like us," his corporal said. "Watch it, Goldie. Hey, Stocky, keep your camp follower in line."

The gate watchers, who seemed more like idlers than sentries, got a laugh at that. Valentine wondered if the Gray Baron kept his men deceptively undisciplined, or if this was an unusually free-and-easy Kurian Zone camp. Even the most backwoods Arkansas militia unit showed more discipline on winter exercises.

"Sergeant Stock, see to it our kite-tail gets properly billeted," the officer told Stockard. "Usual post-patrol liberty when you've turned them over."

"Sir," Stock replied. He picked up a field phone near the gate and scribbled something on a clipboard.

They waited, listening to insects and the buzz of conversation from the men at the gate, who treated their arrival as a chance to show off beautifully rolled cigarettes in virginal white paper. Valentine sat, dispiritedly, with his back to Sergeant Stock, but he walked around in front and took another look. He could see, up a little hill, a big structure but didn't want to lift his head and gape.

A man in a plainer, unstained uniform and two Gray Ones appeared. The man had a small bamboo pointer, otherwise none of the trio were armed. The Gray Ones wore cargo-pocket shorts and thick canvas vests with the same vertical prairie camouflage. The human entered into negotiations with Ahn-Kha, offering a four hundred silver-dollar bonus if he joined a group of "Baron's Own" Golden One warriors. Ahn-Kha did his humble trader routine and said he hoped to sell Valentine here rather than to "those Kansas double-talkers and lead-coiners."

"You give a good price, all prisoner come here," Ahn-Kha said.

"Such facility with English! I can almost guarantee a quick promotion to officer."

"Will think it over, chief. I wish to sell this one, then find a bed and food."

The recruiter for the Baron's Own, who held the nebulous rank "officer candidate" laid down the law for Ahn-Kha about visiting his kind. Without membership in the Gray Baron's forces, or swearing to the First and Second Understandings—it was with that casual remark that Valentine learned what the Golden One articles of surrender were called—Ahn-Kha would be treated like any other potentially hostile tribesman, Gray or Golden, who might wander in out of the grass.

Ahn-Kha agreed not to leave the Golden One sub-camp save under guard, to obey any command by one of the Gray Baron's officers that did not endanger his or another's life, and to refer any disagreements with his own kind to one of the Gray Baron's officers before matters escalated into violence.

"May I endure three more hells in life or death if I break my word," Ahn-Kha said, in the proper Golden One manner.

They walked through the stronghold, the officer and Ahn-Kha in front, the officer candidate beside him, still mentioning the honors and rewards that would go with membership in the Baron's Own. Valentine led on a line in the middle and the two Gray Ones trudging behind, with Sergeant Stock bringing up the rear, as usual.

At last Valentine had a chance to look around.

The stronghold was a great wheel, pivoting around a green, planted, and landscaped central campus made out of an old, heavy-timbered megachurch.

Valentine had seen his share of rural megachurches, but whoever had built this one was a visionary. It reminded him a little of a snapping turtle sunk on a muddy hillock with its nose raised high to catch a gulp of air. Two outbuildings formed the creature's legs; a sort of ski jump of a steeple rose between overlooking what must have been a courtyard with a fountain; and the worship area itself formed the plated arc of the turtle's back.

Brick, structural steel, thick interlocking slate on the roof and canopy rigging to keep off the worst of the summer sun, heavy beaming and concrete-wrapped terraces of decorative prairie earth built up to the roof—this Baron had chosen his headquarters well. Nothing short of a heavy artillery barrage would put much of a dent in that monstrosity. Valentine wondered how many could be gathered under that titanic roof.

Of course the Gray Ones had added their own touches the original architects never intended. The decorative garden beneath the steeple sprouted monoliths of bones, skulls, and captured weapons. Victory columns, Valentine guessed. Female Grogs scrubbed their broods in ample pooling space of the fountain's spray. An aged attendant skimmed dirt out of the sluices and others waded to the fresh flow at the top to fill jugs and jars.

The Gray Ones had also added their own fetishes. They didn't go for brass idols, but rather markers like over-thick spears or harpoons with knot work and mixtures of leather and wood dangling from spars that reminded Valentine of pictures he'd seen of medieval samurai warriors with banners attached to their armored backs. There were bones, teeth, dried fingers, and even a preserved penis or two among the tokens of triumph.

Valentine had never seen the like in the Kurian Zone proper, where discretion about bodies both kept things hygienic and the populace settled. The men who handled bodies were typically selected and supervised by the Church, with a doctor or nurse on hand to add an air of medical authenticity. Only in the worst New Orleans slums were bodies left for discovery by rats, or those eager to plunder a corpse for its socks and hair. The Gray Baron was essentially saying *death is our business*, with a display like that on the doorstep of his headquarters.

There was an old pre-22 chain hotel that looked like it served as quarters for NCOs, judging from the men coming and going and lounging in the pleasant spring sunshine, eating or playing games or reading or cleaning guns. Small armies of servant Grogs worked in shacks nearby, polishing and resoling boots, laundering and patching uniforms, even shaving and cutting hair for the men. The Gray Baron's men had it good.

Valentine got a glimpse of the alleyways of the Gray One quarters. He'd never seen Gray One urbanization before, and he wished he was at liberty to take a better look. From a distance, their ghetto reminded him of a creative child's stack of blocks. Prefabricated housing trailers were grafted on, dug in, suspended over, and bridging older human single-family homes into what looked like a haphazard pile, but probably had something to do with chiefs and sub-chiefs and their clans. The ghetto clattered and buzzed and smoked. There was electricity in most housing, but for water it looked like the residents had to use troughs and pumps set out in the yards of the older human houses.

Back in the hills behind the headquarters megachurch, Valentine saw a few more elegant houses, presumably the Baron and his main lieutenants lived there, several barns of various types, and an expansive training area on the distant hills. He saw groups of Gray Ones, antlike in the distance, moving upslope and down, crossing various sorts of obstacles, breaking up and re-forming like waves striking rocks, and some hand-to-hand tussles.

Of the Golden Ones he saw nothing; though up by the dust and clatter in town he did see the giraffe necks of cranes and a vaguely pyramidal structure rising next to them.

Before he could get a better look at the distant, dust-shrouded construction, Valentine was brought before a little cinder-block building with a sod roof. GUARD AUXILIARY MONGO STATION ARRIV-

ALS read the stencils on the door lintel. It had a hand-painted sign out front as well: *ABANDON ALL HONOR, YE WHO ENTER HERE—AND RETIRE RICH*. Even the doormat had a legend, Valentine noticed, but the letters were mostly obscured by mud.

OAR

In the "Arrivals" blockhouse, they negotiated Valentine's sale in the time it might take Valentine to turn in a bag of laundry and his best uniform at a Southern Command Laundromat.

Valentine submitted to the usual once-over. They looked into his eyes, ears, checked his teeth, combed through his hair looking for vermin, looked at his nails and tongue and toes.

They didn't like his limp and made him walk, run, and hop along the spring mud flanking the blockhouse.

After a good deal more argument they settled on a price, it seemed. Ahn-Kha walked over to Valentine.

"I claimed you fought me like an evil spirit and you'd no doubt won your scars in battle," he murmured, removing the lead. "They claim you're fit only for use as a draft block in a doorjamb, but I suspect they are pleased to have you."

Ahn-Kha insisted that their price for such a healthy specimen wasn't satisfactory, and the manager there finally accepted a deal where they would see how the captive worked, and if he lived up to Ahn-Kha's promises, they'd meet his price.

Ahn-Kha leaned on the counter so heavily Valentine could hear nails working free. "He's to be well treated, until my price is met."

They sprayed off the mud with a power hose they kept at the

gate to the motor vehicle revetment. Valentine rather enjoyed all the mud being blasted off, though his skin felt like it had been sandpapered after. The towel they gave him to dry off was rough and stiff and had not met soap since the previous March, but it was as clean as well water could make it.

Sergeant Stock hung around, watching, which seemed a waste of time for a man due for liberty.

He threw the towel over his head and shoulders, assuming that his nakedness would draw attention rather than his face. If there were still wanted posters out for him, they were for a much more youthful face and long black hair.

A corporal with another odd variant of a short whip—it looked like a stingray tail Valentine had seen in the Gulf—led him to a white-painted prefab with a Quonset-hut-style roof. Valentine noticed a red cross painted on the roof—as if Southern Command or the Grogs had an air force that might bomb the Baron's headquarters—and took him inside. Valentine's nose smelled rubbing alcohol and Kurian Zone disinfectant of the sort that came in fifty-gallon drums sweetly reeking of artificial lemon.

He was glad the place sparkled and smelled. At least he wouldn't be probed with a blood-encrusted finger.

"Wait here," the corporal ordered, shoving him into a folding metal chair.

Stock, who was still watching, spoke up. "Easy there, Corp. This Scrubman's been a broke horse the whole march in." Turning to Valentine, he said, "Relax. Didn't you read the doormat? *No fear.* Goons over with here. No Reapers. Savvy?"

With that, he walked out of the building.

Was that a code, Valentine thought? Relax, I recognize you, your secret is safe? Or is he just kindly to human captives. The Molly Carlson he'd known wouldn't have married a brute, not after what she'd been through; if anything, she'd only be courted by the most gentle of men. Probably just his nature.

More waiting. Valentine grew ever hungrier, and his stomach growled. The corporal's knuckles whitened on the whip handle, but he otherwise didn't move.

At last, a cough preceded a medical man, with an orderly trailing behind carrying a tray full of instruments and some jars.

The doctor, a gray-hair who looked terribly frail for a forward military camp, examined Valentine. The medical man knew his business. He looked into his eyes, ears, and throat, listened to his heart and breathing through a stethoscope, tut-tutted over the old steam burns on his back, palpitated his scrotum and had Valentine cough, and ran some sort of irritatingly dry swab up his rectum.

He paused over the old gunshot wound in his leg. He cocked his head first to one angle, then another as he looked at it. He reminded Valentine of a pigeon he'd once watched in New Orleans, deciding if a dropped coin was edible.

"Bad, this. How old is it?"

Valentine dropped his mouth open wide and acted as though he'd been asked to construe Wittgenstein. "Errrrrrrup—not baby to manhood. Baby to hunting age."

"In years, please. Four seasons equals a year."

"Four. No, ten. Tenteen?"

The doctor sighed. "Never mind. It still gives you trouble?"

"No run long," Valentine said, which was close to the truth.

"Could have been worse, Scrubman. It might have hit your femoral artery. You would have been dead in seconds. Next time you have the opportunity you might want to sacrifice a chicken or whatever you do to appease fortune."

Valentine didn't mind being talked down to. It meant the disguise was working, at least so far.

The doctor took out a white instrument like a thick pen. He folded it open to reveal a little screen on a swing arm.

"Orderly, starting SSI scan."

The orderly picked up Valentine's clipboard and a pencil.

The instrument passed from temple to temple. Valentine felt a crackling presence across his skin, like a piece of wool that's built up a strong static charge.

"Subject fifty-one-eleven, Mentation weak A. That's interesting. Too bad he didn't get some education. Emotional weak C, no, I'll call that a strong D—he's seen a lot of stress, by the look of it, and he's got it buried deep. I've gotten strong Ds out of semi-sentient Grogs. He either tortures critters or he cries at the sight of a dead baby bird, I'll bet. Delta signal—whoa there, strong B." Valentine felt the instrument touch him midforehead. "No, weak A—no, strong A . . . dropped back to B again. The hell? This SSI needs a factory recalibration, that can't be right with a Scrubman. And we're back at A, steady. I think this SSI's crapped out."

He tested it briefly on the orderly. Valentine watched its screen travel from green to pink, with little arrows and letters appearing as he moved it across the man's forehead. "Hmmm," he said.

The doctor turned and stared hard into Valentine's eyes.

"You're not a Kurian agent, I'm guessing, unless our dear Baron's made some powerful enemies. An agent wouldn't dink around in the labor pens. He'd walk right into headquarters."

Valentine tried to look blank and uncomprehending, and offered a nervous smile. "Haircut now?" he asked.

"Wonder who whelped this pup and who his father was," the doc mused, folding up his instrument again.

The stingray-whip corporal took a firm grip on his upper arm and led him past a small motor pool filled with rebuilt trucks—the sleek twenty-first-century panels had been replaced with brutally ugly corrugated steel painted in that same vertical camo scheme—to a pole barn filled with shipping containers and tables.

They issued Valentine a set of plain white canvas pants and a shirt, along with some mass-produced sandals that he'd last seen in Xanadu. The shirt, probably once stiff and uncomfortable, had been washed down to an almost flannel smoothness. Valentine noticed there was a patch sewn on the right breast, shaped to look like a shovel-head with a number 3 on it.

"Don't worry, in the winter you'll get boots," his corporal said.

"No kill? No eat?"

The corporal cracked a smile for the first time. "Believe me, this isn't the end of the line for you. Getting roped by that Grog's the best thing that ever happened to you. Getting any of this?"

"Yes-yes," Valentine said. "Littles."

"Do as you're told and you're entitled to three hots and a cot. If you're doing heavy labor, you get snacks, even. I grew up in Illinois, farm labor, and we didn't get that unless our families snuck it out to us, so appreciate it. We only send screwups back north. We've had some guys come out of the pens and make sergeant. I don't suppose you can read and write—"

"Read, yes, read good."

The corporal chuckled. "Well, they'll test you, so let's wait— Hey, look alive, if you know what's good for you, here's the man himself. That there's the Baron, Scrubman, he owns your ass now. You do what he say, you can rise right up to a piece of Iowa heaven. Cross him and you'll be turned into pig feed."

Two four wheelers and a pickup truck rolled through camp at a gentle pace. Valentine assumed that the Baron was in the first car, the passenger seat of a polished, high-clearance jeep-style vehicle. He wore a long legworm-leather duster of a reddish-brown hue with its brass-tipped collar turned up and the brim of his old military-style scrambled eggs cap down low. He wore big reflective sunglasses, in fact, put a corncob pipe in his mouth, and in that cap and glasses and Valentine thought he might pass for General MacArthur.

The corporal saluted as the cars passed and Valentine aped him, poorly. The Baron gave no sign he'd seen them.

The rear truck had a camper on the back with old bulletproof vests fixed over the windows. Valentine supposed some Grog body-guards were within, looking out at the world through concealed firing slits.

The corporal looked pleased with the salute.

"Seeing as it's your first day, we'll let you get settled in quarters."

The corporal took him to an old basement that had been timbered over with sod. Two ventilation pipes stuck up, without any sort of cover to keep out the rain. The corporal pulled back a tarp and brought him downstairs.

It smelled like body odor, wet wool, and possibly ferrets within, but to the eye it was clear enough. There were window wells, partially blocked up to prevent someone from sneaking out, that admitted some light. Most of the furniture was bunks, but there was also a big five-gallon plastic water barrel with a permanently stopped spigot hole. Instead of that there was a siphon hose and a cup.

"This is Hole Three. Can you say that?"

"Hole threes," Valentine repeated.

"Remember that. Any bunk without a blanket you can take."

Valentine decided he had to choose between light and fresh air and warmth. He chose light and fresh air, and took an unoccupied bottom-bunk near the door.

"Here, you won't eat until breakfast," the corporal said, rummaging in one of his big cargo pockets and pulling out something wrapped in foil. "Unless you're in the hospital, you only eat on the job site. Don't know if you're too smart or too dumb for all this, but I appreciate you not fussing and spitting, Scrubman."

The outer wrapper had a label with a picture of snowcapped mountains. It tasted of real cocoa and sugar and had plenty of peanuts in it. If a corporal in the Gray Baron's command could afford to give away chocolate like this to a prisoner as a kindly afterthought, they must be doing very well indeed in the Kurian Order. Valentine had sipped ersatz cocoa with many a New Universal churchman, even in Louisiana with its access to ocean trade.

Valentine ate half and saved the rest.

†

Everyone called him Scar.

Hole Three was run by a fleshy man known as Fat Daddy. Valentine wasn't sure of the source of his authority, as he went directly to his bunk and didn't move, even to urinate. His urine was collected and dumped into the basement urine bucket—he later found out every drop was saved, it went to a fertilizer manufacturer—by an injury-hobbled old man called Pappy.

They were all wary of him at first, in his clean new clothes. Fat Daddy distributed the soap ration, and there was none left once his own ample body and that of his rather gorgeous, bewigged golden boy were taken care of. A mix of servant, jester, and lover, the effeminate youth slept like a dog on his plastic-covered mattress at the foot of Fat Daddy's pushed-together bunks. Everyone called him Beach Boy and he was the one who gave Valentine the "Scar" moniker.

"Just do like Fat Daddy says and everything'll work out swell," Pappy advised him.

Valentine suspected they'd sniff his chocolate out sooner or later. Better to give it up voluntarily than be put in his place in the pecking order by having it taken from him forcibly. Despite his lurking hunger, he offered it to Pappy.

"You looks hungries, grandfathers," Valentine said, offering.

"Naw, I couldn't," Pappy said. He shot a glance around, most of the workers were stripping and hanging up their clothes so they'd dry out by morning, or they were taking drinks from the plastic bucket by letting a siphoned jet of water spray into their mouths so as not to touch the plastic end. Pappy still eyed it, licking his lips.

"Give it here, Pappy," Fat Daddy said. Valentine wasn't sure they were even watching.

Pappy grabbed it and brought it over to Fat Daddy in his bunk. Beach Boy—though Valentine didn't know the name yet—took it, smelled it, and insouciantly popped a chunk in his mouth before handing it to Fat Daddy.

"Naughty boy," Fat Daddy said. He tasted it. "This is good stuff, new meat. Hey, Boy, new meat needs a name."

Beach Boy made a great show of licking his lips. "Scar."

†

Valentine liked the work. Maddeningly so.

He spent his days working with excrement, or drying it and then transporting it to the fields, rather.

It was filthy stuff for a man as fastidious about his own cleanliness as Valentine, filling a trailer with liquid "hot honey" and raking it out into a field to dry with other organic waste in the sun. The better job, in some ways, was taking the dried version of it, known as "brown sugar" out to the fields, though in spreading it some dust would get up and you'd have to spend the day with a rag tied around your face and the uncomfortable thought that you were blinking feces out of your eyes. There it was turned into quick-growing heartroot, or other more traditional Midwestern vegetables and grains—there were even paddies for rice. Most of the heartroot was broken up and added to scraps for pig feed or to granary leavings for the chickens the Gray Ones kept in little household coops or vast stacks in the pole barns.

The work was done by men because Grog warriors would not be stained by such duty, fit only for slaves. So the men of the forced-labor group, a collection of criminals, last-chancers, and sold-off Grog slaves of dubious origins such as himself, did work no warrior would take up, and the few Grog females in the Baron's stronghold were too valuable to sully with such labor.

Valentine followed orders, took his three hots and a cot, and waited in absurd, smelly happiness. They ate their meals outdoors, in the sun in good weather, under a tent or inside available transport in bad. He felt his body toughening under the dawn-to-dusk days, and there were no worries beyond his being recognized. There was a part of him that hated responsibility, the endless choices between bad outcomes that came with military life, the paperwork that no one ever read, useful only to the creators of file cabinets and document storage boxes.

His work wasn't limited to agriculture. Anything having to do with shit would cause an officer or a Grog chief to call in the forced-labor group. Valentine and Pappy were sometimes called into the Grog Quarter to deal with a stuffed-up toilet drain. He'd crouch to walk under lofted housing, or pass through alleys just wide enough to allow two Grogs to face each other and squeeze through. He smelled delicious steak and vegetable kabobs being cooked on tiny charcoal stoves and took cover when raucous games of throw-and-block or breakgrip burst out of multihome courtyards and into the streets, paths and alleys. He smelled tobacco and hot iron and applewood smokers. The Gray Ones loved pine and orange oils in their homes to cover the scent of a stopped drain.

"They also slosh around a lot of oil and burn it when the she-Grogs go fertile," Pappy said. "Grogs theyselves don't cause too much trouble about mating if there are no eligible females about, as long as they don't smell 'em. But if they get a whiff, it's Katie bar the door, 'cause you're about to get plugged in like a surge protector."

He also saw the Golden One quarters. Many still lived in tents, but more permanent housing formed of bricks reclaimed from the town and the output of a new Golden One–run sawmill was going up. Their quarters were laid out with more precision than the Gray One piles of housing, but each Golden One had less space. A whole family of six would be put into just a half basement.

Valentine felt for them. It was never fun to sleep in the same place you cooked.

Once, when their spreader flatbed broke down near headquarters, Valentine got a look at "the model."

It was on display in a peaceful garden, and as nobody seemed to mind him wandering within sight of the disabled truck, he went into a little Grecian temple, or maybe it was a small theater or music platform, and took a look at the wooden blocks carefully arranged on the three-dimensional plan.

The Baron had something grand in mind for his headquarters. There would be columns worthy of the Romans, a pair of arches that modernized the famous one he'd seen in pictures of Paris to include friezes of Grogs on one side, humans on the other—the Gray Gate and the Golden Gate, and, dwarfing all else, the Missouri Throne.

When his officer for the day called him back to the others, Valentine asked him about the pyramid.

"Going to take years to build, if it ever gets done at all. Even with all these Golden Ones going at it full-time. You wouldn't believe the hour cost in moving a city's worth of giant bricks into a single pile, Scar."

It would sit atop a staired Aztec-style pyramid, and the officer told him it would be visible, in some directions, from twenty miles away. The Baron could communicate with the Kurians from the top of it by reading the stars and planets. Or so the officer said.

†

Some days, Valentine saw Sergeant Stock out doing calisthenics on the athletic field near the forced-labor dugouts. A near mountain of dirt and gravel stood at the edge of the field, for emergency washout repair to the patched-together camp road network after a bad rain. Stock was one of a few who ran up and down the gravel hill, sometimes carrying a dummy gun, trying to keep his footing.

One morning, it was Ahn-Kha there, sitting atop the gravel mound, eating an orange from a bag of them.

Valentine got permission to try and cadge a couple of oranges from his old master, and trotted out to the hill.

Ahn-Kha made him go through the effort of climbing, sliding, and reclimbing the gravel pile.

"There is a difficulty, my David," Ahn-Kha said.

"What's that?"

"I have spoken to a few old friends, and last night I met with the Speakers of the Castes. They will not take up arms against this Baron. Here." He passed Valentine an orange.

"He has them working like slaves!"

"Yes, he has them working, but he has kept up his part of the bargain. When they surrendered, there were to be no reprisals, no mistreatment, we were to live within his sight and build in return for our keep. It was all laid out in the First Understanding, and then when that was completed successfully, the Second Understanding became law. None would be sent off to the Kurian Zone, and any generations to come would choose whether to live in his domain or depart. His execution of the bargain is faultless."

"They can't wait to help his army, or the Iowa Guard. The Kurian Order, in effect."

"My people were defeated, my David. They accepted more generous terms than they would have received from other Gray One tribes or the Iowans."

"Well, did you at least get a count?"

"Some seven thousand and two hundred. There were losses in the fighting, and some managed to flee into the sand hills to the west rather than be taken. But those number in the hundreds, mostly those without family to think of."

"What would your Speakers like?"

"Like? I do not know that 'like' signifies. They will uphold their end of the bargain as long as this Baron does."

Anger surged up in Valentine. He'd travelled all these miles, killed, sent himself naked into the Gray Baron's camp, when he might as well have stayed in Kentucky, for all the good it would do. Stiff-necked—

No, that wasn't right. It was his fault for thinking he could steer history, the way he tried steering one of the Tennessee boats they'd stolen.

"What if the Baron doesn't keep his end?" Valentine asked.

"The peace and captivity would no longer be valid. They would be only too glad to go to the soft green hills of your Kentucky."

†

Valentine spent the rest of the day disgruntled and itchy.

With Ahn-Kha's help, he was fairly sure he could escape. Ahn-

Kha still hadn't formally accepted a price for Valentine's sale, so he could demand his return at any time. Though the men on base were few in number, Valentine guessed fewer than a hundred were in camp at any one time, with a few dozen more strung out on the rail lines and back north in Iowa. The Golden Ones wouldn't rise and the Gray Ones couldn't. The Gray Baron was their chief's-chief, their warlord, and they liked it that way.

That night, Fat Daddy picked the wrong moment to humiliate Valentine.

Maybe because he'd seen Valentine eat an entire orange without saving half as an offering to the Lord of Dugout 3.

"Forget it, Pappy," Fat Daddy said from his usual prone position, rippled as a sea lion sunning itself. "Have Scar take the piss pot tonight."

"I don't mind, Big—," Pappy began.

"Give those knees a peaceful easy," Fat Daddy said. "Let the Groggie's pet handle it."

"I don't mind," Valentine said.

The worst part was he had to kneel down; Fat Daddy's joined bunks sagged so with the man's weight in it. Kneeling and leaning forward with the sawed-off water bottle made his bad leg hurt.

Beach Boy giggled as Fat Daddy filled the bottle. Disgusted, Valentine felt the plastic go warm in his hand.

"Give him a tap," Fat Daddy ordered.

Valentine pulled the bottle away.

"Don't you hear right, son? You're slower than a wooden Indian. I told you to tap it off. Now me sheet's all soiled."

"Ah-ah-ah," Beach Boy said, waggling his finger in Valentine's direction from behind the garden-slug form of his protector.

For a man who had taken the whole group's soap ration, his bedding was remarkably dirty. Valentine threw the contents of the warm jug into Fat Daddy's face.

For a full ten seconds Fat Daddy remained frozen, as though his brain couldn't quite absorb the splashed urine as well as the sheets and his shirtfront.

"You cunt!" Beach Boy spat.

"You'll regret that!" Fat Daddy bellowed, a rising tide of flesh coming for Valentine.

Valentine's only regret was that he didn't leave a few ounces for Beach Boy's concealer-coated face.

He backpedaled and bounced off the chest of one of the other laborers, who'd gathered to get a look at Scar's humiliation.

"Excuse me," Valentine said, but the man shoved him toward Fat Daddy.

Fat Daddy got a grip on his shirt and started slapping him, hard, back and forth. Valentine lashed out, felt his fist glance off a meaty pectoral rather than the chin he'd been aiming for.

"*Oh, will you,*" Fat Daddy snarled. The slaps turned into closed-fist blows, hard, into the painful sweet T between nose and eyeline.

Valentine went momentarily blind. He felt more hands grabbing at him, a hot panting.

"Finish his ass-face off, Daddy," Beach Boy said, strong fingers suddenly pulling at his hair.

The smooth-chested bastard twisted his ear, hard, as though trying to tear it off. Something that must have been a brick struck him in the jaw, and through sheets of rainbow lighting Valentine saw Fat Daddy pulling back for another punch.

Then it came. The red rage. It flooded through Valentine's bloodstream from somewhere behind his liver. When it hit his chest and heart, he felt as though his hot muscles might burn through his skin. Valentine had Bear blood in him by way of his father. A lifetime of unconscious emotional training held it in check—but when some combination of pain, fear, anger, and sweat washed through him, the shadow monster slipped its leash.

He pulled the two men pinning his arms down to the ground—hard. Fingers closed on a forearm and he felt a snap, his fist tightened as though he were pinching off a flowing garden hose. With his right hand he grabbed something—anything—and got a finger. He twisted and it popped off like a banana squeezed out of its skin.

Beach Boy shrieked and hopped away, injured hand clasped between his knees.

Fat Daddy looked down in horror. Valentine saw his snarl reflected in the formerly eager eyes.

Valentine spun on his hip so his body faced opposite Fat Daddy's, got his instep across his throat, and kept a hold tight on the chunky arms.

A horrible crushing, choking sound from his windpipe: *Kckchckhhh* . . .

Whistles and calls of *fight! Fight in the pens!* sounded like the distant roaring of falls in a canyon far below.

Valentine rose, picked up Fat Daddy by the waistband and neckhole, and threw him around like a tackling dummy. Thunk—up against the wall. Then Valentine tested the man's ability to cushion an attempt to bust through the cinder blocks. He smelled blood.

The cinder blocks didn't give but something in the man did and Valentine upended him onto the floor and came down after him, leading with a hard-driving elbow as though trying to knock a new drain hole. Again, the floor resisted the blow, but a cartilaginous sound like a thick sheaf of paper tearing showed that his victim's body saved the floor from its punishment. Valentine picked him up again and saw men scattering, threw the broken body through one set of bunks and knocking down a second.

Valentine raged around an ever-widening circle of men in white scrubs. Some sane sliver of his consciousness realized he was foaming at the mouth.

Then the floor rose up and hit him, hard. He felt water pounding up his back and realized the cleaning hose had been turned on the room.

†

Of course there was an inquiry into Fat Daddy's death. Pappy broke the silence of the labor gang.

"Was two-on-one, chief. First blood was on Fat Daddy's fists."

Looking at the damage to Hole Three's boss, the inquiry evidently assumed some sort of group justice had taken place, and Valentine, being the new guy, was "volunteered" to show some damage and had his lights convincingly punched out. The query was closed as quickly as it was opened, at least insofar as the healing Valentine could tell.

The men in the pens seemed to assume that Valentine wanted the strongman-leader position vacated by Fat Daddy. They took to calling him Fast Scar and offered tobacco, toiletries, even tin cups of sack-made fruit-cocktail wine that might be mistaken for some sort of acidic drain cleaner.

Valentine wasn't interested in having toadies or allocating who would change whose bedsheets and when in exchange for downcast eyes whenever he passed. But he did see to it everyone had their soap again.

"Sort it out yourself," he said with a shrug to other matters.

The food was dreadful, the worst kind of Kurian Zone canned, waterlogged vegetables and freeze-dried shoe leather passing as meat. Only copious amounts of ketchup, the one condiment available (no need for salt; every dish tasted like it had been dragged through an oceanside brine pool).

†

Valentine had earned himself a reputation as a fighter. They sometimes gave him the day off, then at night he'd be taken to the old entry rotunda on the megachurch, an octagon that might have been a modernized Globe Theatre in that three levels of audience could look down on him from balconies leading to various spaces in the headquarters building. There, under strings of lights hanging down from the skylight, he'd go up to three rounds in a boxing match or a no-holds-barred fight. Valentine gave a good account of himself, despite not being able to box, though the gloves and soft toes of the kickboxing boots often left his face swollen and painful.

He found, in his fights, that it took a few blows before his blood started jumping. For all his years as a fighting man, he wasn't much with his fists, the more skilled boxers shed his blows like a slicker kept the rain off. Only once his nose was bleeding and body blows making each rib come alive in pain did it come. Then, no matter how skilled his opponent, it was just a matter of harrying him into a corner and beating down his guard with blow after blow after blow until the ref pulled him off. The men in his corner took to throwing an ice-cold towel over his head like a panicked horse.

"He's like some kind of fuckin' machine," a spring-steel hard sergeant gasped to his own corner when Valentine knocked him down the second round, under the eyes of the Gray Baron himself, watching from a balcony. The sergeant was Mongo Station's reigning boxing champion and fought any weight. "Gasoline on a fire. The more you put into him, the harder he hits back."

The reputation came with its rewards. They finally issued him some sheets and a pillow, for a start. Ahn-Kha reported that his price had suddenly been met, and he'd had a second offer from the big Gray One Deathring tribal leader, an aging veteran of a hundred battles named "Danger Close," that he'd like Valentine as an armed bodyguard. Danger Close hadn't named a price specifically, but it seemed an obligation to him was a good thing to have, whatever the color of your skin and fur.

"They're getting suspicious," Ahn-Kha said.

"I have a feeling I can get away from the labor gang easier than this Danger Close. Take the money and get back to the camp. Tell Duvalier that she may need to start poking around headquarters, if she hasn't already. Assassinating this Gray Baron might be our only out."

Ahn-Kha didn't make any obvious comments about the difficulty of killing a warlord in his own headquarters. "Even if that happens, as long as the order my people made their agreement with exists, they will be bound to it."

"No discontent at all."

"Well, some grumbling. Those born since the surrender are not bound to its terms, and may leave at maturity if they wish. The men are recruiting them to be in athletic contests and pretend marches and that sort of thing, handing out many toys and prizes. Their elders do not care to see the young ones seduced into being little more than prouder versions of the Deathring Tribe."

"I need to get going," Valentine said. "Try and set up a communication system with the ratbits. They should be able to get into the camp at night without much difficulty. If there are any dogs other than strays living off scraps, I haven't seen them."

"If you get into difficulty, try to set a smoky fire. Chieftain can arrange a diversion, and you should be able to escape."

"No heroics this time," Valentine said. "If I get stuck in here, I'll just follow orders and bide my time."

There was another benefit, as Valentine found out when they brought him out of the hole on a warm, three-quarter-moon night.

At first they walked in silence, but as the cavernous headquarters building receded, they started joking about Valentine spending the night on stud detail.

"Don't worry, buck. With a woman," the older of the two said.

They brought him to a small trailer house at the base of the hill behind headquarters. It was one of several in a little, politely fenced grove. Valentine heard a woman singing through an open window, and a pair of lusty young voices, wailing away into the night.

They stepped up to an aluminum door. Little Gray One fetishes were tacked three-deep all around it, offerings of teeth and fingers again. "Time to do your duty, Arms," one of them called through the screen door, rapping.

"'Bout time she earned a pink or blue star," his comrade said. He'd had some sort of dreadful wound to his cheek, running from the corner of his mouth almost up to the ear.

No one answered the call, or the rapping. Valentine smelled new paint and stale tobacco coming from inside the trailer home. He noticed that the electrical system for this cluster of trailers consisted of what looked like extension cords running on poles back to a concrete platform.

"Bet she's out dancing in the moonlight, again."

They took Valentine out around the trailer and up along a little creek. The cool evening air poured into him like a fizzy tonic after spreading shit all day, washing up with a cake of soap seemingly as invulnerable to water and lather as aluminum.

They traced the creek back to a natural spring, or perhaps a natural pool that collected water from the hills. It lay in a little, thickly wooded dimple on the hillside.

A woman splashed in the water there. It took Valentine a moment to realize she was dancing in the ankle-deep pool. She did a routine displaying a rope around her arm.

No, the darkness had fooled him. It was a snake.

She was a diminutive little thing, smaller even than Ediyak. One of his escorts whistled.

"Hey, showgirl. Biological duty time."

She turned her head just enough to take a glance.

"Biological each other, why don't you. I'm busy. It's Warmoon Feast in three days, if you didn't know. Gotta dance for Danger Close."

"This comes from the Baron himself, sweetie," the one with the scar-lengthened mouth said.

"Don't bend her too hard, buck," the other said quietly. "She's little, but she's like one of them snakes."

She stopped her dance, lowered her head, and took a deep breath. After a moment, she turned.

She was wearing an oversized undershirt and as far as Valentine could see through the wet clasp of damp cotton, nothing else. She waded up, making no effort to hide her body.

"I don't know you," she said to Valentine.

"You will soon," scar-mouth sniggered.

"Forced labor? Really? What, am I a last request? He gonna get shot at sunrise?" If she showed any resentment at being ordered to service someone at a moment's notice, she was hiding it well.

"Nothing like that. The Baron just liked the cut of his genes."

"Not bad looking, either," she said, tickling the copperhead wrapped about her arm. It was a "Her face wasn't beautiful, but she could be called pretty," and an energy crackled out of her through the clinging T-shirt. It was easy for Valentine to imagine her being the source of the bubbling spring, a kind of Lady of the Lake. Or, going back a couple millennia in the literary world, holding an apple in her bower.

"Our beloved Baron gave up on Captain Coltrane becoming a father, I guess," she said. "I don't have my glasses on, stranger, but you're a finely formed blur. Should I keep my glasses in their drawer, Porter?"

"He's chewed up, but tasty," the scarred man answered. He cupped Valentine on the butt cheek.

"Keep it off base, Private," the other said. "Just because the Baron looks the other way . . ."

"My snake's cold," she said. "Let's get going."

She led them back down the path to the trailers, silent. She had a grace to her, her gait had a rhythm, even on the uneven trail. The singing had stopped and the crying had changed to the sound of a woman telling a story about an ugly duckling.

"First time in the harem?" she asked, over her shoulder.

"Yes," Valentine said.

She waved the escort off at the door. "When will you pick him up?"

"Morning," the one in charge said. "Well after dawn, so don't be afraid to—"

"Give him breakfast?" she said.

They left.

The trailer had more Grog art in it. A tiny corner kitchen at one end, with a bathroom opposite it, and a built-in folding table with a pair of small chairs covered eating and expulsion. At the other end, a long couch hid a bed. She had some bookshelves made of planks and bricks filled with battered books, mostly reference works and fiction. Several of the paperbacks were held together with rubber bands.

"Why do you do your routine in the water?" Valentine asked.

"Good workout for the legs. I had the guys bring up some sand, so the footing's not too bad, and most of the year enough water is moving to keep it clear from water weed. That and it takes care of the sweat, so I don't have to wash after."

"I practice when it's cool," she said. "They're happy to just hug my arms for a few minutes."

She had three aquariums filling a wall of the trailer, warmed by a space heater. Valentine peeked inside and recognized a diamondback rattlesnake and a cottonmouth, plus something near black he'd never seen before.

"What's your name?" Valentine asked.

"They call me 'Snake Arms.'"

He wasn't sure he'd heard the name correctly and asked her to repeat it.

"Snake Arms. They tell me it's how the Grog name is rendered in English. Tethmot or something like that, with a purse of the lips and a spitting sound before or after to signify that I'm a captive. Hope you don't mind Grog spittle, every time you get an order you'll get a sprinkle."

"I'm guessing they gave you that name."

"I'm a praise-dancer. I've got a way with rattlesnakes and such. Can we get this over with, I need to hunt mice for my creepies and if I go to the grain pits after they close they might think I'm stealing."

Valentine wondered how much to the hilt he'd end up playing this role.

"They call me Scar. You—fine reward," he said, keeping to his role as an ignorant Scrubman who was learning fast.

"Your first time in a Grog pit? The Baron's not interested in your pleasure. He wants strong, healthy babies for his next generation of soldiers. It's Orders. They want some offspring combining valuable traits."

Valentine had experience with this sort of thing. Southern Command ran a controversial program for a period before the return of a few Lifeweavers where they tried to breed a new generation of hunters by pairing up likely candidates. As one of the very few male Cats, he was called on. It wasn't unpleasant, but it made him feel like a prize bull.

"Like dogs," Valentine said.

"How do you think they ever made Shepherds. They picked two mutts with features they wanted and got a litter. The Baron's thinking long term."

"Hey, I'm off all duties but sewing while you're trying to impregnate me, so I'm happy with it. Under all the wear and rust, you ain't half bad looking, plus you have that intense Indian thing going, so I've got no problem with taking it twice nightly for a while if he wants me knocked up. Thing is, I have to check in at the doc's dripping spunk, or they'll take me off procreation and put me to berry picking or beekeeping or cleaning chicken coops and so on, and that's sticky work. We only get two hot baths a week. Otherwise it's a basin and rag, or the spring when no one's drawing water."

She disrobed as she spoke. She was a little on the fleshy side—Valentine couldn't help but think of milk-skinned Molly, that summer in Wisconsin—but nicely proportioned. She'd probably been chosen for her hips and breasts.

"I'm kind of looking forward to this," she said, approaching him. Her eyeline only came to his midchest, he could look down and see the direction of growth in her hair.

"You smell—sweet," Valentine said.

"I dusted a little lavender in my hair. It's in bloom now."

Her body, soft and ripe and smelling of the spring water and salty sweat, suddenly seemed to be touching his, from toe tips to eyeline, as though they were magnets with perfectly aligned poles and curvatures.

His hands started at her shoulder blades and explored south.

She had deceptively strong muscles under that jiggling flesh. He felt one buttock tense under its padding, it might have been an oak banister carefully curved by some woodworker. They fought a brief war, her leg against his hand, and she let him win, bringing her calf up and tight against his own, tucked in between buttock and thigh.

Valentine had experienced all kinds of sex in his travels. Tender and tentative, loving, exhausted, mechanical, professional, enthusiastic, angry . . .

For him, it was a form of oblivion. He could wipe away everything when between a woman's thighs the way some lost themselves in drink or drugs.

But this woman, a gift to him in his labor pit, was outside his experiences. She reminded him of one of those Old World robotic toys, where once plugged in or batteried up, lights roamed across it and noises sounded from hidden speakers and it began to buck and jump.

The first few strokes of penetration seemed to trip a hidden "on" switch within Snake Arms. She suddenly came alive and apparently grew another set of legs and arms, like some Indian idol. Were those hands or legs on his buttocks, and if they were hands, what on earth was clasping at his latissimus muscles.

Still, he stayed gentle. She seemed like a bird in a cage, tucked under the arc of his limbs.

"Faster and harder, Scar. I can take it . . . All of it, now."

"I much bigger than you," Valentine said.

"Tougher than I look." She made a face, as though trying to remember a foreign expression. Valentine felt her inner muscles work him, pulling at him.

"Jesus," he said.

"It's the dancing. Works your core."

She'd gone impossibly wet, running like the spring where he'd seen her dance in the moonlight. He gave her his all.

"Fuck yeah," she squeaked.

He had to agree.

Now they were both moving, grinding together, a steady meeting of hips like some obscene musical instrument.

The lavender must have been mostly pollen. Valentine gave a soft sneeze.

He pulled her off him, for some reason needing to taste her. He hugged her salty mount with his mouth, savoring her.

Suddenly she bucked and scooted away from his tongue. When her eyes opened again, he reentered her, aroused by her climax, and in a few brief strokes it was his turn.

His mind cleared in the afterglow.

"Work, work, work," she said into his arm. "Dawn to midnight." Then she seemed to relax into sleep.

Now he could think. A rough count of the armed Grogs made him wonder if an uprising by the Golden Ones could even be successful, given the forces the Baron had. A force two or three times that of the Baron's would be required to smash this feudal Grog-human war machine.

The Baron would have plenty of warning and the advantage of rail-fed interior lines of communication on that arc he patrolled between the Mississippi and Oklahoma. No such army existed north of the Missouri, even if he could somehow unite the Gray Ones running wild north of the Missouri valley.

No, the destruction would have to come from within. The Kurians had managed the trick any number of times. Could he manage it here?

Not on his brown sugar.

After a day's work in the fields that no longer seemed quite so delightfully mindless, he was rinsed and brought to the little trailer park enclave again. This time, he thought he saw a shadow watching him from the woods sheltering the trailers from prying eyes.

It was laundry day. There were bedsheets drying on every line. She showed him a tub of iced beer. "Present from the med staff. Doctor says it's the right time in my cycle, so you've got me for the next two nights. Let's enjoy ourselves."

"Sure. But later, let's talk. Alone. Quiet," Valentine said, still not sure of her.

"If your tongue's not too tired. And don't go getting lovelorn. You're here because the Baron wants it so. Don't be surprised if when you're done with me, they move you on to another, or get you jacking off into a cup. They'll make use of those balls while you still have 'em. Soon as you knock a couple of us up, you're getting snipped high and sewn up tight. Washtub gossip says you're going to be guarding the officers' harem."

CHAPTER TEN

*T*he Grog Auxiliaries: the Kurian Order keeps its place through its Church, police forces, riot squads, troops, and of course the Reapers. Some might say the paperwork and permits of existence in the Kurian Zone is a form of control, a little less obvious and more debilitating than the policeman on the street or the riot cop at his fire hose. Fear has its role too.

Of course, the Kurians sometimes have difficulty getting men to shoot down other men, especially in the early days of their advent. They brought the Grogs over through the Interworld Tree, telling them that a rich planet was theirs for the taking if they'd evict an indolent and degenerate infestation of scrawny humans.

So the Grogs came, though where they expected to frighten and herd away the humans (as their scouts who'd gone among the confused, starving multitudes in a few devastated areas had reported) they found resistance. But Grogs take to new modalities of warfare like ducks to different-sized bodies of water, and soon modified human weapons for their own use.

The Gray Baron's "Missouri Division" is a recent construct. The Grogs in central Missouri now recognize no law but their own, and are *quite happy to raid north, south, east, or west—and the rich lands of Iowa have valuable cattle and swine worth stealing. Starting with nothing but a starving, co-opted Western Missouri clan of Grogs known as the Wrist-Rings, he built them up into a formidable fighting band over the course of a decade, absorbing bands of Grogs along the Missouri Valley with promises of easy duty—when not fighting.*

He kept that promise. His warriors enjoy an enviable lifestyle, only chieftains south of the river live in the manner of his lowliest fighter. As for the clan chiefs, some believe they've died and returned to Earth as demigods, so much wealth and wives and slaves do they have at their command.

The next generation of fighting Grogs and their human masters is training even now, while a third is being selected and bred. What plans the Gray Baron has for them perhaps not even his human lieutenants may say.

†

Valentine wondered if Snake Arms's comment was a plant, to make him anxious. Or perhaps it was a warning about crossing the Gray Baron.

If he hadn't seen him in his command car, Valentine would have suspected the Gray Baron was a creation, a boogeyman developed by the Kurians to keep both their Grogs and soldiers in line.

Ahn-Kha was true to his word, as always. Two nights later Valentine was awoken by the discreet scratch of Patches. The ratbit had a little pack made out of a zip-up eyeglass case, and in it was a pad and paper.

Valentine had spent some time thinking about the vulnerabilities of the Baron's human/Gray One legion. For the first message, he just passed word of the supplies he needed them to gather from Brostoff's forward Wolf base. They might not be able to spare guns, but they had plenty to eat and drink . . .

Valentine puzzled out why there were no Grog overseers. Men ordered, and sometimes struck men; the Grogs did the same for and to their own kind.

He had plenty of time to give it thought, under the orders and the implied threat of short whip, knotted rope, or crop in the hands of some ill-tempered NCO.

He'd seen, all too often, one race or species used to supervise another. It focused the subject people's animosity in the right direction—at least in the tyrant's terms—at a powerful tormentor. Every shortage, every injury, every illness could be blamed on the people charged with policing. The group on top had to be fiercely loyal to the existing order, or they'd fall—and a bloody, hard fall it would be.

Seemed crazy of the Gray Baron not to use this system on his human forced labor. But instead, a few men and women with clipboards and kepis kept quiet watch, little brutality required.

Probably the Gray Baron wanted to make sure his fighting Grogs didn't get any ideas about pushing men around. In Valentine's experience, all Gray Ones considered themselves superior to puny humans, most of whom weren't even as strong as a prepubescent youth.

Valentine wondered if the Gray Baron wasn't sitting on a throne of sweaty dynamite. If only he were more sensitive to the unspoken currents among Grogs—he might be able to find an ambitious revolutionary among the Deathring Tribe.

Over the next two days, Valentine paid more attention to the young people he saw in camp. Teenage and preteen humans and Gray Ones worked together, dressed alike in either green or blue overalls, putting up utility poles, working in the kitchens and laundry. They looked healthy, intelligent, and strong—they reminded him of the Kurian Zone propaganda posters where everyone had firm jaws and full heads of hair.

The cooperation between the younger humans and Gray Ones was the closest thing to symbiosis Valentine had seen. The juvenile Gray Ones did much of the heavy work, with the human youths directing and checking and correcting. But when not engaged in work, the roles were reversed and the Gray Ones ate first while humans served and poured, with humans cleaning their ears and nails and teeth, making sure the bedding was clean and the chamber pots empty. Perhaps to the teens, the Grogs were glorified, highly trainable pets that needed care, and to the young Gray warriors, the human allies were their slaves once the enforced egalitarianism of action was over.

The Baron's stronghold didn't feel like a Kurian Zone. The elements were there, a survivor at the top with absolute power, his close advisors and guards just below, then the common herd scratching for any kind of advantage or notice to climb up the next rung of the ladder.

Valentine had his chance to step up a rung with the Warmoon Festival.

It was his first time inside the old megachurch that served as the Baron's headquarters. He was, to his surprise, the Baron's new champion human bare-handed fighter, and despite his lowly status as forced labor, he'd won a front-row seat at the festivities. Even more oddly, Sergeant Stock was to lead his small party, which consisted of a teenage girl who had finished studies at the top of her class in the stronghold's school and a Youth Vanguard military track student commander who'd travelled all the way from a little town near Buffalo on Lake Erie to join the Baron's forces.

Again, a less Kurian Zone establishment could hardly be imagined. It reminded him of some of the older, forgotten corners of Southern Command, where staff inspectors were rare and the men built a little military world they liked. There were captured weapons and pieces of uniform hung on the timbered walls, hunting-lodge style.

Trying to get out of the press of flesh moving for the big central arena, he stepped off the corridor and into a sort of museum-cum-trophy hall. Some of it was a little gruesome. There was a collection of human scalps in one case, an early souvenir of the Deathring Tribe. Valentine saw some photos of piles of corpses, bodies lying in the streets in front of apartment buildings, one plummeting to earth after being tossed out by corpse-disposal teams, what looked like a wild band of ravies victims, shot down Goya-like and frozen in time and space, white eyed and screaming, in a photographer's flash.

The only time you ever saw photos of corpses were in Church museums featuring the sins of the Old World, such as the Nike and Coca-Cola corporations' slaughter of laborers in the sugar plantation killing fields of Cambodia or the murder of the Tutsi nation in central Africa by a New York diamond consortium.

Valentine guessed that the genesis of the Baron's organization was a body locator and gravedigger's unit, judging from some of the pictures and souvenirs in the first cabinet.

The "Warmoon" to the Gray Ones was the first crescent moon after the vernal equinox—the fang that signaled the start of the season when their obscure cosmology looked favorably on fighting.

Snake Arms found him looking at some early Gray One weaponry and armor, much of it cut from car parts and old utility tools.

"Future father of my child!" she called. She was dressed, if you could call it that, in a costume made out of silk patching, snakeskin, feathers, and lines of beads, both atavistic and glamorous somehow. She had multiple, thick layers of makeup on, giving her face an otherworldly whiteness.

"Baby come?" Valentine asked.

"Just kidding. Women don't know so fast, you know."

"We go again now?"

"What are you, punchy? You don't want to be seen arriving late under the Baron's nose."

He kept glancing down at her costume.

"Like it? The enlisted ranks do. It's what keeps me in my trailer with some of the other wives. If they hauled me to the officers' whorehouse, I think there'd be a riot."

"Top come off, you'll see riots plenty," Valentine said.

"I have to get backstage. See you later."

Valentine caught up to his group and they entered the big auditorium.

Perhaps next to the Memphis Pyramid's stadium, it was the largest indoor structure Valentine had ever entered. Unlike the Pyramid, smoke hung heavy in the air and it smelled like a pig show.

The main auditorium of the old church reminded Valentine of a gigantic pup tent. Thick wooden beams, six of them, rose to the

246

ceiling, where skylights admitted the evening light at the pinnacle. There was a balcony—one part glassed in, presumably for the families with small children when it served as a church.

Valentine was surprised to see the cross still there. It was a simple one, made of the same thick, wrought-iron bolted beams of the ceiling, and it hung down at an angle over the congregation, making Valentine think of a set of last rites he'd seen performed by Father Max over a dying woman in his youth. He'd held the cross before her face at just that angle. Whether that had been the original architecture or a recent change Valentine couldn't tell.

There was too much activity to look at.

The Gray Ones, for the most part, filled the lower level. The church's pews had been turned into benches to better accommodate them. A few clan leaders of the Deathring Tribe had their own furniture brought in, or perhaps it was permanently placed there, waiting for them, great perches like oversized Roman chairs.

The human soldiers inhabited the balconies, emblazoned with painted battalion symbols and specialist patches. The iconography was fierce, colorful, and oddly Midwestern, featuring hawks and foxes and coyotes and an out-of-place cobra. More humans sat upon the old altar riser, which projected out into the pews, though that part of it was empty for now.

Valentine marked the Gray Baron from his seat off to the Baron's right on the main floor. He sat in a plain, high-backed chair, flanked by two flag bearers, human and Gray One, the Grog with what looked to be a red-and-black checkerboard design with a few spiky icons stitched in the square's contrasting color, and the human holding the other, the modified tricolor of the Iowa State flag, featuring a pair of sharpened parentheses crossing each other—the locked bull horns, he'd heard them called, but it might also be stolen from a pre-2022 Chanel handbag.

Valentine thought he looked like something out of another age. He could see this man sitting on a smoky Tatar's throne or commanding some cut-off Victorian regiment in Afghanistan.

He had a heavy, sloping forehead and a mountain spur of a nose hooked like a hawk's talon. But even the oversized nose was nothing compared to the Pancho Villa mustache. It was like a curtain obscuring his upper lip and the sides of his mouth. It made his expression rather difficult to read; Valentine couldn't tell if he was smiling or frowning.

A network of scars crisscrossed his face as though a maniacal game of tic-tac-toe had been played with an assortment of scalpels. Valentine had enough battle wounds to know they couldn't have been accidental. Unless the Gray Baron had stuck his head into an oversized lamprey's mouth, someone in his past had made a point of cutting him up into shreds.

Flanking him, discreetly behind the flags, were three Reapers.

Valentine had never seen Reapers like this. They were fleshy—he thought fat Reapers didn't exist, it seemed the Kurians drained off calories along with the *vital aura* the Reapers transmitted. Despite the bellies and love handles, their faces shone hard and alert, yellow eyes watchful of the few empty square yards in front of the Gray Baron's throne. Rich red, white, and black war paint striped their bodies in a series of Vs, and their claws and a band across their eyes were a deep blue.

The Gray Baron had a woman next to him, a rather hard-faced

brunette with an athletic build. Her hair was piled up tight atop her head, bound together by a pair of stilettos in Asian hairstick fashion. Valentine wondered if the blades were just for show. She had her own stool, but chose to drape herself over the back of his chair, playing with his hair.

Next to the Gray Baron on the stage was a feeble-looking old Grog gone white and bent—Danger Close, Valentine guessed. He tried counting bullet wounds in the thick old hide and stopped after nine. He was attended by a bevy of six she-Grogs, wives, daughters, concubines, or some combination. They all carried little ceremonial working blades, like the skinning knives native tribes of the Arctic north use to separate seal blubber from skin.

A few Golden One representatives watched the celebration, stone faced. They stood apart from both the humans and the wild Grogs. The celebration was like some fantasy of a black mass. Grog warriors ran up with linked bags of netted heads, tossing them so the line hung over the massive cross at the front of the church.

A gong sounded, and the auditorium began to go quiet. From somewhere behind the curtained "stage" Valentine heard kettledrums pound slowly, a deep and thrilling sound that touched you in the pelvis. It grew louder, or perhaps the crowd grew quieter, and then the Gray Baron led Danger Close out on the platform projecting near the center point of the auditorium.

"My brothers . . ." he began.

Danger Close repeated the words in a Gray One dialect Valentine more or less understood.

The Gray Baron kept it brief. The most auspicious season for war had begun.

Danger Close translated, but not exactly. He expressed the same sentiments, but in a Gray One idiom.

This would be another year of building and training. They would venture regularly to Springfield and the Missouri River, even to the outskirts of Saint Louis, yet fighting only when another sought to fight. Otherwise they would be peaceable, friendly, even helpful. A Gray One clan with a broken water tank? Fix it! Illinois bandits stealing cattle or goats? Drive them off and return the livestock. In time their legion would be thought of as a two-headed dragon, not just because one head was human and the other Gray One, but because one head was smiling upon friends, the other biting and rending enemies. Then would come a time of alliances, and in a very few years, the strength to whip the true enemies, the humans of the Ozarks. Addled by fevers, radiator-still whiskey, and backwoods religious monomania, an army with patience to gather and strike would crumble them like a hollowed egg.

They finished to applause and Grog stomps of approval.

Then some Gray One storytellers spoke, giving anecdotes of the importance of treating the seasons with respect. Not all could fight even at the best of times, and those who'd already won great glory fighting might wish to take a season off and enjoy their wives and increase their herds and teach youngsters the stern tasks of warfare so that they might survive to win their own glories and wives.

The storytellers met more approval from the main floor than from the balcony.

The Gray Ones had several stomping patters, and Valentine's quick mind enjoyed puzzling them out. There was one for hearty approval, and another that might be characterized as a nod, and a quick one-two that asked for more of the same.

Then there was a display of captured weapons and torn-off service patches. Valentine felt a pang when he recognized a Zulu-Company patch and a Logistics Commando wagon wheel on a helmet, but he applauded with the rest of the humans.

"Trophies are great indicators of luck, to the Gray Ones," Stock explained to the boy from Buffalo. "A poor year for trophies one year will make them more conservative about what they attempt when the next spring's warmoon rolls around. A good year means they'll be more aggressive."

"Last year was a good one?" the kid asked.

"No, but it wasn't our fault. Southern Command quit trying to supply Omaha or move into Kansas, and the days of them slipping recruiting teams up to Minnesota or the Dakotas are long over. The Baron thinks that Southern Command's lost the will to fight, and wants to take advantage of it, but the Gray Ones will be hard to convince."

Hoots and yelps broke out. Valentine saw Snake Arms step into the open space on the main floor. She had a rattlesnake wrapped around each arm.

"Snakes are big juju with the Groggies," Stock said.

The kettledrums started up again along with something that twanged and the familiar scraping of a well-played fiddle. She began to dance.

It was a fascinating routine, as most of it played out from beneath her rib cage down. Her arms stayed statue-steady so as not to disturb the serpents, heads pointed out at the crowd, black eyes glittering. Her head moved as though on a gimbal-mount with her lower limbs, but the torso and arms opened and closed only occasionally.

The Gray Ones watched in silent reverence. Even the emotionless Golden Ones leaned forward in their seats.

Valentine could just hear the quiet rattle of their tails as she moved, if he really sought the sound.

After the dance came a combat display, Grogs wrestling, fighting with sticks, and finally swordplay. Valentine wondered if on their home world they used swords or if they'd adopted the weapons from machetes and such captured after 2022. Their fighting style, at least in this theatrical display, involved cuts and parries in precise, ever increasing tempo time. The Gray Ones in the audience became increasingly excited as the more furious blows and parries drew accidental blood.

After that came a bloody sacrifice.

Animals were slaughtered, starting with chickens and moving up to an ox and a captured eagle. They made a great show of presenting the eagle's feathers to Danger Close.

"A few deaths prove that they're serious about getting on the good side of all the invisibles," Stock said. "Don't let it scare you."

He glanced closely at Valentine. Valentine looked down to see that some of the spray from the sacrificed ox had struck his shirt, peppering it in red.

By now the crowd was excited.

They brought a huddled line of shorn men and a few Gray Ones out onto the pulpit projection. Two of the proposed victims were brought in on stretchers.

"Bad head injuries," Stock said. "Sometimes they're considered prophets, but if they're only barely responsive, they're done away with."

Men with riot guns stood behind, and the Baron's three pet Reapers flanked the column and stood at its head.

Valentine recognized one of the sacrifices. It was Beach Boy, from Hole Three. He hadn't seen him since the fight with Fat Daddy, though he'd heard he'd been put in another hole to stave off further fighting.

The Baron stepped forward, carrying a bamboo cane. A string with some weighted feathers hung from the handle end. He grabbed it by the base, and held it up over the first man in line. The feather just touched the top of the convicted man's hands as the two Reapers held him, one at the ankles and one at the elbows, with the third behind.

"Raminov, knifed a man over cards," Stock said to his party.

There was some hooting from the Gray Ones. A voice cried out from the balcony: *I'd knife a man who was cheating at cards too!*

Some applause and whistling broke out from the men, with a faint boo or "open him" shouted.

The feather moved on to a shorn Gray One behind him. Fierce growls broke out among the Gray Ones.

"No idea what he did," Stock said.

The convict fell back. He gave one violent shrug. The fist of the Reaper behind him exploded out of his chest in a shower of blood. Valentine noted, rather coldly, that the Reaper had discreetly locked its teeth at the Grog's shoulder and appeared to have its tongue wedged beneath one of the thick rhino-hide plates of cartilaginous armor.

The auditorium roared approval.

It was a revolting ceremony. Valentine decided it wasn't so much a sacrifice, or an execution, as a final appeal. Valentine noticed the crowd went silent for some of the victims. Someone from the audience would shriek out a plea for mercy, and if that met with approval there was a great stamping of feet. The Baron never failed to heed the collective verdict, either way.

Valentine, tired and nervous and sick to his stomach, tried to keep his meagre dinner down. Hot-blooded killing was one thing, but execution as grand theater . . .

He'd seen his share of executions. There were several combat-zone offenses that could get one shot, or a civilian hanged, in Southern Command military jurisprudence. He himself had been under a death sentence, thanks to escaping trial and the rendering of an *in absentia* conviction. Arguably, he'd performed them himself, as some half-awake sentry at one end of an unlit bridge was just as helpless against his knife as a chained convict. You didn't execute men like this, in front of the next one in line with a holiday crowd roaring.

The feather moved over Beach Boy.

"He was in your hole, I think," Stock said, looking at Valentine. "He's in for shirking. They found him sleeping under a truck on his shift. When you're forced labor, that's it."

Beach Boy was a silly little toady, certainly, but how many in the audience knew him by anything deeper than sight? Perhaps enough had seen him in the fields to know he played the fool, always with the softest jobs and gentlest duties, to better preserve his supple, scented skin for Fat Daddy.

"Give him another chance!" Valentine shouted.

The growls and angry murmurs grew louder.

"Chance! Chance! Chance!" some others began to shout. The chant picked up voices, and the feather moved on. Beach Boy looked skyward.

He could guess the thoughts of every man in the audience: if it was me up there, how would I take it? Tears? Pleas for mercy? Reasoned argument? A final mouthful of spit?

"Just like you, Valentine, trying to save a worthless little dicksicle like that," Sergeant Stock said out of the side of his mouth.

†

The rest of the ceremony was mostly a blur. He was enlisted to carry the glass box with Snake Arms's reptiles back to her trailer.

So, Graf Stockard knew his name. He must have seen a picture through Molly, or looked him up sometime or other at headquarters. Perhaps he'd even met him at some point or other before either of them knew Molly Carlson, and Stockard remembered and Valentine didn't. Much of his life before becoming a Wolf had a vague, dreamy feel to it these days.

Stockard had whispered a few words about speaking to him in private. He'd used the word escape, at least Valentine thought so. The din of the Warmoon Festival as the sacrifices were offered to a successful summer of battle made the word difficult to pick out.

"Warmoon Festival's going to last for five days. I think they'll cut you off before then. My fertile period this month's almost over."

"Have they tried to breed you before?" Valentine said, slowly, as though thinking over every word.

"I'll let you in on a secret, my lash-worn prince. About half the guys here are bent as jackknives. It's kind of a haven for the rugged, outdoorsy ones."

"I don't understand."

"They don't like girls. They don't like them so much, fucking's about out of the question."

Valentine pretended to puzzle it over for a bit. "Ahhh," he finally said. "Men's men."

"Exactly."

She murmured something into her pillow about being like Dorothy, all the men she met were missing either heart, courage, or brain.

†

Valentine heard Snake Arms's door open and came into alarmed wakefulness. He sat up so quickly, he half-rolled her off the bed, where she was sleeping atop the sheet.

A flashlight shone in his face.

"Yeah, it's Scar all right," a man said.

The dazzling light made ghostly circles on his optic nerves and gave him an instant migraine.

"Whassat?" Snake Arms said.

"Baron wants to see ya, Champ."

This time it was four who escorted him, two from Snake Arms's trailer joining up with two more waiting outside. These men were neater and a good deal more alert than the Baron's usual human soldiers who supervised the labor gangs.

They let him dress completely and didn't put him in handcuffs, so perhaps the Baron was having some sort of private after-midnight celebration.

They brought him to a different part of the camp, in the wooded hills behind the church. They walked him on a pavement path big enough for a single truck up a hill and down into a hummock between two higher hills.

A glow of lights frosted the red oaks and maples. Valentine got the sense of some kind of compound. The planting of the trees did a good job of concealing it, but he suspected heavy fencing stretching off into the woods. It looked like someone had planted quick-growing, thorny trees of some sort along a double line of razor wire a few years back. The trees turned the wire into a messy tangle that was difficult to spot at night.

The ground flattened, and they came to a second line of fencing, nice-looking iron railing, gated at the trail. Valentine smelled dogs, but didn't see or hear them. His escort nodded to a sentry at a shelter and was waved in.

Valentine got his first look at the Baronial residence.

It looked like a hunting lodge or a small hotel set in the pretty wooded hills, with decorative rather than security lighting.

He passed under a threshold. The posts and lintels were covered with deep-burned Gray One markings, wedge-writing like cuneiform. Valentine recognized one for "victory" and one for "health."

The inside was just as rugged. Slabs of limestone and great, river-smoothed rocks in a sort of hunting-lodge meets prairie-style that the Gray Baron seemed to favor.

He was taken into an office-cum-game room. There was a pool table with a low electric light hanging just above it and a dartboard at one end, and a great semicircle of bookcases high enough that they needed a ladder with a desk in the middle at the other. A beautiful button-backed leather sofa sat near a massive stone fireplace, partly in the office, partly in the gaming area.

The books looked dusty and not in any sort of order. Valentine wondered if they were just for show.

"Welcome to my home, Scar, isn't it?" he said. Valentine nodded in reply. "Sorry to keep you up so late. I'm a night owl. Useless in the morning. Coffee?"

"Whiskey spirits?" Valentine asked.

"Not when I'm working," the Baron said. "Sit."

The woman he'd seen draped behind his chair shuffled papers.

"Chuckles here has three degrees," the Baron said. "You know what a degree is?"

"Hot," Valentine said, wondering if he looked wary enough.

"No, it's a piece of paper that says you know better than someone who's been in the field their whole life. But she makes everything I do look right on paper. Keeps the generals in Iowa happy. I don't imagine you know any Iowa generals, but they expect the paperwork correct. Murder all you like, just file it in triplicate."

The dark woman came out with a wooden tray. A little chrome-and-glass pot and some cups sat on it.

"Three degrees to serve coffee," the Baron said.

"And five technical certifications, plus security clearance," she said.

Valentine sipped the coffee. It was rich stuff, but he felt a slight lift that wouldn't be explained by caffeine as it warmed him. Probably a few drops of some KZ happy/alert mix favored by higher-level Quislings.

"Why did you speak up for Beach Boy?" the Baron asked.

"Knew him, room, gang same-same," Valentine said.

"That made you like him better? He's been a problem since he hit the recruitment office in Davenport. He's been here nine months. Never bothered to learn the first thing about military discipline. We tossed him into labor after his three months probation was up, figured he could serve out his term there, then let him muster out. But sleeping on the job—that's a death sentence, whether it's a sentry on duty, a rail switchman, or a guy with a shovel."

Valentine shrugged. The dark woman was staring at him. It made him uncomfortable.

"You're clearly tough, well-muscled, healthy. I'm impressed with your reflexes. I think you're a lot smarter than you're letting on. I'd like you in one of my service uniforms."

"Soldier—no good," Valentine said. "Fighting—dead quick."

"Let's drop this pidgin shit, shall we?" the Baron said. The dark-haired woman handed him a red paper folder. He unhooked a binding band.

"David Stuart Valentine. Born date unsure, probably in 2047, Boundary Waters region, Northern Minnesota. Father Lee Valentine, formerly of Southern Command, formerly of the United States Navy. Mother—well, that's a bit of a question mark, isn't it? Mother is suspected to be Helen St. Croix, much of her information isn't available to a mind of my level and capabilities, as the Kurian Order styles it. Recruited into Southern Command by guerilla fighters—"

He turned the open folder around. Valentine felt cold sweat running over him, started to nerve himself for a fight. There was nothing on the desk that might be used as a weapon. There was an old picture of him, eyes closed, looking beat up, both full face and profile. It must have been when he was captured in Nebraska by the Twisted Cross, after the bullet to the leg in the General's rail yards.

"You might say I inherited it from your old friend the General. My Groggies used to guard his trains, sometimes. Valentine, let's be civilized about this. We're just talking."

"When do the Reapers show themselves?" Valentine asked.

"Not giving away all my secrets, but yes, my bodyguard is nearby. There are other forces I'm a lot more worried about than you. I don't think you understand the nature of my power. I determine my own destiny. I'm better than those ring-holding rabbits on their estates in Iowa with their board meetings and balls and cotillions. Those precious, precious, *my precious* rings. The Kurians can take those back.

"No one, no one, can take my power away from me. I can lose it, through inattention, bad luck, bloody Christ, some Grog witch doctor might even declare me an evil spirit if he thinks the graybacks'll stand by him. Have you ever drawn a truly free breath?

"Out here, there's no law but what I say is the law. I say I want seven new wives brought in and three old ones carried out, hippety-hoppety it's done.

"Want to know the secret of my success?

"I employ oddballs. There are two kinds of oddballs in the world, those who are weird because they got nothing else going for them, and those who operate on a level where they just don't fit in seamlessly with something like those Kurian ant farms. I'll take both kinds and watch 'em for a bit, just to see if I'm mistaken about which group they belong to. But I can find a place for either.

"I'm not asking you to join my team, Valentine. I'd like you as an ally, with that crew that's about to get kicked out of Kentucky. I know you're more open than most Southern Command military ticks to working with Grogs. I could arrange for you to take back Saint Louis. Think of all the human captives you'd free. You'd be the biggest liberator since Lincoln. All I'd ask in return is your help taking out a few Kurian towers of my choosing. The Rings in Iowa are worried that they're about to get muscled, since they're the only east-west connection left north of the Gulf, unless you count that patchwork in Minnesota connected to the Pacific Northwest through Oregon."

"Mind if I take a nap while you finish jerking off? That couch looks a lot more comfortable than those kennels." Valentine had the odd feeling that he'd been called a bastard, if that word applied for the ridiculous circumstance of having one's own mother unknown. Of course he was the son of Helen St. Croix, he had her cheekbones, hair, and dusky skin. He wished he had her kindness, or the gently teasing way she kissed fingers and toes as she put him and his baby sister to sleep.

"Play the hard-ass, Valentine. I have some exciting news. There are several parties very, very interested in getting you back for a variety of reasons. Don't worry, they think you've been captured in Minnesota, trying to get back to your birthplace. I have a smaller contingent up there, too. Bids are pouring in. The Ordnance in Ohio, the Lich King in Seattle, assorted lordships and illustriousnesses from New Orleans plus the plain old Coastal Marines, and one fat old rug runner in Michigan who resents what happened to his glorious, God-favored Moondaggers."

"An embarrassment of bitches," Valentine said. "Don't tell me there's not some Twisted Cross colonel over in Nebraska or Kansas who doesn't want his pound of flesh too."

"My Golden Guard did too thorough a job on them, Valentine," the Gray Baron purred. "Before they had the good sense to come under my protective wing. There are some Twisted Cross in the Alps in Europe and the mountains of Asia Minor, I understand, but they have no special grievance and are muchly occupied with another tiresome Polish rebellion. No, I'm limiting myself to Kurians, I think. They have the most to offer, and will probably be the most creative in making use of human vermin. I don't believe in hell in the classical sense, of course, but the Kurians can keep you alive and screaming for what seems like an eternity. Several human lifetimes of torment might be in your future."

"I imagine there's an unless coming up."

"I can think of several. Unless you're clever enough to kill yourself before a down payment is arranged and delivery worked out. Unless you escape. You've done it before, so I'm considering welding you into your cell and putting napalm somewhere where it can be delivered into the cells in a hurry in case of a disturbance."

"Or unless I join you."

"That makes me into a video villain, and a not very imaginative one at that. I do wonder if it wouldn't be better to release you, at that. To my knowledge you've been involved in some very unlucky operations. Very unlucky indeed. Southern Command is much the worse for wear thanks to the David Valentines of its officer corps. Full of plots and plans ahead of them and lines of silent, shallow soldiers' graves behind."

Valentine yawned and sat. "Mind if I stretch out? I'm not as much of a night owl, even with some of your drugged coffee."

The Gray Baron shrugged. "I don't expect you to weep and crawl, but some recognition of the relative balance of power between us would be in order. Since I'm running a silent auction for your hide, I might not take the highest bidder and instead send you to whoever has the most vicious way of dealing with your brand of nuisance. You know, Valentine, when I risk something, I try and make sure it's a pawn or a bishop at most. That's why I lead Grogs. There are always more Grogs. That bright young lieutenant, Rand—how many more like him are in Southern Command? Or somebody like William Post—there's an active, intelligence man who'd be an asset to any headquarters. He's reading intelligence reports from his wheelchair these days, I believe."

Valentine put his feet on the elaborately knobbed armrest of the sofa. "You have my full attention. If you're going to offer an alternative to winding up in Seattle's rooftop aquarium, I'll be happy to hear it."

"Your name and abilities intrigue me, Valentine. You have some kind of understanding of Kurian Zone politics, I believe?"

"I don't keep up with the latest alliances and betrayals," Valentine said. "It's all I can do to stay current on *Noonside Passions*, and that has much prettier actors."

The Gray Baron smiled. "We can agree on that, Valentine. I've always had a bit of an obsession with that Barbara Diamate. Leggy and hippy, but it makes that Youth Vanguard Directing Executive uniform skirt look so much better during her walk and talks. Slit higher than regulation, of course, but that's television for you. I've asked for a publicity tour in Iowa, of course, but they're much too busy."

"We could have a Christmas Truce to watch it together, Baron."

"Back to business. I mean to say—I and the Iowans have certain enemies . . . Kurian enemies . . . who it would be expedient to be rid of, or at least see greatly weakened in power and influence. Now, I could provide you with information, possibly even a contact or two on the inside, and you and your barefoot little Kentucky band could, what's the phrase—*choke a bitch* for me."

"My troops aren't barefoot," Valentine said.

"Then perhaps someone's been feeding me bad intelligence. Since my sources are in Southern Command proper, I'd suggest keeping your own superiors more up-to-date."

Valentine needed to buy time. He said he would have to consider their conversation carefully, at leisure.

"Tell me one thing. What clued you in?"

"Something funny happened. After you spoke up for Beach Boy, Sergeant Stock here asked for Scar to be assigned to him for a day. Except he didn't call you Scar. Called you Valentine. I mentioned it to Chuckles here and she recognized the name and dug up your file."

†

They took him to a no-fooling jail car in a wired corner of the rail yard. It was well lit and noisy from the sound of work on the trains.

He reviewed the conversation. Whoever was feeding the Gray Baron intelligence wasn't doing a very good job of it. Or perhaps they were passing on misinformation.

Should have kept my fool mouth shut, Valentine thought. Well, he'd been playacting the laconic, insolent veteran and let it get away from him.

†

They let him stew behind bars for two days. Then, on the final night of the Warmoon Festival, they put him in irons again, under gunpoint from a pistol close, a shotgun at the door, and a rifle outside the bars.

"You got another fight on, buck," his guard said.

On the way to the headquarters, they saw that festivities had spilled out in front of the headquarters, where a throng of Gray Ones and some men were gathered around parked vehicles.

"Hey, the roamin' emporium's set up already," he said.

Valentine couldn't believe they'd arrived so quickly. He'd figured it would be another few days at least.

They were parked there, bold as brass in a line of thick-wheeled trucks in the vehicle loading lot between headquarters and the motor pool. Valentine recognized two of the trailers from near Brostoff's headquarters.

Frat rode on the hood of one, sitting cross-legged with yards of woven hair and necklaces of dog teeth and ear-reamers made out of shinbones. God knew where he accumulated the Grog trade goods, probably from some back room at Hobarth's Truckstart and Trading Post.

"Name's China Jack, they say," the guard said. "Sergeant Major Quince knows him from Kansas City."

Valentine wondered if this was some strange ability that went with Frat's background as a Kurian agent. As far as these men were concerned, he was somebody they knew from way back.

"I met him south of Omaha. Got a great pair of boots," the shotgun man said.

"Bought my kids a baseball and two gloves from him, couple years back, at Hannibal," the rifleman put in. "He's upgraded his vehicles since then. Used to be old truck frames pulled by horses."

Bee rode shotgun in the first truck, Chieftain in the second. Chieftain had toned down his look a great deal, and wore some greasy mechanic's overalls.

The third truck had ROOT BEER in giant black stencils on a white sheet. That had the largest crowd around it. Valentine almost smiled. The Baron's headquarters was in for a wild night.

Already, the Gray Ones were lining up to buy.

†

They brought him to the atrium. A temporary wire cage had been set up, the sort of thing used to keep dogs in, about eight feet high.

The Baron looked down on it from a balcony.

Again, it was mostly Gray Ones on the main floor, though in the smaller atrium there was a good deal of shoving and standing on flower beds and other interior decor of the old church to get a view. Men and Gray One elders were ringing the balcony.

The Grogs were unusually agitated, pushing each other and snarling. Some were idly digging daggers into the woodwork.

Luckily there were few women in the Baron's command. Valentine hoped Snake Arms wasn't dancing in the moonlight tonight.

They turned down the lights and some brighter spots were focused on the white floor in the cage. Valentine was led in. He saw Bee outside the cage, looking at him, fighting off paws reaching for her. She snapped her teeth at the more aggressive suitors.

Snake Arms came into the cage and began to unlock his shackles with a key. They must have figured she wouldn't kill him.

"We've arranged a special fight tonight," the Baron said. He saw a commotion next to him, caught a flash of one of the Baron's pet Reaper faces.

They threw a figure off the balcony. It pivoted neatly in fall, and landed on its feet.

Duvalier!

She had a bandage on her left hand and an ugly bruise on her chin, but otherwise looked healthy. Like Valentine, she was stripped to the waist. Unlike Valentine, she was armed, with a Kabar-style fighting knife.

"We caught one of Southern Command's finest sneaking around the woods in civilian clothes," the Baron said. "By rights, she can be shot as a spy. But we'll give her a fighting chance against our champion, here. Only one of these two will leave the cage alive, tonight. The other's head will go up on the ancient cross for Warmoon!"

"Sorry, Val," Duvalier said. "Whaddya suppose they'll do to us if we don't fight."

"That's easy. You all three die. Snake Arms, too," the Baron said.

Snake Arms flew to the cage's door, but a chain closed it. "No, this isn't part of the deal! I could be pregnant! You can't—"

"We'll fight, all right," Valentine said. "Bee, tell the Gray Ones what I'm saying. Speak my words!"

Bee nodded. She swung up to the top of the cage, standing balanced at the joints with one arm bracing herself, like King Kong atop the Empire State Building.

Valentine smiled at the hubbub. The Gray Ones were putting their heads together and muttering.

"I'll give you all a fight," Valentine said. "I've mated with a woman under the Chief's protection. I'm part of the Deathring Tribe now, and demand my rights."

He patted Snake Arms on the belly. He had no idea if she might be pregnant, nor had enough time passed for her to have an inkling either, he suspected, but the Grogs understood the gesture.

"Don't talk tribe to us, buck," one of the Iowans said. "This is a military organization, not some Grog's head hut."

"To you, perhaps," Valentine said. "I'm challenging the Chief's leadership." He switched to his poor Gray One dialect and repeated it. "Has he ever had to fight to win it or defend it?"

A few laughs broke out among the humans, but the Grogs began to go quiet. He spoke the words again, louder. Bee amplified them.

"When night stalkers come, does Chief protect? Does he give? Where are herds, where are wives? Deathring Tribe fight hard for no reward. Where are the wives?"

The excited Grogs digging their daggers into the woodwork and pawing at Bee looked up and began to bellow at the Gray Baron.

"You fucking idiot," his dark assistant he called "Chuckles" said in his ear.

"Honor much. Weapons taken and kept," the Baron said.

"Wives! Wives! Wives!" the Grogs chanted.

"Oh, screw that," the Gray Baron said, reaching for his shoulder holster. He pulled his pistol and fired at Valentine.

Valentine needed every iota of his hair-trigger reflexes to throw himself sideways and down out of the path of the bullet.

A hail of plates, bones, and bottles rained on the Gray Baron and his officers. *One of the Chief's clan had issued a challenge all could understand, and the Chief had neither pacified the malcontent nor met him in fair fight! No wonder his teeth had turned black and lies came from his mouth.*

The cage suddenly collapsed. Grogs pushed, prodded, and poked Valentine. It felt uncomfortably like the way he'd seen an old Wolf cook testing hung meat. Were they planning a mixed buffet barbecue?

A massive shape loomed over him, blotting out the light.

"Dvfud," it mouthed.

Bee!

She reared up on her hind legs and shoved the Gray Ones apart. Valentine basked in the air and space that two muscular arms the length of a good road bike could provide.

Bee put her back to him and began to talk, loudly and quickly. To Valentine, Grog speech always sounded like old boards being pulled apart and melon-sized rocks being tossed into a pond.

Then Ahn-Kha was beside him. A hairy arm wrapped about his chest, took him carefully under the armpit, and lifted him clear of the mass of Grogs.

Valentine ignored Ahn-Kha's rescue, mesmerized by the sight of Bee. Usually she remained quietly at heel, like a companionable older dog who simply enjoyed watching events rather than creating them. This new version of Bee might be mistaken for Snake Arms doing her dance. She talked with mouth, arms, fingers, and foot stomps, half dance and half speech.

"What's Bee saying? Or is it just a protective display?"

"Her dialect is a little difficult to follow, my David, but in general, she's saying that you put the moon in the sky. This is the first I've heard of you rescuing her from a circus."

"I didn't know warrior Grogs listened to females."

"They do. Bee's at a respectable age, where she becomes—the human word would be 'Auntie.' That is an important title."

"Auntie Bee?" Valentine said. His head was swimming. "Why does that sound familiar?"

"You don't speak much of your family. I am not sure. My David, did you intend for Gray Ones to come to Kentucky as well?"

"No, only your people."

"Well, I don't think Bee fully understands your plans. She is talking up the place in the manner of a—what is that title?—real estate salesman."

Yips and hoots broke out among the Grogs.

"What excites them?"

"She's talking about how many legworms there are, and that the humans are friendly and welcoming to Grogs."

Valentine looked at the Gray Ones. They were spellbound. Or perhaps still under the influence of the Kurian aphrodisiacs. Bee had them riveted as she spoke to the ring, turning every moment or two on one vast forearm to face a different part of the audience.

The hundreds of Grogs broke out of their circle, forming groups, calling, pushing, pulling, and cajoling. Others loped off in a four-legged run to acquire friends and relatives for the scrum.

"I think a new Grog tribe is being formed, my David."

"Would your people mind having them along, or does it mean interspecies warfare?"

"We look on the Gray Ones as rustics. Some we find charming and congenial, others—not so. As long as they are not highhanded. Some of the habits of the Gray Baron's army will have to be changed."

†

The camp was in chaos. Gray Ones were chasing the few available females. "Chuckles" was missing. Valentine hoped for her sake she'd made it out unmolested. But Gray Ones had been known to make do with human females and other livestock, when desperate . . .

They'd patched up Valentine as best they could without a surgeon. He'd heal, if he could just eat and drink enough. He still felt light-headed, but he had to help bring order to the camp. The Golden Ones were freed, by Valentine's word as new Stronghold Chieftain, and he'd promised Danger Close that once everyone who wanted to leave did, the headquarters would be his.

But first, he wanted to give the Baron the same chance he'd been given. Now it was his turn to feel the weight of shackles and uncertainty about the future.

"Okay, what happened?" the Baron asked. "How did you turn my army into a Spring Break party?"

Bee had told him that the threat to Snake Arms had also motivated them. She was strong juju, in charge of the spirits who'd died in the Baron's service.

"The Root Beer," Valentine said. "We dumped a case of Kurian aphrodisiacs in it. We weren't sure of the pharmacological effects. By the books, by my beliefs, you're my enemy. I don't feel it in my guts, however. My gut tells me you're a friend."

"A friend?" the Gray Baron said. "Give me a knife, and I'll spill your guts and have a look, see what the problem is."

"I've taken a bullet from you. I wouldn't want to return the experience."

"One thing I know about the Kurians. They're not a forgive-and-forget race. They'll suck the life out of their own mother as soon as she reverts back to being a father, if the parent's dumb enough to let them. I've sent as many of your forces in the field as I can get in touch with off to the west. It's full spring now, and the Grogs in the Missouri Valley will be feeling their oats. How soon before they head north to make a warrior's name for themselves?"

"The way I see it, you have three options. First, I can leave you behind to explain things as best as you can to the Iowans. Second, I can take you prisoner and drop you off with Southern Command. I'll assume they have nothing on you, other than you being a high-ranking Quisling, which will probably mean you'll get a few more appeals before they shoot you. Third, you can come with me."

"Ha!"

"You told me once you liked the taste of real freedom. I don't think you know the meaning of the word. I'm part of a sort of ex-perimental formation that gives Quislings a second chance, if they want it. You choose a new name, swear under it, and serve six years. You can serve more if you want a chance at a pension or a land grant, later. You're a good leader. You'd probably even still be in command of some of your same Grogs. We sure could use a man like you."

"I'm no turncoat. So there's honor involved. You talk about land allotments? Like some patch of Texas scrub can compare with what the Kurians give?"

"What do they give, really?"

"Eternal life. Not some mystical Jesus hoo-ha, either. Life you can see and touch. The churchmen said that if I can pacify Missouri, they'll get me a brass ring and the power to extend my life as long as I like."

"Feeding on your fellow men?"

"There are other ways. No shortage of pigs and dogs. Pigs are more emotionally developed than we think. I met one of their archons, Japanese and Korean guy; he was born in the 1920s and he lives off pigs."

"You think that offer is still open? Suppose I order a couple companies of your Grogs to go burn some towns in Iowa."

"Their officers know better. They'd march right back here to see what was wrong."

"Well, either way, you're coming with us. When we get back to the bootheel country, I'll let you make up your mind—a Southern Command military prison or freedom in Kentucky."

"Bootheel country's a long way off. That's a tough march with all these Grogs."

"We'll manage."

"Now you're the one jerking off, Valentine. You think everyone's just going to settle down, happy? A couple of lambs will go missing, and there'll be bloodshed, and somebody's going to get their head chopped off. Then it's all-out tribal warfare. Just wait and see. You want to build something that'll last, I'd suggest a permanent hierarchy. Humans on top, then the Golden, then the Gray. That's what I was working toward."

"You left out the Kurians."

"I said working toward, Valentine. Till you screwed everything up."

†

Valentine left the Baron in an evil mood matching his own.

"I have a message for you, sir," the Wolf said. "Repeat from Colonel Lambert at Field HQ."

Valentine read the block pencil letters. The coms tech had lined out the code phrases beginning and ending the message that acted as filler to make decryption more difficult.

BROWN BEAR BROWN BEAR WHAT DO YOU SEE. GENERAL HEADQUARTERS TO SENG/ LAMBERT THROUGH EASTERN OPERATIONS. PERMISSION FOR GG TRANSPORT AND SUPPLY DENIED. PRESENCE OF NONHUMAN FORCES CONSIDERED DANGEROUS AND PROBLEM- ATIC FOR CIVILIAN MORALE. RIVERINE ELE- MENTS WILL PROVIDE LIMITED SUPPORT FOR TRANSFER TO KENTUCKY. CONGRATULA- TIONS ON ACTION IN N. MISSOURI—SIGNED MARTINEZ FOR HE'S A JOLLY GOOD FELLOW WHICH NOBODY DARE DENY.

Valentine wondered if the scrambler chatter at the end was a simple mistake or the headquarters code clerk sending his own secret message.

Anger throbbed, tightening his chest. The general had

done it to him again. *That bastard. Maybe he knows I'm involved, somehow.*

"Well, my David?" Ahn-Kha asked.

"We can't land in the Ozark Free Territory," Valentine said.

"Odd that they'd be so nervous about it. Chances of more than a few civilians seeing them are slim, there's not much civilian presence near the river in the bootheel country."

"We must still go ahead. My people's dice are cast. They are trapped between enemies."

CHAPTER ELEVEN

*T*he *Grog Express: The Gray Baron's rail line describes the chord of his defensive arc running from the Mississippi River to the Missouri south of Omaha.*

It is an unusual railroad, in that it connects no cities, Kurian Zones, or resources. Much of it did not exist before 2022; it's purely an invention of military necessity. The Gray Baron wanted a fast way to link his vast operational area and defend it with a comparatively small force. The answer was mobility.

The Iowa Guard believed it couldn't be done—a rail line largely built and worked by Grogs. The Gray Baron, with a few hired engineering guns and a lot of backbreaking labor, proved them wrong. With it, legworms even pull loads, drawing laden flatbeds in the manner of horses hauling barges on a nineteenth-century canal.

The Grog Express runs two kinds of trains. Fast diesel locomotives pull the battle trains, designed to shift artillery from one point to the next with his best-trained Grog and human elites. Slower-moving supply trains shift his companies of fighting Grogs, legworms, and the wounded and injured and supplies for other formations.

The Grog Express is fed through two supporting lines. One runs

up into Iowa, the other to the Mississippi River, where it ends near the
riverside wharf of a little town called—nowadays—Grog Point.

†

David Valentine watched the progress in the rail yard with something like satisfaction.

The day promised another thunderstorm. High white mushrooms above, a griddle of blue steel flat as the prairie beneath.

The Baron's Stronghold had a small but functional yard, communicating with his personal line and running back up to Iowa. The first order of business was to send Chieftain and a few Golden Ones a dozen miles up the line and tear up track, to prevent a surprise attack.

Unlike their Gray cousins, who had a Byzantine tribal network, Golden One families organized themselves generationally, making organization of the flight somewhat easier. Postpubescent males and females each formed a "circle" as Ahn-Kha translated it, then newly mateds, then females with the unborn, then families with young unable to survive without their parents help, then families with older offspring, then those who had lost one or the other mate, then senior males and females, and finally the truly elderly who needed the care of a younger generation. Each such "circle" had leaders and adjudicators who found help and settled disputes and spoke for their circle, more or less. The circles called on other circles for help, ancient "links"—such as widows and widowers naturally supervising the unmated youths, pregnant females seeking help from the senior females, unmated youth looking after the elderly . . .

Little of it was codified; it seemed to be a tradition with the Golden Ones.

"What happens if a newly pubescent male doesn't feel like making sure one of the toothless elderly's food is properly mashed?" Valentine asked.

Ahn-Kha's ears went back. "Very little, as long as there isn't thievery or brutality of any sort. Just talk. But if such a link breaker should ever need assistance themselves, they may have difficulty finding it outside blood relations."

Graf Stockard had made himself useful as a sort of sergeant major in the confusion. He assembled the Baron's men under guard of a couple of armored cars and Valentine made the usual offers to take volunteers. The others would be locked up, packed into the old forced-labor holds and secure warehouses to be turned over to whichever of the Baron's forces or Iowa Guard reclaimed the camp. Valentine had more than enough to do without a few hundred extra prisoners to take care of. It wasn't quite lawful, but it would have to do.

Somehow, the difficulties of organizing the move sorted themselves out among the Golden One circles. Valentine and his team stayed furiously busy answering questions, often in mime for not one in ten Golden Ones even knew a few words of English. They wanted to know about weapons, about the trains, about canned heat and water purification, about tentage and cordage . . .

The scattering of humans and masses of Golden Ones were slowly coming together as a team. Nothing like breaking a good sweat together in the outdoors to start an alliance.

They were such gentle giants, too. They reminded Valentine of horses, very careful of how they placed their feet and shy to the touch. As he explained coupling and uncoupling railcars and the attendant safety chains, a pair of juveniles, easily the size of a smallish man, held a plate of mashed heartroot and a pitcher of instant lemonade, ready to give arificially-flavored-and-sweeetened refreshment.

Whatever last doubts Valentine had buried in the recesses of his mind about the Grogs' ability to adapt to Kentucky were dispelled. The Kentuckians like those in the Gunslinger Clan would welcome such neighbors. Well, probably.

It occurred to Valentine that it would have been a good deal easier to simply relocate the Kentucky Legion to Northern Missouri than move the Golden One population to the more hospitable Kentucky soil. But the idea of abandoning Evansville and the Army of Kentucky . . .

He wondered if the same doubts had plagued his father at the birth of the Ozark Free Territory.

†

They were able to organize two trains, plus a small third flatbed worked by powerful Grog muscles like a giant handcart. The first was full of warriors and had the fastest engine. Valentine and Ahn-Kha briefly considered attaching the armored battle cars and filling them with warriors, but the weight would slow the train. They elected to have it look more like a fast-moving troop train, with the warriors crammed into boxcars and a single armored caboose bristling with machine guns. A twin 40mm cannon on a crated-and-sandbagged flatbed was pushed by the engine.

Only one of the Baron's patrols came in during the process, and they were taken prisoner by armed Golden Ones before they comprehended the changes to the fortress. Thanks to the Warmoon Festival, there had been only a few patrols out. Every Gray One wanted to take his part in the rites to enhance his chances in the coming season.

Ahn-Kha thought it best if the experienced Golden One fighters stayed with their people and the "Express" was stuffed with Gray One warriors. The Golden Ones would be at ease with their families and the familiar command structure of their elders around.

The Golden Ones' commander-in-chief was a meaty, shrapnel-scarred veteran named Wu-Dkho—no human could say his name on the first try. Valentine thought of him as "Napoleon." He was a little shorter than most of the Golden Ones, and he wore a heavy, pocket-lined coat with his chin tucked into his chest in a manner that made Valentine think of a painting he'd seen of Napoleon retreating from Moscow. Ahn-Kha explained that his stance was a little intimidating to most Golden Ones—to them that body language was more Gray One than Golden, indicating an angry bull-Grog ready to head-butt.

Valentine made contact with *Cottonmouth* and told them *Buffalo* would be on the move. He hoped to cover the forty air miles with his advanced elements overnight, and have the rest of the Golden Ones to Muddy Landing in three days.

"Muddy Landing," Captain Coalfield's voice crackled back. Valentine couldn't tell if there was relief in his voice. "Seventy-two hours."

"From dusk tonight," Valentine said.

They held a final meeting in the command caboose of the fast train. A chalkboard with a tracing of the eastern spur of the Grog Express was filled with the latest information about the expected schedule and the distribution of the population and soldiers between the trains.

On a sideboard, the Gray Baron's expensive array of ports and whiskeys had been cleared away and replaced with heartroot, nuts, and strawberries, plus the inevitable instant lemonade common to every Kurian Order organization Valentine had ever visited.

Old sweat clung inside his uniform. He wanted a shower, badly, but a sponge and a basin would have to do, and even that could wait until the Express was moving.

Duvalier stood in front of the chalkboard, looking like a small mannequin displaying the wrong-sized coat, examining the time-tables with her arms crossed.

"Forty miles in three days with this bunch is pushing it," she said. "We'll be crawling at foot pace."

Frat was there, along with a human engineer who wanted out at Saint Louis, Ahn-Kha and a messenger Golden One, Duvalier, Stockard, and Pellwell, the last because she and her ratbits were already designated to ride in the command car.

"Who cares if we're slower than shit," Frat said. "With those big bastards properly armed, nobody's going to mess with us, at least nobody who can concentrate in time."

"We'll move in shifts," Valentine said. "Apart from those riding full-time, we'll stop every three hours to let a few hundred rest."

"A drop in the bucket when you're talking about ten thousand—," Duvalier said.

"Nine thousand two hundred and seven, though we might see

a birth very soon," Ahn-Kha corrected. "With enough water it can be done. Water is the key."

Which led to a technical discussion about the conversion of a pair of ten-thousand-gallon diesel tank cars to carry water.

Pregnant females, mothers of infants would ride in some comfort in the barracks cars.

"One problem remains," Valentine said. "Already, there are probably phones ringing in various Iowa headquarters about the silence from Gray Stronghold. If we could keep up some radio chatter, the usual business traffic between here and Iowa . . . I wouldn't want to be in the coms bunker when the next Grog patrol comes in, under the Baron's officers."

"I'll do it, sir," Stockard said. "I've been trained on coms procedure."

"Thought you wanted to come with us, Captain? Get back to your son?"

"Yes. Very much. But having someone staying back, manning the radio will increase your chances that much more. They know my voice in Iowa. I've pulled my share of shifts in the com bunker."

"As long as you don't flip back to the Iowa side," Duvalier said. "A guy could win a brass ring, letting them know what happened and where we're headed. Once a Quisling—"

"Enough of that," Valentine said.

"You're too quick to judge," Frat said, glaring.

"I've been my own judge, jury, and executioner out there often enough," Duvalier said. "I don't trust. That's why I'm still around."

"Time is fleeing," Ahn-Kha said. "Perhaps we can bicker once we are on the waters of the Mississippi."

Valentine was tempted to ask Duvalier if she'd stay. Of all of them, she could be relied on to press, but not extend her luck. She knew Missouri well, and could either make a fast break for the Mississippi, get to Saint Louis, or take the short route back to the Wolves in the hills to the south and then make her way back to Kentucky at leisure.

Provided her health held up. She'd been limping, and her stomach wasn't keeping much down.

Then again, she didn't know radio procedure, and there were few women in the Gray Baron's command. Best to leave it to an experienced hand. But Valentine still wanted to give Stockard an out.

Valentine reached for a handful of nuts. His stomach was gurgling and suspiciously unhungry. "Nothing has to go down on paper about the circumstances of you rejoining Southern Command, Graf," he said. "On the report you'll be just another prisoner of the Grogs who was brought out with the Golden Ones."

"My son thinks his father's a hero," Stockard said. "If I make it back to him, I'd like to do it being able to call myself that as well. I'll stay. Leave me a bicycle?"

"Frat, scare him up some transport and fuel. Double- and triple-check it."

"No, a bike's fine," Stockard said. "I was in the bike troops in the Guard, back in the day. I still do it for exercise. Motors get noticed by our Gray friends on both sides of the Missouri River."

Ahn-Kha leaned over and whispered something in Stockard's ear. His homely face took on a shy smile.

"I'll stay as well. Two can travel more safely than one," Frat said, trying various field jackets of the Baron's troops. "I took a good look at your prisoner and heard a few words from him. Short of one of them showing up in person, I should be able to confuse the issue for those wandering into camp." He pulled a slouch hat on low and stared into Valentine's eyes. For just a second, he shimmered and Valentine saw the Baron's eyes and Pancho Villa mustache.

"Neat trick," Valentine said. "Teach me, sometime, when you get back."

"I would, if I only knew how I did it," Frat said.

†

By nightfall they were loading the trains with the riders. Supplies, weapons, and ammunition were distributed among the cars.

Valentine put the Baron in the first train. There were several grim, barred cars designed for transporting captives. Only one showed any sign of recent use, the rest were badly rusted. The Kurians were all too used to shuttling bodies around on rails in their aura-based economy, where humans served as currency.

It looked biblical, like something out of Exodus. The Grog elders organized their march so all the herders were on the outskirts, the craftspeople and food makers in the center, the very old, sick, pregnant, and very young on the train with their doctors and attendants, and the youths expending their energy running messages between the groupings.

Valentine wondered if Moses organized the Exodus with a headache and a mild case of cramps.

He suspected he picked up a nasty amoeba in the food or water. Both the Golden Ones and Gray Ones had good toilet habits—they dug shallow pits and buried, like cats—but their hand washing left much to be desired and the tufts of thicker hair at the knee and ankle joints would get befouled.

Had he been feeling better, he would have taken the scout glider up and tried the Missouri air. There was a fresh spring breeze the wide, nearly weightless wings could ride.

It was a fascinating device occupying its own flatbed on the command train. When the train was up to full speed, the glider could be launched into the wind at the end of a tether, rather like a kite, and rise and rise in altitude where a tiny ultra-lightweight electric motor could be turned on or off for extra power. The sailplane could easily scout for an hour or two then return to the train for recovery.

Valentine had done a good many hours while learning to fly with Pyp's Flying Circus in the Southwest, where gliders were towed to an appropriate altitude by a larger plane so new pilots could be trained without risking a precious aircraft.

Well, it would be dangerous to fly at night, or, more accurately, land at night.

At last the Express pulled out, with Valentine giving himself a sponge bath in the caboose and grateful for the built-in toilet.

The company of Gray Ones, the new Headring Clan, whined for action like hounds waiting to be shipped. Valentine did not know if they enjoyed fighting or were eager to prove themselves to their new master, but as the Express pulled out they hooted and yowled out their eagerness for action.

Bee, always eager to be of use, ululated her excitement with the rest.

"Rest now. Eat now. Fight later," Valentine told them as the train lurched into motion behind the armored diesels.

†

Everything depended on seizing control of the two strongpoints between the Baron's monuments and the Mississippi. There was a third strongpoint at the terminus on the river, occupied jointly by the Grogs and the Iowa Guard.

The strategic plan reminded Valentine, far too closely for comfort, of an allied disaster from the Second World War.

Valentine had studied the Market Garden—called by some of the soldiers "Hell's Highway"—operation at the War College. The plan, unfortunately, resembled his own in that everything depended on maintaining control of the rail line and seizing the strongpoints, rather than bridges, along the line.

The Allied Forces had managed to take the first fairly easily, had a bitter fight for the second, and never made it to the third, where the British Paratroopers lost eighty percent of their forces by the time their withdrawal was completed.

Valentine would have to do much the same thing, only without benefit of paratroops.

One predictable, but unplanned for, consequence of the Train March amused Valentine as mile after mile of train track twisted and burned behind his rear guard. With the Gray Baron's army decapitated and divided, every tribal chief called on his cousins to hurry and raid into the rich Iowa estates before control of Northern Missouri could be reestablished.

Valentine would sit and listen on the Iowa Guard shortwave channel and the AM stations in the larger cities, sending out muster orders for emergency home-county defenses.

Valentine stopped the car twice to run assault debarkation drills, once with unloaded weapons and then again with bullets in their guns.

When he was satisfied with the performance, he let the Grogs have the fun of knocking some cans off sticks with their weapons on fully automatic.

"The Baron didn't trust Groggies with full auto. Too much ammo for too few hits."

"Are you always this cool and collected?" Pellwell asked.

"How do you mean?"

"Bullets flying, Grogs running everywhere, and you're in the toilet shaving."

"I thought I should make an appearance," Valentine said.

Word passed around. Valentine heard two Wolves muttering to each other that he'd been so confident of victory he'd stepped into the bathroom so he could change his shirt and shave in order to tour the scene.

†

The second strongpoint was found abandoned. A halfhearted attempt to blow up the tracks had been attempted, but the railroad-working Grogs knew their business. An entire train car was devoted to railroad equipment, and they simply took rails and ties from a siding and transferred them to the main line.

They found a looted warehouse with a pair of fresh Grog cairns behind.

"Looks like word is spreading, my David," Ahn-Kha said. "I think those are Missouri Valley clans."

†

They found Grog Point defended, but not by Grogs. A hasty line of defenses was drawn up in a hummock between two hills that might charitably be called a pass, but it was hardly Thermopylae.

They backed the train out of sight and Valentine dropped out of the armed flatbed, field glasses in hand to take a closer look.

Valentine could make out red caps among the hastily constructed head logs and machine gun positions.

He deployed his Grogs and set up the light artillery. He sent a screening force forward to probe, with instructions to fight, then return and report what kind of troops they faced. His real infantry strength he kept back with the train and guns.

Pellwell tried to convince him to wait and let her ratbits explore the lines—they could get an exact count of men and machine guns—but Valentine wanted to probe and attack before they could be reinforced. They were so close to the Mississippi they could practically smell it, and the flotilla was waiting downriver for him to radio that the town had been cleared.

Firing broke out all along the line of fortifications. Sustained, panicky firing.

His probe pulled back as though they'd touched an unexpected flame, without firing. No need to reveal positions to the wildly firing machine guns. A grenade detonated somewhere in the middle and Valentine saw a rabbit run for the hills.

High-pitched cheering broke out along the defensive line. They went up and over their fortifications, some calling the others forward, others waving them back. They had camouflage ponchos, so oversized they looked like caftans, pulled over black uniforms.

"They're advancing?"

"Send the Grogs forward. Bring the train up for cannon support," Valentine told Chieftain.

Chieftain was getting along like a house aflame with the Grog Warriors. He pushed and shoved, showed his blades to get the toughs to back down, and head-butted others to laugh off a mistake.

The main force of Grogs went forward and a few confused seconds of shooting broke out. The ponchos didn't retreat, they ran. The armored train came forward and the cannons opened up on the fortifications. Explosions and black plumes rose from the machine gun positions.

They went forward cautiously. There were still a few sporadic shots from the head logs, but careful Gray One fire silenced the snipers.

They advanced into horror. They'd been fighting children, in neat, unblemished black school uniforms and red kepis. They lay in windrows, a fragile, fallen fence.

"Poor kids," the Wolf communications tech said.

Chieftain took the hat off one, ran a gentle hand through a boy's sun-white hair. "We just killed the local choir," Chieftain said.

There were a few disarmingly sweet, freckled female faces among the dead.

"What the hell are those?"

"Now what was the point of that?"

"Who are they?" Pellwell asked.

"Youth Vanguard. Jesus."

Two had survived their wounds. They were all nine- to fourteen-year-olds, the next generation out of the Ringwinners and Quislings in Iowa, proving their worth to the Kurian Order.

"Patch 'em up and take them along," Valentine said, taking his youngest POWs, ever.

†

Grog Point was theirs.

Valentine learned from the wounded that a military school in southeastern Iowa had turned out, and been rushed to Grog Point to keep order. They were supposed to be joined by Illinois troops and some artillery coming across the river, but the Illinois men never showed up. The school had either been sacrificed uselessly with lies, in the hope that they'd hold long enough for men to come down-river, or been caught up in a Kurian Zone double cross between rival Iowa and Illinois factions.

It took all the sweetness out of seeing the rest of his charges arrive and start to board the river barges. Valentine spent the next thirty-six hours with a bilious taste in his mouth, working like a fury to get the population organized and into the boats.

They'd put together quite a river fleet. Three huge, multibarge tugs under Captain Mantilla protected by six armed craft, plus the firefighting tug rigged out with a few guns, to do double duty as a close-in armed boat and emergency tug, if the need arose. The flotilla was under overall command of Captain Coalfield, a veteran Mosquito Fleet boatman whom Mantilla tempted out of retirement with the prospect of the biggest riverine operation Southern Command had ever launched.

Valentine was astonished to see Gray Ones taking precedence over the Golden Ones in space in the barges, tentage, and bedding. They even ate and drank first.

"None understand the Golden Ones," Ahn-Kha said. "We are peaceful looking—even our sports and games have none of the knockabout, violent energy of human and Gray Ones contests. We don't roar out our accomplishments in battle. When the hot blood comes, it comes fast and hard and fades again, like a flash flood."

Still, the Gray Ones weren't behaving as he would have liked. Clearly, he'd gotten the outcasts, all but the most ambitious or the outcasts had stayed with Danger Close. He'd try the Baron again, in the hopes that he'd take charge of the lot.

†

The Baron smelled. He hadn't shaved or washed himself.

"We're getting on the boats, Baron," Valentine said. "Nice easy trip on the water. You might avail yourself of it.

"A few days ago—was that all it was?—you told me you thought I had potential," Valentine said. "I see the same in you. I could use a man like you in Kentucky.

"What is your real name, anyway?"

"Ricard Anthony Alido, but my father's last name was Mairpault, of the Ithaca Mairpaults."

"I take it the Mairpaults were important," Valentine said.

"My father's brother chaired the Council of Archons for North America. Church politics. I was an embarrassment, so they sent me to a military college in Wisconsin. Always wanted a title, the Maripaults were always dropping titles like trump cards in bridge. Bridge is very popular with the churchmen. They sip their white tea and play bridge and eat sandwiches made of cucumbers and bread that's mostly air."

"I could use a good officer for these Gray Ones. Pick any or all of those names, and swear under it. From then on out, you're a new man. Like the Baptists pulling you out of a river."

"I told you I don't think too much of your definition of freedom. I was scratching-poor at the school and didn't care for it."

"Better than a POW camp in Arkansas."

"You'd hand me over to Southern Command's inquisitors? I've heard some funny things about you, too. Would your record survive that close a look?"

Valentine looked him in the eye. "No." He reached into his pocket and took out a key, knelt and undid the leg irons, unthreaded the chain to the wrist restraints, then undid those.

Quick as one of Snake Arms's serpents, he whipped the chain around Valentine's throat. Valentine felt a hand fumbling for his holstered gun.

Valentine let him get it. The gun came out of the holster and the Baron released the chain around his throat and backpedaled.

"Now you're—fuck!" the Baron said, fumbling with the plastic trigger lock Valentine had put on it. Quite an ordinary precaution before entering a prisoner's cell with a firearm.

Valentine drove a solid chain-wrapped right into the Baron's jaw, followed it with a roundhouse left. The gun fell, and Valentine kicked it back behind him.

"Can we stop this nonsense?" Valentine said, rubbing his chafed throat under his chin.

He quieted the soldiers calling from outside. "Stand down, we're fine in here. Coffee!"

They shared a cup—coffee was almost always decent near the river where traders and smuggling boats could come and go at will.

"We're boarding the barges. Next stop is Southern Command," Valentine said. Technically, the next stop would be Saint Louis, but no point revealing too much. He grabbed a small rucksack from one of the men standing guard on the car.

As they walked along the ticking, waiting train, Valentine took an extra step away from the Baron and removed the trigger lock from his pistol.

"Kind of you, Valentine," the Baron said. "I'd prefer the back of the head, if you'd oblige."

Valentine said nothing, but nodded to the man on the scout-plane car.

"Won't be the first ragged-ass general to wind up shot in a ditch. I'm in distinguished company."

"Not my style, Baron. We're saying good-bye now, but not the way you think."

He climbed up onto the flatbed with the glider. It sat on a little platform with a heavy spring. A line was attached just behind the landing wheel tucked into the bulbous canopy.

"You checked out on this thing?"

"I practically invented it," the Baron said, testing the air with a wetted finger. "We used to screw around with these as cadets in the kettles of Wisconsin. Just tell the engineers that in this light wind we've got to be doing over forty, or I might end up in the treetops."

Valentine tossed a gun belt containing one of the engineer's .357

revolvers into the Baron's lap and followed it with a box of shells. "There's a survival kit and dried food and water under your seat."

He gave a wave of the arm, and the engineer put the train in motion, taking it back to Missouri, or at least a siding where it would be derailed and have the driving wheels blown off.

Valentine watched the train pick up speed. The train had shrunk to the size of a dime held at arm's length when he saw the winged dot rise perfectly. It altered course to better catch the light wind and rose.

He felt a little jealous.

After turning a few lazy circles, the glider turned and headed back for its launching platform. For a brief moment, Valentine feared the Baron would end his flight in a suicidal crash dive into the engine, but he simply swooped low over the train to land in the clear of the siding.

The glider came to rest in the crackling rush of grasses passing under its smooth, glossy belly.

Valentine hurried to the cockpit, but the Gray Baron was already climbing out

"You called my bluff, Valentine. Always had this weird feeling we were going to end up working together, from the first I laid eyes on you."

He handed Valentine the gun belt. "I appreciate the gesture of letting me go, though I'm guessing you know I couldn't go back to the KZ, and scratching a living in the sticks isn't my style. Truth is, I love commanding those big brave bastards, and if there aren't perks that go with the job already, I'll earn some. How do I swear into this chicken run you call an army, anyway?"

CHAPTER TWELVE

The East Bank, May: Across the river from Saint Louis lies a collection of settlements known as the Tangle.

It's watched over by a lone Kurian tower, a growth on what had been a bank building in East Saint Louis. The Kurian there is an odd one—weak, reclusive, and of little import to the scoundrels and smugglers across the river from the Grog metropolis. He has but a Reaper or two, rarely glimpsed, no police force, only a few toughs with well-maintained armored cars to shuttle his mouthpieces and churchmen about. Southern Command's intelligence service, insofar as they think about him at all, believe "Eastie" is some fallen Kurian exiled to a disputed area chiefly to keep his eye upon the Grogs across the river and maintain some manner of relations with them.

Which is just as well. East Saint Louis marks the farthest north Southern Command's "Skeeter Fleet" will operate, facilitating the activities of Logistics Commandos buying, begging, borrowing, or stealing items from the industrial centers around the Great Lakes. They have been known to tie up in Eastie's domain and deal with the shifty traders found on the Illinois side of the Mississippi riverbank.

When the barges full of well-armed Golden Ones, plus the new-

found Headring Clan of Gray Grogs, tied up their barges under the shelter of the east half of the old McKinley bridge and occupied an old, gap-roofed warehouse near the river, there was not a great deal Eastie could do about it.

As it turned out, he did, however, report to the rest of the Kurian Order the mysterious flotilla of barges and their odd occupants.

†

Night still flowed down the Mississippi. The wind died at midnight and the air filled with mosquitoes and other night fliers, clustering around *Number One*'s running lights.

Bats, drawn by the mosquitoes, ventured far out into the river. Valentine, watching the hazy moon through the moist night air, imagined he could hear their cries as they echolocated.

Eating distance, even in the frustratingly zigzagging manner of this great intestinal river, gave him a sense of satisfaction. Watching the riverbanks slip by without the effort of crashing through brush and bramble, with food and water a couple of steps away and a blanket and pillow that would allow him to both sleep and cover mileage brought back memories of the old *Thunderbolt* and its endless coastline patrols. Back then he'd marveled at the ease of water travel as well.

Even the deceptively empty banks of the river comforted. The river, running near wild here, had pushed all but transient fishers, trappers, and the river traffic back. Of course, the occasional shed showed so many bullet holes from River Patrol machine guns it looked as though the spots were part of a paint job.

Thumps, calls, clanks, and hammering noises from the barges travelled across the gentle river water.

"What are them Groggies up to?" an idling River Rat wondered.

"Making themselves bunks, I expect," his mate on watch said, watching the barges with the boat's sole pair of binoculars. Their strap had its own flotation strip, and someone had added some extra rubber cushioning to the housing. Optics were hard to replace.

The convoy travelled in two parts. *Cottonmouth* were the boats exploring where the barges were heading. *Exodus* were the barges themselves, with the support of the armored firefighting tug. Then *Rattler* covered the convoy from upriver, a mere two boats and the slowest ones adapted for riverine fighting.

Valentine was tempted to ask for the glasses, but he was nothing more than a glorified passenger in *Number One*. Besides, if he was feeling too relaxed and lazy to dig around in his dunnage for his own glasses, it couldn't be that important.

He decided to make conversation. His mind kept drifting to Snake Arms, and those hard muscles under that deceptively soft flesh.

"Back in the Wolves," Valentine said, "when I was trying to convince Captain Patel that I knew my ass from a knothole, I learned a saying, 'If a Wolf doesn't have it, he makes it. If he can't make it, he captures it. If he can't capture it, he'd does without.'"

They all watched the tug begin another careful turn, its paired barges in front reminding Valentine of a cargo wagon with an eight-horse team, following in the wake of the pilot boat.

If only we'd grabbed another tug or two. We'd be able to make better speed. Shorter cargo barges would mean easier turns.

Still, the amount of space they'd covered in a single night's run was nothing short of astonishing—a steady five miles an hour thanks to the smaller boats feeling their way forward. They'd be north of Saint Louis sometime before noon.

"That's the worry, Valentine," Captain Coalfield said. Like most men who spent their lives on water, he was darkly tanned and seamed. Rather wispy hair gave away his years—his body certainly didn't. Coalfield was all muscle. "There's a River Patrol station at the mouth of the Illinois River. We got by it northbound by tying together, dousing all our lights and using trolling motors on all but one boat in a dark run. Unless they're all drunk as Milwaukee brewers, these barges aren't getting past without the River Patrol having something to say about it."

According to intelligence, there were no heavy cannon at Alton. Mortars, machine guns, and light cannon protected the base itself from potential Grog raids, but trained artillerymen and their pieces were needed at other borders of the Kurian Zones. The River Patrol relied on their fast, hard-hitting boats to command the Mississippi.

"You don't need much to take out Grog canoes and flatboats," Coalfield's executive officer said when briefing Valentine on Alton.

Captain Coalfield shifted his grip again.

He would have made a bad poker player, Valentine decided. There were all kinds of "tells" that he was uncertain.

"We've never made the run past the mouth of the Illinois River with such a big flotilla before," Coalfield said.

"That may be to our advantage," Valentine said. "Three big barges, loaded, an escort of combat vessels—it's coming from the wrong direction for anything Southern Command would do."

"Could be they were alerted by riverbank spies."

"I've been up that riverbank as a lieutenant. There are a few gangs of headhunters, but they have to watch themselves. The Grogs raid across the river into the bluffs all the time. There's nothing worth guarding on that bank until you get to the big farms in the flats."

Weather came to the rescue of their doubts. As they approached Alton, thunder began to crackle. A line of fast-moving storms boiled up from the south, and soon rain turned the boat into a one vast drum.

"Better go down in the cabin. Lightning on the river can be dangerous," Coalfield said.

Morse lamps were flashing back and forth between the barges and the escorts.

Hair running with water, Valentine complied, as Coalfield made a note on a plastic-covered clipboard next to the ship's wheel. "We're all reducing speed," Carlson told the man at the wheel. "Tighten up on the pilot boat."

Valentine, stripping off his shirt in the cramped, food-stuffed cabin, had a strange flash of Frat Carlson and Stockard sheltering in an old farm shed. If they were being tracked, the bad weather would put the pursuers off, and hopefully buy them time to rest for the remainder of the overland trip.

✝

Valentine always thought of Saint Louis as "the Green City."

He'd seen two great ruins in his life: Chicago's downtown and Saint Louis. The buildings of Chicago's downtown, while sporting tufts of green here and there, never became too overgrown, mostly because the unfortunates dumped there cultivated every bit of useful soil. Potatoes and onions grew in the old boxes that had held trees; tomatoes grew from old sinks propped up in glassless windows.

Saint Louis could not have been more different. The Grogs did not utilize the higher floors of the city's great structures, except for thrill-seeking youths looking for risky reaches to prove themselves. They liked to see vines and bushes clinging to the sides of concrete and glassless windows bearded by kudzu and creepers. The growth sheltered insects, birds ate the insects, and hawks ate the birds. The Grogs, in turn, captured and trained the hawks to hunt waterfowl.

Valentine went ashore with Mantilla, the riverman who'd delivered letters to Narcisse when he could not visit Saint Louis himself.

They paid their usual brief homage to a fat old Grog chieftain Valentine thought of as Blueball—he painted himself in blue dye, put gold flecks about his face, and had a human slave who whitened his fangs and brushed out his hair and polished his nails to flaunt his wealth and power—and obtained a foot-pass for both of them. The price was some Kevlar liberated from the Gray Baron's stores.

Humans had to carry a token in Saint Louis, either signifying their ownership by a particular clan or tribe, or to show they passed through the city with the permission of a chief. Valentine had learned in his years of visiting Blake that certain Grogs who sold foot-passes cheap had influence only on the waterfront, or the market, and if you ventured into the city with some nobody's foot-pass you could get cuffed about and kicked back down the hill toward the riverside. Blueball was one of the more influential chieftains, being a slave trader, and his passes were recognized even in the hills to the south and the suburb country to the west.

This trip, Blueball's foot-pass was a piece of Christmas decor, some old sleigh bells on a bit of dingy leather with the red velvet flaking off. But they still chimed a merry accompaniment as he and Mantilla crossed through the market.

It was a little like Dickens, come to think of it. As painted by Maurice Sendak. Grog children gamboling underfoot while groups of females sorted and bargained and stored, trading weights of salt and tobacco and bullets for foodstuffs and goods.

Valentine looked forward to a happy day. He'd bring Blake and Narcisse with him when he left, this time.

Of course, a young Reaper at the fort would be strange for the men. He hoped that with so many other new arrivals, Blake would pass without comment, perhaps as a pale and sickly child.

"Haven't had a letter from them in a while. Haven't you been north?" he asked Mantilla as they passed through the Grog trade stalls of the riverside market. Valentine made a show of carrying his Type Three—a foot-pass was a useful necessity, but Grogs had their criminal classes, too.

"Narcisse had other concerns," Mantilla said. "She had to move back into town. The Jesuits are giving her and Blake shelter at the cathedral. She asked me to explain it to you. No other choice."

Valentine didn't like Blake being so close to people—even if most of them were unarmed slaves—and Grogs.

An old downtown cathedral, Father Cutcher's domain, stood near Cass Street off a park on the North Side. Valentine knew the Jesuit somewhat from his travels into Saint Louis over the years.

Ostensibly, he ran a mission ministering to the Grogs' slaves, offering solace to body and soul alike. He had a few sisters offering nursing and midwifery, and traders and the very few travellers in this part of the country could bed down in the mission and avoid the snake pits of the waterfront ghetto.

Valentine sniffed the incense as he entered the Narthex—it was the official Vatican stuff, not the wild spice mix his old Catholic guardian made do with on holidays.

A pair of bent old women gave their boots a glance.

"Wipe that river mud off, ye drips," one said with a hostile squint. "That's what the mat's for."

Other elderly filled the nave. The pews had been removed and replaced with rockers, lounges, and card tables. Former slaves, aged enough to be given their freedom before death takes them, but too old for a journey, washed up at Cutcher's door.

A nun directed them to Father Cutcher. They had to climb some rickety stairs to reach him in the bell tower. The Jesuit wasn't trying to pray closer to God, he was fiddling with a shortwave radio with one of his elderly.

"Leave off, Father," the electronic tinkerer said. "I think it's atmospherics, not the antenna. If it were the antenna, we wouldn't be getting anything south or west, neither."

"Major David Valentine. Captain Sebastian Mantilla."

"Sebastian?" Valentine asked Mantilla, as they trailed the old man down.

"Don't know how the old *coglione* ever found out. None but my old mom used that name."

Narcisse and Blake had taken up residence in an old third-floor room that was practically an attic, though it did have a view of the park. Wobble, Blake's dog, limped over to Valentine, wagging his tail and licking.

Narcisse, her head wrapped in its usual colorful turban, made a special blend of coffee for her visitors. Valentine sipped carefully, more to savor the drink than because he was suspicious of ersatz. He could taste nuts, citrus, and chocolate along with the coffee beans.

"Eats like a goddamn meal," Mantilla said.

Blake, as usual, was wide-eyed and wary for a few minutes. Narcisse put an encouraging hand on his shoulder, and suddenly he was all hugs.

"You have a magic touch, Sissy," Valentine said. "I remember that time in the Caribbean, after Captain Boul's men stomped me. Your hands on either side of my head."

Though in years still a toddler, the top of Blake's head now came up to Valentine's rib cage, and he was astonishingly strong.

"Ouch. Blake, careful, gentle like with Wobble."

"*As petting*," Blake said in his whispery voice.

Narcisse sat tiredly, her eyes closed. She'd aged since he'd last visited, distressingly so.

"You all right?" Valentine asked. "Can I get you something to eat, or look for medicine?"

"You know me, Daveed. Did you not ever wonder how I could control a toddler who could break my arm at sixteen months?"

"You had such a gentle way about you," Valentine said. "I figured he loved you."

"Yes. Most of the time, the gentle way works. But sometime, heem too emotional, Daveed. Not listen for my voice, not mind my words. Then, other ways."

She looked closely at Mantilla. He nodded. "Good a time as any, Sissy."

Narcisse patted the shriveled skin stretched across her breast. "I am weary, Daveed. This old body is ready to give up. It was ready to give up some years ago, but I keep it going."

"If you're feeling sick—," Valentine said.

"No, not sick. Tired. Not much left in these bones, I think."

She unwrapped one of the colorful turbans her head never seemed to be without.

A Kurian rested upon her bald, scarred head, an obscene cap that glistened and pulsed in the candlelight.

Or perhaps it was a Lifeweaver. They were the same species, with the same powers and potentials. Only by their actions could they be distinguished.

It resembled an animatronic, prickly cucumber more than a Kurian. Valentine, to his everlasting horror, had seen dead pregnant women and the children who had died *in utero*. This—entity—had the same misproportioned, squashed look—a melted model of the adult version. Its webbed arms were still tight-wrapped next to her body, only tiny hook-digits at the end clung to her skull.

The head, with its two cloudy topaz eyes so large it was a wonder they didn't roll right out of the soft flesh surrounding them, turned toward Valentine.

So we meet at last.

"Face to cephalopod," Valentine said. "Who are you?"

A survivor, the David. A survivor. I am a scion of one of the last Lifeweaver holdouts on Kur.

I will not take from sentient creatures. Indeed, I only consume other living beings with regret.

I do not have many years left, I think. Perhaps I would be dead already, were it not for Narcisse and her concoctions, and the scraps of lifesign from the chickens and rabbits and squirrels the Blake takes.

Valentine tried to comprehend speaking to a being who was alive when Julius Caesar walked the earth. No wonder the Kurians could look upon mankind as livestock. The endless cycles of war and killing, cruelty and hate. Distant observers, they. All they'd know is battles and pogroms, having never sat and listened to the audience laugh at *A Midsummer Night's Dream* or hummed the "Toreador Song" from Bizet's *Carmen* while digging in the garden the way his mother once had.

"You look like you need some air," Mantilla said.

They went out into the night. Valentine smelled Grog cooking on the breeze out of the city.

"There is one more caste, you know, Valentine. Beyond the Wolves, Cats, and Bears."

"Kurian agents?"

Mantilla smiled. "Not quite, though there are some similarities. No, we're talking about one that's been under a variety of names, but considering your time and place and background, we'll call it a 'Raven.'"

"You're one of these?"

"I am."

Valentine wondered if he could survive another passage to some new level of Lifeweaver mysticism. Did he truly trust Mantilla? Perhaps Frat Carlson wasn't the only Kurian agent who'd been close to him.

"What do you do?" he said, temporizing.

Mantilla looked skyward. "How shall I describe it to you? We bring messages from the Lifeweavers, and can talk amongst ourselves, after a fashion. Like Ravens of old, we flock to where the battle is thickest. Not to feast on corpses, but to report and intervene as needed. We are tricksters, able to take on a different appearance, at least for a brief time and with some help from the more gullibly minded."

"Like the Lifeweavers and Kurians—and their agents." Valentine didn't mean to cause offense, but Mantilla scowled at the comparison.

"In a sense. It comes down to us in the legend of shape-shifters, or the Rakshasa in India, where they may have been the last enclave of Kurians from the first invasion."

Valentine went back over his encounters with Mantilla. He'd hinted and hemmed and hawed about certain abilities in the past. Valentine gave him time to continue his explanation.

"Every Freehold has a Raven or two watching over it. I was, for a time, one of three in Southern Command. Then I became one of two. It was then that you met me for the first time, on the Arkansas River fixing my barge. Now I'm alone, save for a man who comes up from Texas from time to time. If a new freehold is established in Kentucky, it will need a Raven, for there's little chance a Lifeweaver can be found to guide it, at least anytime soon."

"So you act as substitutes for the Lifeweavers?" Valentine asked.

"It's rather more complicated than that I'm afraid. Have you ever heard the term 'symbiosis'?"

"Yes, it's two organisms of different species who survive better by cooperation. Like a bird who picks ticks off the body of a rhino. The bird gets to eat the ticks, plus I suppose the protection of something the size of a rhino and the rhino has parasites picked off."

Mantilla slapped an exposed brick wall and dust flew. "*Verdammnt*, I think you're in the wrong profession, my friend. You should be a teacher. Most shape-shifter legends involve duality of one kind or another. The poor *sukhim* is cursed with this other side living within. It is like that with us, though whether it is a curse or not . . . How about the reproductive cycle of the Kurian/Lifeweaver beings? Do you know anything about that?"

"I heard they budded off—like self-cloning."

"Not quite. They shift genders, briefly, when they need to reproduce. If conditions are right, two 'males'—though they're not really sexed that way, they're way beyond pricks and pussies—who have found themselves in affinity decide to reproduce. One shifts into 'female' mode long enough for a combination of genes. Sometimes it will be two joining with a third serving as brood-parent as well. In extreme cases they can self-fertilize, but that is more risky. In any case, a small carbuncle is fertilized and it grows into a new Lifeweaver. Or Kurian."

"You'd think we'd have a lot more around, then," Valentine said.

"The Kurians practice very strict population control. Centuries of being trapped on Kur forced it on them. Only the most clever and vicious survived to reproduce. As for the Lifeweavers, they've so successfully extended their already long life spans that they put it off more and more often than not never get around to reproducing. It takes a lot out of them and they'd rather spend their energy on art and science."

"Or get a piece of us."

Mantilla took a deep breath. "Sometimes, a bud doesn't develop properly and dies. Other times, if it is taken off early, it does not develop normally, but remains in an arrested state. It can attach itself to a host and live off the host. In return, it helps the host survive, though it acts more as an agent of the host's will than on its own."

He talked more of the Ravens—how they sometimes just knew a truth, or had an unusually vivid dream depicting the future and the course they should take. "The trick, of course, is to shape the actions of others. You're already accomplished at that. Perhaps your mother's influence passed down to you."

"No thanks," Valentine said, after turning it over. "I feel like I've given enough of myself to the cause. There's only a tablespoon or two left."

"I'm afraid, then, David, you condemn Blake to the life of a wild Reaper. Narcisse will be gone soon, no matter how hard her symbiot tries to keep her alive, and Blake is like a young child in a supremely powerful body. Sooner or later he'll succumb to the temptation to run down a Grog or two. Unless you choose to keep him in chains, of course, and throw him a dead chicken every other day."

Mantilla, in some ways, was as clever as Brother Mark, finding the chinks in his emotional armor and sleeping sensibilities. Did Brother Mark have something riding in him?

"Perhaps I could try it?"

"Of course. The one on Narcisse detaches at will."

They ate a meal of vegetables. Slave food, the Grogs called it. Valentine had been ravenous since being wounded by the Baron, and wanted something in his stomach before trying any new experiments.

When he had his nerve worked up, he allowed Mantilla to take the dwarf Lifeweaver from Narcisse and place it on him. Valentine tried not to think that it would be the work of only a second for it to drain the vital aura from his body, leaving him twitching on the floor until his heart quit.

A light-headedness seized him. It reminded him of coming out of a sound sleep and jumping to his feet. A controlled swoon.

"How do I know where you end and I begin?"

Such vitality. I feel a millennium younger, David Stuart Valentine.

"What do I call you?"

I do not know. I as this flesh am part of a larger identity. Narcisse called me "Makak"—I rode her like a monkey.

Would you like to see the world through Blake's eyes?

"Let him be."

I would no more control him as my others would a Reaper than I would have used one of these nerve hooks to bleed the aura from Narcisse. I correct him, calm him when he is anxious.

"When he eats a chicken?"

The aura in a chicken is more trouble than it is worth. It is like the smell of real food to you, David Stuart Valentine. Does it sustain you, or make you wish to eat your fill?

"Suppose I were linked to you, and knifed someone. Close enough to smell them."

I cannot say; it depends on many variables. I may benefit. I may shrink in fear of the violence. You may benefit. I expect you have already.

Why do you think you thrill so, when you survive a combat? That is a splash of vital aura washing across you as it is released.

Valentine flushed. He felt greasy where it was touching him. "Get off me. Now."

He handed the double-handful of over-intelligent calamari back to Mantilla.

"Sorry, Mantilla. You'll have to find another symbiot."

CHAPTER THIRTEEN

*T*he Mississippi: *The mighty river south of Saint Louis to its meeting with the Ohio is practically unrecognizable to a riverman of the twentieth century.*

Thanks to the great New Madrid quake in '22, the river doesn't even match old maps, having shifted both east and west in a few spots, closing down old loops, creating new islands, and leaving new fields and sloughs where once the river flowed. There is also very little in the way of dredging, so during the driest months it takes an experienced river-reader to navigate its twists and turns in an eighteenth-century style.

These banks are deep Grog country, owned by wild tribes who settled there shortly after the last great North American Grog-Human battle outside Indianapolis of the Old World in its death throes. The Illinois bank is owned by a tribe of Amazonian crossbreeds, another failed experiment by the Kurian Order.

The Grogs on the Missouri side are tough Gray Ones. For decades, they fought Southern Command tooth and nail, but both sides eventually exhausted themselves and discovered they could live in wary neutrality, with neither disturbing the other too much. Yes, bold young Grog warriors still prove their fighting and thieving skills by raiding down into the rough wilds of the New Madrid area, where no two bricks still stand atop each other after the massive 2022 earthquake. And yes again, Southern Command tracks, captures, and shoots the raiders, sometimes practically under the eyes of their home village, but the days of launching large counterraids to burn out Grog settlements and recover trophies of earlier raids have been over for years.

An informal demilitarized zone exists, where each side understands the other is fair game.

The river is another sort of zone, with a different set of rules. On the run between Cairo and Alton, Illinois, directly north of Saint Louis, it is understood that any craft on the water are inviolate. However, any vessel that becomes entangled with one or another bank is fair game. Crews are usually allowed to escape in a smaller boat, as long as they abandon their craft quickly enough to satisfy those onshore that cargo is not being taken off.

This has led to some Grogs acting in the manner of old wreckers on forbidding coasts, placing obstacles or faking the marker lights of another barge or boat in an effort to draw river traffic into the banks and disable it so plunder may be taken.

Now, in the critical spring of 2077, the snags and shallows are less of a hazard, as the river is at its fullest. Heavy spring rains and melting snow from farther north have turned it into a swollen, turgid beast, with many a birch- and poplar-filled spit turned into an island or chain of flooded trees. This is good smuggling time, for it's easy for small boats to take shelter behind the many temporary islands and short-lived lakes thrown off by the waterlogged river. But the Grogs on both shores are also ready for the increased traffic as well. On every bank there are eyes and ears watching the traffic, legitimate and illicit, sensitive as sharks detecting fish in distress.

†

The frustrating part was that the exodus could have been over by now, had Southern Command just cooperated. Lambert could have set up a landing at some friendly stretch of river, with a small mountain of foodstuffs and medicines. Blake and the rest would be resting in safety and comfort while they organized the final trip through Western Kentucky.

Instead, they'd have to pass the Missouri bootheel country and turn up the Ohio. All those "highways"—the Mississippi, the Ohio, the Tennessee—Lambert had mentioned could be used to attack the vulnerable transports. By now the Kurian Order would know what they were and where they were going.

Coalfield lowered his glasses. "Shit. They've strung a boom across the river."

"'They' who?" Valentine asked.

"Grogs maybe. Or the River Patrol. Looks like junked boats, most of them," Coalfield said, looking through his glasses.

"How do we get rid of it?"

He warned the following barges, out of sight on this twisted stretch of river, to backwater.

"Ideally, we just run up to it, board it, and blow a hole wide enough for our craft to get through."

"Bad stretch of river for them to do it. Lots of Grogs on either side taking potshots," Valentine said.

"Which is your bet?" Coalfield asked.

"Missouri side. Better cover, and the Grogs there are a little more amenable than the Doublebloods on the Illinois side."

†

Valentine had to admit, it was a perfectly executed ambush.

It had rained off and on through the afternoon, and thunder began to rumble. Good weather for the attempt. Still, they waited for the cover of night. *Cottonmouth Four*, the fastest of the boats, swept down the west bank to draw fire, then ran close to the boom.

Not so much as a single Grog potshot came from the bank.

"Very odd," Coalfield said. He'd put extra rivermen into boat *One*, along with the dynamite.

They moved forward cautiously, covered by the other four boats of *Cottonmouth*.

As the demo teams disembarked, Valentine examined the boom with a hooded light. It was simply a series of waterlogged boats filled with buoyant. The real danger came from the chains connecting them below the waterline. They would either hang up a boat or cause damage to the propeller and rudder.

A sudden flash and a thunderclap lit up the valley.

Valentine heard the engines first, coming from a loop on the river on the other side of the boom.

Every eye on *Cottonmouth One* looked across the sodden boom, downriver.

"Get back on board, here," Valentine told the demolition team.

"We can do it, sir!" the senior called back, wiring his charge.

"That'll just open it for them."

Fast-moving River Patrol attack boats were heading for the boom. In the center of them, like a foxhunter's horse among its dogs, a ship as big as a barge could be made out. It seemed to be moving impossibly fast, throwing up three different bow waves.

"Evasive pattern," Coalfield ordered into his radio to *Cottonmouth*. "Make smoke! What the hell is that?"

Valentine finally received his chance to tell the riverman something he didn't know.

"That's the *Delta*. Chinese-built littoral craft. Triple catamaran hull. Crew of twenty, or thirty if they're expecting ship-to-shore fighting. I knew her when I was with the Coastal Marines. She's River Patrol, but back when I knew her she alternated between Mobile Bay and the Mississippi Delta. Before my time it was called the *Delta Queen*, but some Biloxi Church busybody pointed out that queens and all that were part of the Old World everyone was supposed to forget, and by naming a boat after one, they were treating royalty and aristocracy as a aspiration, rather than a blight to be wiped off the earth. So it became the *Delta*."

"Get that smoke going, there," he called to the sailors aft, securing their explosives.

"Smoke won't help. She's got radar-controlled guns, rapid-fire cannon—two of them, one on each side just forward of the bridge."

Cottonmouth broke away from the boom.

The two sides exchanged tracer fire across the blockade. The *Delta* moved fast; either her captain was a reckless bastard or he was unusually sure of the Mississippi's depth. Of course, the catamaran hull helped.

"Shit!" the gunner roared as brass casings fell into the canvas recovery bags. "What's that thing made of, moon rocks?"

Valentine had never heard that moon rocks were bullet resistant, but the man was under stress.

A hot hand washed across *Cottonmouth One* and the gunner was gone, whisked away by bullets like a strong breeze plucking a loose piece of paper off a desk. Valentine heard distinct splashes as bits of the gunner struck river, his eyes blinded by the white streaks of tracer fire. Miraculously, he'd avoided being hit.

He jumped into the blood-splattered position, feet finding purchase on the rough platform. He checked the drums on the twin machine gun and opened fire.

The Atlanta Gunworks Type Three had more of a kick. The gun gently chattered in its mount. The hardest part was keeping aim with the boat rushing across river. As *Cottonmouth One* heeled he had to constantly adjust elevation.

The rain came down harder, shielding them from both visual and radar—or at least Valentine hoped for that to be the case. *Cottonmouth* limped upriver, leaving a single boat to watch matters at the boom.

†

They held a dispirited council of war at an abandoned riverside bar.

Some entrepreneur had tried to make a go of it as a rest stop for boatmen and River Patrol. It had been painted in the past ten years, and there was signage up, huge block letters advertising EATS BEERS MUSICS in block letters big enough to be read on the other side of the Mississippi.

The Delta's flotilla had paused near the boom, ready to protect it tonight or open it in the morning—if not sooner, with the weather clearing.

In the open waters of the Gulf, the *Delta* would have made short work of the *Cottonmouth* flotilla, where its speed and accurate fire would have reduced the boats to blackened wrecks in a quarter of an hour. But on the twisting Mississippi, she couldn't make use of her speed and even her supremely light draft only allowed her to use the relatively narrow barge channel. *Cottonmouth* boats could float on a heavy dew, as the rivermen phrased it.

Cottonmouth One had been so badly damaged by gunfire that Coalfield—himself with a painful splinter wound—had transferred flotilla command to *Cottonmouth Four.*

"We could just abandon the river, right?"

"They just saw us run and hide," Chieftain said. He'd seen it from *Cottonmouth Five.* "To me, that seems like the perfect time to attack."

"Except for those guns on the *Delta*," Coalfield said. "We'll be as waterlogged as those hulks on the boom in two minutes."

"A lot can happen in two minutes," Chieftain said.

"He has a point," Valentine said. "I wonder if something could be attempted."

"Not with our flotilla."

"I was thinking—more like a canoe. Have to find out what kind of swimmers those ratbits are, first."

Their watch boat reported that the River Patrol flotilla and its giant weren't chancing the boom in the dark and storm. But God knows what they would try tomorrow. If the *Delta* got in among the crowded barges . . .

Valentine stood, gripping the rail, looking at the beached barge, listing under its load of rusted containers.

Containers.

He'd have to swallow his pride and ask Makak for his assistance.

†

Valentine practiced with the ratbits on the back of *Cottonmouth Four*.

The hardest part was getting the line to float in such a way that the ratbits could use it. Though small and discreet, they weren't strong.

Valentine reconciled himself to spending the night cold and wet. The Mississippi in April would be unpleasant, especially on his still stiff wound, but it would be a vacation compared to the wild river trip raiding Adler's headquarters, when he'd been in and out fast-moving snowmelt for three days in an insulation suit.

They found him a green-painted aluminum canoe on *Cottonmouth Three*. It had a couple of bullet holes in it but was otherwise sound. Valentine would have preferred a plastic composite—less sound when scraping against branches or if he accidentally banged it with his paddle, but it was not to be.

"Don't suppose you can make me feel warm," Valentine asked Makak as it rode clinging tight to his belly.

I can make you not mind the cold so much. It is like a stiff drink, however. It will slow your reflexes and brain activity.

"Then forget it," Valentine said.

Pellwell rode in the front of the canoe, paddling. She'd insisted on coming along on this final mission.

They clung to the Missouri bank. A quarter mile from the boom, they portaged to the downriver side. Pellwell stumbled noisily but held up her end in more ways than one.

On the downriver side they paddled north toward the boom. There were sentries on the bank, watching the ropes fixing the boom to some sturdy tree stumps, trunks, and sunken anchors.

Pellwell slipped into the bottom of the canoe.

"I need to start playacting."

Just imagine yourself a Reaper. Move as it does. Scan as it does. I will do the rest, Makak advised.

Valentine had seen enough Reapers to fake the exaggerated, long-limbed movements. He turned the canoe toward the bank and stared hard at the River Patrol guards there, as if he were checking them and not the reverse.

Cigarettes were hurriedly extinguished. If the guards had looked any more alert, they would have pissed voltage.

Silently, Valentine turned out to the boom. He felt as naked as if he'd stepped out of the shower under all those eyes, but the ruse, whose effects were invisible to him, seemed to be working.

They found some floats and old, moldy life jackets helping hold up one of the wrecks. With them, they formed a makeshift float for the rope.

Then it was time for Valentine and the ratbits to go into the water. He cheked their gear one last time. Everything depended on a Miskatonic researcher and her chittering little creatures with brains that would fit into the palm of his hand.

†

They came at first light, sure as sunrise.

Valentine stood on the prow of *Cottonmouth Four,* daring the tracers to intersect on him. *Cottonmouth Two* pushed a little ahead of *Four* on a turn, wetting him with spray, before Captain Coalfield opened her full out.

According to Pellwell, the ratbits had done their job and fixed the lines to each of the rudders. From there, they swam back to the boom. He'd warmed their tiny little bodies, hugging them tight while they chittered and gave him little thumbs-up gestures.

The *Delta* trailed soggy hulks like a puppy with tin cans tied to its tail. Its prow swerved this way and that under the drag. Catamarans were not famous for their ability to tow.

He could tell the river sailors were nervous at their guns. Coalfield was busy directing the boats, especially deciding on the key moment for the fire tug to get under way, so it was up to him to do something colorful.

He clambered up onto the slick cabin roof at the front of the racing boat and took hold of the fore anchor line.

"Hiy hiy hiy-yup!" Valentine hallooed to the line of boats, closing fast on the *Delta*. Not that they could hear him.

Some feral part of him lost itself in the yelling. If he yelled, he didn't think about the second stream of tracers emerging from the *Delta*, or the third, or what would happen in the next few seconds once the radar control on the guns corrected for wind and temperature.

Here it comes . . .

Two streams converged, fast, ready to tear him and *Cottonmouth Two* into scrap, blood, and food for the catfish and gars.

Flowers of bullet-torn water closed on *Cottonmouth Two* as though a phantom horse approached. All Valentine could do was howl defiance, hanging on as Captain Coalfield worked his throttles to dart out of the way.

The streams lifted from the water, passed overhead with the low susurration of torn air.

Valentine forced himself to believe his eyes. The *Delta* lurched; one of the boom boats it was towing was hung up.

With the beast pinioned, Valentine played his floating trump card.

The fire tug motored forward, shielded by barges piled high with rusting containers full of sand. The Golden Ones had labored through the night, while Valentine was occupied on the river, filling the containers with tree limbs, driftwood, brush, rocks, anything that might stop or deflect a bullet once it punched through the thin side of the shipping container.

The *Delta* managed to get one gun pointed at the approaching hulk. A stream of fire lit up the glimmering dawn.

From across the water, Valentine heard the buzz-saw sound of bullets striking the containers.

But still the tug pushed on, absorbing the punishment of the cannon fire. All around it, river combat raged as the smaller craft tore each other to pieces with machine-gun fire. Valentine saw blood splattered on windscreens, dead men lolling at their guns, debris, dust, and splinters kicked up by bullets tearing through boat superstructure. Without the support of the big catamaran, *Cottonmouth* was winning, as two of the River Patrol boats had gone to the aid of the *Delta*.

It closed, and the fire nozzles started. The first few seconds of flow came limp and desultory, little more than a drinking fountain. Then the water went bright white, and arced up into the air over the barrier of container ships.

Three mighty jets of water fell across the *Delta*, with such force it pushed even the triple-hull of the catamaran over into a list.

The *Delta* crabbed sideways, pushed into the shallow banks and riverside snags.

Valentine saw two crewmen, caught on deck, swept overboard by the torrent.

The barge with its single container full of Grogs pushed forward, smaller boats whizzing around protectively.

It sidled up to the *Delta* under the arc of water, an oddly festive maneuver.

The fire tug shifted the flow of water, rather than cutting it off and having a few hundred gallons dropped on the boarders, knocking them down and interfering with their footing.

The boarders threw lines up and grapples fell across the rails of the catamaran. The barges were of such a height that the necks were nearly equal, and the handpicked Golden Ones and Gray Ones were more than equal to the task of bridging the gap with leap and grasp.

They splashed through the water still pouring off the decks and seized the guns. With the guns under control, the *Delta* was defanged. They could round up the remaining crew in a few minutes of blows.

Valentine watched figures drop over the side, chancing the Doublebloods on the Illinois shore over the fury of the Golden Ones.

†

They learned from captured crew members that the *Delta* had been rushed upriver by the Georgia Control. Somehow they'd learned of the approaching reinforcements for Western Kentucky, and decided to stop them weeks short of the target, in overland terms.

Coalfield was all too happy to transfer command of *Cottonmouth* to the big catamaran.

"Let's give it a new name," Valentine said.

"There is only one," Pellwell said. "The *Goliath*. After all, David slew it."

"The ratbits slew it," Valentine said. "I just paddled for them."

CHAPTER FOURTEEN

*E*pilogue: *The exact provenance of the word Kentucky is a matter of dispute. The popular translation used by Civil War historians that the word means "dark and bloody ground" is almost certainly false.*

For purposes of this history of Vampire Earth, it may be most appropriate to use the alleged Iroquoi-Wyandot phrase "land of tomorrow." What began to take shape at what Lambert called the heart of North America's great rivers as summer came on hot and dry and lush, was the first sprout of the new world that would have to take shape, should the Kurians be overthrown.

Man and Grog, ratbit and Reaper, horse and legworm, radio and newspaper, clattering petro-fueled engine and brown-water-churning propeller, community and its defenders came together that spring in something the world hadn't seen before, at least at the scale envisioned by Brother Mark. Like the ingredients in a stew, each took on some flavor from the other after the heat of action.

Kentucky would see more violence. Atlanta wouldn't give up their plans for the conquest and incorporation easily. Kentucky lived up to its misnomer as a dark and bloody ground in the following years, but like a vigorous new hybrid, its thrived in the churned-up soil.

After false starts in the swamps of Arkansas, the plains of Central Asia, the shores of Lake Victoria in Africa, and the islands and coasts of Japan and Alaska, the seeds of the future at last fell on fertile ground in Kentucky. Fate and the necessities of duty would soon separate some of the actors who gave what would become the Great Rivers Freehold its vigorous birth from their newborn republic.

But most would return, in time.

For now, we shall return briefly to the last few steps of a series of weary marches and passages by our no-longer-so-young major.

†

David Stuart Valentine felt each of his thirty years as he walked back up from the river landing to Fort Seng. His leg and back hurt. An old pain, one he hadn't had since a Reaper nearly took his head off during the escape from Xanadu, throbbed at his jawline.

Even echoes of the stomping he'd taken in a jail cell in Haiti courtesy of Boul brought a dull ache to his ribs.

Fort Seng buzzed as he crossed the old highway on its west border, at the edge of the thick woods on that side. The Kurian Missionary's doughnut stand had been turned upside down, looking like an odd mushroom with its tacked-together wood-pallet foundation.

He smelled cordite and shell everywhere. Clearly, there'd been some kind of action.

The fragrant smell of dough in hot fat set his saliva running.

"Kur bless you, Major," the missionary said.

Fort Seng looked like a whirlwind had hit it. It was the air raid all over again, redoubled. Headquarters was more or less intact, but looked scorched with several windows blown out and a hole in the roof.

The road to the fort was lined with cheering Bears and a healthy smattering of Wolves, drawn up in neater company lines. Valentine had never seen so many Hunters gathered in one place before.

The barbecue pits were ringed by furry lumps of hair, muscle, and weapons clothed in the ragged mix of Reaper cloth, Kevlar, leather, chain, and pig iron that passed for Bear duty uniforms— rumor had it that the entire Bear regiment had only three A uniforms, cleaned, swapped and returned as needed like a rental tux.

A rough count numbered them in the hundreds.

"Stevens, acting captain, Company A, First Bear regiment," a bearded little man said, stepping forward with a rather abashed and bootless Major Grace behind. "Only why it's called the first when there's only one nobody ever told me, Major. Elements of Companies C and D. Bravo's still down around Houston. Them Texans said they'd leave the UFR if the Bears got pulled out of the fighting line."

"Acting?"

"Formerly top sergeant," Connoly said.

"So you're here without orders?"

"Oh, I got you beat on that, Major. We're here specifically against orders. Written, verbal, signal flags, smoke signals. I think they tried everything."

"Except shooting at us," another Bear called.

"Nobody dared."

"Then you're volunteers," Valentine said.

"Men who want to fight. Seems like you're the one piece of Southern Command still in this war to win it. Though when we got here we were a bit surprised to find the place turned over to them

Atlanta jaspers. Major Grace here was in the middle of surrendering it to a crew of them. We lit our fires and ran 'em off."

"Hear tell it, you're gunning to take on Atlanta," a Bear corporal with a strange facial hair pattern—he'd shaved off one eyebrow and half of his pencil mustache on the opposite side—put in. "We thought we'd get the ball rolling for you."

"We'll be glad to have you at Fort Seng."

"Infestations of Quislings is pract'lly our speciality," a Bear chimed in. He tightened a hook-studded leather glove.

Lambert greeted him in front of the bullet-riddled headquarters, Ediyak at her knees keeping order among the messengers reporting in and asking for instructions. The elegant old mansion had fire damage around two windows and smoke still trickled up from one glassless window frame. Lambert had an interesting dirt pattern about her eyes and smelled of sweat and gunfire. No one could accuse her of being unbloodied in battle ever again.

"Hail the man who opened up the Missouri-Ohio junction," Lambert said. "My map's looking better and better."

"I'm glad we have something to come back to, sir."

He saw Gamecock and a couple of Bears stacking captured weapons and equipment in the parking lot. There were several Pooters and some new light armor vehicles parked there, not much the worse for battle damage. Blood caked on the window of one.

"Atlanta rolled the dice. They almost won, too. Most of the Evansville milita collapsed—there was another air attack, and I don't think anyone expected them to be able to fight helicopter gunships. But half the Lifeweaver-trained hunters of Southern Command showed up at an opportune moment, and nobody objected to attacking without knowing much about the opposition. Luckily it was just recon stuff backed up with garrison troops."

He could tell she was holding something back.

"Who did we lose?" Valentine asked, suddenly anxious. "Where's Captain Patel?"

"Patel's fine, according to his last transmission. He's handling the pursuit with some Wolves and legworm riders."

"Then what?"

"From the very top, Valentine," Lambert said. "I just received new orders. I guess Major Grace gave us the thumbs down right before he surrendered the joint."

She handed him the communication tech's transcription. Block pencil lettering had a date, time, and code confirmation. Below that were the bare words:

WITHDRAW TO RALLY BASE. AT ONCE.
CONFIRM SOONEST.
(S) MARTINEZ, GHQ

Valentine didn't know whether to retch, faint, or shoot himself. Gamecock, up to show him a vintage combat shotgun, steadied him with an arm. "After all this? The river's open now. Between the *Goliath* and the boats, we can hold the river, now."

"Not 'defensive stance' enough," Duvalier said, appearing from nowhere, in her usual style.

"What about the Golden Ones?" Valentine asked. "We'll just abandon them here?"

"Must have been garbled. Doesn't make any sense," Lambert

said. She turned to her communications staff. "The equipment must be to blame. Find the fault in our long-range gear. Take it all apart if you have to, and go over it piece by piece. I don't care if it takes a year to finish the job."

"That transmission was confirmed received," Valentine said. "Somebody might call that mutiny. They can shoot you for that."

"You seem to be healthy enough with a death sentence," Lambert said. "Operation Javelin's going to succeed. Maybe it'll just take a couple tries. But if they want me to stop, they'll have to drag me out by the heels."

"Us by the heels, suh," Gamecock said.

"Dots Lambert ignoring orders," Valentine marveled.

"Can't withdraw anyway," Ediyak put in. "We're in action."

"And will be the rest of the summer, I expect," Lambert said.

They watched Fort Seng fill.

The Golden Ones filed in, walking in the football-shaped formations of the fighting Grog march. A ratbit rode on broad, fauncolored shoulders here and there. The Gray Baron led his Grogs in, Snake Arms dancing with her reptiles at their head to Bear whistles, the warriors perhaps not as orderly as they'd been at the Gray Stronghold, but time would improve them from war band into soldiers.

What fascinating pieces to a yet-unknown future mosaic, Valentine thought. Smelly, disorderly, ragged—like Kentucky, with a full year of warfare washing over it. But toughened and slowly coming together, and unlike the silent, oppressed masses to the south, every one of them could be trusted with a gun and a knife.

He almost felt pity for the Kurian Order. He certainly felt it for the poor bastards who'd be sent up against them.

GLOSSARY

Bears—The toughest of the Hunter classes, Bears are famously fero-
cious and the shock troops of Southern Command, working themselves up into a berserker rage that allows them to take on even the
Reapers at night. Also famous for surviving dreadful wounds that
would kill an ordinary man, though how completely they heal varies
slightly according to injury and individual.

Cats—The spies and saboteurs of the Hunter group, Cats are stealthy
individuals with keen eyesight and superb reflexes. Women tend to
predominate in this class, though whether this is due to their bodies
adapting better to the Lifeweaver changes, or the fact that Cat activities require the ability to blend in and choose a time for acting rather
than more aggressive action is a matter of opinion.

Golden Ones—A species of humanoid Grog related to the Gray
Ones. Golden Ones are tall bipeds (though they will still sometimes go down on all fours in a sprint) mostly covered with short,
faun-colored fur that grows longer about the head mane. Expres-
sive, batlike ears, a strong snout, and wide-set, calm eyes give them
a somewhat ursine appearance, though the mouth is broader. They
are considered by most to have a higher culture than their gray re-

lations. Their civilization is organized along more recognizable groups, with a loose caste system rather than the strictly tribal organizations of the Gray Ones.

Gray Ones—A species of humanoid Grog related to the Golden Ones. Their hair is shorter than their relatives, save for longer tufts that grow to warm the forearms and calves/ankles. Their bodies are covered in thick gray hide, which grows into armorlike slabs on some males. They are bipeds in the fashion of gorillas, with much heavier and more powerful forearms than their formidable Golden One relations, wide where their cousins are tall. Unless organized by humans otherwise, they tend to group into tribes of extended families, though in a few places (like Saint Louis) there are multitribe paramountcies.

Grogs—An unspecific word for any kind of life-form imported or created by the Kurians, unknown to Earth pre-2022. Some say it's a version of "grok" since so many of the strange, and sometimes horrific, life-forms cooperate. Others maintain that the term arises from the "graaaaawg!" cry of the Gray Ones when wounded or calling for assistance in a fight. In most cases among the military of Southern Command, when the word "Grog" is used it is commonly understood to be a Gray One, as they will use other terms for different life-forms.

Hunters—A common term for those humans modified by the Lifeweavers for enhanced abilities of one sort or another. Up until 2070, the Hunters worked closely under the direction of the Lifeweavers in Southern Command, but after so many of them fled or were killed during Consul Solon's incursion, the Hunter castes were directly managed by Southern Command.

Kurians—A faction of the Lifeweavers from the planet Kur who learned how to extend their life span through the harvesting of vital aura. They invaded Earth once before in our prehistory and formed the basis for many legends of vampires. Although physically weak compared to their Reaper avatars, Kurians are masters of disguise, subterfuge, and manipulation. They tend to dwell in high, well-defended towers so as to better maintain mental links with their Reaper avatars. Face-to-face contact with one is rare except for their most trusted Quislings. Some have compared the Kurian need for *vital aura* with an addict's need for a drug, especially since the consumption of vital aura sometimes leaves the Kurian in a state of reduced sensibility. Most Kurians live life on simple terms—are they safe, do they have enough sources of vital aura, and how can they gather a large supply and keep it against their hungry and rapacious relatives?

Kurian Agents—The Kurian answer to the Hunter class, Kurian agents are very trusted humans, often trained from early childhood to utilize psychic powers similar to their masters. There are reports of Kurian agents able to assume the appearance of other races and genders, confuse the minds of their opponents, and even read minds to uncover traitors.

Lifeweavers—A race thought to have populated some nine worlds, modifying or creating an unknown number of life-forms. They appear to be some form of octopus crossed with a bat, equally at home in the water or gliding between treetops. A faction of Lifeweaver scientists on a planet called Kur created a schism when they began to use the *vital aura* from other living creatures to extend their life span. Soon open warfare broke out. The Lifeweavers were successful in keeping the Kurians confined to Kur for millennia, but they managed to break out and invade Earth and an unknown number of other Lifeweaver-populated worlds in 2022, our time.

Legworms—Long centipedelike creatures introduced to Earth in 2022 that reach lengths of more than forty feet and eight feet of height or more. They are a useful but stupid creature, able to bear heavy loads, but can be urged to move at a pace only above a walk by a skilled rider and constant prodding. Their chewy flesh from around the hundreds of clawlike legs is high in protein and edible, barely, and the skin from their eggs makes a tough, breathable form of leather that is a valuable trade good if harvested before the newly hatched legworms consume it. They lay eggs in fall and become sluggish and torpid in winter when they gather together in masses to shelter their eggs.

Lifesign—An invisible signature given off by all living organisms, in proportion to their *vital aura*. Reapers can detect it, especially at night, and are able to home in on humans from miles away. It is possible for a human to train herself to reduce lifesign through mental exercises or meditation, and it is possible to camouflage lifesign by hiding in densely wooded areas or among large groups of livestock. Earth and metals do tend to block it. There are some who maintain that a sufficient quantity of simple aluminum foil can conceal lifesign, especially if one keeps one's head properly wrapped, but empirical evidence is lacking, since individuals who try to sneak past Reapers relying on layers of foil rarely return.

Logistics Commandos—A branch of Southern Command that concerns itself with acquiring difficult-to-obtain supplies, mostly medicines and technology. They do this by purchase, trade, and outright theft. It is common for veteran Hunters to go into the Logistics Commandos as a form of retirement from fighting.

Miskatonic (the)—A fellowship of scholars devoted to studying the Kurian Order and categorizing Grogs. While the Miskatonic contains its share of academics, there are also "field" people who accompany Southern Command's forces to act as advisors and record evidence. Researches at the Miskatonic have developed more effective weapons for killing Reapers, mostly thanks to the discovery of Quickwood and its derivatives.

Moondaggers—A religious military order that fights for the Kurians. They were created and closely directed by a branch of the New Universal Church that is more patriarchal and theocratic than the typical churchmen. Famous for their brutality, they were key in putting down the revolts in the Great Plains Gulag in 2072. They were nearly destroyed, however, when they resorted to similar tactics against the legworm ranchers in Kentucky in 2075–76.

New Universal Church—A religious order of trusted Quislings who help manage the spiritual and intellectual needs of the human subject populations in the Kurian Zone. Much of their time is spent rationalizing the deaths of those taken by the Reapers and keeping the human breeding stock quiescent. Higher-level churchmen are often trained by the Kurians in similar psychic skills as those used by Kurian agents.

Quickwood—An olive-treelike plant that acts as a catalyst in a Reaper's bloodstream, freezing it in place and killing it quickly. The only drawback to Quickwood is its rarity, as the small supply that Southern Command managed to acquire was virtually destroyed by Solon's forces, though some seeds were saved and a few plants now are thriving both wild and in controlled and defended environments. The Kurians are working on modifying their Reapers to be immune to Quickwood, but for now the Reapers deal with a Quickwood wound by a fast self-amputation, if practicable.

Quislings—Humans who work for the Kurian Order. There is a great deal of dispute as to what exactly constitutes a "Quisling," but usually someone at the bottom rung of the social ladder who just follows orders is not considered to be actively supporting the Kurians, even if he happens to drive a collection van for the Reapers. Quislings are more commonly held to be those actively working for their Master Kurians in pursuit of immunity for themselves and their families. Quislings who do great service in the name of their Kurian lord are sometimes awarded a "brass ring" granting immunity from the Reapers to themselves and their immediate family.

Ratbits—A short-lived Kurian experiment to create a rodent with a higher concentration of *vital aura*, possibly as a replacement for difficult-to-control human populations. They are approximately raccoon-sized and combine the features of a rat and a rabbit. They have a level of intelligence that is measurably close to that of a human child in grammar school. They were bred in a vast expanse of Texas Hill Country known as "The Ranch" but resented being harvested as much as humans did and escaped into the wild, eventually forcing the abandonment of the Ranch.

Reapers—The avatars of the Kurian Order, Reapers are very powerful humanoids that form the basis of most of our vampire legends. With only a vestigial reproductive system and a simplified digestive process based on the consumption of blood and a small amount of flesh, Reapers are fast, strong, and deadly, particularly at night when the connection with their Kurian Master is strongest. They are strong enough to tear through metal doors and hatches, can jump to second- or sometimes third-story windows, and can run as fast as most cars can move on all but the best-maintained roads. Hunters find Reapers most vulnerable during daylight hours when the Kurian connection is weaker, especially directly after a feeding, when the Reaper is sleepy from the blood intake and the Kurian relaxing in the flow of fresh aura.

Twisted Cross—A military faction of the Kurian Order, the Twisted Cross use trained humans to operate fighting Reapers in a manner similar to a Kurian Lord. The Twisted Cross activities in North America were stillborn when the Golden Ones revolted and destroyed their base in 2067. There are reports of more successful Twisted Cross military formations operating around the Black Sea and in southeastern Europe and Asia Minor, the Asian subcontinent, and Japan.

Vital Aura—The energy created by all living things, but enriched and refined in sentient, emotionally developed creatures. Thus a human will have a much more *vital aura* than, say, a much heavier cow or pig. This energy is what sustains a Kurian over their extended, and seemingly limitless, life span.

Wolves—The great guerilla fighters of the Hunter class, Wolves are famous for their endurance, sense of smell and hearing, and ability to operate without logistical support. They can cover a good deal of ground in their all-day runs, often evading even mechanized opponents.

FREEHOLD—Any area in active resistance to the Kurian Order. Every man, woman, and child in a freehold tends to be familiar with the use of a variety of weapons, securing their homesteads, and highly motivated to keep out of the clutches of the Reapers. Freeholds vary in size, but the largest ones in North America are the United Free Republics in the Transmississippi and the old Quebec/Maritime provinces of Canada.

GEORGIA CONTROL—A Kurian Zone known for its high-quality weapons and trade goods covering much of the old Southeastern United States. Unlike most Kurian Zones, management of this region is left to Quisling human "directors" who keep the master Kurians fed through meticulous record-keeping of the health, productivity, and reliability of the human population. Their world is one of gruesome and remorseless "bottom lines."

GREAT PLAINS GULAG—An ill-defined region running roughly from South Dakota to North Texas, Eastern Colorado to the Ozarks. It is a patchwork of Kurian Zones, mostly made up of fortified farms, mines, and oil and natural gas fields, with Nomans-land in between. The Kurians there are mostly a passive problem for Southern Command, but they react to any attempts to take over territory with scorched-earth tactics and depressingly thorough slaughter of civilian populations. It is also one of the Kurian Zones with the widest gap between the freedoms and lifestyles enjoyed by the privileged Quislings and the subject labor force.

IOWA RINGLANDS—A Kurian Zone almost completely devoid of Kurians, the Ringlands are a collection of vast, rich, and highly productive rural estates given to Brass Ring winners from all over North America. They have a small but well-trained military known as the Iowa Guard and a superb education system for training the next generation of Quisling leadership. Young men and women brought up in Iowa are often chosen for the best positions in other Kurian Zones when their ringwinner parents encourage them to move out and earn their own rings.

KENTUCKY FREE STATE—A freehold comprising much of the old United State of Kentucky, minus much of the Bluegrass, some parts of the Jackson Purchase, and the area around Louisville and with the addition of Evansville, the small industrial city in southwestern Indiana and some of the more mountainous sections of northeastern Tennessee. Previously it was quiet, neutral territory where the legworm ranchers feuded with each other more than the Kurian Order. Thanks to the heavy-handed actions of the Moondaggers in pursuit of Southern Command's formations in 2075–76, the Kentucky revolt broke out and resulted in the formation of the

Army of Kentucky. It, with the support of a single Southern Command brigade in the western half of the state, established the first new freehold east of the Mississippi in decades.

KURIAN ZONE (or just "The Zone")—There are many different flavors of Kurian Zones, but they all have a few things in common. The remote Kurian Lord and his Reaper avatars are at the top of a pyramid of power. Below them are a few trusted Quislings and the New Universal Church high officials directing a slightly larger middle layer of functionaries and police. Kurian Zones tend to have only small groups of well-armed soldiers, relying on club-wielding police, mercenaries, and special traveling military cadres like the Moondaggers to protect themselves.

MIDSOUTH ZONE—A weaker Kurian Zone comprising Memphis on the Mississippi and Nashville and the areas in between. It is considered an ally of the Georgia Control, maintaining its independence by providing military assistance to the Georgia directors now and then.

NOMANSLAND—Any area not part of a Kurian Zone or a freehold is generally considered Nomansland. This can include stretches of useless, postapocalyptic wasteland inhabited only by a few bandits or dangerous Grogs to the bigger Grog lands of Saint Louis and the northern half of Missouri. Frequently, headhunter gangs roam across Nomansland areas, looking for runaways from the Kurian Zone to return for bounty or sell to the highest bidder.

One mistake the unwary make in venturing into Nomansland is assuming that there is little chance of meeting a Reaper. Kurians who wind up on the losing end of a power struggle or are ambitious offspring of a powerful Kurian can sometimes be found in Nomansland zones, trying to incorporate that region into the Kurian Order or simply hiding out from powerful enemies.

NORTHWEST ORDNANCE—A collection of old rust-belt states around the Great Lakes, excluding Chicago and Wisconsin and including some bits of Southern Ontario. The Northwest Ordnance is viewed by the rest of the Kurian Order as something of a "sick man of North America" and jealous eyes are watching it from all directions, waiting for it to fall so that its more valuable parts and populations might be divided up.

SOUTHERN COMMAND—Not so much a geographic region as a military command and operational zone, Southern Command was one of the first networks of military resistance formed after the Kurian Invasion in 2022, and in pure manpower is the largest. It maintains contact with other freeholds and formerly cooperated with them when possible, but after several disasters and reverses in the last few years it has adopted a "defensive stance," concentrating on better defending the United Free Republics against Reaper and Grog incursions and training.

UNITED FREE REPUBLICS—Once considered one of the bright spots of North America, the UFR has retreated into a well-guarded neutrality. The United Free Republics had a tumultuous birth, when the collapse of Consul Solon's Transmississippi, which had overthrown the Ozark Free Territory, caused a ripple effect in the surrounding Kurian Zones, especially in Texas. After ridding themselves of Consul Solon through a mixture of luck and planning, the Ozark Forces plunged into Texas and Eastern Oklahoma in response to uprisings there, managed to surround and then occupy Dallas, and plunged south into parts of the Rio Grande Valley. Shortly thereafter the United Free Republics were formed, somewhat along the lines of the old states of Arkansas, Oklahoma, Missouri, and Texas. Military reversals led to new elected leadership and a new direction for UFR's military arm, Southern Command, but most believe it is only a matter of time before the UFR manages to link up with freehold in Colorado and the newly organized rebels in Kentucky.